# KAIJU RISING II

## REIGN OF MONSTERS

EDITED BY N.X. SHARPS & ALANA ABBOTT

OUTLAND ENTERTAINMENT

KAIJU RISING II: Reign of Monsters

Outland Entertainment | www.outlandentertainment.com

Founder/Creative Director: Jeremy D. Mohler

Editor-in-Chief: Alana Joli Abbott

Publisher: Melanie R. Meadors

Senior Editor: Gwendolyn Nix



Published by Outland Entertainment

5601 NW 25th Street

Topeka KS, 66618

Paperback: 978-1-947659-30-8

EPUB: 978-1-947659-31-5

MOBI: 978-1-947659-32-2

PDF-Merchant: 978-1-947659-33-9

Worldwide Rights

Created in the United States of America

Editor: N.X. Sharps & Alana Abbott

Cover Illustration: Tan Ho Sim

Interior Illustrations: Frankie B. Washington

Cover Design & Interior Layout: STK•Kreations

Printed in the PRC by KrakenPrint

*Dedicated to the memory of Haruo Nakajima,*
*without whom Gojira could not have stomped.*

# CONTENTS

**FOREWORD**
*Robert Hood* ........ IX

**INTRODUCTION**
*N.X. Sharps* ........ XIII

**THE GHOST IN THE MACHINE**
*Jonathan Green* ........ 2

**WINTER MOON AND THE SUN BRINGER**
*Kane Gilmour* ........ 36

**RANCHO NIDO**
*Guadalupe Garcia McCall* ........ 62

**THE DIVE**
*Mari Murdock* ........ 76

**WHAT EVERYONE KNOWS**
*Seanan McGuire* ........ 98

**THE KAIJU COUNTERS**
*ML Brennan* ........ 120

**FORMULA 287-F**
*Dan Wells* ........ 160

**TITANS AND HEROES**
*Nick Cole* ........ 186

**THE HUNT, CONCLUDED**
*Cullen Bunn* ........ 236

**THE DEVIL IN THE DETAILS**
*Sabrina Vourvoulias* ........ 266

**MORITURI**
*Melanie R. Meadors* ........ 292

**MAUI'S HOOK**
*Lee Murray* ........ 322

**SOLEDAD**
*Steve Diamond* .......... 358

**WHEN A KAIJU FALLS IN LOVE**
*Zin E. Rocklyn* .......... 382

**ROGUE 57: HOME SWEET HOME**
*Jeremy Robinson* .......... 416

**THE GENIUS PRIZE**
*Marie Brennan* .......... 444

FOREWORD:

# WHEN MONSTERS RULE THE WORLD

ROBERT HOOD

**GIVEN THAT YOU'RE READING THIS** awesome book, you're probably of the school of thought that says, "Giant Monsters Rule!" right? It's a popular attitude, and one that's grown ever stronger in recent years. But when did this monstrous reign begin?

We like to fantasize that the earliest humans co-existed with those prehistoric giants, the ever-popular dinosaurs, whose rule lasted for something like 135 million years. Think of the Titanosaurs in particular (such as the Argentinosaurus, which is said to be the largest of them all), though the Brontosaurus and T-Rex are still the most popular dinosaurs. Is the popularity of giant monsters some sort of genetic throwback to distant ancestral memories? Alas, not only did nothing even vaguely human exist until a few million years *after* the dinosaurs died out, but also none of the earliest human beings looked anything like Raquel Welch in a furry bikini. Sad but true.

Of course, facts never hinder the human imagination, and in lieu of actual living giants, it didn't take humanity long to begin populating the world with monsters of the mind and soul. Consider, for example, the famous monsters of Greek (and Roman) mythology, such as Cyclops, Cerberus, Talos, and the Hydra. Several of these were the children of the Titans Typhon and Echidna ("the Mother of All Monsters"). Typhon himself was described as one "whose head brushed against the stars" when he stood erect.

But that's not all. Dragons, those huge winged serpents of many a fantasy, are almost universal in cultural legends, both as supernatural bad-guys and deities. Aboriginal Dreamtime legends contain Kulpunya, a giant dingo spirit, as well as the better-known Rainbow Serpent. Norse mythology has many humanoid giants, but also such monsters as Jörmungandr (the Midgard Serpent which encircles the earth). Sea-dwelling giants were plentiful, too, the Kraken being a popular foe. Another is the Finnish sea-monster Iku-Turso. Better-known is Leviathan of Biblical fame. Giant myth-based monsters, largely born of gods, were spawned on nearly every continent.

Things changed for giant monsters with the on-set of film-making—though in becoming the subject of entertainment rather than religious belief, they served a similar role, at least in some respects: both mythic tales and acknowledged fiction explore metaphorically the worries, uncertainties, and hopes of their various cultures. And they are all a reminder of our own fragile hold over the planet.

Ironically enough, the modern rule of giant monsters began with a dinosaur. In 1925, Harry O. Hoyt directed the first film version of Arthur Conan Doyle's *The Lost World*, which ended with a Brontosaurus rampaging through London, creating a precedent of city-trashing for many giant monsters to come. The creator of the beast, Willis O'Brien, would go on to create the titular monster in 1933's *King Kong*, the first *real* giant monster film. Then in 1953, as fear of the consequences of the atomic bomb kicked in, Eugène Lourié directed *The Beast from 20,000 Fathoms*, with FX by Willis O'Brien's apprentice Ray Harryhausen (who would go on to create many other giant monsters). The success of *The Beast*, in turn, inspired Japan's Toho Studios to produce *Gojira* in 1954 (released in a re-worked form as *Godzilla, King of the Monsters* in the U.S.). *Gojira* director Ishirô Honda's film was a deliberate reaction to the 1945 destruction by atomic bomb of Hiroshima and Nagasaki, generalised to address the consequences of "dangerous" science. The worldwide success of *Godzilla* inspired Toho to create a plethora of increasingly bizarre monster films, known in Japan as *kaiju eiga* (monster films) or *daikaiju eiga* (giant monster films). Godzilla films are still being made today, both in Japan and the U.S. Meanwhile, other Asian countries began to film their own (generally less successful) giant monster flicks, the U.K. followed suit with 1961's *Gorgo* and others, and Hollywood during the 50s and beyond continued to create many more. The gradual development of complex CGI effects has, during the past decade or so, given a push to the genre that sees such films reigning over the box-office.

In the 1960s and 70s, comics starring giant monsters became popular, too, most notably such Marvel titles as *Where Monsters Dwell* and *Tales to Astonish*, with the most iconic of these monsters drawn by the master, Jack Kirby. Naturally, written giant monster stories—both short and long-form—followed suit, often honouring the overwhelming Japanese influence on the subgenre by using their term: *Kaiju*. The first anthology to publish original giant monster stories was the award-winning *Daikaiju! Giant Monster Tales*, edited by myself and Robin Pen, in 2007. Two sequels followed. In the intervening years, many more anthologies have appeared, few as awesome as the best-selling *Kaiju Rising: Age of Monsters*, edited by Tim Marquitz and N. X. Sharps, and now its sequel, which you hold in your hands.

*Kaiju Rising II: Reign of Monsters* contains a plethora of great stories, written by some of the best writers in the field. You will be awed, amused, thrilled, terrified, inspired—emotions integral to the subgenre.

I'm glad to say the latest Age of Giant Monsters is in good hands.

# INTRODUCTION

N.X. SHARPS

**IT'S BEEN FIVE YEARS SINCE** Guillermo del Toro's *Pacific Rim* stomped onto the big screen, popularizing the term "kaiju" amongst large swathes of Western theater-goers, and inspiring me and the team at Ragnarok Publications to create an anthology dedicated to a Japanese film genre featuring giant monsters. With the support of 444 backers, we successfully crowdfunded that anthology and released *Kaiju Rising: Age of Monsters* into the world. Plenty has changed since then but with *Pacific Rim: Uprising* and a bevy of other giant monster movies on the horizon (including a film adaptation of the beloved arcade game *Rampage* and the long-awaited showdown, *Godzilla vs. Kong*) now seemed like the perfect time to unleash a sequel of our own.

Editing a project like *Kaiju Rising II: Reign of Monsters* is gratifying on so many levels. It's an exciting exercise brainstorming what authors might best fit the overarching theme of the anthology while still managing to deliver their own unique style. And once the submissions start rolling in and you get to read original fiction by your favorite authors before anyone else will? Talk about sublime! I knew the anthology would be good, but it wasn't until I started to read the submissions that I realized just *how* good. I held some expectations for what the stories of *Kaiju Rising II* might offer, but authors, beautiful beasts that they are, have a tendency to surprise you.

Rewinding a bit, let me just say that one of the things I love most about the first book, *Kaiju Rising: Age of Monsters,* is the degree of diversity in the content of the stories. It's a feature that is frequently mentioned in reviews, and I whole heartedly believe it's the anthology's greatest strength. I'm glad to say that *Kaiju Rising II: Reign of Monsters* only builds on that (hopefully earthquake-resistant) foundation. It's a leaner predator than its big sister, more King Kong-sized than the Godzilla that is *Kaiju Rising: Age of Monsters,* but the stories printed on the following pages still manage to span an assortment of genres—action, horror, post-apocalypse, alternate history, and science fiction. We've got stories of love and loss, revenge and redemption, duty and sacrifice, conservation and annihilation, all united under the aegis of kaiju. In the true monster movie tradition, our kaiju range from villains to victims, creatures of instinct, forces of nature, and in the words of *Jurassic Park's* Muldoon even a "clever girl" or two.

All books are a team effort, but none more so than an anthology. I've already touched on the incredible stories written by our amazing line-up, but I'd be remiss not to mention the hard work by those who made *Kaiju Rising II: Reign of Monsters* a reality. Alana Joli Abbott, my co-editor, really knows her craft, and her abilities have covered for any of my own shortcomings. Tan Ho Sim's awesome cover art is a perfect match for this anthology, and I'll be proud to display it on my bookshelf. Frankie B. Washington has all the experience needed to illustrate kaiju, and his interior art evokes the essence of each of these stories. Without the determination and marketing expertise of Melanie Meadors, it would have been a much steeper hill to climb to reach our funding goal for the Kickstarter campaign. Shawn King's design sensibilities are second to none, and I'm astonished one of the big traditional publishers hasn't snatched him up yet. Outland Entertainment's fearless leader Jeremy Mohler deserves credit for deciding to take a risk on this project, and I'm eternally grateful that he did.

But perhaps the greatest member of the team is you. Yeah, you. Whether you backed the Kickstarter campaign, bought a copy after, borrowed this from a library, or stole it from your friend (don't give it back, just convince them to buy another copy)—we couldn't have done it without you. Without a reader, there's no audience, and it doesn't matter how good the book is or how much time and effort was sunk into it. So, thank you, even if you skipped ahead to dive straight into the stories like I would in your position. If you're a fan of kaiju I sincerely believe you will appreciate what these authors have achieved. If this is your first exposure to the genre, I hope *Kaiju Rising II: Reign of Monsters* can be your gateway drug to a wider, weirder world.

And with that, I am honored to introduce *Kaiju Rising II: Reign of Monsters.* The Age of Monsters has arrived, and the Reign of Monsters has begun.

N.X. Sharps
March 6, 2018

# THE GHOST IN THE MACHINE

JONATHAN GREEN

**THE JUKUNG CUT THROUGH THE** waves like a spear, the outboard motor purring as Keoni kept his hand on the rudder and his eyes on the horizon. And then the interminable blue and green of sky on sea was broken by the surf-lapped outcroppings of the atoll.

The ring-shaped island was a near perfect circle, the weather-worn tips of the exposed reef dusted with the accumulated sand of crushed sea-shells in some places, while in others a few determined plants sprouted. But the real life lay beneath the waves, where the reef descended like a calcified cliff towards the seabed, which was why the Redmonds fished these waters and were never short of food. And the desalination plant aboard the *David Redmond* that formed the nucleus of the sea-borne community meant they never went without fresh water either.

The wind tousled Keon's thick mop of sun-bleached hair

FBW20

while the burning disc high in the sky warmed his skin, and the sea spat its salt-spray into his face.

He looked every part the hunter, his lithe, muscular body toned and tanned, his steely gaze focused on the approaching atoll. At fifteen he was almost a man, but his skin was as yet unblemished by the scars that would one day mark him out as a hunter of Redmond tribe.

The only clothes he wore were a pair of baggy breeches and his favourite leather waistcoat, but then he didn't need anything more. The only other item he wore was his shark's tooth talisman, suspended from a leather thong about his neck. In fact, it was on this very atoll that he had found the tooth, all those years before. Remembering the lucky find, Keoni unconsciously put the talisman to his lips and kissed it.

As the outrigger drew closer to the island formation, Keoni caught sight of the natural opening that gave access to the lagoon at the heart of the atoll. Even from this far out he could see the distinct difference in colour between the waters surrounding his boat and the unplumbed sapphire depths of the lagoon.

Some said that there was no bottom to the Great Blue Hole, others that it led to the depthless dark domain of Dakuwaqa himself. But whatever the truth, Keoni knew that within the Blue Hole was where the hunter would find his prey.

As he steered the boat towards the break in the atoll wall, the youth cast a glance back over his shoulder at the receding ship-city. Parts of the *David Redmond* were still visible beyond the horizon, but then the floating city was huge. An agglomeration of ancient vessels, moored together to form a many-tiered floating platform a thousand metres across, at its widest point, and twelve tiers high in places. The mountainous platforms were supported by the jostling decks of the rocking ships, with Chief Turi's tented apartment lying on the topmost tier. The great, calico-white awning shone like a beacon in the light of the climbing sun.

Keoni could scarce imagine a bigger settlement anywhere within the bounds of the Coral Sea. But then he had never travelled further than the outlying trading post of Ovation and the pirate-port of Prelude.

Easing off on the motor, Keoni carefully brought the outrigger to the entrance to the lagoon, before cutting the engine altogether.

A coconut bobbed between the hull of the canoe and the starboard float. "Must be my lucky day," he mused.

Fishing it out of the water, he reached for his machete, lying alongside a steel box, beside a pile of oilcloth, ready to cut it open and enjoy its bounty. As he did so, the tarpaulin moved.

Warily taking hold of one corner of the tarp he yanked it back. Lying there, in the bottom of the boat, blinking in the sudden sunlight, was the slight form of his sister.

"Kaimi? What are you doing here?"

"I should ask you what you're doing here!" Kaimi countered, shielding her eyes from the blazing sun with a hand.

"You know what I'm doing."

"Are you mad? Father says you're not ready."

"I'm ready!" he snapped back at her.

"Father said you must wait until your sixteenth birthday.

I knew what you were planning," she went on accusingly. She was younger than him by four years, but the way she spoke to him now, she sounded more like their mother, the ancestors keep her. "That's why I stowed away. Someone has to talk sense into you or father will feed you to the fishes!"

"I have to prove myself," Keoni said, thin-lipped.

"You dishonour the gods by coming here!" His sister gave a dramatic sigh. "What are you hoping to catch anyway?"

"Toki!" Keoni replied, with a measure of embarrassed pride.

"Toki? You would dishonour Dakuwaqa by killing one of his children?"

"They prey on us, so why shouldn't we prey on them? No one has ever brought a shark back from the sea. When I do, the elders will have to accept that I am as great a hunter as any Redmond has ever known!"

"You sound like that idiot Tamati. The toki do not prey on us," his younger sister chided him. They only attack when we enter their territory. And if you brought one back, dead, to the *David Redmond,* even if that were possible, I think Chief Turi would exile you from the tribe!"

"Well I don't," countered Keoni.

"Well I do."

"Well we'll just have to wait and see then, won't we?" Keoni said, using an uncapped flare to light the stick of dynamite he had taken from the box in the bottom of the outrigger.

He quickly let go of the dynamite and it entered the water with a plop, its fuse still fizzing. The flare followed it a split second later.

The siblings watched as the dynamite sank into the blue depths, quickly vanishing from sight, although the pinky-red glow of the sputtering flare remained visible much longer. They both heard the muffled boom of its detonation and felt the surge of the sea beneath the boat as the shockwave rose to the surface. A great column of water burst from the submarine sinkhole before raining back down again in a sudden deluge that drenched Keoni, Kaimi, and the boat.

"You idiot!" Kaimi shouted as she pulled her soaking hair out of her eyes. "Are you trying to kill us?"

"I have to do something to shake Toki from the comfort of his sea bed," Keoni said.

Water sloshed about in the bottom of the boat between them.

"So now what do we do?" his sister grumbled, peering over the side of the jukung at the fathomless depths beneath them.

"We wait."

And so they waited.

**"HOW LONG HAS IT BEEN** now?" Kaimi asked for the umpteenth time.

"I don't know!" Keoni snapped. "About thirty seconds since you last asked? Just shut up, okay?"

It had been several minutes since he had dropped his dynamite lure into the ocean, certainly longer than he had thought it would take to stir his prey from its lair, and he was suffering the comedown from the adrenaline peak he had experienced at coming out to the atoll, without his father's permission.

Since dropping the dynamite into the sea, he had

remained standing in the boat, but now his legs ached from maintaining his balance and, disgruntled, feeling that his plan had all come to naught, he sat down on one of the bench seats that crossed the hull.

Kaimi lounged with her head lolling over the side of the boat. "What's that?" she asked.

Keoni stood again and moved to the edge of the boat. He looked down into the water, between the hull and the canoe's portside lateral support float. He could see beads of light twinkling in the dark depths far below. And it was then that he saw the grey shadow beneath the waves, moving at speed towards the jukung.

The shark rocketed out of the sea with the force of a torpedo, its gunmetal grey, bullet-shaped head all gaping jaws as it exited the ocean.

Kaimi screamed while Keoni scrabbled for his spear, not because he thought it would serve him well against the Great White, but just because he didn't know what else to do. The terrifying selachian cleared the waves for a moment, a moment that slowed in Keoni's mind as his adrenaline-heightened senses took in every detail, from the remora sucking fish clinging to the monster's pale belly, and the scars striating its flanks and muzzle—the legacy of previous submarine battles—to the soft, pinky quality of the flesh inside its mouth, the rolling rows of serrated teeth, and the creature's oblivion-black, soulless stare.

And then it was dropping again, the intimidating mass of it blotting out the burning white disk of the sun for a moment, casting a great shadow across the outrigger. Keoni was aware of Kaimi screaming as the fish hit the water again, sending a wall of water crashing over the boat, as it landed a mere hand's breadth from the outrigger's port boom, and setting the vessel rocking.

The young hunter's blood was pumping now, his whole body shaking as he raised his fishing spear, ready to plunge it into the shark's eye-socket the moment it broke the surface again. But when the tentacles burst from the boiling sea in the shark's wake, Keoni was paralysed into inaction.

The rubbery appendages writhed above the surface of the water, as if tasting the air.

Keoni had set out that morning to catch a shark and prove himself a hunter, but now he found himself facing the proposition of dealing with another leviathan born of the deep ocean, some colossal squid!

Kaimi's screams shook him from his reverie. "Get us out of here!" she managed to articulate between her howls of horror.

For the briefest moment, Keoni wondered if he could take on a fully grown giant squid and win, but when he saw how far away it was and how long the writhing, suckered arms must be, he thought better of it and ran to the back of the boat, scrabbling desperately at the outboard's starter cord.

His first tug summoned nothing more than a throaty belch of engine fumes from the outboard.

"Come on, Keoni!"

He turned and saw the panic writ large across his sister's face. Following her horrified gaze, he expected to see the writhing limbs moving through the water towards the boat, but what he saw instead froze him to the very core of his being, despite the heat of the blazing sun beating down upon him.

As brother and sister watched together, more writhing limbs emerged from the sea at the centre of the atoll. They were coloured with rippling patterns of pink, orange, and yellow, and there were far more than was normal for a giant squid.

Suddenly several of the tentacles whipped out across the water, elongating with elastic fluidity, and shot past the outrigger. Kaimi screamed again as the muscular appendages struck the water. The surface of the sea became a seething turmoil as something was dragged, thrashing with all its might, back to the surface.

Keoni gasped. With the appearance of the strange tentacles he had momentarily forgotten all about the Great White. It suddenly surfaced again beside the outrigger, threatening to smash the port boom to matchwood as it fought to free itself from the tightening tentacles. The huge fish twisted and turned with such force Keoni worried that, even if it didn't destroy the outrigger with its desperate thrashing, it would swamp the boat with seawater and sink it just the same.

The shark snapped its jaws open and closed, as if in a feeding frenzy, but still it could not free itself from the clutches of the tentacles. Inexorably it was dragged backwards through the water towards the centre of the atoll, where the water was darker.

The sea frothed and foamed as the shark continued to fight the tentacles—a fight it could never hope to win.

But if witnessing what he had thought was the apex predator of the Coral Sea being captured by this half-seen tentacled leviathan wasn't shocking enough, what happened next expanded Keoni's understanding of the truth of his world in ways he could never have imagined when he set out that morning.

As the shark was hauled in, the tentacles began to rise out of the water, impossibly high for a giant squid, or even an overgrown octopus.

It very soon became apparent that no mutated squid had caught the shark, but something much, much bigger.

As the tentacles rose, Keoni saw that they surrounded a vast mouth that made the monster look more like a gigantic starfish, or some impossibly large anemone. The writhing limbs were there solely to feed food into the gaping maw, and as Keoni stared dumbfounded at the leviathan emerging from the Great Blue Hole, he saw the frantic shark disappear inside.

The strange creature was already taller than the outrigger was long, and yet still it continued to rise from the ocean's unplumbed depths, the roots of the tentacles fusing into what at first appeared to be a serpentine body, until it broadened out into a vast trunk-like structure, and Keoni realised that what he had taken to be the thickness of the creature's entire body was in fact only its neck. And still it continued to rise.

"Keoni!" Kaimi's scream reminded him that rather than staring at the monster emerging from the sea, he should be getting them out of there.

The starter cord was loose in his hand. He gave it another tug, and this time the engine caught. Gunning the throttle expelled any lingering sea-water from the engine and got the motor running up to speed.

The outrigger began to move towards the heart of the atoll, towards the towering monster.

Keoni pulled hard on the outboard, angling the propeller so that the boat described a tight arc across the choppy waves, the pitch of the engine changing as the boat bumped over the surges, rippling out from the centre of the Blue Hole.

His sister's screams had been replaced by terrified, heart-rending sobs, as she stared up at the monstrosity rising above them, taller now even than the *David Redmond*, blocking out the sun, its shadow stretching far out across the sea.

And then they broke from the shade and passed into blinding sunlight again, and in that moment Keoni dared hope they might escape the fate the shark had suffered.

Massive limbs, like boneless arms, peeled away from the sides of the creature, four in total. As it rose still higher, another pair of vastly-thick tentacles split apart to form a pair of rudimentary legs and the towering agglomeration of asteroidae-like flesh took its first long stride after the outrigger.

There was nothing Keoni could do other than gunning the throttle and keeping his eyes firmly on the familiar, ziggurat shape of ship-city on the horizon.

Seawater cascaded from the body of the beast in a dozen waterfalls a hundred feet high.

The monster's "leg"—for want of a better word—didn't break the surface of the sea but dragged through the water as the creature waded through the shallows beyond the atoll. And then the colossal limb passed by the boat.

As it did so, Keoni got a closer look at the entity and its writhing flesh. Everywhere Keoni looked, the rippling orange-pink-yellow flesh of the thing was made up of wriggling coral-like polyps, a million microcosms of the creature's head—a ring of tiny tentacle-like growths surrounding puckered sphincter-mouths.

"Lusca!" he gasped as a childhood memory surfaced once more.

He remembered his grandfather regaling him and Kaimi with tales of the lusca, monsters from the abyssal depths of the ocean, and the battles they had fought with the guardian gods of old, but he hadn't really believed those stories to be true. Now he wasn't so sure.

As the creature left the boat behind, Keoni wondered whether it was even aware of the outrigger. Or was it simply that it had detected something more deserving of its monstrous attentions on the horizon?

Keoni had no idea how the thing sensed the world around it, whether it was through vibrations, smell or sight; just because it didn't have any obvious eyes on a scale to match its vast body didn't mean that the billions of polyps that formed its flesh didn't have myriad eyes—or at least light-sensitive cells—of their own.

The primal terror he had felt upon witnessing the monster's rising from the Great Blue Hole now became a burning dread as he realised where the creature was headed. Keoni had no idea how its mind worked—or what form such a mind might take—but something was drawing it towards the *David Redmond*, whether that was the smell of the cook-fires and the reek of diesel or the scurrying movement of the people on the deck, who were surely aware of the monster's presence by now.

"No!" Keoni screamed, as the beast closed with the sea-borne settlement.

The distant rattle of gunfire carried to the pursuing outrigger across the waves, underlined by a chorus of shrill human screams.

Keoni gunned the throttle again but in truth there was nothing he could do, other than point the outrigger towards the *David Redmond* and keep going, even though it meant putting not only his life at risk, but that of his sister too. For the *David Redmond* was their home, and without it they would have nothing.

**EVEN BEFORE THE OUTRIGGER BUMPED** against the floating jetty, Keoni leapt from the trimaran canoe onto the pontoon and sprinted towards the steel staircase chained to the side of the ship. "Stay there!" he commanded Kaimi.

"No, I'm coming with you!" his sister retorted, throwing a loop of rope over a mooring post before chasing after him.

Keoni gave an exasperated sigh and raced up the stairs, two steps at a time. Upon reaching the deck he was greeted by the clamour of the unfolding horror, as he entered a once familiar world now run to chaos.

The barter-market was a scene of utter devastation. The stalls and makeshift structures of the bazaar had been swept aside by the lusca's attack. People were staring up at the towering creature in abject terror, their minds broken by fear. Others desperately scoured the deck for missing loved ones, or ran back and forth, searching for an escape from the horror.

And there, in the thick of things, Keoni saw their father, his face red from shouting as he tried to direct people to safety.

"Father!" Keoni called as he ran towards him, despite the obvious danger, Kaimi close on his heels.

The older man turned, hearing his son's voice, a look of hollow-eyed dread on his face. "Keoni? Kaimi? Oh thank the ancestors, you're alright!"

"Daddy!" cried Kaimi running into his father's arms and hugging him.

"Where were you?" their father demanded, meeting his son's own horrified stare.

"I'm so sorry, father," Keoni said, the guilt and remorse suddenly too great to bear. "I only meant to catch a shark, to prove to you that I *am* a hunter. I took the outrigger. I didn't know Kaimi was on board, I swear."

"What?" His father's face darkened, as if a storm cloud had passed across the face of the sun. "I told you not to," he growled. "You're not ready!"

"I know. I'm sorry. I had no idea it would lead to this," Keoni said, unable to stop the tears.

"What do you mean?"

Without really considering what he was admitting to, Keoni told his father everything, how he had taken the boat out to the atoll, how he had used dynamite as a lure, and how the shark had risen from the deep blue depths closely followed by the monster that was even now attacking the *David Redmond*.

Despite the turmoil swirling around them, Keoni's world suddenly became very small and still as his father stared at him, clearly appalled, not saying a word. He hugged Kaimi even tighter to him.

"F-Father?" Keoni stammered. "I didn't know..."

"You did this?" his father said, his voice barely more than a whisper. "You, and your overreaching ambition, brought this doom upon us all?"

"Father…"

"Do not speak to me. I told you you weren't ready." Still his father did not raise his voice, and that only made it that much worse. Keoni could see his father shaking as he fought to maintain his composure.

"I didn't know!" Keoni protested.

"You were told!" his father suddenly roared. "I told you not to go out there! I told you you weren't ready and you didn't listen to me! And now this—" He took in the deck of the *David Redmond* with an expansive sweep of his hand. "—this is the result!"

"Father!"

"I said, do not speak to me but *still* you disobey me! Do not speak to me ever again!"

"Daddy?" Kaimi sobbed, pulling away from his father's embrace, as the force of his words began to sink in.

"Hush, Kaimi. We must get to safety," their father said.

"But what about Keoni?"

Their father hesitated before answering. "What about him? He is no son of mine."

After having shock after shock piled on him, Keoni was barely aware of the screams that heralded another strike against the ship-city by the lusca. A split second later, an octopoidal appendage struck the deck, sweeping aside habitations and capturing more unwilling victims on its underside with a million tiny sucker-like protuberances.

Some of the men manning the *David Redmond's* defensive towers fired harpoons into the beast, or hosed it with flame-cannons, but only the latter seemed to have any real effect on the creature. Where the burning napalm hit, the wet flesh of the creature rapidly dissolved, accompanied by a shrill hissing sound, as if the colony animals that formed the monster's body were screaming as they burned. But the lusca was huge, and the flamethrowers were few, and while pieces of the creature burned away as quickly and as surely as if eaten by acid, such injuries were only the equivalent of grazes and scratches to a human being.

Keoni turned his gaze from his father, retreating across the deck, dragging Kaimi with him, to the ship-city's doom as the towering creature struck again. The force of the blow from its gargantuan, starfish-like limb lifted people into the air, only for them to hit the deck again moments later.

Keoni crashed down on his hands and knees. Rolling onto his back he found himself staring up at the titanic beast as something else emerged from the sea behind it.

Two flattened silver horns broke the surface, catching the light of the sun so that they seemed to burn with a magnesium-white flame, and Keoni had to shield his eyes to see precisely what was rising from the ocean behind the colossal creature.

The horns surmounted a finely-sculpted helm, the eye-slit of its visor glowing a barely-discernible ice-blue. The head was joined by a neck of articulated metal plates to a torso just as angular and sculpted, the shoulders tapering to triangular metal points. These were swiftly followed by a slender, yet just as strongly-armoured, torso, and elongated legs, the metallic muscles seeming to flex and bunch as Keoni's own muscles did.

He stared at the giant, all thoughts of his family and the chaos consuming the *David Redmond* forgotten in that moment. Where the coming of the lusca had provoked a horrified reaction within him, the appearance of the silver colossus brought forth only awe.

As the metal giant rose from the sea, two slender arms detached from its sides, and with a sound like a fishing spear being sharpened on a whetstone so loud it rang out across the entirety of the ship-city, two slender blades slid from sheathes in the giant's arms. Keoni found himself blinded by the glare coming off the twin swords.

Without announcing its presence, the silver giant struck, sinking both blazing blades into the body of the lusca. Where the weapons struck, they had the same effect as the napalm flamethrowers, burning away portions of the hideous creature's body.

A near ultrasonic scream rose from the creature, a squeaking hiss like that made by a squid thrown onto a hot skillet.

The giant withdrew its blades and struck again. Aware of its presence now, the lusca swung its heavy arms at the giant, each one ten times as long as an outrigger. But while the creature was the larger, the silver warrior was the more agile. The giant ducked the wind-milling limbs of the lusca and swung its twin sword-arms again, with a speed that Keoni would not have expected from something so huge.

One of the superheated blades sliced through the meat of the lusca's body. The second caught one of the four thick tentacles, carving a gobbet of coral-pink flesh from the flailing limb.

Keoni followed its descent as the chunk of anthazoa-flesh thudded down on the *David Redmond.* It was bigger than a man and a smelled like frying octopus.

With the ship rocking under him, Keoni warily approached the lump of flesh. He could see more clearly now the tiny coral-like creatures that made up the shapeless mound, a writhing mass of tiny tentacles and pseudopods, the milky undulating flesh rippling with bursts of stress colours.

As he watched, it became even more amorphous, as some of the exposed white meat continued to blacken and shrivel—so hot had been the blade that had sliced it from the colossal creature that the excised lump was still cooking—it seemed to Keoni that the rest of the mass was dissolving, as if the surviving polyps were trying to detach themselves from those that were already lost.

A reverberating crash that sounded, and felt, like two ship-cities colliding jerked Keoni's attention from the dispersing mass of lusca-flesh to the battle raging between the two colossi off the bow of the ship-city.

He gave a cry of panic and disbelief as he saw the silver giant come crashing down towards him. In a desperate attempt to escape the giant's scything, sun-hot swords the colony-creature had hurled itself bodily at the machine-man. Both taller and heavier that the sun-blade warrior, the impact of the monster sent the giant toppling onto the *David Redmond*.

People screamed as the colossus they had taken to be their defender became the author of their demise. The giant crashed down on the ship, its feet clearly losing all purchase on the seabed. As it fell, its right side towards the vessel, one of the guardian's burning blades struck the deck too.

Keoni heard the grinding hum of hidden mechanisms housed inside the vast robotic arm as the giant tried to retract the weapon, but it was still only halfway back in its sheath when it hit, the exothermic blade slicing through the deck plates, the steel becoming molten in seconds. Smoke and steam gouted from the entry point as the sun-hot sword vaporised the substance of the ship.

The blade slid through the ship, cutting through the decks below, severing powerlines and rupturing water pipes. Any poor tribesfolk who found themselves in its path also found their flesh and blood flash-fried by the massive heated blade. Flames erupted from the fissure gouged in the deck as a fuel tank ignited somewhere below. And then slowly, yet inexorably, the *David Redmond* started to sink.

Where the lusca acted with the instinct of a cornered animal, the robot behaved as if driven by a reasoning human intelligence. Even as it fell beneath the weight of the monster, with a grinding of gears the vast machine twisted at the waist—the piston-powered digits of its colossal hand crushing the side of the ship as it arrested its fall—and swung the blade still extruded from its left arm in a one-hundred-and-eighty-degree arc. It brought the blade backwards first—skirting dangerously close to the hull of the *David Redmond* as it did so—and then swung it up behind it to bring the sword down on top of the beast.

The blade struck the lusca on the top of what passed for its head, slicing through the tentacle fronds surrounding its cavernous mouth. A smell like shellfish left too long on a fire assailed Keoni's nostrils as the white-hot weapon burned down through the body of the monster without showing any sign of stopping, bifurcating the creature, until the superheated blade touched the sea, sending great clouds of salty steam into the air and obscuring the titans from view.

The clouds parted again, and Keoni saw the two halves of the monster peel away from each other and flop into the sea, sending a great wall of water washing over the hull. The creature's pallid flesh had been burned to a blackened crisp where the blade had done its dreadful damage. But at the same time, Keoni saw the silver giant convulse, as if gripped by a paralysing seizure. Its fluid movements stiffened and then, just as if someone had flicked the off switch, the guardian slumped onto the *David Redmond*, striking it with a dreadful, death-knell clang that rang out across the ship-city.

Keoni stared at the felled giant, its head resting on the deck of the slowly sinking ship, not twenty yards away, in bewilderment. It didn't make sense; how could the lusca have crippled the silver giant? Surely hitting the side of the ship couldn't have caused it damage catastrophic enough to put it out of action like this. There was no smoke emanating from within its metal shell and no erratic electrical discharge. Keoni had not even heard the grinding of worn gears or struggling internal mechanisms. There had to be some other reason why the giant had fallen.

Staring fixedly at it in disbelief, he approached the helm-head of the silver giant, where it lay, on its right cheek-plate, facing him. A dim ruddy glow of hazard lighting replaced the blue glow that had emanated from its visor-slit.

Now that the warrior was out of action, and Keoni was no longer dazzled by the brilliant sunlight reflecting from its gleaming armour, he could see that the shell of the giant was in fact pitted with corrosion, rust-red patches visible here and there between the interlocking steel plates, while strange faded shapes had been stencilled in a line down one side of the giant's metal torso; Keoni supposed it might have been a name.

"Keoni!" came his sister's voice from across the deck. "What are you doing?"

He didn't answer her but kept walking purposely towards the head of the silver colossus.

As he approached it, he was able to make out a delineation between the metal plates forming the giant's head. It was unmistakeably a hatch. Was there someone inside the silver giant? Once he had the thought, there was no way he couldn't open the hatch and find out.

There were discrete indentations hidden between the metal plates, inset steps that enabled him to climb up to the hatch, even though, due to the way the head was resting on the deck, it was like climbing up the underside of an overhang.

Holding himself against the side of the huge head with one hand, he activated the opening mechanism of the hatch, which swung open with a hiss of changing air pressures, and a gust of stale air, redolent with the potent aroma of age-old sweat, assailed him. He gagged and swung away from the opening, taking in great heaving breaths to clear the foul air from his lungs.

Steeling himself again, he peered inside. The open hatch led to a metal shaft that angled up towards the interior of the robotic head.

"Keoni!" Kaimi was standing in the shadow of the huge head, billows of thick black smoke blowing across the deck behind her.

"Go away, Kaimi!"

"What are you doing?"

"Go away!" he repeated more emphatically.

Taking a deep breath, and turning back to the shaft, he climbed inside.

After only a short distance the shaft opened into a cramped cabin space. Keoni wasn't sure what he had been expecting to find inside the silver giant's head, but it wasn't this.

Strapped into a leather seat at the heart of the cabin, in front of a bank of blinking lights and bathed in the ruddy glow that permeated the cockpit, was a man. He was wearing a loose vest and combat fatigues, similar to those worn by the sentries on board the *David Redmond*, and he was old. He appeared to be little more than skin and bone, his scalp almost hairless, and his features appeared strange to Keoni. The man's face was flatter than the faces of the people of Keoni's tribe, with a small nose and wide cheekbones.

On his head was a helmet that descended from the roof of the cabin on a flexible cable. Through the helmet's face-covering transparent visor Keoni could see that his eyes were closed and if it hadn't been for the straps holding him into the chair, Keoni would probably have found the man lying on the floor of the cabin, so slumped was he within the harness.

What was the old man's purpose here? Was he the guardian's pilot?

Using grab-handles bolted to the curving walls of the cabin, Keoni eased himself into the cramped space.

"Is he alive?" came a small voice from behind him.

"Kaimi!" Keoni snapped. His sister peered down at him from the top of the shaft.

Suddenly, as if in response to Kaimi's question, a sound

like twittering electronic birdsong echoed around the cabin, making them both start.

"What was that?" The buzzing sound came again. "It sounds like talking."

The electronic voice ignored Kaimi's interruption and suddenly, mid-sentence, they were both able to understand what it was saying.

"Austronesian language detected," came the voice, soft-spoken and feminine. "Eastern Polynesian."

"I can understand it now but at the same time I still can't understand it, if you know what I mean," Kaimi said, tipping her head to one side as she listened.

"Tahitic."

"I know what you mean," said Keoni, equally bewildered.

"Maori selected," the voice pronounced, was silent for a moment, and then said, "Greetings."

"Hello?" Keoni said warily, taking in the entire interior of the cabin, searching for the source of the voice.

"Greetings," the voice said again. "I am the Guardian Interface Protocol Program."

"What's a Guardian in-your-face?" Kaimi asked the air.

"The Guardian Interface Protocol Program bridges the gap between the pilot's consciousness and mechanoid's machine-mind. It relays the pilot's thought impulses to the Guardian, and relays damage indicators to the pilot's cerebral cortex, enabling man and machine to operate as one."

"Who's he?" Keoni said, his eyes fixed on the man currently slumped in the pilot's seat.

"His name was Yurei Ishiguro," said the interface.

"Was?" queried Kaimi.

"Yurei Ishiguro suffered a cardiac arrest. All attempts to restart his heart failed. Yurei Ishiguro is dead."

Despite the electronic voice maintaining the same neutral tone, Keoni couldn't help feeling that something about the way it made the pronouncement of the pilot's death made it sound almost sad.

"This is why the Guardian shutdown. To be fully operational, the *Kaiju Killer* needs a pilot."

**"WHAT ARE YOU DOING?" KAIMI** asked, horrified, as Keoni punched the release button on the dead pilot's harness, allowing his body to fall to the floor of the cabin.

"I'm going to do what I can to make amends for all the trouble I've caused," he said, as he climbed into the cracked leather seat himself.

"But you can't know it was your fault."

"Father thinks it was." Keoni pulled the straps of the harness over his shoulders, fastening them at his waist. "Go to father. He needs you."

His sister looked up at him with tears in her wide eyes. "And I need you, big brother."

"I have to do this, Kaimi," Keoni insisted. "Alone. Please try to understand."

"Are you sure?" she said, gulping back a sob whilst taking his hand and squeezing it.

"I need to fix this. I need you to be safe."

"Please put on the interface helmet," chimed the interface.

First kissing his shark tooth talisman, his heart beating like a tribal drum against the cage of his ribs, Keoni carefully lowered the helmet over his head.

"Calibrating," came the voice of the interface through the helmet itself.

Warily, Keoni closed his hands around the control levers, testing the feel of them in his palms.

The crippling stabbing pain arrived without warning. It was as if someone had thrust a frozen fishing spear through the middle of his brain as a bolt of pure information was uploaded into his cerebral cortex.

A host of images filled his head as data, in its purest form, flooded his mind. He saw newsreels, internet news feeds, broadcast bulletins, a host of headlines, footage of battles between men and the "kaiju"—that was the word he saw and heard repeated over and over again—the strange creatures that Keoni knew as the lusca. The information pumped directly into his brain core so that it remained there, readily accessible, as if he had always known it.

Keoni gasped for breath, physically shaking with the strain of the cerebral download, sweat glistening on his dark skin.

He understood everything now...

**CENTURIES AGO, THE WORLD REACHED** a tipping point. Humankind stood at the precipice of an environmental disaster. If it took that final collective step into the void, there would be no going back. And so, at long last, the nations of the world combined their scientific know-how after their leaders signed the Gaia Treaty.

Balance had to be restored. Renewable sources of energy were the only ones available to humankind now. Plans were put into action to ensure the relentless destruction of the biosphere ceased for good. But there were many parts of the world where Mother Nature would need to be given a helping hand to repair the damage left in the aftermath of centuries of humankind's pillaging of the planet's natural resources. In some parts of the world, that meant attempting to restore the dead coral reefs that had lain bleached and lifeless for decades.

And so the Proteus Project was born. Geneticists and marine biologists worked together to re-engineer the base DNA of numerous corals, giving Mother Nature the means to reclaim her reefs. But in the rush to reverse centuries of ecological ruination, in his hubris, Man over-reached himself once again.

At first Project Proteus was hailed as a great success; the corals quickly reclaimed what had once been theirs and the seas around them soon teemed with life again. But the genetically-modified *corallium novum* did not stop there. They continued to grow and multiply, reaching beyond their reclaimed reef homes to lay claim to uninhabited island chains and outlying coastal communities, growing in size all the time, mutating, evolving to combat whatever obstacles stood in their way, just as they had been genetically programmed to do. And when they encountered resistance, their approach became more aggressive.

Before the scientists knew it, the lusca—as some had christened the creatures—turned their attentions to the land. The outlying coastal communities were the first to be swallowed up, their inhabitants becoming food for the rapidly mutating monsters.

Those who could took to the seas to escape the fast-replicating coral-creatures, heading far away from any landmasses, that they might escape the monsters' seemingly inexorable advance. But isolated pockets of the world's military fought back.

A scorched earth policy was applied, but in the long term this only made the problem worse. It turned out that an entire medusa-genoform lusca could reform itself from the tiniest polyps—the organisms coming together to form new lusca colonies, reproducing rapidly and growing exponentially day by day—and bombing runs, or attacks against the creatures utilising heavy ordnance, merely helped to spread the polyps further afield.

The only thing that the lusca seemed truly vulnerable to was intense heat, but deploying fire and fury, like the world had never seen, against an enemy that was either already located in, or could rapidly retreat to, the sea, proved nigh on impossible. The sun's rays focused into killing heat beams by satellites in orbit around the planet had some effect, but on the ground ordinary weapons were not sufficient And so, as human society began to collapse across the globe, a last ditch attempt was made to fight back against the monsters.

Something was needed that could get right to the heart of the problem, meeting the lusca head on in single combat. In Japan, and surrounding territories, this dire need led to the development of the Guardian Programme; giant mechanoid war machines that could fight back against the monsters face to face, modelled after the feudal warriors of old, each guided into battle by a human pilot.

But it was too little too late. The islands of Japan were among the first to fall to the lusca, and those Guardians that survived went their separate ways; some banded together to seek vengeance against the monstrous invaders, others went it alone, ronin now, pursuing their enemies and eradicating them wherever they might be found.

The *Kaiju Killer* was one such warrior mechanoid and, piloted by Yurei Ishiguro, it had pursued its relentless quest for years. But while the machine had been built to endure for centuries, the man that piloted it had not, and now he had made the ultimate sacrifice in an effort to fulfil the oaths he had sworn following the Fall of Japan.

But now the *Kaiju Killer* had a new pilot to help it hunt the monsters, and the people of the *David Redmond* had a new champion.

**A THRUMMING HUM FILLED THE** cabin, and the blood-red hazard lighting was supplanted by a neon blue glow.

"Get out of here!" Keoni shouted at his sister. "Tell father... Tell father I did what had to be done."

"Keoni?"

"Go, Kaimi!"

"You are coming back though, aren't you?"

"Go! I love you!"

A shudder passed through giant mechanoid as its systems came online again. A startled Kaimi slid back down the shaft, half-leaping from the hatch, and landed in a roll on the deck of the sinking the *David Redmond.*

She watched, dumbfounded, as the robot heaved itself upright, the blades retracting into its arms. It swayed for a moment as if finding its balance, the sunlight reflecting from its curving horns, and the hatch hissed shut.

The pride that filled Kaimi's heart, as her brother took

charge of the towering silver avatar of war, was matched only by the horror that gripped her stomach as she saw the lusca rising from the sea behind the colossus. Where before there had been just one, now there were two.

Though they came from two halves of the original attacker, the half-formed lusca were distinct from one another. Perhaps, given time, they would have both come to resemble the original colony-creature, but in their half-grown state it was easy for Kaimi to tell them apart.

When the giant robot had seemed to kill the parent organism, the Guardian's attack had bifurcated the monster's body, but not into two equal halves. One half retained the majority of what had passed for the monster's head, with its writhing fringe of pseudopods and tentacles. The other was left with the bulk of the lusca's trunk-like body and three of its four writhing arms.

Clearly, as the colony-gestalt regrouped beneath the waves, elements that made up the whole had taken on new functions within the two lusca. In one, fresh mouthparts had formed where one would have expected to see a neck, and there was already the nub of a fourth starfish-limb protruding from the side of its body.

The other creature had shapeshifted, re-absorbing the tentacle-arm left to it, so that it now resembled a huge worm, its head nothing more than a gaping maw surrounded by long, rippling feelers.

As the Keoni-piloted Guardian turned, ready to finish them, the monsters struck with horrifying speed.

The original lusca had been bigger than the Guardian in every way; the twin horrors now assaulting it were shorter than the towering mechanoid. But there were two of them, both still at least as tall as the *David Redmond* was long.

As the starfish-like tentacled lusca lumbered in, the snake-like lusca-worm elongated, its elastic body narrowing as it stretched itself thin, its writhing mouthparts arching over and coming down towards the silver giant's head.

While the two creatures might once have been one, the individual colony-organisms coordinated by something akin to a gestalt consciousness, the two half-formed monsters now operated independently, even if their overall aim was the same.

The lusca-star barrelled into the giant robot, the sheer weight of the coral-creature sending it staggering backwards towards the ship-city. The worm's darting head struck, its clutching tentacles closing on thin air, as the Guardian fell away from it.

Then the silver titan rose once more. The lusca-worm lunged, its feeder-tentacles writhing with febrile convulsions, but Keoni was clearly ready for it this time. The Guardian crouched, avoiding a flailing blow from the wind-milling arms of the lusca-star, and the mechanoid's right arm described a broad arc through the air. The superheated blade made contact with the worm, slicing cleanly through it, the two halves of its body tumbling back into the sea, the mouth-tentacles still wriggling with sickening autonomy.

But now the lusca-star wrapped its boneless limbs around one of the giant machine's arms and pulled hard. The Guardian appeared unbalanced by the monster's assault, as it stumbled towards the creature. But then Kaimi saw it for a bluff—or simply an opportunistic act on the part of her brother?—as the robot brought its blazing right blade round again, severing one of the tightening tentacles at the root. The limb hit the edge of the deck before splashing into the sea.

Kaimi thought she heard something like a shrill scream rise from the beast, and not just from its mouth but from every part of it, as if the rippling skin of the creature was convulsing in agony.

Even as parts of it recoiled from the Guardian's attack, the lusca-star's remaining pair of tentacle-limbs kept a tight hold of the robot. But Keoni wasn't finished with it yet.

The Guardian thrust in again with the steaming blade—residue from the severed tentacle carbonising on the superheated blade—once, twice, three times.

The lusca shrank from before the Guardian, its physical form twisting into impossible shapes as the blazing blade struck again and again and again, the colony-creatures trying desperately to escape its burning touch.

The left arm-blade suddenly shot out of its sheath, bursting through the meat of the creature between its remaining pair of limbs. As the arms released their hold on the worn armour, the Guardian brought both blades to bear at last.

A flurry of blows followed, as the giant robot delivered so many burning wounds to the monster that the colony was no longer able to maintain cohesion. But even as the creature came apart and slid into the sea, so the tentacled mouth of the lusca-worm emerged from the churning waves and, latching onto the giant's leg like a leech, began to haul itself up the armoured greaves.

Its warrior swords blazing as bright as the sun, the Guardian thrust both blades into the sea and the remains of the lusca that lurked under the water. Great clouds of steam rose around it, the salty fog drifting over the ship-city, obscuring the giant from view as the sea boiled.

When, at last, the breeze coming in off the sea dispersed the clouds, the colossus stood alone. Not a single polyp of the reef-monster remained, the lusca having been boiled alive in the cauldron of the ocean.

"Kaimi!"

She turned, hearing her father's voice again, and ran to his open arms, the tears flowing freely.

"I thought I'd lost you again!" he cried, glancing back over his shoulder as he hurried her away. "We have to get off this ship. The *David Redmond* is sinking."

She let him lead her away this time, but as she did, she turned once to see what had become of their Guardian.

The robot stood there, off the starboard bow, tall and proud. And in that moment, she was sure it was looking down at her.

**AS THE DISPARATE ELEMENTS OF** the ship-city began to break up, freeing themselves from the doomed and sinking *David Redmond*, Keoni took one last longing look at his home through the view-screen of the Guardian's cockpit.

"Goodbye, little sister," he said.

Yurei Ishiguro's mission was his mission now: there were other monsters to fight, and he would not—*could* not—relinquish the responsibility laid upon his shoulders. He was honour-bound to keep up the fight until every last one of the kaiju were dead.

The Guardian turned away from the dispersing fleet and

set off again, its feet carrying it across the seabed, sinking with each step as it headed for the deep ocean, until its torso, shoulders, and finally its horned helmet head were entirely submerged, and the *Kaiju Killer* was gone.

# WINTER MOON AND THE SUN BRINGER

KANE GILMOUR

**WINTER MOON PULLED HER FLEECE** blanket around her shoulders and stared into the crackling bonfire before her. Dark, straight hair hung down from her head, covering half her face, like always. At seventeen, she was old beyond her age, haggard and tired, the past four years packed with chaotic events. She shivered in the crisp December air, but she knew the weather could be worse. Much, much worse.

The other teens gathered around the robust fire all knew that her appearance under the perpetual curtain of black hair was not her real story, only the result of it. They would get the full tale tonight when she was ready to begin speaking. Tonight, on the winter solstice, she would pass on her knowledge and her wisdom, before her eighteenth birthday came—when she would forget the true face of the world.

Moon held court around the glowing fire, as if all her subjects were Abenaki, like her. But six of the eight

surrounding her were not even Indians. They were white kids from the hipster suburbs of Burlington, but if they were willing to hear, and willing to pass on what she would tell them, then she was happy to have them here. The mission was more important than ethnic identities or labels, even though she had been raised by her grandfather to believe that her ethnic identity was of paramount importance.

She cleared her throat, and even though the gathered teenagers had been silent before—the only noise filling the circle that of the crackling, spitting fire—now she could hear them settle, and they became even more still. It was as if they feared to even budge on their picnic table benches, a stray rustle from their clothing ruining the solemnity of the night. Either that or they were just all afraid of her. *Celebrity has its perks*, she thought. Then she spoke at last, diving right in to the good stuff.

"The 2000 U.S. census suggested that there were only around two hundred Abenaki Indian teens in the country. And yes, I said 'Indian.' That's what I am, and I prefer to be called that over 'Native American,' which is a bullshit term someone in Washington thought up for a Census in the 1970s—long before I was born. The name Indian came from Christopher Columbus either being a halfwit and thinking he'd landed in Asia, or possibly as a linguistic assimilation of his Spanish expression for 'People of God.' *En Dios*. Who the heck knows anymore? But if it's a choice between 'Indian' or some bullshit euphemism from a bean-counter in DC, I'll take Indian. But what I really am is Abenaki, and like I said, twenty-some-odd years ago, there were only two hundred Abenaki teenagers. No one knows for sure, but we guess that now there are only ninety."

She paused for impact, raising her head and looking at each of the teenagers with her one good eye. Her audience was rapt, and no one was diving in with questions yet, so she plunged on, taking a deep breath of the pine-scented air.

"Out of those ninety, it's anyone's guess how few are actually First Born teenagers with the sight. But I can tell you this. Out of all the remaining tribal peoples in this part of the country, I'm probably the only one who was there when 'Hurricane Irene' struck."

Kanozas, one of the two other Abenaki in the circle, was just thirteen, and she had gained her sight only a few months earlier. The girl had a short, bob-style haircut, and wore jeans and a flannel shirt. She looked just like any other Vermont kid, as her Abenaki genes had been muted by generations of interbreeding with Caucasians. But she was aware of her heritage, and she was a keen student. The girl raised her hand, clearly loaded with a question.

A smile spread over Moon's curtained face. "You don't need to raise your hand here. This isn't school."

Kanozas dropped her hand into her lap and quickly looked around to see if any of the others would make fun of her. No one did. No one would.

"What is your question?" Moon prodded the young girl.

"I know I'm jumping the gun a bit, but it wasn't really a hurricane, right?"

Moon nodded. "Correct. All of us here are First Born children. All of us have the sight. We see the world as it truly is, but we only carry the vision until around our eighteenth birthdays, and then it fades. Then we forget what we knew and go about living like our parents do: seeing natural and man-made disasters, instead of the truth."

One of the Burlington boys, a seventeen year old with shaggy blond hair and a battered leather jacket mumbled to himself. "Monsters."

He had muttered the word, but everyone heard him, and they all nodded their heads. A gust of cold breeze sent a spiral of smoke from the bonfire in Moon's direction, and she held her breath until it passed. Then she also nodded and spoke again.

"Yes. The world is full of monsters. And we are the only ones who know."

Noli, a fourteen-year-old boy, and the only other Abenaki present, frowned like he didn't follow what was going on. She understood that. He had only had his sight for a year, and this was the first major telling he had attended. Up until now, all his knowledge consisted of rumor and whatever any of the older, more experienced kids had told him. And sometimes they were too busy trying to stay alive to pass on what they knew.

"Noli, you understand how the Perception Filter works?" Moon asked him.

The boy shook his head. "I thought no one knew how it worked."

"That's right," Moon confirmed. "We don't know what it is or where it comes from. We only know that it *is*. The 'Perception Filter' is what we call it. Adults don't see what we see."

"What about little kids?" One of the white girls, Suzy, asked. She was slender and plain, but her knuckles showed that she had seen battles already. "I've heard they can sometimes see."

"Small children sometimes get empathic feelings about what they *can't* see," Moon corrected her. Her voice was soft, and the older kids nodded in agreement. "They might sense a monster in an old abandoned house, but they never actually glimpse it, even if they know it's there. People have attributed those sensations to the paranormal for generations. But we know that for some reason, they simply cannot see what *we* can, and the Filter makes them see something else. Only First Borns. Your younger siblings won't ever see what you can. If you die early, they may not inherit the sight from you. If you try to tell them about what you can see, they even hear a different story. You could write your little brother a story, but he'll either see different words on the page or none at all. We don't know why. But we know that for some reason, it has been this way since the beginnings of recorded history. We do what we can to protect those who cannot see, because their perceptions of reality are altered."

Moon stood up, tossing her curtained hair out of her face and over her shoulder, allowing the others to take in her scarred visage. They knew about her injuries, and no one gasped or stared, but they all looked, confirming what they had heard. She did not feel any sense of shame from her looks, though. These were battle scars, and she stood proud and erect, allowing the others to gaze upon the burned tissue. The entire right side of her face was covered in thick ripples of it, her eye socket empty and black.

"And on nights like this one," she continued, "we pass on what we have learned. A history of oral storytelling stretching back centuries. Because every newly sighted teenager is rightly terrified of the sudden inexplicable vision they gain. They, like each of you, begin to see the creatures that secretly inhabit this world. And as you all know, those monsters can wreak havoc on the world, but other people will only see the results of that damage, and they will experience different causes for it. They think a teenager murdered by a rampaging hydra had a drunk driving accident. A cyclops tears up a suburban backyard, but the homeowners see fallen tree limbs from a storm that might not have even happened. Blood stains become grass stains. An attack becomes a mugging. And in the cases of the truly immense creatures on this world, their passing becomes epic storms. Their battles, war. Or in my case, a rare hurricane in Vermont."

"What really started Hurricane Irene?" Noli asked.

"Terror."

**MOON HAD TURNED THIRTEEN A** week earlier, but now she was running for her life. She was sprinting down a trail in the woods with three other teenagers, all older than her, sweat pouring off all their faces.

Her next-door neighbor, Mark Roman, ran at her side. He was seventeen, had his own car, and was the most popular boy in U32—the regional high school, where Moon would be attending, in just a year. He had always been friendly with her, despite their age gap, but as her birthday had approached, he'd begun hanging out with her more. As she found out, he had known she was going to gain the sight, and he wanted to ease her into it, being present and available to explain the new world to her. Once she had seen her first creature—a massive worm, the size of a school bus and three times as long—she had been both flabbergasted at the sight and incredibly grateful Mark had gone out of his way to ease her transition into being sighted.

But that was two days ago, before the world started to end.

"What *is* that thing?" Moon shouted.

An ear shattering rumble pursued them, shaking the ground and dislodging pine needles from the trees around them, showering them as they ran. All four of the teens clapped their hands to their ears against the shrieking, roaring sound, until it faded a moment later.

But no one stopped running, so Moon ran, too.

"Terror!" Mark shouted.

"I know, right?" she said. The creature behind them was hundreds of feet tall and reptilian in appearance, with giant spikes stretching out backward from its head, neck, and forearms. There were spikes pointing upward from its hips, and the creature's tail looked like a jumbled pile of giant bones in a tapering deadfall. All over its upper body were glowing dots of red light, which was how she had first spotted the thing moving through the distant mist. But then its head had cleared the cloud and it had opened a terrible maw full of teeth as tall as buildings. It roared. The others had noticed the creature, then, and turned to flee. That was twenty minutes ago. They were still running.

"But what is it?"

"That's its name," Scott Ferriver called back from ahead of Mark. He wore a black leather jacket that concealed a curved scimitar-like sword on his back, the handle sticking out of the collar like one of the creature's bony projections. Unlike

Mark, Scott went to Montpelier High, and so did the Abenaki girl with him, Saba. She was the oldest of the group. Nearly eighteen. Saba carried a set of knives on her hip. Mark had explained that a lot of the kids in Montpelier carried blades that were coated in monster blood. Adults, susceptible to the Perception Filter, couldn't see the weapons, and the teens used them to protect themselves from monsters—or in the case of Saba and Scott, to protect others.

When Moon had asked whether she would have to carry a weapon, Mark had told her "We'll get to that." She wasn't sure what good a blade would do against something taller than the mountains all around them, but she still wished she had something with her now.

"Okay," she shouted. "But what *is* it?"

Saba slowed, letting Mark pass her, and she placed her hand on the back of Moon's neck. The girl spoke to her in Abenaki, "Run now. Questions later!" Then Saba gave her a push, as if lending Moon some of her speed.

Although there was no actual transference of ability, Moon intuited the urgency in that shove and found a reserve of strength she didn't know she had. Her breathing became regular, and her strides longer. Soon she overtook Mark in a wide spot of the path, Saba right beside her.

The ground shook as they ran, the tremors increasing in frequency and severity, until she was sure she would turn an ankle.

Then came a furious burst of wind in her face, as if all the air was being sucked out of the world. Running against the wind was nearly futile, but they all struggled, like insects caught in sticky honey. The wind shrieked past them, building to a crescendo, a high keening pitch.

Then suddenly all the wind resistance in front of them dissipated. Scott fell forward, scrabbling in the dirt. The others managed to keep their feet, but just barely. Mark rammed into Moon's back. Then Scott was back on his feet, running faster than before.

Moon took a single step forward without the wall of wind in her face, when the world behind her erupted with heat. She felt like the clothes on her back would burst into flame. The wind came back again, this time superheated. The breeze was like the air coming out of an oven that had been cooking a roast all day.

Saba grabbed her arm and shouted at her, but Moon couldn't hear what she was saying. The noise filled the world, a reverse of the horrible shriek from a moment ago. And now the world was darkening, a massive shadow filling one half of Moon's vision. Saba ripped her jacket off and started swatting at Moon with it.

Moon was too stunned to do anything but raise her arms in defense.

The burst of heat faded, and was replaced with extreme cold, the right side of Moon's body aching from it, as if she had just stepped out into a sub-zero winter. But it was April, and Saba kept beating her with the jacket. Then she threw it on the ground.

Noise returned to the forest in a surge, Mark screaming incoherently, and Scott shouting far ahead of them that they were almost to the car. Saba was crying and panicked. "Oh God, oh God, oh God."

Moon looked down at the jacket on the forest past. It was

steaming, and singed. Curls of smoke whipping off it in the direction of the parking area up ahead. Then Moon turned, looking behind her, where Mark rolled on the ground. At least, she thought it was Mark. His body was black and charred, with glowing orange pockets in the strange bark-like folds of what used to be his skin. A gurgling noise came from his throat, and then he fell silent, his arm flopping across his chest and onto the smoking ground. Behind him, for what seemed like miles, the forest had been obliterated. Trees were aflame. The air was scorched so badly, she could taste soot in her mouth and on the air. A cloud of black hung where there should have been trees.

Beyond it all, miles away, Terror's head loomed above the blackness, still touching the sky. Liquid orange flame appeared to drip out of its mouth, like saliva, glowing and casting odd shadows up the creature's reptile face. The mouth hung open, huge teeth scoured clean by the purifying fire that had erupted from the beast.

Then Saba was dragging Winter Moon forward again, down the trail, as the horrific Terror took another rampaging step in their direction. The ground rumbled and wavered under her feet. Finding some kind of rhythm was impossible. She half staggered and was half dragged the rest of the way to the car in the parking lot. Scott backed the yellow Ford Mustang up and turned it, the passenger side door wide open. Saba pushed Moon inside, and she struggled to climb into the back seat while Saba rammed into her from behind, screaming "Go, go, go!"

The ground shook again, and the Mustang's wheels spun on the dirt and gravel of the lot, before the car lurched forward, throwing Moon to the floor of the back seat. The acceleration made righting herself difficult, but she got up in time to see the rest of the forest set ablaze, an immense stream of reddish-orange jagged light reaching from the blaze up to Terror's face. She couldn't see past the glow in her left eye and the dark in her right, but Moon was sure the monster breathed the liquid napalm like some sort of dragon. Orange billows of curling flame larger than the car, interwoven with black smoke, expanded sideways. The fire clouds stretched into the trees, vaporizing everything they touched.

And then, even as the car raced away from the scene at manic speed, the fire began to chase them. The road was melting just behind them, the heat palpable even through the rear window. Moon watched fascinated. She was in shock, she knew, but the curling, swaying flames were simultaneously beautiful and terrible to behold. She knew they were all dead. In just a few moments, the fire would outpace them, consume them, and turn her and the others into their component atoms. There was no escaping it. So instead of freaking out, a calm settled over her.

Winter Moon reached out her right hand to touch the window and was surprised to see a limb as shriveled and blackened as Mark's thrashing corpse. She had just a second to wonder about her skin, and then she extended her hand anyway, as charred as it was, to touch the glass and meet the flames as they leapt up to touch the rear of the car.

Then the strangest thing happened.

The flames stopped, right in the middle of the road, as if rejecting her touch. They stood up straight and then recoiled backward, as if in horror at the thought of finishing the job they had started on her. Then the world slowed down, the car sliding sideways, and Moon was thrown against the driver-side rear door. She hit against her blackened arm, but was surprised she could feel nothing. No pain. She did feel her stomach lurch, as the Mustang's passenger-side wheels left the ground. Her senses felt heightened. She could smell the strange halted flames, and hear the roar of the wind and the scratch of the tires on the dirt road, as the car tipped. She felt certain they would roll now, but everything froze in place, her anticipated direction not matching the world's decision yet again.

Moon had just enough time to see with her left eye that the flames had not only stopped, but retreated, ripping away from her and the side of the car, as if yanked back by their horrific creator.

From her right eye, she saw nothing.

Then the car slammed down on its passenger-side wheels, and lurched forward again, twisted, and returned the scene of the fleeing conflagration to the back window. Moon could see the fires still retreating, but the smoke behind her completely obscured the terrifying creature in the distance.

Scott kept his foot mashed on the accelerator, putting a mile between them and the fire before propelling the car up a steep hill. At the top the road curved. He slowed the car to a stop, and both he and Saba looked out the passenger side window.

It was then that Winter Moon fully comprehended that she could not see out of her right eye. She touched her left hand to her face and felt hardness and wet softness, but not her skin. She craned her head up and saw her reflection in the rearview mirror. Half her face had been charbroiled, leaving sticky patches of blood and pulp amidst the blackened swirls and ruptures.

*Just like Mark*, she thought, still dazed, but calm.

Then she turned her entire face so she could see out the window with her good eye, and she forgot all about her hideous new visage.

From their vantage point on the giant hill, they could see the spot where Terror's breath had annihilated the forest. And Moon understood why the creature's rampage began.

It was being attacked.

Her first thought was that the airborne creature was a giant bald eagle, but she soon saw that wasn't exactly the case. Easily the size of Terror, the bird-like thing filled the sky. Hundreds of feet tall, it had the smooth white head of a bald eagle, and a bright yellow beak. Its muscular upper torso was brown, but instead of feathers, the creature looked like it had a lion's mane of hair around its neck. Below the torso, the thing had tiled, reptilian skin, still brown, but mottled and plated, tapering down to vicious yellow talons larger than a school building, and an armored and spiked tail like a stegosaurus.

As the bird-creature flapped its massive wings and swooped in to take a nip at Terror's shoulder, the wind from the giant, spread appendages staggered the monster on the ground. Now Moon knew what had stopped the car, and nearly flipped it. She understood that the fire hadn't retreated—it had been blown backward by a force ten gale.

"Kisosen," Saba whispered.

Winter Moon knew the name—not from any teaching the other sighted teens had given her, but from her grandfather's

Abenaki tales. Kisosen was the solar deity, who opened his wings to bring the day and closed them to bring the night. Kisosen, in Abenaki, meant the Sun Bringer.

But she knew that if a being the size of Kisosen was fighting something the size of Terror, they would bring only one thing to the world.

Devastation.

Terror swept a brutal clawed arm upward, the long, talon-like fingers tearing through the feathering of one of Kisosen's immense wings. The massive bird-creature shrieked in anguish, then flew up out of Terror's reach. Moon wondered if that would be the last of it, but Terror turned its terrible maw upward and unleashed a blast of red-orange liquid flame at Kisosen as the Sun Bringer dove downward, talons extended for the kill.

Just before the first lick of flames touched the mighty bird, it swooped left, only the tip of its outstretched wing getting singed—and then only slightly. But next the bird reversed angle, just as easily, and swerved upward, raking its deadly claws up Terror's back, between the deadly spires.

Now Terror shrieked, and the three teens clapped their hands to their ears, the deafening sonic assault powerful enough to shatter the windows on the Mustang behind them. As glass tinkled to the ground at their backs, in front of them, the fight raged on. Terror threw itself to the ground, rolling and lashing upward with the massive spiked tail, just as Kisosen struck with his own barbed appendage. The spikes on each tail locked, and Terror rolled back the way it had come, its scaled tail tugging the soaring bird out of the sky, and down to the ground.

"Who is the aggressor here?" Winter Moon wondered aloud.

"Most likely Terror wandered into Kisosen's territory," Scott said, not taking his eyes off the action. "She has a habit of going wherever she wants around the globe. No one's seen her in the United States for at least thirty years. Kisosen's normally quiet; it takes a lot to bother him."

Terror tugged the giant avian creature downward, rolling her own tail around her body, until Kisosen's talons raked her again. But now Terror rammed an elbow joint backward, its massive spike thrusting deep into Kisosen's torso.

The bird's keening shriek was deafening, and it instinctively flapped its powerful wings harder, lifting both creatures up into the air. The action sent a powerful wind toward the nearby hillside, and the teens had to lean forward to not be blown back into the side of the car.

Terror threw its immense head backward, the huge spikes on its crown also impaling Kisosen, and the glow from the three rows of strange lights on Terror's head illuminated the impact, even in the swirling smoke from the forest fire below the combatants. Moon could see an arc of crimson blood launch out of Kisosen's white plumage when the spikes hit him.

Then Kisosen struck with his deadly beak, pulling a chunk of flesh from the back of Terror's neck. Terror struggled in pain, and in doing so, her tail came loose from its lock on the bird creature. Kisosen nipped again, but already Terror was falling back toward the ground.

When she hit, the shockwave was so severe it *did* knock the teens down. But Terror took the impact in stride, rolling and blasting another tongue of fire into the sky from her mouth. Kisosen had risen out of range, but the burst was impressive. Then the bird once again plunged downward in an attack dive.

Terror clambered up and set her feet in a wide stance, her face tensed into a squint, but her mouth was not open. Maybe she had no more liquid fire to spew. Moon climbed to her feet and watched as Kisosen rocketed out of the sky, his deadly talons ready to drive right through his reptilian enemy.

Just as Kisosen closed the distance, Terror's armored arms shot upward, and her gargantuan clawed hands passed the talons, reaching around the upright stem, and clamping shut. Just like that, both combatants froze for a split second. With Kisosen completely immobilized Terror wasted no time. She pivoted, twisting her body, and swinging the now flightless Kisosen. At the 180º point of her arc, Terror released Kisosen, throwing him toward a stand of still burning trees.

Soot, soil, and feathers erupted in a cloud from the impact site. Then with a powerful flap of those several-hundred-foot-wide wings, the Sun Bringer rose, leaping high into the air to prevent being nabbed again. Instead he turned in the air and seemed to hover for a minute before flapping his wings hard and firing a blast of air downward that nearly knocked Terror over. Trees—both those untouched by the conflagration and those aflame—ripped out of the ground and pelted the giant reptile. To a beast the size of Terror, hundreds of feet tall, the trees were like a small pile of toothpicks hurled at her. Even the flaming pines were beneath her notice, and they all bounced harmlessly off her armored hide.

But the torrent of wind that the flying creature's wings created unsteadied her. Terror's feet slid backward against the force of the gale, and the winds reached to where Winter Moon stood. She ran behind the Mustang, and the others followed her lead. As the wind buffeted the car, they crouched down, Moon hiding behind the additional protection of a large boulder to the side of the car. The others stayed tight against the metal doorframe, still peeking through the car to see the battle far on the other side—but Moon had seen enough.

She ducked down lower behind the boulder, curling herself into a tiny ball. She squeezed her eyes shut, at the howl of the wind ripping up the mountain. It was all too much. Mark's death, the fire, the monsters, the wind, and her burns. She could feel herself shutting down.

Then she felt rain patter on her face.

*But the sky was clear before,* she thought.

Winter Moon opened her eyes to see storm cloud swirling above her. Each new flap of Kisosen's powerful wings affected the moving clouds above.

*He's actually changing the weather.*

She could feel that the temperature—which had been higher from the fires—was colder now. The rain that hit her upraised face was like tiny needles of ice, although on the right side, where she had been burned, she felt nothing at all.

Moon stood up, grasping her boulder. She could see through the body of the car, to the distant battle between epic creatures that should not exist. Terror blasted the sky with unnatural bursts of demonic flame, and Kisosen retaliated from the air, with flapping gusts of wind so strong they tore the world apart.

It all seemed so wrong to her.

*They will kill everyone if they don't stop.*

As if to prove her point, Kisosen swooped in low, his talons grasping Terror from behind, and lunged into the sky with his heavy load. Terror thrashed in the gigantic bird's grasp, tearing and stabbing with the spikes all over her body until the Sun Bringer unleashed the reptile, flinging her at the mountain.

At the car.

Winter Moon started to shout a warning as she ducked behind her boulder, but the only word she managed before Terror's miles-long tail swept the hilltop clean was "Look—"

The car rolled into the air, clearing Moon's head and her boulder, and flipped sideways into the distance. When it landed, it was so far away that Moon couldn't see where it hit.

Terror rolled down the hillside, back toward the battle, and Kisosen again battered the former forest with powerful gusts of hurricane wind. Moon looked around the bare hilltop for Scott and Saba, but she was alone with her boulder and the stumps of trees that had been shaved off the mountainside. She was alone, and the two gigantic monsters battled to the death, unaware of the destruction they caused and the human lives they ended. She gave a quick thought to the damage that the weather was causing and the lives that would be lost as the monster brawl spread into the nearby populated areas of Montpelier, Berlin, and Barre.

Then Terror unleashed another roar, this one filled with rage.

The ground shook, and Winter Moon clasped her hands over her ears.

She found herself sprinting down the far side of the mountain, weaving and dodging through trees, unaware that she had even fled the hilltop. Branches and leaves slapped at her as the sounds of battle continued behind her.

At some point she realized her hands had come away from her ears to bat wet branches away from her face, but her legs kept pumping, and she ran on, through the pelting rain.

Finally the shock of the day's events overwhelmed her, and Winter Moon collapsed to her knees in the mud. She stayed there, facing two mounds of dirt, side by side, each the size of a house. Beyond the mounds, in the distance, was a large hill with smaller mounds all over it, as if she were in a graveyard pocked with ancient burial cairns.

The wind whipped around her, Kisosen's storm now in full fury, battering her with sheets of vertical and horizontal rain. Each powerful gust of wind brought another sheet of dampness, and the cacophony of battle in the distance grew closer. Her nose was filled with the scents of leaves, pine needles, fire, and mud. Her skin was either burnt to a crisp or rippled with goosebumps.

She heaved for air on her knees in the mud, as lightning crackled through the sky.

"Someone help me," she said.

**"I CAN HELP YOU."**

The disembodied voice sounded like it came from everywhere, all at once, booming in her ears. Or in her own mind. But it felt... alien. Different. *Other*. The voice was deep and rumbled like the same quaking ground as when Terror had chased her earlier in the day. Deep, but even with the limited number of words, she could tell that the inflections were wrong.

Winter Moon knew that she had not thought the words.

Something else had.

"Where are you?"

"How is your face, Pebonkas?" the voice asked, everywhere and nowhere. This time she knew the words resounded in her mind, not her ears. The sounds of battle and the howling wind faded.

"My name is Winter Moon. Pebonkas sounds horrible coming out of Vermonter mouths. And worse in Massachusetts. So I use the English translation."

The voice chuckled. "And your face?"

"I can't feel it," Winter Moon said. "Who are you?"

"I have many names, but you may call me Kashikoi."

The voice was in her head, but its accent was foreign, its enunciation slow and precise. As if the unseen speaker was from far away and was still mastering the language.

"Where are you?" She asked again. "How can you help?"

"I am here," Kashikoi responded. "What is it you need?"

"Are you in my head?" Winter Moon asked.

A long delay. The sound of the storm and the battle beyond it were almost gone now, blotted out by a soothing wave of calm in her mind.

She began to wonder if she had imagined the voice.

But then it spoke again.

"Yes," the words came even slower. "I can see inside your head."

"Then look," she said.

Winter Moon thought about all that had happened, the deaths of her friends, and all the chaos and devastation the people across New England would suffer if the two behemoths did not cease trying to murder each other. She thought about her burned face, and the fact that she'd only had the sight for a week. She thought about how Mark had introduced her to Saba, and how Saba had explained that even though some teenagers with the sight fought the smaller creatures to protect humanity from them, it was the Abenaki job *not* to engage. They were the oral storytellers, the ones who passed knowledge down from generation to generation. Their duty was to absorb all the knowledge and pass it on to the others who would come after.

On the verge of tears, her thoughts swirled with panic and outrage, loss, grief, and confusion. She wasn't supposed to be witness to two mega-creatures destroying the world. She just wanted everything to stop.

The dirt on the house-sized dome in front of her trembled, and cascaded down the large hillock, as if something on top of it had disturbed the ground by treading on it. Then two immense golden eyes opened in the hillside, staring right at her.

"I see."

**TERROR SANK HER JAWS INTO** Kisosen's armored tail, scrabbling up the back of the bird-creature with her claws. The Sun Bringer cried out in pain, flapping his mammoth wings harder, and kicking backward with his talons, dislodging the attacker. Kisosen turned and nipped at Terror's face with his gnarled yellow beak, the razor-sharp tip gouging deep into Terror's left cheek.

Terror responded with a point-blank blast of fire from her mouth, the flames billowing out around both creatures' faces until they broke from their embrace. The fire scorched them both, but unarmored, the giant eagle creature endured the worst of the damage. Once again taking a higher vantage point, Kisosen flapped his terrible wings, swirling storm clouds around the battleground, the water scouring down in nearly solid sheets.

The storm rampaged all around the massive creatures, and the wind and hammering rain spread over the land for miles, wrecking homes, uprooting trees, flooding valleys, and killing wildlife. Terror hunched down against the blasts, holding her ground, while Kisosen appeared content to blast the creature with the elements from above instead of coming within range of the monster's humongous claws.

"STOP."

The voice boomed through the valley, drowning out the deafening thunder and the howling wind. Terror turned toward the voice, and Kisosen flew down to the ground, landing on his yellow talons.

A massive, hundred-foot tortoise-like creature approached them. Its shell was steeply pitched with erupting lumps, like mutations or boils. Its powerful scaled legs resembled a cross between a typical tortoise's leathery limbs and the reptilian muscled legs of a monitor lizard or Komodo dragon. Two dragon-like heads on separate necks stretched from thick folds at the front of the immense shell. Thick bony horns and ridges lined the twin heads, protruding backward along the jawline. Triple fins topped the rounded heads, while gnarled bird-beak jaws slowly opened, dripping a viscous pea-green saliva that burned holes through the ground wherever it touched. Golden eyes on each head crackled with golden fire.

But the voice had not come from the mammoth tortoise creature.

Standing on the shell of the slow-moving third combatant was a thirteen-year-old human girl, holding up her hand toward the gigantic foes. The double-headed tortoise had amplified the voice, but it had belonged to the child.

**"WHAT HAPPENED NEXT?"**

Kanozas asked the question, but everyone in Winter Moon's audience wanted the answer. She adjusted her fleece blanket against the chill in the air. The fire was dying down, and they would need to go inside soon.

"There are many great, omega-level creatures in the world," Winter Moon said. "We do not know all of them. But we know of Terror, and the Sun Bringer, and Kashikoi, the Great Tortoise. Well, I say 'tortoise' but Kashikoi is more like a cross between a turtle and a dragon. He sleeps on land, but he is just as adept in the water as he is on the ground. We know of the great spider creature of Central America, and the enormous elephant-reptile creature of Africa. There are giant squids and even a huge serpent with a head at either end that attacked Japan at the conclusion of World War II."

"How many do we know of?" Noli asked.

"Ten," Winter Moon replied. "The giant bear in China is dead. First Borns found its skeleton in the nineties. And the Ouroboros is also believed to be dead. The Sun Bringer is the only one of these gargantuan creatures to live in North America. Terror was just passing through. But when they encounter each other, these mighty beings can destroy whole nations. In this case, those without the sight construed the fight between Terror and Kisosen as Hurricane Irene. The Perception Filter took the devastation and presented it only as rain and wind to those who cannot see."

"How did the fight end?" Kanozas persisted.

Winter Moon smiled. "I don't think any of the others can speak in the minds of people or creatures, the way Kashikoi can. But he let me speak, and he projected the words and ideas to them, beseeching peace on behalf of the world. Both of the creatures stayed still long enough for Kashikoi to project my words and thoughts and images."

"Did it work?" The blonde girl with the battle-scarred knuckles, Suzy, asked the question on everyone's mind. "Did you stop the fight?"

"No. It was a hurricane. And that moment? It was just the calm in the eye of the storm."

Dylan, the shaggy-haired Burlington boy, shook his head. "Terror never stops."

"She did that day," Winter Moon surprised them all. "It was Kisosen who refused to back down. The giant eagle swooped up into the sky, and for a second, I thought the message had been received. But Kashikoi projected another thought to me alone. To hold on. The Sun Bringer launched skyward and then turned, talons extended, wings swept back in an attack plunge."

Kanozas had been sitting so far at the front edge of her seat that she fell out of it and onto the snowy ground.

Winter Moon laughed.

"What did you do?" the small girl asked from the ground.

"I rode that mighty creature into battle. Terror stalked away, off into the forest. But Kisosen turned his assault on Kashikoi. With two heads, though, Kashikoi would have had enough golden fire to blast the both of them. On his own, and with flammable feathers, the Sun Bringer really stood no chance against the benevolent tortoise. The fight ended in minutes, with Kisosen finally taking to the skies in retreat. First Borns sighted him later in the Pacific Northwest."

"What about Terror?" Noli asked. "Where did she go?"

"No one is sure. Sometimes she dives deep under the waters of the ocean and sleeps for decades."

Suzy asked the important question at last. "What did you learn from Kashikoi, after the fight?"

The bonfire still crackled, but it was getting low. All the assembled teens in the circle shivered from the cold. It was time to go inside the cabin. Winter Moon stood up and stretched her neck. The signal was understood, and the others all stood as well. They were all cold and looking forward to hot chocolate and warm beds for the night. But tradition dictated that the passing of a life's knowledge happened outdoors. They were here at camp for the week, and Winter Moon would tell them more the next night, sitting around a new crackling fire.

"I learned many things that day, about the monsters in this world, about loss, and danger, and fire, and pain. But I also learned about strength and courage and fighting for what you believe in. Kashikoi told me many things and let me ride on his back the next day, too. While Vermonters picked up the pieces from the damage the monsters had caused, he answered my questions, and told me stories of battles long past. I'll tell you those stories tomorrow. But the most important thing he told me was that not all the creatures of this world are bad. Some of them are friends."

# RANCHO NIDO

## A BORDERLANDS KAIJU ORIGIN STORY

GUADALUPE GARCIA MCCALL

**PEOPLE SAID RANCHO NIDO WAS** cursed—infested with creatures from outer space, winged demons that fell from the dead of night, creatures that crawled out of the corroded stars that ignited the darkness with their glowering blue fire as they descended.

"Everyone who gets near that place ends up dead. You can't buy it, compadre. That place is evil," Crecencio Aldrade told Hernan Valdez. But Hernan didn't care what they said about Rancho Nido. It could have been infested with alligators and snakes, and Hernan would have bought it anyway. The opportunity to buy a large piece of land at such a low price was just too good to pass up.

"I don't believe in such things," he told his wife, Licha, when she complained.

Licha was scared. "I won't move there," she told him. "I'm staying right here with my mother. And so are the girls. I'm

not taking a chance with the girls."

"Come on, woman, you don't really believe in magical creatures, do you?" Hernan paced the dirt floor of the cottage they'd lived in during most of their marriage: a cramped, two room house he'd built behind his in-laws'. "That's just bullshit meant to scare people. Machinations thought up by the rich back in the day, politicians and clergymen who wanted to keep the Indian in us from getting ahead. But the world has changed, Licha. This is the twenty-first century. I'm not letting my children grow up listening to any more superstitious nonsense. I bought it and you're going to live in it."

Licha tried knocking some sense into Hernan. She cried, begged, threw fits, but nothing worked. At the end of the month, they put all their belongings in the back of the truck, loaded up their children—two girls with hollow cheeks and watery eyes—and headed north along the border, from Matamoros all the way up to Reynosa.

They drove through the borderlands, stopping only to buy a few groceries, ammunition for Hernan's rifle, kerosene for the lamps, and a new axe. Aside from hunting, which he was good at, Hernan knew that everything he needed to make a better life for himself and his family at the ranch could be cut down and given shape with the sharpness of the blade of that new axe.

"It's bigger than I expected," Licha told him when he walked her through the main house in the light of day. She touched the weathered curtains, tested the wide windows, and bit her lip. "We'll need to reinforce these. They are weak from age."

"You like it, don't you?" Hernan said. "Come on, don't

pretend. She's pretty, isn't she? And sturdy. She's been here over a hundred years and she's still standing."

"It is pretty," Licha admitted, and she smiled. Licha's obvious love for their new home, the way she put all her energy and strength into cleaning it, pleased Hernan, and he felt vindicated in his decision to buy Rancho Nido from that crazy American woman.

On their first night there, the girls woke up the whole household with their screaming. "There was something outside our window," they said. "A very mean face, with giant yellow eyes, just staring at us in our bed."

"It was big," Lucia, the younger one, whispered. "Bigger than you or dad. Taller than this house, even."

"What about you? What did you see?" Hernan asked his older daughter, Paty.

Paty shook her head. "I don't know," she said.

"It was black, with giant wings," Lucia said, nodding toward her sister. "Like a bat."

Hernan brought his rifle down from the wall and went outside. He checked everywhere. There was nothing out there. Only brambles and an abundance of tiny, star-shaped grass burrs that he had to peel off his pants at the kitchen table, cursing the whole time, while the girls kept their lips tightly wrapped around spoons full of sugar to chase away the fright that had them shivering in their nightgowns.

"I told you," Licha said, later that night, when they were back in bed. "You should never have bought this place."

Because the women in his life were scared, Hernan stayed close by the whole next day. He didn't do any work if it meant getting far from the house. The field didn't get cleared, the fence on the south end of the property didn't get mended, and he had to milk the one skinny goat they'd brought with them until he had a chance to go back to Matamoros to bring up the rest of their cattle.

While Licha cleaned the cobwebs out of the barn, she found a large trunk. She flipped the lid open and discovered an arsenal. What in the world? She asked herself. There was enough dynamite there to start a revolution. Hernan didn't know what to make of it. He moved the trunk to an old tired shed on the property. He thought he might sell it in town if things ever got lean.

Superstitions be damned, Hernan told himself as he went to bed that night. The next day, he got up at dawn, mended the fence, and headed down to Matamoros. He had a group of men waiting to help him load up the herd in a rented cattle truck so they could drive them back to Rancho Nido.

"When will you be back?" his wife had asked that morning. "Before dark, I hope."

"I don't know," he had said, because he was an honest man and used honest words. "You'll be all right. Just stay in the house. There's plenty to do there."

Hernan had no intention of taking all day. The drive to Matamoros was an hour and a half. The biggest part of his day was spent rounding up and loading the herd. There were men willing to do the work, but only three of them agreed to come back to work for him on the new ranch.

There was a lodge, with a small kitchen and six bunk beds on the property. The workers would be well paid and well fed. Perhaps in time, when Rancho Nido prospered, more men would come work for him. Yes, Hernan told himself. He would go down in history as the man who brought Rancho Nido back to life.

It was dark by the time they drove in through the gates. His old friend, Jorge, was driving the cattle truck following behind him. He was hauling forty-five head of cattle with him. Behind him were two more ranch trucks. They belonged to two young ranch hands, Betin and Nando, who had agreed to come work for him.

As the men made their way down the dirt road to the main house, Hernan was perplexed, and a bit exasperated. There was no light coming from the windows of his home. How could his wife and children go to bed before he got back? She had to know there would be men with him who would need to be fed.

He sped up. The headlights on the trucks shone brightly on his home, and he could see as they drove up that the place was wrecked. He stopped, jumped out of his truck, and ran up the porch steps. The front door lay on the ground to the right of the open threshold. Glittering shards of broken glass from the two front windows crunched under his boots. The curtains, tattered and blood-stained, hung out of the gaping holes, lifeless and spent in the mute, breezeless night.

But Hernan didn't have time to look for his wife and children, because something loud and thunderous sliced through the air, heading toward them. The men looked up at the sky and saw several large, black forms looming overhead, and the workers ran to their trucks.

They heard shrill screams, like screeching or squawking, and the violent flapping of wings as two gigantic bird-like creatures descended on them. Betin and Nando shot at the creatures, again and again, before they got picked up, screaming and kicking, their torsos encircled within the ebony claws of the giant beasts that flew off with them.

Hernan stood frozen on the porch as two more gargantuan black monsters with enormous leathery, bat-like wings and long, shiny beaks toppled over the cattle truck, clawed through the metal box like it was tissue paper, and fished out his livestock.

Hernan ran into the house, rushed from room to room, looking for his wife and children, but there was no one there. Only broken windows, a gaping hole in the living room ceiling, and bloody handprints welcomed him. Outside, the sound of incessant, flapping wings, squawking creatures, and cows bellowing in distress was deafening, but Hernan was indifferent to all of it. He fell to his knees in the darkness of his broken home and wept.

In the morning, when the sun crept through the shambles of his home, Hernan lay crumpled into a fetal position on the wooden floor and blinked. Something filtered in with that first ray of light, a distant thought, a memory.

Dynamite.

Hernan ran to the shed and opened the door. There, cowering in the corner, clutching a rifle to his chest, was Jorge, his oldest and dearest friend. "I'm sorry, Hernan" he said. "I couldn't help you. I had to get away."

"You did the right thing," Hernan said. "They would have killed you if you hadn't.

"Is your family okay?" Jorge asked. "I know those things hauled off Betin and Nando, but what about your wife? Your girls?"

Hernan shook his head and tightened his jaw. "We have to kill those fucking things," he said. "I have dynamite, here, enough to blow up half of Reynosa. We just need to find out where they're coming from. They're some kind of birds, right? They have to nest somewhere. They probably have hatchlings. Why else would they need to haul so much of the cattle?"

"They looked more like bats to me," Jorge said.

Hernan nodded. "Well, if they're anything like ordinary bats, they're roosting. They have to be up there in the hills somewhere."

Jorge stepped aside and watched Hernan open the trunk. "Holy shit, what are you doing with that much dynamite?" he asked. "What are you involved in?"

"Don't be an idiot," Hernan said. "It was already here when we bought the place. My wife found it in the barn. I thought I'd never need to use it."

"I'm sorry, Hernan," Jorge said, "but you're going to have to do this alone. I'm going home. Is my truck okay?"

"Every truck's on its side, torn open and gutted out," Hernan said. "You can walk back up the road if you want, see if someone will give you a ride. I'm going up the hills to find those damn things. I could use the help, but I understand if you'd rather run."

"So what's thc plan?" Jorge asked him, picking up a stick of dynamite and smelling it.

Hernan shrugged. "No plan," he said. "Just gear up and figure things out as I go along."

"So that's it, then," Jorge said. "You're going to do this? Alone?"

Hernan closed the lid on the trunk. "Listen, either help

me load this up or get out of my way," he said. "I don't have time to waste. If those things hunt at night, they must sleep by day. I want to make sure they never hunt again."

Because Hernan was his one true friend, Jorge decided to stay. They loaded up the dynamite, rifles, ammunition, and binoculars, stomped around in cow dung, and smeared mud on their faces. They didn't want their body odor to rustle the monstrous beasts out of their nests.

They hiked up the hills, walked around the mouths of caverns, and looked through their binoculars for two hours before they spotted the nesting site. There, on an overgrown steep slope of a hill where the dirt road gave way to thick brambles and weeds, amidst tall mesquites, sat four enormous creatures, black and shiny as tar. Their eyes were closed, but inside the folds of their leathery, black wings Hernan could see several odd-shaped heads.

"Just what I feared," Hernan said. "They have mouths to feed."

"What should we do?" Jorge asked. "We have to get close enough to toss these at them."

Hernan winced. "Tossing them's not good enough," he said. "Not to kill all of them at once. And we have to do that. The live ones will come after us if we don't."

"So you're saying we have to go out there?" Jorge's eyes widened, and he shook his head as he spoke.

"Yes," Hernan said. "We have to lay the groundwork, run a long line, and blow it all up at once, like the revolutionaries used to do. Let's go. We can do this."

Jorge didn't let his trepidation stop him from following Hernan up the hill carrying a sack full of dynamite. They walked slowly, careful not to snap twigs or roll any pebbles as they stepped through the woods. Bits and pieces of carcass, broken bones, and hollowed out heads of cattle lay in their wake as they crept upward.

The nose-numbing smell of rancid and spoiling meat turned their stomachs. They pulled handkerchiefs out of their pockets and wrapped them around their heads, covering the bottom part of their faces, before they continued upward on the hillside.

At the base of the cluster of trees where the two pairs of bird-like monsters were nesting, Hernan found a piece of red gingham cloth. He picked it up. It was a piece of Lucia's dress. He grasped the cloth in his fist and closed his eyes. He fought the urge to scream and tossed it away. He would blow up every last one of these damned things if it killed him.

Together, Hernan and Jorge planted wrapped stacks of dynamite between the branches of the two trees with the nests. They ran fuse lines out, gently, back to the bottom of the hill. Jorge lagged behind, but Hernan was ready. He crouched behind a huge boulder anchored deep within the side of the hill. He had the box of matches out, but he couldn't understand why Jorge was going back to the first nest.

"What are you doing?" Hernan called out quietly.

"Hold on," Jorge said. "I want to put one more stack on that one. Got to make sure there's enough to blow up the whole lot all at once."

Hernan shook his head. "Don't," he said. "Come back here. We're ready."

Jorge got too confident. He crept up a little too fast. He made too much noise because, as he reached the first nest,

Hernan saw one of the bird-monsters open its eyes. It shook its head and looked down at him. Jorge had just finished placing the last stack of dynamite between two crossing branches when the huge creatures stood up, extended its enormous wings, and reached down.

Fingers!

Hernan did not know the things had hands. Long, clawed fingers, like black, hooked machetes, reached over and grabbed Jorge by the collar. The monstrous creatures yanked him up until Jorge dangled in the air. He kicked and screamed so loud he woke up the other creatures, who looked on as the giant beak opened and closed down over Jorge's head.

The monster pulled at Jorge's torso and snapped off his head with its beak, much the same way a man might snap a grape off a vine with his teeth. Then the vile creature cracked Jorge's head open in its beak, crunching it into bits and pieces, which he dropped into its hatchling's beaks. The other creatures squawked in their nests. One of them stood up and flew across to the nest of the monster who was holding Jorge's dangling body. They fought over Jorge, pulling him apart, limb from limb.

Hernan tightened his lips and fought the urge to run out screaming and cursing at the beastly things. Trembling with rage, he took a match from the box and lit the fuse on the boulder before him. As the creatures ripped and gorged themselves on Jorge, the lit fuse line ran upward. Hernan watched the fuse burn; upward and upward the spark ran until it was inches away from the dynamite.

Hernan turned away. He folded himself into a fetal position, pressed his back against the massive rock, and held his hands against his ears. When the dynamite went off, popping off one by one like fireworks, the boulder shifted. He heard a crackle and he reached up, clinging to the sliding mass even as it slipped sideways. He pushed against it, but his boots slipped. The last explosion ripped the boulder right out of his grip and thrust him sideways, away from the boulder.

Hernan went tumbling down the hillside. He rolled off an incline and flew over the edge of the cliff. As he descended he reached out, his fingers grabbing at every leaf and tree limb he saw as he fell, and then, miraculously, he wasn't falling anymore. He had managed to grasp a long, desiccated tree limb on his way down, an ancient thing, thick and gnarled as a crone's hand. In vain, he kicked at the air as he held onto the crumbling limb with both hands. But no matter how hard he tried, he couldn't get himself close enough to wall of the ravine to climb back up.

He hung suspended in mid-air, sweating and thirsting for hours. In the late afternoon, the crept over the steep incline of the ravine, blinding Hernan as it descended toward the horizon. Hernan fought the heat and the pain that it brought, not just to his eyes, but to his entire body. At last, when the sweat and the tears were too much, he opened his eyes and looked straight into the face of the merciless sun. He thought he saw angels emerging out of the center. The heavenly creatures swirled and spiraled out of the light and floated outward, drifting off to do their duty in all four quadrants of the world. They vanished as they headed in all directions, dissipating like fog into the horizon.

Hernan's watched them, entranced. His arms were beyond pain, and he feared he had no other choice than to give in to the descent. Perhaps that was what the angels had wanted, to bring him to light. Perhaps that was why they had not helped him.

Taking one last breath, he closed his eyes, lowered his head, and let go of the branch. He felt himself falling, but he refused to open his eyes. He hit the ground too hard, too soon, too fast to react. His lifeless body rolled, thrashing through bramble and star-shaped grass burrs, to finally came to a stop at the bottom of the gorge.

The series of explosions made the neighbors get in their vehicles and drive over to investigate. They met at the gates of Rancho Nido and talked about what to do. In the end, they decided that crossing property lines without permission onto a cursed estate was not worth the risk. They had families to take care of, mouths to feed. This kind of thing was better left to the police.

It took the authorities several hours to get to Rancho Nido. They didn't understand why a man would kill his family and blow up half his cattle with dynamite up in the hills like that. Perhaps it was a desperate attempt to hide his crime. Or maybe he had other illegal affairs, and this was an attempt to wipe the slate clean.

"Who knows how many bodies were destroyed with that huge blast?" they said to each other, again and again. "There isn't enough man-power to collect samples and run DNA tests. We have bigger problems along the border than a crazy man killing his own kin and cattle on a 'cursed' ranch."

In the end, Rancho Nido became the place it had been since Señor Nido died: a sad, abandoned place, full of mystery and ghosts. A place no one wanted to buy. A place that inspired fiction and lore. A place of death.

# THE DIVE

MARI MURDOCK

***"...SCAPHOGNATHUS GORGOLODON, COMMONLY REFERRED** to as Georgie, the flying kaiju nesting on Mount Kumotori just outside Tokyo. This is not the first time Georgie has swallowed sea vessels. However, the Japanese government's confirmation of the freighter's size makes this the largest ship this particular kaiju has swallowed to date..."*

"Kevin! Turn that down. I'm trying to work!"

Kevin Schroeder looked up from his newspaper to see his six-year-old daughter Lexa standing five inches from the TV, the shaky helicopter footage of the famous 70-meter flying monster reflecting in her eyes.

"Lex, turn it down. Mommy's working."

"Hey Dad, could Georgie eat our house?" She held the TV remote in her chubby fists, not listening.

"Turn down the TV, Lex."

Lexa kept dancing in place, her eyes glued to the kaiju. "Could he eat our car?"

"Kevin!" Kevin's wife Claire yelled from her home office. "Now!"

"Lexa, turn it down now."

"But is he big enough?"

Kevin snagged the remote to turn it down for her.

"Dad!"

"What? Yes! Probably. He could swallow anything he wanted. But he lives in Japan, sweetie."

Lexa turned to her toddler brother Trevor on the couch. "He could eat you too, bitch!"

"Lexa, don't call your brother that!" Claire yelled. "Where did you learn that word?"

"Not from me," Kevin muttered, falling back into his chair, the remote dangling from limp fingers.

He sighed. He couldn't really blame his wife for their... state of affairs. He'd been an unemployed nuclear engineer for nearly five years, because no one was hiring in a kaiju economy. He thought he could go straight to the military with his expertise, as that was the only really booming industry these days. However, some Russian biologist had discovered nuclear energy sources actually attracted kaiju, making nuclear engineers just as bad as kaiju these days—everyone blamed you for the state of the world, and everyone ran the other way. Kevin couldn't believe his luck, graduating with his doctorate at MIT just in time for his entire profession to go out of commission. He got to sit on his butt and watch the world end as the U.S., France, South Korea, and Japan had their populous city centers hit with these enormous monsters, hungry for… well whatever they got from fission reactors. It just wasn't fair.

Luckily, Claire's job as a closed captioning stenographer had taken off as interest in the news exploded, keeping their family afloat for a little while. But having appeared nearly a decade ago, kaiju were old news. Georgie was old news. At least, not news enough to disrupt Kevin's Thursday morning crossword puzzle. Kaiju were somebody else's problem.

He turned his attention back to the paper, tuning out the TV, his kids, his wife, and… his phone? Kevin snapped to his feet and grabbed his cellphone before it could ring a third time. Was this a job?

"Hello, Kevin Schroeder speaking," he stammered, trying not to sound too excited.

"Dr. Schroeder," a stern but not unfriendly voice pealed on the other end. "This is Chief Master Sergeant Miguel Andreas with the U.S. Air Force. I'm calling about a job opening that might interest you."

"Wow! Yes! Great!" he couldn't help bursting out. With his legs shaking, he began to pace. Lexa had trundled over to see what his excitement was all about.

"Why are you so happy, Dad?"

"Not now, Lexa."

"Dr. Schroeder, this job only requires two things really: expert knowledge of nuclear technology, both American and international, and the ability to work under extreme pressure. Now, I've heard from the instructors at your institution that you definitely have the former, but how are you with stress?"

Claire had come out of her office to yell at him some more

for still being loud. Seeing him on the phone, she thought better of it.

"Who's on the phone, Kevin?" she asked, crossing her arms.

Kevin stared at her, dazed. "Uh… Stress?" he stuttered into the phone. "Yeah, stress. I can handle it, sir. Pretty good at that whole… stress thing…"

"Kevin," Claire hissed. "Who is it?"

"Good to hear, Dr. Schroeder. Sounds like you're our man. We'll send a helicopter for you. It'll be there in about an hour."

"An hour?"

"Kevin!"

"Yes, one hour. Good bye." The phone went silent. Kevin could feel the nerves in his fingers throbbing as he struggled to set down the phone without dropping it.

"What was that about?" Claire demanded, picking up Lexa, who was mimicking his wife's creased eyebrows.

Kevin just crushed the both of them with his arms, almost lifting them from the floor. "I got a job!"

**"YOU WANT US TO DO** what?" Starla Jurgensen shouted, slamming her briefing folder onto the desk. Kevin shuddered along with the glass on the conference room's windows. "You're crazy! Marshall, tell them they're crazy!"

Marshall Montgomery, a thick-necked giant rendered soft from his own sedentary unemployment, waved his ham hand at her. "I think they know, Star. They're just yanking our chains."

Kevin blinked, still unable to believe the last thirty minutes had actually happened.

Chief Master Sergeant Andreas, a small, muscular man with receding hair and suspicious eyes, glared right back at them, his protocol etiquette slowly melting away in impatience. "Dr. Jurgensen, given the creature's roosting proximity to Tokyo, we have no choice. We can't kill the thing until we have neutralized the nuclear threat inside—"

"—Sir, let me get this straight," Kevin interrupted. He pulled his hands out from where he had been sitting on them for the last half hour to stop himself from pulling his hair out. He couldn't believe the words that started coming out of his own mouth. "Sir, you seriously want us… to fly in a plane alongside a kaiju, parachute into his mouth, slide down his throat to his stomach, find the Russian submarine he swallowed, and deactivate its nuclear missiles?"

Andreas nodded. "You four are leaving just as soon as your equipment is ready."

"Kevin," Starla demanded. "Tell them it's nuts! This is not what I signed on for!"

None of them had signed up for this kind of job. Starla and Marshall were friends of Kevin's from long ago, former classmates at MIT's graduate program. They made up three of the four nuclear engineers the U.S. Air Force had wrangled for today's recruitment circus. The fourth, Hiroshi Sato, a frowning, elderly fellow sent by Tokyo, rounded off the posse.

Kevin tried to gulp down his fear, but his mouth was dry as a sheet of paper. "Sir, there must be a different way. Don't you have… uh… personnel for this kind of thing? Have you tried reaching out to the Russians?"

Andreas' face hardened. "Our ranks of competent personnel have diminished due to years of sustained kaiju activity, Dr. Schroeder, and there's been no communication with the Russians, military or otherwise, since Georgie scooped their sub out of the Pacific. It seems they aren't taking responsibility for violating the International Nuclear Decommission Pact by having an active nuclear reactor in international waters, and we don't have time to make them clean up their own mistakes."

Kevin flinched. The unanimous world response to uphold the INDP at any cost was the reason they were all unemployed. Here it was, back to bite them in the ass afresh. Only this time, he had to enforce the INDP himself… after willingly feeding himself to a kaiju. Talk about adding insult to injury.

"We have no idea how long it will take that thing's stomach acid to compromise the warheads," continued Andreas, "and if we lose Tokyo to an accidental nuclear catastrophe, we start losing the war. We can't take that chance. We have no choice. *You* have no choice. This will be your greatest act as patriots to this planet, and you cannot refuse."

Starla smashed a cigarette between her thin lips. Marshall swore under his breath some more. Sato nodded his assent, though his frown faded to more of a despair. "We will do what we must," he mumbled in his accented English, as though to bolster his own spirit. "Our lives will be worth the effort."

"Cut the ass-kissing," Starla snapped. "This is not a kamikaze suicide mission. This is a homicide mission!"

"Your orders stand as given." Andreas stood to leave. "You suit up at 0100 hours."

With a slam of the door, he was gone, and the engineers sank into their steel seats. Kevin didn't dare meet eyes with his colleagues.

"I don't like our odds," Marshall said to no one in particular after looking up from some figures he had been scribbling on paper. "None of us have field experience, let alone combat experience."

"Oh, and who are you planning on fighting, sweetie?" Starla laughed. "You gonna wrestle Georgie first to make him lie down?"

"This is no laughing matter," Sato muttered. "Millions could die. Our duty is given to us. Our task must be fulfilled."

"Do you even know your way around a warhead?" Starla bellowed, flinging her cigarette across the room. "Let alone on a half-digested Russian sub trapped inside of a flying rollercoaster?"

"That's enough, kids," Kevin said numbly. "We can argue all night. The odds of success suck, and they're going to continue to suck even if we planned this until Doomsday... It's just an impossible task. But they're still going to send us regardless..."

Starla growled and Marshall sunk further into his chair. Sato eyed Kevin warily as if contemplating how soon Doomsday was actually coming for them.

"Come on, guys," Kevin finished, standing up and squeezing his fists together. "Work is work. It's better than waiting to die."

Kevin looked at his watch. There was only a few more hours of training and nuclear disarmament study standing between him and being Georgie's lunch. Well, that and a call to Claire telling her the position was just a temp job.

**BEFORE KEVIN COULD EVEN BREATHE,** Clarence, the paratrooper strapped to his back, edged them to plane's hatch. The door opened and wind whipped around his head. Though his helmet and diving suit shielded him, Kevin felt naked.

There was Georgie. Like a pterodactyl, the enormous creature glided on leathery wings below, his black—and gold-striped skin covered in noduled scales glistening in the setting sun. His enormous beak bangled with razor sharp teeth opened, releasing an ear-splitting screech. The reverb thundered through the plane, through Kevin's body, like electricity, and he felt as if his intestines melted.

"God, help me," Kevin prayed. But *this* was a god, wasn't it? Facing Georgie in his 230-meter glory, Kevin nearly wept.

"Maybe we'll miss!" he thought, hoping that his paratrooper would overshoot the mark, and they would fall past the peril into the city below. But Kevin could see Georgie's six red eyes locking on to the plane now, locking on to him, and he knew they couldn't possibly fail. Georgie released another piercing shriek before pulling up, intending to swallow their tiny plane whole. He zoomed up to meet them.

"*He's taken the bait!*" Kevin heard on his headset. "*Now now now!*"

Kevin's paratrooper waited a second longer before flinging them both out of the hatch and into the void. Kevin wanted to close his eyes, but all he could do was stare at the abyss below them. Teeth! So many teeth! He thought he could hear Starla screaming about a few meters behind him, but he wasn't sure it wasn't his own voice, sounding so far away as his mind retreated into the back of his head.

A sudden gust of wind slammed into their trajectory, and the buckled pair started spinning out of control. Clarence shouted commands, but Kevin heard nothing, lost in the chaos of screaming wind, blurred colors, and shining teeth. He finally succeeded into shutting his eyes, just as the kaiju's hot breath signaled the final moments before oblivion.

He defensively slammed his arms up before his face as his body made a slippery landing. The heat was suffocating, and all around him he could feel ripples of muscles and gravity undulating behind him, beside him, twisting him this way and that. He fell for so long, bouncing in totally new directions until he couldn't tell which way was up or down, and he wailed as the heat and stench of sulfuric acid and rotting pressed into every crevice of his body. He vomited inside his helmet, which immediately slapped him back in the face, once, twice, a hundred more times until finally he fell unconscious, his brain unable to stabilize in this vaulting, reeking hell.

***"STATUS UPDATE. KSK... I REPEAT.*** *Status update. Zzzzzz... Can anyone hear us? Anyone alive in there?"*

Kevin didn't dare open his eyes, but the radio in his helmet tickled his ear enough to rouse his sense of alarm.

"Ugh..." he whimpered. He felt another tickle near his neck, but this felt more like a garden hose being pulled past him. He opened his eyes. The inside of visor had been slopped with vomit, leaving him a blurry window through which he saw he lay on a long black road.

"Where am I?" he whispered.

A muffled clanging nearby caught his attention, and he focused his vision on that. Black shapes with thick curves and shining skin moved toward him, flames pouring out of where their eyes should be. Their footsteps rang like bronze bells as they lumbered along the long black road toward him. Closer and closer they came, until Kevin couldn't stare into their flaming eyes any longer. Kaiju! There were kaiju coming to get him!

"Kevin! You're alive!"

He squinted, focusing his vision through his dizzy haze. It was Marshall. His friend knelt to unbuckle his restraints, propping him upright.

"We thought you were gone!"

Then Kevin remembered where they were. He looked down, and the black road was the hull of the Russian submarine. Sato, Starla, and a paratrooper followed close behind, wary of the darkness beyond their headlamps. They'd made it.

"Sir, this is Adams," one paratrooper called in on the radio, her voice steadier than Kevin's insides felt. She shoved him off Clarence, helping her friend to his feet. The soldier groaned as he rose. Apparently, he'd broken Kevin's fall. "We found Dr. Schroeder and Clarence alive. That makes six total. Blitz and Wolden snagged on the fangs on the way in."

"*Good. More than we hoped*," the radio buzzed as Andreas' voice echoed in all their heads. "*Now, Georgie's roosted on Kumotori for the night, so you shouldn't be bouncing for about five hours. But work fast and get out before he wakes up. What's the status on the sub?*"

"The sub actually looks to be in pretty good shape," Adams answered. Her headlamp whizzed around as she scanned the area. Kevin grew nauseous again and shut his eyes. What he wouldn't give for a glass of water. "Right now, it's actually sitting right-side up. We have a hanging ceiling about a meter from our heads, and there isn't a lot of stomach acid around."

*"Yeah, the zoologists guessed the sub might still be in the proventriculus, waiting to be digested. Good thing Georgie didn't catch your plane, or you might've had to go swimming in his gizzard."*

"Well, the sub looks pretty lodged in here. The conning tower and rudders are caught, so we're pretty stable. And no gutworms in this part of the digestive tract."

Kevin's eyes shot open. "Gutworms?" he stammered. "What are—"

Marshall suddenly screamed and dropped Kevin. The garden hose near his neck had coiled around Marshall's forearm. A mass of ropes seemed to explode as sinewy tendrils and dozens of tiny legs tumbled loose from its body as the creature scrambled up Marshall's arm, each tearing tiny holes in his suit. Adams and Clarence jumped in, knives in their hands, but the moment they caught a hold of any bit of the gut worm, it wriggled free from their gloved fists. Several gaping maws emerged from between the fibrous coils, each latching on to Marshall with needle-long teeth. The engineer fell, rolling in agony. Clarence slashed the worm in half, his blade easily slicing through its body, but the severed halves ignored the wound, continuing to tunnel through Marshall's suit.

Kevin ripped a screwdriver from the tool cache at his side and jumped on Marshall. He pried at the gutworm, but his friend screamed as the needle fangs refused to unlatch. Suddenly, the tendrils sprayed a purple slime all over Marshall, globules smoking wherever his suit had an opening. He screamed anew as the gastric sludge melted his skin.

"Don't touch that!" Adams yelled, jumping and dragging Kevin back as the purple secretion pooled around Marshall.

Kevin could only watch helplessly as his friend writhed, entangled in the gutworm's coils.

Suddenly, Sato leaped forward, his own knife drawn. However, instead of cutting the creature into pieces, he slashed down the side of the worm with surgical precision, splitting it lengthwise in several places. The worm wriggled for a moment longer before hanging limply from Marshall's still twitching body. Sato seized the worm chunks and yanked them away, throwing them far into the darkness.

Marshall moaned, his body contorted into unnatural angles, seizing for a final moment before laying still. Sato, careful to avoid the purple slime, inspected the downed engineer, muttering in Japanese under his breath.

"*Status!*" the radio bleeped. "*What the hell is going on in there?*"

"Gutworm, sir," Adams responded, spinning around to search for more of them. "It got Dr. Montgomery."

"Marshall," Starla cried. "Are you okay? What's happening?"

Sato stood. "Dr. Montgomery is dead," he said, putting his knife away and stepping out of a pool of blood that had emerged from Marshall's body. "I was too late."

Kevin caught Starla as she staggered.

"Oh God," she bawled. "God, oh God. What are we going to do?"

"We are going to do our job," Adams snapped.

Clarence put a hand on her shoulder, cutting her off. "Hey. Civilians, remember?" he whispered.

Adams frowned and turned her head.

"Breathe, Dr. Jurgensen," Clarence said calmly. "Don't

let Dr. Montgomery die in vain. We've made it this far on miracles, so let's not give chance another minute to change its mind."

Adams nodded. Mourning time was up. "Let's move."

She signaled, and Clarence followed, both moving toward the hatch. Sato made to go, but Kevin caught his arm. He locked eyes with the Japanese engineer, whose grim countenance adopted more of a stoic visage.

"How did you know how to take down that gutworm?" he asked, suspicion rising over his fear.

Sato examined Kevin, staring past the vomit-cloudy visor, seeming to make a subtle calculation before answering. "I received training."

"From who?"

Sato again paused before answering, easing his body into a defensive stance. "My government."

"Bullshit. *Our* government didn't even tell us these suckers were in here." Kevin stood to his full height, as though his larger stature could give him the courage to face the truth he was starting to piece together. "How did you learn about them, let alone get the skills to take one out?"

"What are you implying, Kevin?" Starla asked.

"This isn't your first dive, is it, Hiroshi?" Kevin asked, gripping Sato's arm tighter. "You've done this before."

Sato smiled, twisting his arm easily out of Kevin's grip. "If I have, you should stay close. You might make it back out." He walked off toward the sub hatch.

Kevin's breath caught in his chest. He couldn't believe it. What a fool he'd been. Hiroshi's words shoved the final piece into this miserable puzzle.

This wasn't a Russian sub. This one was theirs.

The U.S. never complied with the INDP. Instead, the public ban on nuclear power had only driven their military nuclear efforts to greater degrees of secrecy! The U.S. would never willingly give up their weapons to the INDP if any other country had the potential for taking control of the planet. And as a fellow struggling country, Japan was helping them cover it all up in a power-agreement against the Russian advantage. Kevin remembered Andreas' words: "If we lose Tokyo to an accidental nuclear catastrophe, we start losing the war." He hadn't meant the war against the kaiju. He'd meant war with the Russians.

"Get your asses over here!" Adams yelled from the open hatch. "We've gotta hurry before Georgie wakes up."

"Kevin, what is it?" Starla demanded, her eyes round with fear.

Kevin just shook his head. "Later. We've got a job to do."

Clarence disappeared into the sub, followed by Sato, Adams, Starla, and Kevin. As Kevin reached the bottom of the ladder, the putrid smell only increased.

"Hey the lights are still on," Clarence observed as he made his way through the control room. "Anyone still here?"

Red and purple stains all over the floor indicated that the gutworms had been through the sub. Adams and Clarence both pulled out their guns.

"No guns," Sato hissed, pulling out his knife. "Firing inside a submarine is too dangerous."

Clarence eyed Adams, who nodded. They traded for their own knives. Nothing moved as they stalked from the control room to the sonar room, though papers and bits of human belongings were scattered everywhere. Kevin thought he saw a partially digested hand, but he couldn't stomach another look to confirm.

Finally, they reached the missile tubes.

"Okay, nerds. You're up," Adams commanded. She pointed to Kevin. "We'll take the missiles. You three take the reactor. We've only got about four hours left, so you better make 'em count."

Starla, Clarence, and Sato disappeared into the next room. Kevin looked at the vertical missile tubes and grimaced. Hah. Russian indeed. He took off his gloves and puke-stained helmet. Time to get to work.

**THE HOURS FLEW BY LIKE** minutes but working with American tech was far easier than buying all the lies about deactivating Russian models. Adams also proved to be an adept assistant, regardless of how often she looked at the door to check for gutworms.

"That should do it," Kevin said, throwing down the tools. He stretched his cramped arms. "I can't believe we made it this far."

"Me neither, to be honest," Adams sighed, momentary pain running across her face. "We lost friends today, and it could have easily been any of us."

"Or all of us," Kevin mused. "By the way, they didn't brief you on an exit strategy, did they?"

"Yeah," she laughed. "We're supposed to basically run out of Georgie's mouth."

Kevin's jaw stiffened. He wasn't sure if she was just pulling his leg and there was no plan. "You serious?"

"She is serious," Sato said. He had just emerged from the reactor room. He was holding a gun. "That's how I got out last time."

Before she could move, Sato shot Adams twice in the chest. Kevin sprang aside, narrowly dodging a bullet before leaping backwards into the next room. He slammed the door shut, retreating into the control room.

"Hiroshi! What are you doing?" Kevin screamed as he hurriedly examined the steel door for locking mechanisms. He wouldn't be able to figure it out before Sato appeared, so he just braced himself against it to hold it shut.

"I am finishing my last order of the day. No witnesses." Sato slammed his body against the door, exhibiting strength the Kevin could barely withstand. He doubled his effort, determined to hold.

"No! Starla!" he called.

"She's gone, Kevin," Sato answered for her. "No one is leaving to tell the story."

"Why? Because it's obvious this isn't a Russian sub? They think we'll tell someone the U.S. violated the INDP?"

"There is more to it than that."

Kevin scanned the room, aching for something to help. A broken coffee mug. A fallen chair. A shoe with a leg still in it. The blinking lights of the control panels. Maybe one of these would help. He needed more time to think.

"Why don't you enlighten me," he shouted, his mind flying through the possibilities of fighting off the armed Japanese operative. Was the chair his best option? He growled in frustration.

"You are smart, Kevin," Sato called from the next room.

"I am sure you have wondered why our world governments have not worked together, to kill all kaiju?"

"The news said something about their bodies being toxic. But since you and I survived this dumpster dive, I'd say that sounds like another lie, huh?" The buttons on the control panel winked at Kevin. The nuclear missiles required upwards of ten commands and two keys to fire, plus he had just spent the last few hours deactivating them. But the anti-ship torpedoes. His eyes flickered to the launch switches. They wouldn't save him against Sato's gun, but…

"Yes, Kevin. Another lie. Kaiju are only animals. And as all animals, they can be controlled by humans."

Another body slam to the door knocked the wind out of Kevin. He wheezed but held fast to the door frame. How could Sato be so strong?

"But why keep them around?" he called, looking back at the switches. It would take him about three seconds to get there and figure them out. Would they still function? "They're destroying everything! You should hate them more than anyone. Kaiju ravaged Japan!"

"It's still more complicated than that," Sato replied. "If you know what kaiju want, you control where they go. And if you control the kaiju, you control the world. The Russians figured that out at the same time we had, but as a mostly land-based country, they have an even greater advantage with their submarines. With them, they have been luring kaiju to Japan to weaken our country. It's only a matter of time before they win. We must fight them."

"So this is just another world domination game? It's not us versus the kaiju! It's humans versus humans!"

"No. This is survival. The Russians—"

"—cut the bullshit, Hiroshi!" Kevin yelled, anger spurring his adrenaline into overdrive. "You murdered Starla, not the Russians. You alone. I'm not going to play that game. If you want to fight, you fight the real enemy."

With that, Kevin leaped from the door and slammed down on the firing switches. A second of silence greeted his attempt before Sato burst into the room.

"Time is up," Sato said, aiming his gun at Kevin's head. "It was a pleasure working with you."

Suddenly, an enormous blast rattled the entire sub as a torpedo shot into Georgie's insides before detonating. Immediately, the now familiar ear-splitting shriek echoed through Georgie's entire body as the kaiju thrashed in pain, sending Kevin and Sato flying. The whiplash tore Sato's gun from his hand, and the world around them shook in a kaleidoscopic whirl. Kevin thought he heard Sato crunch into the ceiling, but he couldn't concentrate on his surroundings as he was flung across the room. As if hurled around by enormous waves, his body crashed back and forth, the world spinning with color and steel surfaces.

"Good boy, Georgie," Kevin thought before his head crashed into something and he blacked out.

**KEVIN WOKE UP TO A** dark room. He bucked for a moment in fear, scanning the room for Sato, for Georgie. But the room was empty. Blinking lights were the only things that moved. The switches? He settled back down into the bed. A bed? He cried out in shock.

The door slammed open, and Claire burst into the room.

"Oh my God!" she shouted, flinging herself onto him, crying hysterically as she smothered his face with kisses. "You're awake! Kevin, you're alive!"

"What the hell is going on?"

"You were in a coma for a month! Oh God, I was so worried."

Kevin sunk back. He was in a hospital. With his wife. Alive.

"The doctors weren't sure you'd make it after the accident."

"Accident?" Kevin's eyes nearly bugged out of his head. "Claire, you're hurting me. What accident?"

"Oh sorry!" She sat down in a chair next to his bed, continuing to babble. "You don't remember the explosion? At the geothermal generator factory? Remember? The military was interviewing you for that position in Japan? Well, they said you may not remember. Or at least, you may remember it incorrectly. Something about trauma? I'll have to get Mr. Andreas. He'll be so glad to hear you made it."

Kevin frowned. She had obviously been lied to. Now his life was a government secret. "Andreas is involved?"

As if by magic, Andreas entered the room, shutting the door behind him. "Dr. Schroeder. So glad to see you awake. How's your head?"

Kevin stared long and hard into his eyes, unsure of what he should be feeling. Confused? Angry? Relieved? He didn't even know if he could walk. "I don't know, Mr. Andreas. Why don't you tell me?"

Andreas smirked. "You look just fine to me. Well enough to get back to work."

"Work?"

"Certainly. You were the only candidate who wasn't eliminated in our interview process, so the job is yours. You will be replacing Mr. Sato. A full-time position. Congratulations."

"That's wonderful!" Claire chimed in. "Oh, I'm so happy."

Kevin shut his eyes. Images reeled through his head at a dizzying pace. Sato. Guns. Teeth. Spinning. Rotting. Melting. Starla. Marshall. Gutworms. Georgie. Was Andreas asking him to do it all over again?

"Well, for now, rest and heal up," Andreas said, starting to leave the room. "The last factory got blown up anyway. Bits of it all over Tokyo. It will be some time before we can call you back into work. Take it easy. I'll call you when we have another office for you."

"Smooth, Andreas," Kevin called out to his retreating form. "Real smooth."

He looked at Claire who had taken his hand and was massaging his morphine-numb fingers. At least she was happy. But if he was the new Sato… They'd need to pay him a lot. And include dental.

# WHAT EVERYONE KNOWS

SEANAN MCGUIRE

**IT CAME OUT OF THE** sea; it destroyed a city; it died. That's the story. That's what everyone knows. It was tall and terrible and incomprehensible and biological and beautiful, and it breathed out gouts of acid like it was nothing, and it tore down our towers with its terrible claws, and its skin was armor against almost everything we had to throw—everything but small-scale nuclear weapons. It melted in the face of our atomic might; it burned and howled and screamed and fled and fell and rotted in the slag that had been the beach. Scientists in hazmat suits picked it apart, squirreling every precious scrap away in secret laboratories, coaxing its secrets from the melted marrow of its bones.

That's the story. That's what everyone knows.

I was a child when the creature stepped out of the sea, defying everything we thought we knew about our place in the world. I can remember the sight of it on the morning

FBW 2018
SEATTLE

news, before my mother screamed and turned the monitor off, saying that it was nothing a child should be looking at. She hadn't understood how ubiquitous it would become. No one had. There had never been anything like it before, tall as a skyscraper, ancient as the moon. It had remade our understanding of, well, everything, and it had done it as easily as it killed two point five million people, as easily as it left Seattle and the surrounding area in ruins.

It came; it killed; it died, and we pulled it apart to see what we could see. That's the other thing I remember about the arrival. Crying because there was this huge, beautiful, dead creature sprawled on the sand after three days of destruction—by that point, my mother had stopped trying to cover my eyes, had somehow managed to grasp that everything was changing—and we weren't going to bury it the way we'd buried my dog when he died. We were going to hurt it, and keep hurting it, until it wasn't anymore. That was how we'd punish it for daring to hurt us. We'd hurt it so badly that it no longer existed.

Biologists looked at the crenulations of its brain and the structure of its neurons and declared it nothing more than an oversized, biologically complex animal, no more complicit in its own actions than a rabid dog.

Physicists and material engineers looked at the composition of its bones and the shape of its skeleton and declared it a miracle of form and function, something we could use to make our damaged towers taller and stronger, immune to future monsters.

Everyone had something to say about the creature, which by that point was known around the world as The Beast.

Parts of it went on display in natural history museums, once the radiation had died down. Cute plush toys were sold, considered tasteless until the manufacturer loudly announced that a portion of each sale was being donated to the trusts dedicated to helping the survivors of Seattle. Movies were made. Genres of science fiction were revitalized.

Time passed.

The nuclear weapons used to kill the creature had been selected because they wouldn't leave the coastline uninhabitable forever. A decade, yes, and residents would need to filter their water and avoid growing vegetables for a decade after that, but those were things that could be worked around. Those were hurdles to be overcome. Seattle began to rebuild. The Beast loomed large in the public consciousness, but the creature, the real animal, was chipped away, worn into nothing one forgotten moment at a time.

We were killing it all over again, feeding it into the great machine of human history, where we always had to be the victors, and anything that challenged the narrative of our own superiority had to be destroyed. We were *hurting* it.

It came out of the sea; it destroyed a city; it died. That's the story. That's the narrative.

This is the truth.

**FIFTEEN YEARS IS A LONG** time. Long enough to clean the radiation from a ruined city; long enough to render an impossible creature into its component parts; long enough for a child too young to understand why everyone is crying to become a marine biologist and be loosed, in her own time, upon the world.

Plane tickets were easy. Explaining why I wanted to go to Washington was hard. I wasn't a resident of the state, had no relatives who had either died or relocated when the creature came, and the maps I had so carefully drawn, so carefully considered, weren't the sort of things I wanted to share. But my thesis had been on the impact of radiation on tide pool invertebrates, and my advisor wrote me a glowing letter of recommendation. After fifteen years of nightmares, I was finally on my way to where they'd started. Not with a wave of destruction that rose from the sea and slaughtered everything in front of it. With a creature that fell, never understanding what it had done wrong, and with the look it had cast down the coast as it died.

The scientists had been so *quick* to say that the creature was only an animal, that it didn't know, didn't understand, couldn't possibly have had any motivation beyond instinct. They had never paused to ask themselves whether it might have been intelligent in its own way, or whether that intelligence might have had a purpose when it came for Seattle. They had seen the same thing I had, the flail, the fall, the last, frantic look along the coast, and they had come to different conclusions.

Fifteen years and six weeks after the creature came out of the sea, I parked my rental car on the overgrown slope of a road that hadn't been maintained in far too long, shielding my eyes as I peered into the towering, mossy forest between me and the ocean. Even before the attack, Washington state had some of the most protected beaches in the country, barricaded by evergreen forests, hidden by the curvature of the coast. Now, after a decade and a half of neglect, those beaches might as well be on another planet. No human has set foot on them since the bombs fell.

Everything happens in its own time. I checked my boots, ran a finger along the line of tape dividing them from my jeans—always tape where there might be ticks; it's only common sense—and started into the trees.

Mosquitoes buzzed among the branches, and deer and rabbits watched me with no sign of fear, so unaccustomed to the presence of humans that they no longer understood that I might be a threat. I wasn't, not yet: it would be another decade, at least, before it was safe to hunt here. Another decade of lazy days and silent hunting seasons, of starvation when the herd wasn't thinned before the end of the growing season. Everything has its dark side, even a cessation of gunfire.

I pushed my way through the woods, fighting for every step against the tangled green that threatened to shove me back out to the road, where I belonged. When the tree line ended, it was abrupt and unexpected: I pushed through a veil of blackberry creepers and was suddenly standing at the top of a sloping hill, leading down to narrow, rocky strip of shore. It would widen as the tide went out, but not much, no, not nearly enough to make this place appealing to developers or vacation-goers or even local families. There had always been better beaches, more accessible beaches, places where they could spread out their towels and enjoy the faltering Pacific sun.

The water here was deceptively deep, dropping from shallows into the abyss with surprising speed, and the undertow was correspondingly strong, sucking swimmers in, pulling them down. It was perfect. From a biological standpoint, it was *perfect.*

I slid down the hillside on the sides of my shoes, banking against my own momentum, until I reached the bottom and the stones turned under my feet, making my footing uncertain. I windmilled my arms, getting my balance back, and stopped, listening.

Nothing.

No boats, no cars, no distant sound of voices; no seabirds calling or dogs barking. The world was silent, save for the sound of the sea. I nodded. This fit my assessment of the area, and more, the assumptions I'd made about the environment I was looking for. Someplace that was open and secluded at the same time. Someplace with certain unique geographic features. Unique enough to lure a creature as huge and inexplicable and important as the one the world had watched die fifteen years ago out of the depths and onto the land.

The beach was long and empty, flanked by hills and rocky granite spikes that jutted like bones where the water had worn the earth away. I started walking.

Fifteen years is a long time. Long enough to make a few hours' walk seem like nothing in comparison, although my legs ached and knees burned by the time I rounded the curve of the cove and saw what I'd been looking for: a cave, not natural, although it could certainly pass for such to the untrained eye, hewn from the rock wall that encircled the small, isolated slice of the sea. Something had reached out with a terrible claw, perhaps coated with the kind of biological acid that developed for a *reason*, a reason bigger and better than destroying cities, and had sliced an opening out of the rock. Something that needed a safe, secure, isolated place.

I pulled the flashlight from my bag and started inside,

the pain in my legs forgotten in the face of the moment I'd been seeking for so impossibly, incredibly long, since I was a child who had somehow been able to recognize despair when she saw it in the eyes of a creature the size of a city.

At the back of the cave, I found them, rolled gently into their cradles of melted, stabilizing sand. There had been three once, each the size of a basketball—so small for what they would eventually become, but not unreasonably so, given what I knew about the life cycles of sea turtles and sharks.

One of them was a deflated husk, its leathery skin cracked and pitted, its contents diffused into the sand around it.

One of them had hardened, undergoing a strange, terrible alchemy that might be as common and necessary for this species as the hibernation of cicadas, the slow incubation of alligators. Maybe when there were multiple healthy eggs, one of them would always turn into a sphere of what looked like solid obsidian, preserving its contents for a time when it would be alone, free of competition, free to grow.

The third...

It was the pale, inviting green of a healthy eel's skin, mottled with paler yellow and deeper olive, a biological tapestry of possibilities. It was slightly larger than either of its flawed siblings, pulsing with its own internal bioluminescence. I moved closer. There was a heavy shadow at the center of the egg, moving slightly, preparing to be born. I hadn't missed it.

"Hi," I whispered, and my voice was a shout in the confines of the cave. "I, um. I knew your mother. I've come to take you someplace safe."

The egg didn't respond. I lifted it from its cradle, and it was heavy and warm and soft in my hands. I nestled it in the bottom of my backpack, making sure it was secure, before picking up the second egg. It felt solid from side to side, and I hoped, however irrationally, that that would mean one day it could soften and swell and hatch. For now…

For now, people were returning to the state, to the coast, and this cave would be found soon enough, by scientists who should have started looking years ago, who should have been asking themselves from the start why something so big, so powerful, so *perfect* would come ashore at all. Maybe some of them had been. I liked the thought. I liked the idea that some people had looked at the arc of her steps, the way she went for the closest, most dangerous population center, and said to themselves, "I'll give them time, I won't attract attention, I'll wait." It would mean I wasn't in this alone.

My backpack felt heavier than the world as I made my way back up the coast to the slope where I'd made my descent. I squinted at it. The idea of climbing it made my thighs ache in anticipated weariness. The thought of spending the night on this rocky, exposed coast, with the Pacific winds doing their best to flay the skin from my body, was worse. With a sigh, I gripped the nearest exposed root and began pulling myself up.

I had a long way to go before I—before *we*—would be safe.

**THE HOUSE I'D RENTED WAS** one of hundreds left empty and barely maintained in the wake of the Seattle disaster, the sole remaining asset of a family that might never choose to return to Washington. They had seen the world turn against them, and they were seeking level ground.

The maintenance that *had* been performed had been

handled by the state, squads of nervous, underpaid contractors visiting each municipality for one week a quarter, patching the obvious leaks and repairing the worst of the damage. Nothing they did could have prevented the slow decay of an unoccupied home, but they'd tried, right up until the moment when the region was declared fit for habitation and the responsibility was passed back to the homeowner. A lot of neighborhoods like the one that was temporarily mine had looting problems now, desperate residents pulling down fences and stealing shingles from the unoccupied homes. They tried to justify it to the media, claiming that they were reclaiming materials that would otherwise have been wasted, blaming the state for its lackadaisical standards and the climate for destroying their precious homes, but most people regarded them as dangerous thieves, and it had slowed down the rate of residents returning to Washington. Empty neighborhoods were still more common than the state liked.

I had been able to get my place for little more than a song. It was too big for me, with a yard that opened onto an incredible view of the Sound, all blue water and endless sky. Opening the front door revealed a living room done up in varying shades of beige, with water stains on the walls and ancient curtains covering the windows. I locked up behind myself, making my way to the back bedroom, which I had prepared meticulously for this moment.

Blackout curtains kept the sunlight at bay, while humidifiers and heaters brought the temperature up to something heavy and tropical. The creature had breathed acid, biological and bright, and the eggs had been nestled in cradles of melted sand, with channels dug around them, as if to keep them dry. I had gambled on the fact that the acid had been a part of the gestation process, intended to tell the babies when it was safe for them to emerge. I removed them from my backpack, placing them in the beds of sculpting foam that I had constructed. There were four beds, a moment of wild optimism given physical reality. I pushed two of them under the desk with my foot and went for my field kit. It was time to take some basic measurements.

The active egg weighed eight pounds and had an ambient temperature of eighty-four degrees. The inactive egg weighed twelve pounds and had an ambient temperature of sixty degrees. I still tucked them both in, putting enough distance between them to mirror the setup in the cave, before leaving the room and scavenging a dinner for myself from the meager supplies in the kitchen. My bed beckoned. Cracker crumbs still clinging to my lips, I collapsed into it without removing my clothes. The work, the real work, was about to begin.

The next six weeks passed in a blur of tests and measurements. The active egg grew warmer by the day, and on day six, it began to swell, growing so quickly that I fancied I could almost see it happen. I cooed to it, increased the humidity, and began wiping it down with a dilute acid bath, helping the shell to weaken and thin. I had made a study of the creature's biology, reading every report, examining every biological breakdown, and the acid had to do *something* other than belch forth to dissolve cities. It took too many resources to be that limited. But as a way to protect the young…

The eggshell was so thick. The acid would wear it away, telling the baby that it was safe to emerge. In the absence of a parent, erosion would do the same thing, but it would take so much longer. So very, very much longer.

I was wiping the mixture of acid and seawater across the shell when the egg gave an almighty shake, almost hopping in its cradle. I pulled back and watched in delighted awe as the shell split and tore under the force of a sharp-jawed saurian head pushing its way to freedom.

All vertebrates practice cuteness as a survival mechanism. Even baby snakes and lizards are adorable compared to the adults, with large eyes, outsized skulls, and a certain rounded softness. The infant creature was no different. It blinked its round, golden eyes at me, all four of its pupils contracting, and made a small, querulous sound. I smiled.

"Hello, little one," I said.

It made the sound again, louder this time, before beginning to chirp, pushing its arms through the remnants of the shell and holding them out to me.

The creature had been bipedal. Its child was no different, built like the hybrid offspring of a human and an alligator, with soft scales in a dozen shades of green, from mellow jade across its belly to deep malachite on its back. It had the beginning of what would eventually be jagged spikes running the length of its spine, and tiny, pearlescent claws on the ends of its fingers. Like most reptiles, it had been born with a full complement of teeth, each one sharp enough to tear through flesh. Strangest of all were its eyes, two large and placed where I would expect on a bipedal predator, two smaller and placed above them, giving it an incredible range of vision. Nothing would ever sneak up on this child of the deeps.

It chirped again. I took a breath. It could be trying to lure me in, to make a meal of me, in which case I would die and so would it, starved and unable to escape the house at its current size. It could also be an imprinted infant, turning to its presumed parental figure, seeking comfort.

"You and me, kid," I said, and leaned forward, scooping it out of the eggshell, into my arms.

The infant creature made a softer sound, somewhere between a purr and a sigh, and pressed its face against the curve of my neck, huddling into the warmth of me. I held it tightly, looking at the wrecked remains of its eggshell, and thought of the people who would give anything, *anything*, to be where I was now, to have this tiny, innocent thing at their disposal. Think of the secrets they could learn by taking a juvenile apart!

I could have anything I wanted with a single phone call. Money, fame, all the attention in the world. I could be the new darling of the sciences, the one who changed the field forever. Or I could have this baby, who was already falling asleep in my arms, heavy and content and absolutely sure that I would keep it safe.

I kissed the top of its head. "You and me, kiddo," I murmured. "We've got work to do."

**GEODE TODDLED AROUND THE BACK** yard on increasingly strong legs, tail waving wildly to help them stay stable and upright. Only a month out of the egg and they were already up to my chest, capable of knocking me over with the innocent enthusiasm of their play. With only two known exemplars of their species, I couldn't have said whether they were male or female, but I had lost the ability to think of them with the dispassionate "it" by the time they were a week old, happily shredding salmon with their talons and trying to lure me into eating the bits they didn't want. They were an individual. Not a human, but not a beast, either.

And they knew me. Geode couldn't speak, but they understood their own name, and all the things I was inclined to ask them for. They even allowed me to continue taking blood samples, despite their dislike of the needle, because I said "please" and promised them their favorite delicacies when I was done.

They tripped over a rock in the yard and stumbled, making a distressed groaning noise that turned into a hacking sound, like a cat in the process of coughing up a hairball. They moaned once, and spat a ball of faintly glowing, semi-solid goo onto the ground, where it began to smolder and sink into the earth. Geode moaned again, now sounding ashamed.

"Oh, no, baby," I said, rushing to their side and rubbing the scales on the top of their head soothingly. "That was a *good* thing you did just now. What a fine, strong baby you are! Why, I'm sure most unidentified sea-dwellers can't make acid until they're *much* larger than you are!"

Geode creeled hopefully. I laughed.

"Yes, you can have some chopped squid as a reward. Greedy little one."

They bumped their head against my sternum. I laughed again, planting a kiss on their cheek before turning and starting for the house.

As soon as they couldn't see me, I let my smile fade. Acid. They were spitting acid. I'd known that was a normal part of their development, but between that and the speed with which they were growing... their childhood was going to be much shorter than I wanted it to be, and there was no way I'd be able to hide them forever. Honestly, I was going to be hard-pressed to hide them much longer. They ate more every day. There were only three stores within reasonable driving distance, and even rotating which ones I went to, and when, they were starting to notice how much fish I bought. The money would run out soon, and that was assuming no one tipped off the authorities to the tourist with the strange shopping habits.

Was it paranoid of me to think that buying too much fresh salmon could bring the government down on my head? Maybe. But I was the only person known to be living in my area, and I was from out of state, and this was a different world than the one that I'd been born into. This was a world where monsters were real.

Geode chirped and nudged their head against my arm, asking for more scritches. Maybe this had always been a world where monsters were real. We were just finally being forced to admit that maybe we'd been wrong about what they were.

**ANOTHER MONTH PASSED IN FURTIVE** shopping expeditions and the increasing hunger of my adopted child. The first time I stepped into the backyard to find them with their head buried in the ripped-open chest cavity of a stag I stopped, heart thundering in my ears, questions of radiation and exposure racing through my mind. It wasn't safe to hunt here. It wasn't safe to fish here. It wasn't—

It wasn't safe to starve here, and I couldn't buy enough meat to keep Geode from crying in the night, or apparently, to keep them from running off to hunt. They were taller than I was, still growing at an incredible rate, and their acid projectiles were no longer accidental, but were instead aimed and fired with pinpoint precision, usually to object to something I had asked, like another blood sample or for Geode to lift their tail out of the way while I worked. We danced through the increasingly cramped house with exquisite care, me trying to keep records of their astonishing growth, them snarling and snapping and shedding strips of too-small skin everywhere. I gathered every single one, the marine biologist's equivalent of a baby book, and I didn't feel an ounce of guilt. Yes, Geode was the scientific discovery of a lifetime. A proper laboratory could have learned so much more from them. I didn't care. They were my responsibility, my adopted child, and I knew how this would end.

I just didn't expect it to end so soon.

We were in the backyard, Geode lying on their back in the sun, me wiping down their belly with a mixture of saltwater and dilute acid—the same mixture I'd used on their eggshell to encourage them to hatch, now used to encourage a shed—and me in a tank top and old jeans, half-draped across the slope of their thigh, which held me up and kept me balanced. It was a beautiful day, that rare Seattle sunshine pouring out of the clear blue sky, warming the both of us to the bone.

Geode was mumbling and whistling, a soft, sweet sound that filled my ears enough that I didn't hear the truck pulling up in front of the house, didn't hear the door slam as the inspector got out. He must have tried the door first, ringing the bell on an empty but clearly occupied house, and when he didn't get an answer, he went looking for the source of the sound. Maybe he was even trying to help, wanting to warn me about the looters that had been seen moving closer and closer to this area. Whatever his reasons, he came around the corner of the house, tablet in one hand, the other hand raised to block out the sun, calling, "Hello? Is there anyone home? I'm from the state, and—*oh my God*!"

His voice became a shout at the end, terrified and shrill and unlike any sound Geode had ever heard a human make before. I had to assume that was why they surged to their feet, pushing me gently behind them, and roared, spitting balls of acid with terrible precision to strike the man in the face, throat, and stomach.

I screamed. The man fell, acid eating the flesh away, revealing blood-mottled bone. Geode looked back at me, as if reassuring themself that I was all right, before ambling over to bend over the body, beginning to rip the acid-softened flesh away.

I turned and vomited into the grass.

Geode was a carnivore. There was footage of their mother eating humans, shoving bodies into her mouth as she continued her rampage through the streets of Seattle. This wasn't a *surprise*. But seeing it happen wasn't the same thing as knowing that it was a possibility, and the inspector hadn't done anything wrong, hadn't offered any threat to my lumbering, rapidly-growing child. All he'd done was startle them.

Geode, sensing my distress, stopped devouring the man and came to crouch by my side, nudging me ever so gently with the tip of their snout. I braced myself with one hand, pressing the other to their scales. My beautiful, glorious, impossible child, the baby I'd dreamt about for my entire adult life, looked at me and crooned, confused and hopeful that I would somehow make things all right.

They were already ten feet tall, and growing every day. They could devour most of the predators they'd find in the sea, and ward off the ones they couldn't fight. The inspector... he'd been the first. He wouldn't be the last. His disappearance would be the trigger that brought down an entire world of trouble on our heads.

"It's time," I said, and Geode creeled, and if they knew why I was crying, they had no way to tell me so.

**THE INSPECTOR'S PICKUP WAS STURDY,** designed to navigate the broken roads and crumbling infrastructure of Washington State. Geode was heavy enough to weigh it down, but not enough to stop it from rolling. They sat in the back, head tilted into the wind, making small sounds of delight as I drove toward the coast as fast as I dared. The hibernating egg was an accusing presence in the passenger seat, concealed inside my half-zipped backpack. I'd known there was no real chance I'd have the time to hatch it, had been half-intending, when this moment came, to leave it with my notes for future scientists to study. Maybe one of them would have fallen in love with its contents the way I'd fallen for Geode. Maybe it would have made it back to the sea.

But that had always been me lying to myself. My love had begun with a glimpse of agonized eyes as Geode's mother fell, with a feeling too big for me to put a name on, but big enough to drive my entire life going forward, to steer me, inevitably, toward a cove and a cave and a child and a conclusion. I couldn't gamble on that kind of love happening again.

We were almost to the edge of the wood when the sirens started behind us. The truck jounced as Geode shifted position, barking their distress and slapping their tail against the side of the cab. I swore, fighting to keep control, and hit the gas harder. We needed to reach the trees. We needed—

They must have been following us for longer than I'd expected. A bullet shattered the windshield next to my head, and my focus became only and entirely stopping the truck before I lost control. I grabbed the backpack and kicked the door open, leaving the keys in the ignition as I flung myself out of the vehicle.

"Geode! Come on!" I ran for the distant tree line like my life depended on it, and Geode ran after me, confused and frightened but still obedient to the only authority they had ever known. They were faster than I was, but not so fast that I lost sight of them as we dove into the trees, beast and biologist both fleeing for their lives.

Well. Not really. I wasn't fleeing for my own life anymore. I was fleeing for theirs. They were the endangered species; they were the promise I had made to myself before my mother turned the news off in that long-ago living room. My own life had been forfeit the moment I sat down with a map of the coastline and the intent to bring a legend home.

The trees slowed Geode enough that I was able to catch up, and we ran together to the place where the forest dropped off, replaced by empty coast. Geode stiffened at the sight of the sea, making a sound that was something like wonder and something like longing and something like betrayal. I grabbed one talon, heedless of the way it sliced into my palm.

"Come on!"

Together, we slid down the embankment, the sound of shouts and sirens echoing behind us, our pursuers growing closer by the moment. I stumbled at the bottom, my ankle twisting on the stones, and yelped in pain and surprise. Geode didn't pause in striding toward the sea, only swept me up in one massive arm, carrying me as easily as I had carried them only a few short weeks before. Their eyes were fixed on the horizon, a soft, humming sound building in their chest. It sounded like a sigh. It sounded like a song.

It sounded like going home.

Bullets bit into the beach. I looked back. Soldiers in olive green were lined up at the top of the bluff, guns drawn, shouting and gesturing to each other. They looked at my precious child and saw only the threat of an unfamiliar species, of competition, when we were all only seeking to survive on this planet. The seas are deep. Geode's mother could have been down there for millennia before she rose to lay her eggs and clear away any predators that might threaten them. We didn't have to fight. We could share.

Geode hesitated at the water's edge, the hum turning confused. I put my unwounded hand against their arm, smiling.

"It's okay, sweetie," I said. "Take me home."

It came out of the sea; it destroyed a city; it died. That's the story.

She came out of the sea; she tried to protect her children; she died. That's the story, too.

As the water closed over my head and my lungs began to ache, I relaxed in Geode's arms, content to give my life for my child, even as their mother had done, so many years ago.

They kept walking, and the darkness grew around us, until there was nothing but the feel of scaled arms around me, and the nylon strap of the backpack in my hand. And then even that was gone, and so was I, part of the deep, drowned world where monsters walk, and promises are made, and stories older than the tide, older than the stone it wears away, are told over and over again, forever.

That's the story. That's what everyone knows.

# THE KAIJU COUNTERS

ML BRENNAN

**TWENTY-FOUR YEARS AS A FREELANCE** kaiju biologist—concurrently bucking and thumbing his nose at the military kaiju science system—left Len Haddrill uncomfortably out in the cold when his private monetary backers were unable to provide what he needed, and he found himself desperately scrounging for any possible string to pull. His own eight years with the Kaiju Defense Force service felt like they'd happened two lifetimes ago, and he'd lost touch with everyone he'd known back in those days. It was, after all, a bit hard to maintain a Christmas card list when you were spending two years living rough in the remains of the city of Bangkok, tagging kaiju sub-adults in a three-person team. Eventually, he'd made a list of every person he could remember serving with and sent it along to his daughter Deanna, who was a pilot with the KDF. She'd checked his list against the catalog of base personnel, and luck was in his favor when it turned

out that one of his old squad partners had spent the last near-quarter-century rising through the ranks. Almost two weeks of daily phone calls later, and he was on a transport plane to the KDF command base in the Swiss alps, hoping that his Hail Mary would somehow pay off.

Inside the Colonel's office and shaking hands, the first part of the speech Len had been mentally reciting for days flew completely out of his head. He found himself instead blurting out, "Fuck, Rabia, we've gotten old."

Colonel Rabia Ashiq looked at him for a long, horrible moment, then threw her head back and laughed. "You haven't changed, Len," she finally said. Then she looked him up and down with a raised eyebrow. "For someone who jumped through so many hoops for this meeting, you don't know how to dress for shit. What the hell is staining your pants?"

"Oh." He looked down, embarrassed. The walk to Rabia's office had been a painful reminder of all the times that his team partners had yelled at him to buy a suit for this trip. "Well, I don't exactly spend a lot of time outside the field, so I'm down to one set of clothes for formal stuff."

"I think you're down to no sets," she said. "Are those bloodstains?"

"Not human," he assured her. "I was a keynote speaker at a Hong Kong conference on kaiju seasonal movement patterns, and an adult female kaiju that had been injured in a fight came up to the local shoreline to die. It was a golden opportunity, so I just headed down to the beach along with the others to perform the necropsy. Didn't really stop to change clothes."

"So, kaiju bloodstains."

"Bloodstains, maybe a little viscera," he agreed. "Most of it came out of the pants, and the shirt really isn't bad at all." At her expression, he said, defensively, "I did get rid of the shoes."

Rabia shook her head and settled back into her chair. Len took that as his cue and settled into the significantly less padded chair on his side of her desk. "So," she said. "This is a hilarious insight into the contents of your closet, but we haven't talked since you took your honorable discharge and promptly went nuts. You want something, so why don't you just spit it out?"

"Going nuts isn't how I'd put it," Len said, slightly stung.

Rabia snorted. "You could've taken your military experience and that degree in biology and worked with the KDF science division, with a budget funded by every government in the world. Instead you went to the shoestring private sector, running around with practically zero backup and security. We had a company pool on how long it would take you to get killed out there."

"I assume you lost."

"Fifty dollars, my old friend." Rabia eyed him. "That was good drinking money, too."

He glared. "Private sector meant less money and fewer resources, but it was open source. All my research and discoveries are shared with everyone who can benefit from them. Considering what the kaiju have done to humanity over the last thirty-odd years, you'd think that the KDF would be more interested in sharing and learning with everyone, and less concerned with military secret protocols." With effort, Len reined in his irritation. This conversation, and more profanity-laden variants of it, were exactly why he'd stopped talking with his old squad mates and friends, and why there were topics that he and his daughter, Lt. Deanna Haddrill, carefully avoided. "But you're right, I'm here for something." He reached into his side bag and hauled out a handful of rolled maps and rumpled calculation sheets, plopping them down on Rabia's already overflowing desk. "If historical patterns hold up, then three months from now the kaiju will enter an eleven-year reclusive breeding season."

Rabia leaned forward, all joking wiped away. The lines in the even brown skin of her face were suddenly deeper, and her military regulation hijab seemed to cast a shadow across her eyes. "You," she said, "are not supposed to know about this."

"Oh, please," Len scoffed, shuffling through papers. "The data is all there, and KDF scientists don't have a patent on reading patterns. Here," he shoved one paper forward. "The kaiju appeared and ravaged our coastline cities for eleven years with only minor seasonal variations. Then, suddenly, they all vanished for eight months. World celebrates, starts rebuilding. Joke was on us, because when they returned, it was even worse. But it was different then before—the whole southern Malay peninsula was overrun by the first sub-adult kaiju we have on record—almost fifty, depending on which reports you believe and what we can patch together. Wherever the hell the kaiju went, they spent that time breeding. Time goes by, the pilot program finally comes together, and coastal cities have a defense system that actually works now. Eleven years on the dot—and the kaiju disappear again. No one knows where. Everyone searches this time—including private sector kaiju spotter teams, not just your pilot rigs—but no one finds them. Eight months later—the kaiju come back, along with a major influx of sub-adults. My team worked on tagging them, and I can tell you that we put ultrasonic pingers and physical tags on almost forty, and had visual confirmation on one hundred others. Now we're heading into the third round of this cycle, and the KDF wants to find the breeding grounds."

Rabia sat back into her chair and steepled her fingers, watching him closely. "All this from public information, Len?"

"All of that, yes," he confirmed. He hesitated a moment, but knew that he had to be cards on the table. "But I had a leak for the next part." Rabia's eyes narrowed, but he pushed ahead and rolled open his map. "KDF has hundreds of teams in mech rigs that can traverse deep water. You're looking for the breeding grounds in the Marianna Trench, El Zacaton, Lake Baikal, the Litke Deep, and everywhere else that's deep and underwater." He looked up and stared at her. "But, Rabia, the KDF is wrong."

"I'm going to ignore your possession of classified information," she said coolly. "For now. But the science makes sense, Len. The kaiju are amphibious, and our scientists believe that they go deep to breed and lay their eggs. Maybe they work in parenting pairs, maybe solo. But it's clear that there's some oversight of the eggs, because they do some moderate protection of the young during the first year on land."

"You're looking in the wrong spot," Len insisted. "I've followed kaiju for almost a quarter of a century. They're almost complete loners—I can count the number of coordinated adult kaiju attacks on one hand. But we have a species-wide coordinated breeding cycle right up there with some varieties of cicadas. And once those young are around, they show up in the remains of Bangkok, in what is essentially a nursery that is guarded for at least a year by a rotating roster of full adults. This indicates a breeding ground used in coordination by the entire species. And I've watched the sub-adults—they stay in shallow waters for a long time. What my team and I believe is that you need to be looking at terrestrial locations for a massive, isolated breeding ground used by the entire species at the same time."

Rabia shook her head. "Len, you have a fantasy here. Nature just doesn't work that way. The kaiju go deep, maybe they go in pairs. If we're lucky and we can locate their most heavily used sites in this cycle, we can hope to start making efforts to cut off the influx of new kaiju in the next cycle."

"Nature *does* function this way. There are species of birds that have all their members in one part of the Arctic at one time. Not many species, but some. And if I *am* right, and if I can confirm the presence of the breeding colony in this cycle, then the KDF has eleven years to plan an attack on the *entire* population of the kaiju during the one time that they will all be in one place and vulnerable."

"And no one has seen this massive, coordinated, terrestrial colony?"

Len pointed to the map. "Not if it's in Antarctica."

There was a long silence while Rabia looked at the map, then at Len. "I assume," she said slowly, "that you have a great deal of research to back up this theory."

He pulled four stuffed three-ring binders out of his bag, which sagged at their removal. "Loads."

She nodded, tapping the binders thoughtfully. "Even if I agree with what I'm about to spend the next few days reviewing, at length, with our own scientists," she warned, "you realize that there's no way that I can pull our teams out of the deep-water search project."

"I figured," Len said. "But you don't have to. All you have to do is send my team in."

She gave a small smile. "I assumed it was something like that. Convenient. Though, of course, you understand that operating as a branch of the KDF is going to require some adjustment on your end."

"I know. And I think that you understand that if I didn't believe in my theory this much, I never would be agreeing to that adjustment and whatever conditions you throw on."

Rabia nodded. "Well, then. Assuming your numbers hold up for my scientists, are you ready to rejoin the fight to save the human race, Captain Haddrill?"

He locked eyes with her. "Colonel Ashiq, I never left that fight."

**FIVE WEEKS LATER, LEN HELD** tight to the straps of his safety harness as the KDF military transport soared toward its destination in Antarctica. His daughter had managed to finagle her way into the pilot's seat for this trip, and every time they hit an air pocket or abruptly dropped in altitude Len wondered whether Deanna was deliberately screwing with him. He pressed his thumb hard against the acupuncture point on his right wrist and focused hard on breathing deeply. He'd ridden just about every kind of rickety rust-bucket that could be hoisted into the air, but somehow the knowledge that the human that he'd been partially responsible for potty-training was at the helm epically increased his motion sickness.

Across the aisle, he heard a low snicker. Cracking an eye, Len glared at his team partner, Thaisa Pequeno, who just grinned wider. Her dark hair was heavily streaked with gray now, but the expression on her face was identical to the twenty-five-year-old Brazilian femme fatale that he'd met in a camp in Panama. The two of them had been assigned together on their first freelance kaiju counting operation years ago, when Len had just gotten his discharge papers and Thaisa had been a doctoral candidate from one of the last surviving universities in São Paulo. There had been almost twenty young volunteers in the operation—by the time the expedition ended three months later, he and Thaisa had been the only ones left. All the other volunteers either died or fled at their first sight of a kaiju. He and Thaisa stuck it out—hanging from treetop blinds and staring through scope lenses for hours at a time, trying to locate identifying marks on kaiju coming in from ocean feeding runs, figure out an accurate count of just how many were in the area, and track their movements. Data like that was critical—it could be passed along to the governments working feverishly on defensive installations for their vulnerable cities and populations, and also to the KDF's newly-minted pilot program that focused on active defense and, possibly, hunting down and thinning the population. Of course, everyone dreamed of extermination, but no one had even known how many active kaiju there were—thus, teams like Len and Thaisa.

Strapped in beside Thaisa, the third member of the team snored, seemingly immune to the dips and jerks of the transport plane. Thaisa had picked Madias Sonkeng up in a bar on the edge of Cameroon about fifteen years ago. Len had discovered that it was more than a one-night stand the next morning, when he'd seen Madias wedged into the back of their Jeep along with all their supplies and equipment.

"She is going to murder us," he'd told Thaisa flatly. "We will get five miles outside town, and her gang will roadblock and murder us."

"No, this is love," Thaisa had responded.

"Oh my god, your hormones are going to get us killed. I am going to be the first man in history who, instead of getting killed because of his own hormones, as is right and natural, got killed because of a lesbian's hormones. I hope, as the machetes come down, that you feel ashamed."

"No, I will feel validated in my decision to somehow fuck over your patriarchal bullshit with my dying breath."

"Bullshit," Madias echoed from the back seat, learning her first word in English. Incredibly, she and Thaisa had lacked even a common language. Thaisa spoke Portuguese and English, while Madias had spoken French and four local dialects.

A week later, Thaisa and Madias were exchanging their marriage vows in front of a local judge, with Len begrudgingly serving as their Man of Honor. To Len's complete surprise, Madias had settled into their expeditions as if it was the most natural thing in the world. Six feet tall, with corded muscles rippling beneath ebony skin that was several shades darker even than Len's, and a knowledge of explosives and detonators that hinted at a very disturbing past occupation, Madias had devoted herself to providing security for Len and Thaisa's expeditions. When the pair of biologists had assured her that they were seasoned researchers and knew all the best ways to stay alive in kaiju-active areas, Madias had just nodded patiently before going about her own business. She'd saved their lives three weeks into their first expedition as a trio when part of their treetop blind suddenly collapsed (they later learned that monkeys had been gnawing at the ropes for days), creating a sudden noise, and, even worse, a direct line of sight for the kaiju. Len and Thaisa had been desperately scooting down the tree, hoping that somehow they could get down fast enough to lose themselves in thick underbrush, when Madias had simply pulled a small detonator from her vest and pressed a button. Seconds later, a huge explosion rocked the forest from half a mile away, completely pulling the kaiju's interest. Kaiju were like that—they'd learned big explosions usually meant that something tasty and human was in the area. Abandoning the small meal in front of it for the possibility of a bigger catch, the kaiju had moved off to investigate—long enough for Madias to guide Len and Thaisa into a spider-hole dug for three that she had somehow constructed without either of the other two knowing. When the kaiju came back minutes later, now royally pissed at the explosion yielding exactly zero delicious morsels, they'd been tucked safely in their underground hideaway.

That was when they unanimously voted in Madias as head of security.

They'd been a team for years—traveling the world, equally at home in dense jungles or in the hollowed-out remains of ruined cities, observing, tracking, learning, and, above all, counting the kaiju. And despite innumerable close calls, they'd managed to survive in a profession that had an average life expectancy of less than eight months.

The gut-churning feeling of the transport descending rapidly pulled Len's thoughts back to the present. Antarctica wasn't exactly known for its plethora of ready runways, and their chosen campsite was almost forty miles from the remains of the old McMurdo station and whatever might be left of its infrastructure. They'd all been warned that the runway-less landing could be rough. It turned out to be more than rough, with Len suspecting that tomorrow he was going to have a set of bruises in the exact pattern of his safety harness, but they got down.

"Well," he said to Madias and Thaisa, "here we go." Through the window, he looked out at the vast desert of ice and rock that made up the last continent, the ocean crashing at the beach, and land stretching out endlessly in every other direction.

That was the last free moment they enjoyed, as everyone swung immediately into the process of getting camp set up. The crew of the transport wheeled out what the team would be using as base camp for the next seven months—a retrofitted trailer, shaped like a one-room horizontal box. Painted white to help blend into the surrounding ice and rock, it was just big enough for a four-person team, the most critical gear, and the stove that would keep them alive during an Antarctic winter, where the temperature would plummet to -58° Farenheit, and the sun wouldn't rise for six months.

They hustled to unload gear and start the all-important task of chaining and securing the trailer to the ground. What couldn't fit into the trailer was tied to the heaviest rocks that they could find, all under the direction of the fourth member of their team and the accommodation they'd made to the KDF—Lt. Luis Carrasco, their representative from the KDF who was in charge of their supplies and, technically, base camp itself. They'd had a chance to meet and talk with him before they left, but Len was concerned that Carrasco, almost three decades younger than the members of his own team, had been available at all. He seemed nice, and the fat binder in his hands, color-coded at that, seemed to indicate that he had a good handle on the packing and organization of gear—but he'd never encountered a kaiju in the field. That in itself was a red flag for Len. In all his years in the field, he'd never been able to predict who could handle the experience of seeing a kaiju. There was an almost existential level of terror in viewing a kaiju—their size, power, and sheer destructive force went beyond seeing any terrestrial animal and became like witnessing a hurricane or a tsunami. Even though they had a definable life-cycle, it was hard to escape the feeling that you were looking at the raw, destructive force of nature—and one that represented a specific desire of nature to fuck over the human species once and for all. When he'd been a student, a professor told him that once a person looked into the eye of a whale, they could never be the same again. Well, Len, had looked into the eye of a kaiju, and he felt that the same idea applied, but less in the world-affirming, new-age fuzzy sense of the whale. To look into the eye of a kaiju was to see a malevolent intelligence focused entirely on killing you and everyone else like you. You could prepare all you wanted for that moment, but when it came, you either stood your ground or you ran. Len had seen battle-hardened veterans turn tail and run, and he hadn't blamed them. You could either take being in the field with a kaiju, or you couldn't. He and his team could take it—but he didn't know about Carrasco. And now they were all together in the most hostile environment on earth, with no one capable of coming to get them before their scheduled eight-month pickup. And they were actually *hoping* that the world's population of kaiju would arrive in about four weeks.

Shit, just going over it in his head made Len's bladder loosen. But a team member from the KDF had been Colonel Ashiq's requirement for putting KDF resources into the mission, and Carrasco was it. At this point, there was no turning back, so Len focused on what he could control—which was setting up base camp.

Four hours after landing, Carrasco swatted him on the shoulder (it wasn't full winter yet, but in the heavy parkas that were necessary outside, tapping didn't register through the sheer amount of padding required) and told him that he was needed on the transport. Len ran up the ramp and into the equipment bay, then made his way up the progressively warmer compartments until he reached the comparatively balmy pilot's station, where his daughter sat at the helm, monitoring her dashboard. Deanna had warned him ahead of time that she wouldn't be able to see him much, since the conditions on the ground required that she keep the engines running for the entire time that the transport remained stationary. Now his daughter looked up at him and put a hand over the mic of her headset. "Dad, things looking good down there?"

"Not bad," Len allowed. The nature of what he did meant that Deanna had spent the majority of her childhood and young adulthood not knowing whether he was alive or being eaten by a kaiju, with gaps in communication that could stretch from days to weeks at a time. He'd tried not to minimize the dangers of what he did, but at the same time he didn't like dwelling on them—which had basically resulted in just not talking about his day-to-day work with his daughter. When she'd joined the KDF as soon as she turned eighteen, Len had wondered if she thought turnabout was fair play, since now he spent his free time worrying about how long it had been since he last spoke with her.

She leaned forward and adjusted a dial without breaking eye contact with him. It made Len proud to see his daughter so in control and confident in her environment—though it made him feel infinitely ancient as well. Deanna's bone structure came primarily from her mom, whose family had fled Seoul during one of the first attacks and had ended up in a refugee camp in Len's native California, but her skin was just a shade lighter than his dark brown. It was an unusual combination, and invariably made Len happy—he liked that he could see both himself and Nari in their child.

"Weather report has just been updated—the storm that was on track for three days from now has gotten pushed up. It should be hitting this area in sixteen hours. We need to be wheels-up in twenty minutes." Her mouth thinned. "This is your last chance out, Dad."

Len put his hand lightly on the back of her head, feeling her short dark hair. "Too important. But get your people out, and I'll see you after we get back to the base."

"Maybe sooner than that," Deanna replied. "I can't promise anything, but I'll try to get the pilot slot for the pickup." She reached back and squeezed his hand. "Eight months, Dad. Put it on your calendar."

"I'll count the days," he promised, dropping a quick kiss on Deanna's forehead. She blinked quickly, and he pulled back, fighting against the moisture in his own eyes. "Okay. Stay safe, Lt. Haddrill."

"As safe as you, Captain Haddrill."

He smiled as they went through their old routine. "Try to be a bit safer than that, honey."

And that was all they had time for, because in exactly nineteen minutes his daughter was coaxing the transport down the rocky, barely clear area that they were using as a primitive kind of runway, pulling up just before the wheels would've clipped a set of jagged ice boulders. The team didn't have any time to spend pondering the level of isolation they were about to endure for eight months—the only four humans on an entire continent. Instead they worked with frenzied intensity on getting the camp ready to endure the kind of storm they'd only read about. The right supplies and equipment inside the shelter, the other stuff tied and re-tied to the biggest rocks they could find, the shelter as secure as they could make it.

When they finally went to bed that night, they were confident they were as secure and ready as they could be.

When the storm hit eleven hours later, they discovered how wrong they'd been.

**RESEARCH INTO ANTARCTICA HAD TOLD** them that the katabatic winds were formed by cold, dense air that flowed out from the polar plateaus and whipped down onto the coast at speeds clocked up to 327 miles per hour. Len and his team had all been through gnarly storms in the past, and they'd thought that they knew what they were in for.

They were wrong.

It was, Thaisa screamed into his ear at one point to be

heard over the din of the winds, like kaiju—you knew on an intellectual level what you were in for, but that was nothing in the moment you actually experienced it.

As thoroughly as they'd secured the shelter, it hadn't been enough. Six hours into the storm, the shelter had begun to shake. Small inches of slack in the chains were exploited by the speed and intensity of the storm, and the shakes that had begun at a small, annoying vibration, increased to bone-jarring thuds whenever a heavy gust hit the shelter. The temperature plunged, with the pilot light on their precious stove blowing out constantly, until they'd finally given up and broken it down for the storm's duration. They zipped themselves into all the heavy clothing that they had brought for the outside elements and resigned themselves to dry protein bars and waiting out the storm.

Fifteen hours into the storm, after an almost completely sleepless night, they were huddled around their electric lanterns and doing their best to keep occupied. Len, Thaisa, and Madias played cards as well as they could with the entire shelter shaking horribly every few minutes. Carrasco occupied himself by conducting a complete inventory of the equipment left inside the shelter. He would open a case, check the contents, check his color-coded binder, and make a small notation with his pen. With no way of knowing how long this storm was going to last, Len hoped this coping mechanism would endure.

It was Thaisa who noticed it first. She nudged Len hard with her elbow to penetrate the layers of engineered cold protection, and jerked her chin at Carrasco, whose orderly inventory had devolved into a desperate tearing through cases, and was pale and sweating even in the cold.

Len got up and made his way over. Under normal circumstances, he would've tried to be subtle, but the howling of the wind and the rattling of metal was too loud. "Lieutenant," he yelled, practically in the man's ear, "What's going on?"

Carrasco turned to look at him, and the expression on his face struck a chill in Len that went far beyond wind and degrees. "The satphone isn't where it's supposed to be."

Len's gut tightened. The satphone was their only link off this continent, the only way to call for help, and worst of all, the only way they had to relay any of the information that they might find before their scheduled retrieval.

Everyone joined in Carrasco's hunt. The case his color-coded binder listed as the location of the satphone was filled with packets of ramen noodles. One by one, with increasing desperation, they opened every other case inside the shelter. Everything was exactly what Carrasco's binder said that it would be.

But no satphone.

"Lieutenant," Len finally said, when there was no more hope that the satphone was anywhere in the shelter, and the winds continued to scream. "Where was the ramen noodle case supposed to have been stored?"

Carrasco's eyes darted to the door of the shelter, and what Len had been desperately avoiding thinking for the last hour was horribly confirmed. Their satphone was outside, in a case secured to a rock. A case that whoever had tied it had thought was food supplies—necessary, but not fragile. Able to take a beating.

Which, no matter what manufacturers might claim, was not a key feature of a satphone.

Carrasco managed three steps toward the door before Len snagged him by the back of his parka. Whatever the man's qualifications were that had convinced someone to assign him to this mission, Len knew in that minute that he'd never been in a situation even remotely like this, because Carrasco tried to fight him, yelling that they needed to get out, to save the satphone.

Madias moved in front of the door, an immovable object if ever one existed. Meanwhile, Len and Thaisa forced Carrasco into a sitting position.

"Luis, Luis," Thaisa yelled in his ear, as soothing as anyone could be in this moment. "Listen to that wind, *menino pequeno*. If you go out there, you won't survive."

"But, the sat—"

"We have to wait," Len said. "After the storm, we can look. We can't go out until then. Hopefully we tied it well enough. But we're not going to risk lives on a piece of equipment that could already be destroyed."

Carrasco stared up at him with terrified eyes as all of them fully absorbed the knowledge that, now, they really were alone on this continent.

And outside, the winds continued to howl.

**ANOTHER TEN HOURS DRAGGED BY.** Impossibly, the storm worsened.

They pulled open the sleeping bags and zipped them together, crawling in while still wearing their parka outerwear in the hopes that communal heat-sharing could make sleep safe in an environment where their breath was visible, and frost was beginning to coat the supply cases closest to the door. At first sleep seemed impossible, but Len's team knew from hard experience that even the terror of death would eventually weaken at the prospect of a nap.

Len didn't realize that he was sleeping until Madias's screams woke him up. He was rolling and moving before his brain even caught up to his body, and it took him crucial seconds to register what was happening—the door to the shelter open, immovable in the crushing wind even as Madias strained to close it, Thaisa also struggling to her feet, and Carrasco nowhere in sight.

Then there was no more time to think, as one of the chains that had held the shelter against the wind for more than a day finally snapped, and the horizontal shelter abruptly slammed upwards by forty degrees, the other chains straining to bear the load. Madias and all the supplies were thrown backwards toward where Len and Thaisa now lay prone. For one awful moment, suspended in time, Len watched everything slide.

Then the impact.

The slamming of equipment echoed over the storm for just a moment. Len experienced a second of white pain and breathlessness before individual nerve endings became red hot beacons of each impact zone. The shelter remained horribly suspended for almost a minute until the wind weakened—just enough for it to go crashing down again, sending equipment and aching bodies flying once more. Before the second round of pain even had enough time to register, old instincts sent the whole team moving. They'd faced death in its many, many incarnations, and they didn't even have to discuss. All three threw themselves against the door, using as much weight and muscle as they possessed to force the door closed. Then they all piled into the weak corner, using their combined bodies to try to keep the shelter from achieving that hideous incline again, all too aware of what would happen if another chain broke thanks to the additional strain.

There was no more sleeping for the remaining seven hours of the storm.

They didn't mention Carrasco, either.

**THEY FOUND HIM LATER, AFTER** the storm finally ended, their battered shelter mostly intact. Madias went right to work on re-securing the shelter, while Len and Thaisa walked in progressively wider circles. The sun seemed to hover just above the horizon, even though Len's watch showed that it was barely noon. Soon, they wouldn't see even that much light.

The equipment, tied to the rocks, remained attached, so it wasn't as bad as they'd feared during the darkest moments in the storm. But Case #100834B, which Carrasco's binder designated as ramen noodles, had had just enough slack in the line that it had spent the entire storm being bashed over and over against the rocks. Ramen noodles would've survived—the satphone had not.

They found Carrasco almost half a mile from camp. He'd come within feet of being thrown over the edge of the hill that led down to the beach, and from there to who knows, but a series of rocks had stopped him. His face and head were covered in blood, but he was still breathing when they found him—they carried him back to the shelter, where they covered him in sleeping bags and tried to coax him to suck on a cloth dipped in water, but he died fourteen hours later, never regaining consciousness.

They took his body to the edge of the overhang, with a view of the beach, then covered him with a cairn of stones. Thaisa murmured some prayers in Portuguese, while Len and Madias watched quietly. Under her breath, Madias muttered that at least now they had 25% more food supplies. Len looked at the cairn and wondered if Carrasco's parents were still alive somewhere, or if he'd had a family tucked away on one of the KDF military bases. Without the satphone, it would now be another eight months before anyone could be notified of his death.

Afterwards, when Thaisa investigated good dump sites for waste (and not the food variety—excrement was always a leading camp concern), Len walked up to Madias, who was still standing near the cairn, staring out over the barren landscape, with the shelter looking painfully out of place and vulnerable.

"What do you think, Madias?" he asked.

She spat on the ground. "This whole thing is shit." For a moment Len thought she was talking about this seemingly doomed expedition, but instead she gestured to their camp area. "We're completely exposed. Other than some rocks and some ice, there's nothing here. One kaiju gets a look at us, and we're fucked."

"Assuming we're right, and the kaiju come."

She ignored him. "Get out the fucking black powder, picks, and shovels. We need at least three emergency spider holes at different distances from camp, and there is no goddamn dirt on this continent—just rock and calcified penguin shit. I want two different explosive nests—half a mile and two miles. If I can get some of the rocks closer to the shelter, I can at least add some camouflage that will actually work. And knowing you and Thaisa, we'll need at least three different observation blinds so you don't get yourselves killed trying to spot identifying marks."

He stared at her. "You don't ever wonder if I'm wrong? If Thaisa and I are just on some wild goose chase?"

She spat again. "*Enculeur de mooches.*" She stomped off, probably in search of the shovels.

There was a long pause as he ran that through his pidgin French.

"*Fly fucker*?" He called after her.

Six weeks later, the sun disappeared, and the kaiju arrived.

**THE AURORA AUSTRALIS, THE SOUTHERN** lights, were painting the sunless sky with weird, glorious ripples of brilliant green and blue when Len saw the first kaiju break the ocean's surface. He and Thaisa had been alternating eight-hour shifts at the scope they'd set up at the edge of the ridge, camouflaged to the best of Madias's considerable ingenuity. When he first saw the dark shape far out from the breakers, he wondered if weeks of looking at nothing, on a continent filled with nothing, in constant darkness, had finally driven him mad. But as he watched, the green light gleamed off of a series of massive ridge horns as they rose over the water, then the immensity of the shoulders, and then he could feel the vibration through the ground as the kaiju set its feet down from the swimming position and began to walk up the beach, hoisting a body that redefined the term "massive" up and onto the continent.

It lifted its head and gave a bellow, that sound that Len always swore he could feel concussively through his chest. That finally convinced Len that it was true—that all those months and years poring over the data, debating points with Thaisa—the timing of the destruction of McMurdo and the other Antarctic bases, the unexplained drop in emperor penguin populations, the grouping behavior of juvenile kaiju—had actually resulted in being right. That they had cracked the greatest and most critical secret in the world and actually located the kaiju breeding grounds.

Len wriggled backwards, keeping carefully below the ridgeline (underestimating the acuity of a kaiju's eyesight was usually the last mistake anyone ever made), then ran back to the shelter. He nearly ran straight into Thaisa and Madias, who had heard the bellow, and all three bellycrawled back up and into the observation blind. Over the next thirteen hours, they remained fixed at the scopes as kaiju after kaiju broke the surface and began making their way up the beach and over the rocks. They moved in an orderly line—shocking for creatures that seemed to want nothing to do with each other once they left their juvenile packs—in a southern direction, heading deeper into the continent. In the light of the aurora australis, Thaisa and Len counted each kaiju that emerged and scribbled down identifying notes—ridge horns, snout shape, eye to jaw ratio, all the methods that they had used and developed over the years to differentiate one kaiju from another in a way definitive enough that it could be replicated and used by other kaiju counter teams. This was the experience of a lifetime—all the subjects that they had stalked and hunted for individually, spending months tracking and waiting for, racing through the ruins of cities and towns to follow the path of kaiju that had avoided KDF pilot teams, now laid out in front of them in an eerily docile line. It was Madias who had to remind them that they needed sleep and force them to trade off naps. She was the one who crept in and out to bring more food for the pair, as they watched and recorded, and the one who brought the dump pot back and forth from the excrement site, so that the observation blind didn't start smelling.

By the fourth day, the kaiju stopped arriving, the last one filing up the beach and down the broken path. Len and Thaisa had counted and catalogued 496 individuals. Finally, Madias convinced them to come back to the shelter, to get some real sleep, to eat hot soup rather than just dry MREs and protein bars. They did it, reluctantly, already planning eagerly for how they could travel further into the continent, to observe what was occurring at the breeding grounds. Already the information they'd gathered was breathtaking, and would shake the KDF, and the field of kaiju science, to its foundations.

Which was the moment that the loss of the satphone truly sank in. No one knew what they'd just discovered. And no one would know until the plane came and got them at the end of the season.

They were holding the biggest revelation, the information that the world was waiting for to plan and mount an attack to take back their planet—but their phone was broken.

**EVEN MORE THAN BEFORE, CAUTION** became the byword for the expedition. The challenges of surviving in an Antarctic winter were compounded by the dangers of having the world's population of kaiju settled in a rock basin a mere ten miles from their campsite, and then topped off with the gravity of having the responsibility of making sure that the information about the kaiju got back to civilization safely.

As they planned their first observation trip to the kaiju breeding ground—which involved careful logistics, and quietly setting up at least three ice-cut resting/hiding stations along the route, with food supplies tucked in—Thaisa raised the possibility of a trip to the abandoned McMurdo base.

They were all tucking into a meal of spicy soup, huddled around the stove in the shelter. The air in the stove's immediate vicinity was balmy enough that they had taken off their outer coats, though they kept their hats and sweaters. They were four months into the expedition, and, with no way to manage more than a periodic sponging-down with a rag and a bowl of hot water, they all smelled horrendous.

"We could look for another satphone at McMurdo," Thaisa suggested.

Len considered it. "We know from the records that they made a distress call out when the attack happened, but it was during the winter, and no one could come down to check. There wasn't any contact after the initial call, so all souls were presumed lost. And after the attacks started on the cities elsewhere, no one wanted to spend the resources to come down here to see what was left."

"So it's possible that there's nothing left of the base at all," Madias said, taking a large sip of her soup and shaking her head.

"Possibly not," Len admitted.

Thaisa wasn't giving up so easily. "Even if everyone was killed, McMurdo was a whole series of buildings. They would've had multiple satphones, at least one per emergency stash."

"Satphones which are now over thirty years old," Madias said. "There's no way they'd still be working."

"Lithium batteries," Thaisa countered. "And they hold their charge longer in the cold."

"For thirty years?" Madias snorted. "They're all dead."

"We've got batteries that were intended for our satphone." Thaisa looked over at Len. "Not all of them were destroyed. And even if they wouldn't work in an older model satphone, we could still daisy-chain a series of the old batteries together to create enough charge to get out at least one call."

Len hesitated, then said, "McMurdo is an almost forty mile hike from our site. We've got maps, but nothing that shows the terrain out there in a lot of detail. Unlike what we're planning to the kaiju grounds, there would be no going there and getting back in a few hours. We would spend days out there. Depending on what happened on the trip, it might be a one-way shot. And we have no idea what we'd find when we got there. Maybe most of the base is there, or maybe it was completely destroyed. It's banking on luck and the unknown."

Madias nodded. "Whereas if we stay here and stay safe, we know the day that the transport plane is due back. We can't call them, but they'll arrive and get us."

"And if they don't, and they've given us up for dead because we haven't been able to make our check-ins," Len added, "*then* we can try to make the push to McMurdo for a phone. After the kaiju leave at the end of their season, and the sun comes back, we could make the trip. If that's our only option."

Thaisa considered, then gave a small sigh and nodded assent. "At least if we end up being trapped on this continent for an extra month or two, we have the food to make it." They all looked down at their soup, thinking about Carrasco, and the 25% portion of the supplies he no longer needed.

"Maybe we should start rationing a little more," Len said, and the others agreed.

**BY THE TIME THE SUN** began to climb into the sky and stay there for three hours a day, the kaiju began herding their offspring down from the breeding ground, across the beach, and into the waves. They moved in small clumps—about twenty juveniles making their ear-splitting screams, the attending adults answering in their massive bellows. At the beach, all the adults but two would split off and disappear into the waves, seemingly unconcerned with the juveniles now. It was the remaining two adults who coaxed and urged the juvenile pack, nudging forward stragglers, offering weird growls of encouragement. Then, one adult leading and one taking up the rear, the group disappeared, almost certainly on their way to the Malay Peninsula, and the area abandoned by humanity and dubbed The Mosh Pit.

Len and Thaisa took reams of notes and discussed the behavior in detail. How did the group determine which two adults would act as juvenile nannies? Were any of those adults' offspring in the clump they led? Without a necropsy it was impossible to determine sex, so what were the sexes of the nannies? Were the nannies mating partners? The unknowns seemed endless.

Compared to the incredible four-day arrival period of

the kaiju, their departure was strung out over a series of weeks, beginning with the return of some daylight. Madias checked their observation posts constantly, adjusting the camouflage daily. While the juveniles and nannies distracted each other, the kaiju returning to the ocean on their own seemed to be returning to their normal behavior—snapping and hissing if another adult kaiju came too close. Three elephant seals appeared at the beach edge one morning just as an unaccompanied adult arrived to leave—only one made it back out to the safety of the waves.

Back at the base camp, Len emptied his bucket of waste out into the dumping ground and wondered whether the increasing daily temperatures and the departure of the kaiju meant that they would be able to set up some kind of primitive outhouse soon. While they'd operated as a team in just about every kind of environment imaginable, seven months of proximity on this close a level was getting obnoxious for all of them. The ability to excrete in even moderate privacy would be a welcome luxury.

He'd just finished his shift at the scope—eight hours as primary observer, then eight hours as note-taker. Now came his eight hours of sleep and eating. So it took his tired brain a moment to register what he was hearing as he shook the last drops of urine out of his bucket. Then all exhaustion was gone, and he stared up at the sky in horror as that distant buzzing hum finally made sense.

The transport plane was coming back—three weeks ahead of schedule.

He was running hard over the rocky ground, staring up as the transport plane dipped down below the cloud layer and began a slow circle over the camp. Len waved his arms over his head, screaming, "Go back!" even though he knew they wouldn't be able to hear him up there. "Go back, Deanna!" he screamed again, straining to see inside the pilot's cockpit, unable to make out more than just a generic shape behind the glass.

As the transport plane started its descent, coming into position to make its landing, Len felt the telltale vibration in the ground, and knew that time had run out. There was nothing more he could do for the plane, and he watched in horror as a kaiju burst over the ridge, missing the observation blind by inches. There was nothing Len could do but turn and bolt for their emergency spider-hole, tucked back against an overhanging shelf of rock. As he ran, he saw the moment the transport plane realized its danger and abruptly nosed up, desperately trying to gain altitude. But it was too slow, and the kaiju swung one massive claw, ripping off the left wing. Len slid into the spider-hole just as the plane spun wildly out of control, plunging down into the ground in a fireball of destruction. The plane was gone, and Len pulled the top of the spider-hole down—it was PVC plastic, which Madias had spent days carefully laying over with ice and pebbles until it looked indistinguishable from the ground around it. Len kept the top open two inches, looking back over to the ridge, where Thaisa and Madias were still in the observation blind, waiting for them to pick their moment and make a run for it. Once the kaiju became enraged, there was no safety in any raised structure that could stick out to them—the only safety was underground, tucked out of sight.

Two more bellows from the direction of the beach. The

destruction of the plane had caught the attention of others. Len knew what the next move had to be, and he counted down slowly in his head, crouching down and putting his hands over his ears, picturing Madias carefully unzipping the pocket of her parka, pulling out her detonator, and imagining her calm voice—*trois*, *deux*, *un*, and—

He both felt and heard the explosion one mile away. It was their big distraction, and they'd thrown two-thirds of their material into that nest. He imagined the kaiju coming up the ridge, turning and beginning to move quickly toward the new stimulus, racing each other to try to be the first to scoop up anything there was to devour. Len propped the top open again, peering out. The original kaiju hadn't moved to investigate the new explosion, but it was ripping at the burning remains of the transport plane, looking for anything edible.

That was the best moment, and sure enough, he saw the figures of Thaisa and Madias running out of the observation blind, as hunched down as possible, heading straight for him. He lifted the top of the spider-hole up further with one hand and gestured desperately with the other. *Run faster*, he wanted to scream, even though he didn't dare even whisper, and even though he knew that they were already trying to outrun death itself. *Oh, Jesus, please let them run faster.*

They were just over two-hundred feet from the bottom of the ridge, then just another short distance from the spider-hole and safety, when Thaisa's foot came down on a loose rock. She tripped, sliding over more rocks, which clattered down in a tiny little avalanche. Madias reached for Thaisa's shoulder as she fell, but missed, and Thaisa kept falling, falling, down to the bottom.

And, at the remains of the transport plane, the kaiju, that eye and ear predator, lifted its head at the sound of falling rocks. It turned, and Len saw it see the two women. He could see that Madias knew it as well, but she went for Thaisa, pulling the smaller woman onto her feet. Something was wrong with Thaisa's leg, and she nearly crumpled at her first step, and Madias hauled her into a fireman's carry, running toward the spider-hole, even as the kaiju bellowed, and began coming toward them.

Len saw the glint of metal in Madias's hand, and seconds later the second and last distraction explosion went off, this one just half a mile away. It should've been enough—but this kaiju refused to be distracted and kept moving toward the tiny prey it saw.

He could hear Thaisa shouting at Madias to drop her, to leave her for it and save herself, and they were close enough that he could see Madias's closed, stubborn expression as she continued to run toward him. They locked eyes, and for a second he thought that she could make it.

Then the kaiju's claw came down, slamming with the weight and force of a city bus, covering both women. Len would've screamed, but there was no breath in his body, and just a strangling whimper escaped him. Then the claw pulled back, and Len saw a smear of blood, thought that he saw an arm, and then the mouth came down and the kaiju was lapping and slurping like a dog eating ice cream off a sidewalk. The kaiju's head tilted, and suddenly Len caught sight of a piece of heavy-duty plastic, anchored behind a head ridge with a hard metal bolt, the kind shot from a crossbow by a biologist. The plastic was the size of a pennant—red, yellow, red. And even though he couldn't see it, he knew that there was a number printed on the other side. This was their tag—he, Madias, and Thaisa had tagged this kaiju nine years ago, outside the ruins of Bangkok.

Len dropped the top of the spider-hole and collapsed onto the rocky floor. He rocked back and forth, hyperventilating, as he heard the kaiju systematically destroy the shelter, the observation blind, and everything else that stood.

At last, hours later, the sounds stopped. He felt the heavy footsteps move away. Knowing kaiju, he waited another hour, then another to be sure. Finally, he lifted the top and peered out.

Utter destruction. Nothing was left standing. The shelter and the equipment were ripped apart and spread for what seemed like miles. The transport plane was in wreckage so complete that looking for survivors would be useless. A bloodstain across the ground and a few shreds of parka were all that was left of Thaisa and Madias. All that was left of what had been their camp was Carrasco's cairn, just visible at the ridge.

Getting out of the spider-hole, Len dropped to the ground on his ass and stared around him for long minutes. The sun was setting, and the twilight shadows stretched around him. He was alone, on the most hostile continent in the world, with a dozen straggling kaiju. His friends were dead. The transport plane, and possibly his daughter, was gone.

He was, quite simply, fucked.

"No," he said finally. "No fucking way." He had information that could save the world. Deanna hadn't been sure about being able to pilot the plane, so he would operate on the belief that she had *not* been aboard that plane. If he could get this information back to the KDF, and *goddamnit, he was going to do that*, then in eleven years all the combined fire and fury humanity could muster would come back to this spot, and every kaiju on the planet, along with their eggs, would die—a fitting funereal sacrifice for Madias and Thaisa.

There was no need to spend any more time thinking. Len reached into the spider-hole and yanked out a backpack. There were three of them in there—their go-bags in case of just a situation like this. Each one contained a portable tent, a small cooker for melting water, food rations for eight days, and the map to McMurdo. They'd always expected to use all three, but Madias had packed these bags, meaning that each one contained exactly what one survivor would need—no more.

Len buckled the pack on and pulled his parka hood forward. The temperature was dropping again, but he had thirty-seven miles to hike, and before that, the beach.

He looked over the edge of the ridge. In the distance, the smoke from Madias's big explosive nest still curled into the air, and in the fading light he could see the figures of kaiju as they circled it. They'd added a vat of beef tallow to that nest—enough to confuse the hell out of the kaiju and maintain interest. It was one of Madias's old tricks, and Len felt his throat choking up again.

But, for this moment, the beach was clear, and he wasn't going to waste Madias's last distraction. He maneuvered down the path to the beach, going as fast as he dared over the loose rocks and sudden ruts. Once he was there, he ran flat out across the painfully exposed area, the sweat that poured down his back equally from exertion and stress. It was too easy to imagine a kaiju turning casually and catching sight of him with one of those falcon-like eyes—a lone chicken McNugget, just waiting to be scooped up and chomped. And none of the kaiju had eaten while they were in the breeding grounds—even more incentive to devour the McNugget.

It was full dark by the time Len made it across the beach and up the opposing ridge. He managed another half mile before the dropping temperature made continuing on unsafe to the point of stupidity, then he set up his tent in the shelter of some rocks and crawled in. Grief had stolen away his appetite, but he forced himself to eat a protein bar, then forced himself not to vomit it back up again. Deanna was counting on him, somewhere on some base where she was alive and fine and eating her own dinner. He needed to survive this trip, make it to McMurdo, and find what he needed.

He hoped that any part of McMurdo had survived to be found.

**WHEN THE SUN ROSE, HE** walked. His parka was pulled up, his goggles were on, and his balaclava covered his face and mouth, but the wind dug into every tiny exposed patch of skin. He walked all day, checking his compass periodically to make sure he was going in the right direction. He stopped twice to pee and to choke down more food, to melt ice for the water he needed to keep going, but mostly he walked.

When the sun set, he kept walking until his feet finally refused to move another step. This time he didn't set up the tent, he just rolled himself into his bivvy bag and remained huddled in the dark, waiting until it was time to walk again. Above him, the stars seemed painfully bright and close. On this continent, if he didn't turn on his electric lantern, then there was no light at all. He wasn't taking off his gloves, but he could tell from the stinging on patches of his face that he already had some frostbite. It didn't matter, so he ignored it.

On the afternoon of the third day, he topped a low ridge and saw McMurdo.

At its height of usage, McMurdo had housed just under a thousand personnel and looked like a series of neatly-laid-out warehouse buildings. Now it housed no one except one irritated elephant seal who snorfled and flapped its way back down to the water as Len passed it, and most of the buildings were completely crumpled and blown down to just a few shreds of corrugated metal that flapped mournfully in the wind.

He checked each methodically, exhaustion muffling his brain from heartbreak or despair. All he could concentrate on was the task at hand. If he finished it and hadn't found what he needed—well, hypothermia was probably just around the corner anyway. He could curl onto his bivvy bag and just sleep his way out of this life.

The further he delved into the base, the more he started seeing actual remnants. The front half of the mess hall was ripped open and destroyed, but inside there were still standing tables, and the piles of serving trays and eating utensils remained set up and ready for the next rotation of eaters—barely visible through layers of ice. He kept going, walking through utter destruction into just mostly destruction, and finally, in one small lab, he found the minimal destruction he'd been hoping for.

There were no bodies, which was a relief. He knew that the base had operated on a skeleton staff during the winter months, so when the kaiju had come there had been just under two-hundred souls lost. This lab had lost one wall, but otherwise stayed intact. There were still papers on the tables, and someone's coffee mug sat next to an easy chair. Microscopes, computers, printers—everything that the scientists had needed, visible through thirty years of ice. And then, the answer to his prayers—a closet door with a sign that, when he rubbed hard against the frost, was revealed. EMERGENCY SUPPLIES. DO NOT TAMPER. FOR EMERGENCY ONLY.

This certainly counted. He used his ice axe to chip away along the seam of the door, then pounded at where the handle was. With the layers of ice coating it, that handle was never going to turn again, and Len didn't have time to struggle with a lock, if the emergency supplies had been locked. After almost an hour, and his shoulders burning, he was able to finally get down to the original wood, and yank the handle out completely. Another round digging at the seam, and the door finally creaked open.

Far away, he heard the bellow of a kaiju. Len looked over his shoulder, through the missing wall of the lab. A kaiju stood just over a mile away, staring straight at him—the only moving thing in the entirety of McMurdo base. Len had cut apart a kaiju's eye and analyzed it—they could see as well as a peregrine falcon. And that meant that it could see him right now.

Len turned back to the supply closet, and started ripping through it. Epi-pens, a portable defibrillator, glow-sticks, candy bars, shovels, hand-warmers—and, just there at the back, a case that he recognized.

Satphone.

He yanked it out and popped it open. In the distance, he could hear the kaiju's footsteps, but he couldn't bother with that now. He hit the on button, but the phone remained dead in his hands. So much for lithium batteries. He flipped the phone over and yanked open the battery compartment. Into his own pack, and out came the small kits that Thaisa had made up for all three of them, just in case this desperate journey had to be made—three fresh lithium batteries from their own ruined satphone. He checked—the battery wouldn't fit into the older model. He'd pulled off his heavy gloves for this, but now he pulled off his inner gloves, the skin of his fingers and hands immediately tightening in the frigid temperatures. But he needed finer dexterity as he carefully wound the wire that Thaisa had left him around the new batteries, daisy-chaining them together, then forming the end into a loop that could connect to the satphone's contact point. His hands shook in the cold, and it took him three tries to loop it where he needed it—and as every second ticked by, a small part of his brain was monitoring the heavier and heavier footsteps coming toward him.

He turned the phone over carefully, making sure not to let the connecting wire slip off, and hit the button again. A long pause—then the phone lit up.

"You blessed little motherfucker," Len breathed. Thirty years in a frozen closet, and it still worked. Whoever had stocked this emergency closet had bought the expensive shit.

With shaking fingers, Len tapped in a number. Then he waited as the ringing filled the room.

Ring.

Ring.

Ring.

Ring.

A huge bellow—not more than half a mile now.

Ring.

Ring.

Then—click.

*"Hello, you have reached the voicemail of Colonel Rabia Ashiq. I'm not in the office right now, so please leave a detailed message. Thank you."*

BEEP.

Len spoke to the phone, but his eyes were fixed on the kaiju as it came closer and closer. It looked back at him, its claws opening and closing spasmatically, its mouth opening to reveal rows and rows of teeth. It was crouching now as it came closer, the better to scoop and drop him into its mouth. This was how he'd always known it was going to end.

Or, maybe not quite. "Rabia, this is Len," he said. "The kaiju are there. Ten miles in from our camp is the breeding ground. Three months after when you dropped us is when you want to make your attack—the entire population is communally brooding their eggs, and they are clustered and unwilling to move. The eggs hatch two months after that, and then the community spreads out along the hills. Once the sun comes back, they start moving out again."

The roof started to tear. The kaiju was opening up the building like a can.

"Rabia," he said. "We're all dead, so don't send anyone. Tell Deanna that I love her. And, Rabia,"

The claw was coming down, the mouth was gaping.

He could smell the kaiju's breath, and see the pupil of its eye contract and focus on him.

Len stopped talking to Rabia. The claw had him, but he still had the satphone wrapped in his hands. He didn't know if the call was still going, or if the connection had been lost, or if the wires had slipped. But this was his last moment, so he looked into the eye of the kaiju, that burning source of awful intelligence and endless hunger, and said, "We're going to fucking kill you all. *Enculeur de mooches*, motherfucker."

And then it ate him.

Eleven years later, the Battle of McMurdo began.

# FORMULA 287-F

DAN WELLS

**THE NEEDLE SLID THROUGH JIM'S** skin with barely a prick, so small and smooth he didn't even feel it. He certainly didn't see it—he had his eyes closed, thinking happy thoughts and controlling his breathing. He hated getting injections more than almost anything in the world—the only thing he hated more, in fact, was watching his daughter get injections. She'd just had her four-year check-up a few days earlier, which had included a vaccination for Cass-5, and watching her cry out of fear of the needle—holding her tightly as she tried to run away so the doctor could grab her arm and force the injection through—had broken his heart. Needles, he thought, were the worst, and in their relatively cushy lives on the Elie Colony certainly one of the most painful experiences his little girl had ever had to go through.

Jim had gone through plenty of things which, he knew, were empirically worse. He'd broken his leg once helping to

FBW
2018

build one of the early habitation domes, and a few years later he'd lost three fingers and most of his hand in a maintenance accident, when he'd been cleaning one of the propeller screws that kept the sewer system running, and it had turned back on while his hand was still inside of the pipe. It had hurt like hell, and the mangled hand had been almost too gruesome to look at, but he'd gotten through that fine. Blood and bones and pain were one thing, but hypodermic needles were completely different. He couldn't explain it, and he knew it was irrational, but that didn't make them any easier to handle. So he closed his hands, and he forced himself to relax and to breathe and to think about other things. The meadow outside the Colony, or the beautiful alien flowers that grew in Elie's mountain valleys. And Doctor Hatfield swabbed his shoulder with antiseptic, and placed her fingers on Jim's arm, and then she stepped away.

"All done," said the doctor.

Jim kept his eyes closed. "You're kidding."

"It's just a little prick," said the doctor. "Barely even a sting."

Jim wanted to rub the spot, but he kept his arms loose and took another deep breath. "I don't know why I hate these so much."

"The good news is, this is the last one." Doctor Hatfield dropped the syringe in a plastic bucket, to be cleaned and recycled, and started stripping off her gloves. "The treatment only has four stages, and you just got number four. No more shots for a while."

Jim opened his eyes. "So it's working now?"

"We *assume* it's working now," she said. "We *hope*. The future of the Colony is... well, maybe not riding on that formula, but certainly pinned to it."

"The corps of engineers will get the communications up and running again," said Jim. "They always do. We'll be fine."

"That's certainly the preferable plan," said Hatfield. "New supplies from Earth could get us back on track and save the whole planet—and I hope it happens soon, because the storms are supposed to be awful this year. But. If the corps of Elie engineers, as vaunted as they are, can't solve this problem their way, the corps of scientists has to solve it in ours."

"And ours includes reckless human experimentation," said Jim.

"Not reckless," Hatfield said quickly. "We have... a handful of recks, at least." She smiled at her joke, probably hoping it would allay any tension. "Our experiments with animals have proven far more successful than even our most optimistic predictions, and while we would not, under ideal conditions, jump to human subjects this quickly, we have every expectation of safety and success."

"I know, I know," said Jim, standing up. "You don't have to sell me on it, doc: I volunteered for this, remember?" He held up his right hand and wiggled his thumb and one remaining finger. "If your formula really can grow these back, I'm all in."

**"HOW SOON IS IT GOING** to work?" asked Bonnie over dinner.

Jim shook his head, took a drink of recycled water, and swallowed. "I don't know. Days, maybe? Weeks?"

"I a spacechip," said Meg.

"You're an awesome spaceship," said Jim, and wiped a finger of porridge from her face. "Careful with your food."

"Weeks is too long," said Bonnie. She drummed her spoon against the table—a nervous tic that Jim had only recently noticed. When had it started? Certainly not their whole marriage. Maybe not even their whole time on Elie. Had she only started it a few months ago, when the crisis went public? Bonnie noticed his eyes, focused on her spoon, and stopped tapping it. "The Colony is running out of...." she glanced nervously at Meg. "F-O-O-D. The storms wipe out all the farms before they have a chance to produce. We're living on the rations from the transport, and they're not going to last forever." She dipped her spoon in her porridge, held up a viscous, flavorless glob of it, and allowed it to drip slowly back into her bowl.

"We knew that colonization would be hard—"

"Of course we knew," said Bonnie, "that's not what I'm saying. This went way beyond 'hard' when they started performing untested gene therapies on my husband's DNA. That's not even legal on Earth."

Jim scowled, not in anger but in grim determination. "We might never see Earth again." He glanced at Meg, feeling guilty for talking like this in front of her, but she was playing happily with her food.

"Maybe we're better off not reconnecting with them," Bonnie said, dropping her spoon in her bowl. "Who knows if they'll even recognize us when they get here."

"Babe."

"We're not even terraforming Elie anymore," she said, "we're just Elie-forming us."

"Babe."

"Who knows if we'll even be human anymore?"

"Babe!"

She stopped, looked at him, and grabbed his hands. "I'm

sorry, honey. You know that I love you, and that was... super insensitive. You're not a freak or a monster, you're saving our lives. And I know that, I just...." She ran her fingers over the scars on his right hand. "I'm just scared."

"I know you are," he said. "I am too. But we're going to make it through."

Meg looked up from her bowl, her face once again covered in smears of porridge. "No be scary," she said. "I hep you. I a spacechip." She grinned, and Jim couldn't help but grin back. Bonnie laughed, and then coughed to hide it as the laughs turned to tears."

"The storms only kill Earth crops," said Jim. "The Elie crops grow fine, but their chemistry is too different for our bodies to use—most of it we can't metabolize, and the few parts we can are toxic." He was repeating the same pitch Dr. Hatfield had given him—the same pitch Bonnie had heard with him, sitting in the doctor's office, trying to decide if they dared volunteer. It was desperation that eventually decided it—desperation and the hand. "If this treatment works, we'll be able to heal that damage faster than the local food can cause it—and we'll be able to heal everything else, too. We can survive the storms; we can survive the snotdogs. We can regenerate lost limbs. We'll be sturdy enough, and resilient enough, to survive on this planet that never wanted us to be here."

"I know," said Bonnie. "I know. But that's what I was saying in the first place: this has to happen fast if it's going to do us any good. Whatever... changes... this treatment makes in your body, it needs to make them now. If it's safe enough for everyone, we'll need to start widespread injections soon."

"Then we'll just have to hope," said Jim. "There's not much else we can do."

"Snot-goggy scary," said Meg, and curled her sticky fingers into claws, twisting her cherubic little face into an adorable approximation of a snarl. "Rarr rarr rarr."

"See?" said Jim. "We don't have anything to worry about. Meg'll take care of us."

Bonnie smiled, but only for a moment.

**"THOSE FINGERS ARE COMING IN** nicely," said Doctor Hatfield. She poked gently at the tiny stubs of fingers on his right hand, and they twitched at the contact. "Nerves work. And the reflexes."

"They itch," said Jim.

"They will," said Hatfield. "The skin's probably being stretched quite a bit—they're growing fast."

"They don't feel stretched, said Jim, and moved them. "They look like baby fingers."

"And yesterday they looked like fetus fingers," said Hatfield. "Stretchy or not, they're growing, and they're growing at an amazing rate." She looked up at his face. "And so are you. You've gained three pounds in a week."

"That's what we're hoping for, right? My digestive system is stronger now, so it's drawing more nutrients from the food."

Hatfield frowned a bit, picking up the flat glass screen that held his medical records. "I suppose. You're still just eating the rations, though, right?"

Jim nodded. "Protein porridge for breakfast, lunch, and dinner."

"That stuff's already optimized for human consumption,"

said Hatfield. "You shouldn't be able to draw anything out of it that you weren't already getting. And our animal test subjects never showed a weight gain this dramatic until after the initial healing process."

"Should I be worried?"

"I'm worried about everything," said Hatfield, setting down the screen. "The fate of our colony might rest on this working, so yeah, it's okay to be worried. But don't worry about this hurting you—it seems to be doing nothing but good. An abnormally advanced response only suggests, if anything, that your body is particularly receptive to the formula, and others won't take to it quite as quickly."

"But I'm not going to... swell up and die, or anything."

"If you do," said Hatfield, "try to do it here in my office. I'll need all the data I can get."

"Thanks, Doc."

Hatfield smiled. "Any time."

**THE CORPS OF ENGINEERS' PLAN** was somehow just as reckless as the corps of scientists—but it made sense, Jim supposed, for everyone to pull out all the stops. The Elie Colony contained nearly a hundred thousand people spread across thirty habitat centers on two continents, and every one of them would die if they didn't do something. Solar flares in Elie's star, Bacci, had cooked their satellites and ruined their transports and disrupted their atmosphere, creating deadly storms both on the planet and in the solar system. And since most of those hundred thousand people were understandably reticent to alter their own genome to stay alive, the corps of engineers had spent every waking moment for months now trying to get the long-range communication system running again. They'd exhausted almost all of their options, but one desperate hope remained: a single satellite, thrown off course but still in a stable orbit, had responded to their hails. If they could get someone up there, they might be able to repair it.

They couldn't get anyone back down, of course, but what was one life in the face of a hundred thousand?

From that point of view, Jim knew, he'd gotten the better deal. He might die; Commander Morelos was definitely dying, even if he succeeded.

Jim sat in one of the common areas, watching the launch in a vast group of silent, nervous colonists. He clutched Bonnie's hand tightly with his left hand, and held Meg on his lap with his right. His fingers were almost full size now, bright pink and completely functional. The scar tissue around them was even receding. Plus his pants barely fit around his waist anymore, which might have been weight gain but he suspected it was something more. The pant legs barely reached down to his ankles anymore.

He watched the screen, where a makeshift rocket sat on the modified landing pad and held his breath during the countdown. *Please let this work. Please let this work.* The formula they'd injected him with was doing what they wanted, yes, but it was doing other things, too. Yesterday, as an experiment, he'd fasted the entire day, not even drinking water. He'd still gained a full pound.

The rocket thrusters fired, and the slim cylinder rose slowly into the sky, Commander Morelos perched in the command module at the top of it like a sausage on the end of a spit.

"Spacechip," said Meg.

"Spacechip," Jim agreed.

They watched it on the screen, smoke billowing out behind it, and soon it was so high they could look to the left and see it in the actual sky, climbing toward orbit with all their hopes pinned on it.

Half of their hopes. All of Jim's. He didn't want to be the reason they failed.

The button on his pants popped off, flying through the air like a flat plastic bullet, and Bonnie shot him a look. "Be careful when you move like that."

"I didn't move," said Jim. "I'm just sitting here." He adjusted his arm around Meg's waist, and his shirtsleeve tore at the shoulder, stretched tight across his back and side.

"You need new clothes," said Bonnie.

The rocket exploded in midair, some rushed system proving too faulty to sustain an actual flight. The crowd gasped, and cried, and one by one they turned to look at him. He was their only hope left. Above them a debris cloud hung in the sky, long tendrils snaking out at odd angles where fragments of rocket had spun off into the air. Jim's heart sank, and his other sleeve ripped.

"I think the clothes are the least of our problems," Jim whispered.

**"WE DON'T KNOW," SAID DOCTOR** Hatfield, shaking her head at the other man in the room: JJ McHenry, the Colony Governor. "He grew two inches in two weeks after the fourth dose of the formula, and now he's grown two more inches just in the day and half we've had him under surveillance."

"Why is it doing this?" asked McHenry.

"We don't know," said Hatfield. "It didn't happen in any other test."

"Is it going to happen to everyone else we inject?" asked McHenry. "Now that the engineers have failed this is our only chance of survival."

"We don't know," said Hatfield. "So far he's the only one, so we've halted all injections until we find what's going on."

"Don't dose anyone else," Jim insisted. "We can't risk it."

Governor McHenry shook his head. "We're fast approaching the point where we can't *not* risk it." He frowned at Jim's body. "How big will he get?"

"We don't know," said Hatfield.

"Is it the growth rate going to keep accelerating, or flatten out?"

"We don't know."

"What *do* you know?"

"That this is far more disturbing than you think it is."

McHenry looked at her a moment, uncertain what to say. "More disturbing than the extinction of this entire colony?"

"He's not eating. We stopped his diet completely when he came in yesterday, but he's still growing. He's put on ten pounds just today, but he hasn't ingested ten pounds of anything."

McHenry looked at Jim. Jim looked back, and after a moment he nodded solemnly

"That's..." said McHenry. "Where is the mass coming from?"

"We don't know," Hatfield insisted. "We don't know anything, really—we know what's happening but not why, and that's because none of this makes any sense. Nothing remotely like this happened with our animal experiments. Jim's results don't just fly in the face of our previous data, they fly in the face of physics itself. He's an anomaly, he's... pure, unchecked growth."

"Like a tumor," said McHenry.

"Tumors use your body's own biomass against it," said Hatfield. "They subsume other cells into themselves. Jim isn't taking over other matter, he's just... growing."

"Matter can't just appear out of nowhere," said McHenry. "Figure out where it's coming from."

Jim shook his head. "Forget about me—you need to focus your attention on making a formula that works, not figuring out why my formula didn't."

"Solving that second problem might give us the answer to the first," said Hatfield.

"Or maybe your formula worked perfectly," said McHenry, "and we just haven't admitted it yet."

Jim raised his eyebrow. "What is that supposed to mean?"

"Are you hungry?" asked McHenry.

"Why does that matter?" asked Hatfield.

"The primary crisis facing this colony is starvation," said McHenry. "We altered Jim's DNA hoping that a powerful and constant regeneration process would allow him to digest and metabolize local Elie biomass. I think it's time we give him some."

"You think this growth spurt is just a side effect," said Jim. "You think the rest of the process worked."

McHenry met his eyes with a passionless stare. "There's only way to find out."

"Absolutely not," said Hatfield. "It might kill him."

"That's been the risk at every stage of this experiment," said McHenry. He looked at Jim. "This is what you volunteered for, right?"

"I volunteered to help you find a replicable solution to an existential threat," said Jim, his anger rising. He gestured at his body. "This is not replicable."

"You don't know that."

Jim's anger continued to rise, and his voice with it. "You want a whole planet full of giants?"

"You're not even seven feet yet," said McHenry. "You're bigger than you were, but you're still within the range of standard human development."

"And if I keep growing?" asked Jim. "If I hit seven, or eight, or ten?"

"Then a hundred thousand ten-foot humans will survive this crisis," said McHenry, "which is a far better outcome than a hundred thousand normal-sized corpses."

Jim opened his mouth to protest again, but he thought about Meg and Bonnie, and he stopped. He'd choose an oversized family over a dead one any day. He paused, and he took a breath, and he looked at Hatfield. She looked back helplessly.

"We don't have a lot of other options," she said.

Jim nodded. "Bring on the Elie biomass."

**THE FIRST SETTLERS ON ELIE** had tried dozens of ways to prepare the local plants, hoping that some new iteration of the cooking process could make them safe for human consumption, but all they'd achieved was a range of side effects from indigestion to gastritis to full on organ failure. Only one of them had died, eating a meal of flash-fried plant stalks the colonists had named whiptails. In what he privately admitted was an ill-conceived homage, Jim requested whiptails as his first experimental meal. The corps of scientists cleaned it, roasted it, cleaned it, irradiated it, cleaned it again, and then ground it into a paste laced with almost as many antibiotics as whiptails, following their earliest recipes to make it as healthy as possible. Jim ate it with no problems, though it was so bland at that point he could barely tell the difference between that and the emergency porridge rations he ate at home. They tried a second batch, slightly less processed than the first, and when he downed that without the slightest hint of pain they grew bolder, giving him sample after sample of increasingly authentic whiptail, until by the end he simply broke off a stalk, washed it in the sink, and ate it raw. Nothing happened.

"Nothing," said Hatfield, "is a very bad thing to happen right now."

"What do you mean?" asked Bonnie. She had left Meg with a friend and come to hear the latest report from the Doctor.

"First of all," said Hatfield, "we need to be clear about what 'nothing' means in this case. First of all, he's had no ill effects from the food: no nausea, no pain, no numbness in the mouth or ulcers in the stomach or bleeding from the intestines. All common problems for humans who've tried to eat Elie food in the past, and all absent here—that's a good thing. On the other hand, he has yet to pass any waste, solid or liquid, in the five days we've had him living in the lab."

"Plus the day before that," said Jim, "before I brought myself in here."

"That's not immediately dangerous, though, right?" asked Bonnie. "He's just a little constipated is all—"

"The ultrasound confirms that he is not," said Hatfield. "There is no buildup of material in his digestive tract—his body is using all of it, even the waste."

"That explains the growth," said Bonnie, and turned to look at Jim—a process that required far more craning of the neck than usual. He'd passed eight feet tall sometime that morning, and Hatfield estimated that he'd pass nine before midnight. He was growing so fast they could watch it on time lapse footage.

"Except it doesn't," said Hatfield. "The growth itself is hardly 'nothing,' but the impact of his diet on said growth seems to be completely nil. We measure the precise weight and volume of everything we feed him—some days more, some days less—and yet he continues to grow at the same rate without regard for anything we do or don't put into him."

"How is that possible?" asked Bonnie.

"It isn't," said Jim.

"At least tell me the rate is slowing," said Bonnie. "He's got to plateau sooner or later, right?"

Hatfield shot a glance at Jim, and he looked back calmly. He hadn't wanted to tell this part to Bonnie—he didn't want to her to worry—but unless something changed very drastically and very soon, they wouldn't be able to hide it from her or from anyone else. Hatfield looked back at Bonnie and shook her head.

"I'm afraid the opposite is true. Jim is growing at a geometric rate, faster and faster with each passing second.

As best as we've been able to model it, this time tomorrow he'll be twelve feet tall."

Bonnie's hand tightened around his, though she could only clutch a few of his fingers in her relatively tiny hand. It made him think about Meg, gripping his index finger tightly as she led him around the house.

"That's... not possible," said Bonnie.

Hatfield took a breath. "Are you a mathematician, Bonnie?"

"No," said Bonnie, "I'm a biologist, which is how I know that this can't possibly be—"

"Are you familiar with geometric scales?" asked Hatfield.

Bonnie nodded, losing her momentum. "Familiar enough. The rate of change is proportional to the function's current value." Her voice became calmer as she spoke, and Jim knew exactly what was happening—she did this all the time, using science like a mantra to cope with something that bothered her. It was one of the quirks that he loved about her, but he knew that it was masking a tremendous amount of pain. "It's called an exponential function," she continued, "because the time interval is the exponent that governs the curve. An exponential graph is—" She stopped, her words choking off. She recovered and finished. "Is very steep."

"The second half is steep," said Hatfield. "The first half of an exponential graph is incredibly shallow—far shallower than an equivalent linear graph. But when it gets going, it... really gets going. We don't know the exact rate of growth yet, and we don't know if that rate will continue or taper or if the process that's fueling it has any limits he might run up against—a wall, or a lack of energy—"

"You gave him a DNA treatment," said Bonnie. "DNA can't do what you're talking about."

"We know," said Hatfield. "It's like I told you—we don't know how this is happening, only that it is. And if he continues as he is now, he'll be too big for this facility by the weekend, and too big for the Colony itself a few days after that."

Bonnie's mouth hung open, as if she couldn't comprehend the grim totality of what Doctor Hatfield was saying. "What.... What does that... mean? What are you saying?"

"They've picked a hard boundary," said Jim. "If I go over it—"

"'They' who?" asked Bonnie. "What do you mean 'a boundary'?"

"I helped them pick it," said Jim.

Bonnie's face was intense. "What do they mean 'a boundary'?"

"Twenty-five feet," said Jim. "If I get any bigger they might not be able to do it."

Bonnie's voice was barely-controlled anger. "Do. What."

"Every test we've run shows that his growth is unconnected to any kind of resource," said Hatfield. "That makes it effectively unlimited—not by intake, not by environment, not by matter or even the laws of physics. And if we hit the back half of that exponential graph...."

"They're going to kill you," said Bonnie.

"I'm a threat," said Jim. "The Colony is already at risk of annihilation from the storms—I increase that risk merely by existing."

"Then we'll go," said Bonnie. "Out into the wilderness

somewhere—this is an entire planet, damn it, there's got to be somewhere we can go that won't hurt anyone—"

Jim shook his head. "Even if I can live out there, you can't."

"Then go alone!" cried Bonnie. "You can live out there and I can... visit you, I don't know! But you don't have to die!"

"You're not listening," said Hatfield, but Bonnie screamed at her.

"What the hell else do you think I'm doing!"

"Then you're not grasping the full weight of this," said Hatfield. "Tomorrow he'll be growing so fast you'll be able to see it with the naked eye. And eventually—and inevitably—he's going to round that corner on the exponential graph and start growing so fast he might as well be an explosion. We're not talking about your giant husband on the other side of the mountain that you can go visit like a patient in a hospital—we're talking about your husband so big he becomes a mountain. A mountain range—"

"That's impossible," said Bonnie.

"We knew when we started this that I might die," said Jim. "We were willing to go along with it then—we have to be willing to stick with that now."

"That was you dying to help people," said Bonnie. "This is you dying to not hurt them."

"They're the same thing," said Jim.

"They're not," said Bonnie. "Our Colony is going to starve to death and killing you won't change that. We're *all* going to die, and this just means that *I'm* going to die alone."

"There's still a chance you'll live," said Jim. "They're working on this non-stop. They still might find something, and there's still time to make it work."

Bonnie's face was streaked with tears. "What's the point without you?"

"Meg," said Jim simply. Bonnie stared up into his eyes, and then nodded.

"Meg," she said.

And cried.

**JIM WAS ALREADY SLEEPING IN** a hoverall hangar when he hit twenty-five feet, and he was growing so fast he hit thirty by the time they got him outside of the colony and out to a safe distance. A group of snotdogs watched from a nearby ridge, always eager to probe the weaknesses of humans who ventured outside the defenses of the settlement, but they didn't approach. They stood warily on the ridge, mucus membranes pulsing as they sensed the air, tusks dripping with thick saliva. Jim looked at them, and they stepped back; he shouted and waved his hand, and they loped back into the red foliage of the forest. He smiled. That, at least, was satisfying. He hated snotdogs.

He laid down awkwardly in the open field, putting his giant head near to McHenry and Hatfield. Bonnie had already said her goodbyes; there was no reason to force her or Meg to see what was going to happen next. His voice rumbled through a throat so wide it sounded like an echo in a cave.

"Where do you want me?"

"In the quarry," said Governor McHenry. "The actual—" he used a gesture rather than a word, as if he didn't want to say it out loud "—will be as quick and as painless as we can make it, but there's no way of knowing if the tissue will stop growing even after you're dead. We're going to try to break down the remains in acid."

Jim nodded. He was long past the point where a casual reference to his 'remains' could bother him. He had to die, and he knew he had to die, and he'd known it since he'd volunteered for the treatments. Maybe since the accident that had taken his hand—there wasn't room in a deep space colony for a man who couldn't contribute. He stood up and walked toward the quarry near the edge of the field, looking at his right hand as he went. It was pristine now—less weathered than his left, but otherwise a perfect mirror image. That was the most frustrating thing about this: that the treatment worked, at least in part. This incredible level of regeneration could have saved the Elie Colony, if the side effects hadn't made it impossible.

But the side effects were too extreme. He was already a foot taller when he reached the quarry than he was when he'd started walking.

The Colony had only a few small weapons, mostly to deal with snotdogs and other local predators, but they also had a small fleet of hovertanks to guard against raiders. They'd turned out to be too far away from the rest of settled space to need them, but three tanks were lined up now, facing the quarry, their main guns primed and ready. Jim sat down, barely fitting inside of the small stone depression, and faced them. He hugged his knees, feeling the stone walls bite into his sides as he grew against them. His growth was accelerating now. The three tank guns swiveled, aiming at a small spot on his forehead. Doctor Hatfield shouted from behind them:

"Thank you for your service to the Colony, Jim. I'm sorry it didn't work out."

"For what it's worth," said Jim, "I'd do it again." He could watch them getting smaller as he grew taller and taller above them. "Now end this before it's too late."

Hatfield nodded, and McHenry gave a signal, and the tank guns erupted in a brilliant flash of light, so bright that all three blended into one. The metal slugs were magnetically accelerated—no smoke or explosions like Earth's ancient weapons, just a hum and a flash and a brutal, staggering impact. Those guns could punch holes in mountains, and the last thing Jim remembered was a blinding light and an excruciating pain, and then everything stopped.

And then....

And then....

And then it started again. He blinked, and daylight flooded his eyes, and he brought up a hand to cover them, and to rub at the piercing ache in his forehead. He was regenerating too quickly for a single shot to kill him. The tanks fired again, and again he blacked out, but not as long; they fired a third time, and he didn't even go unconscious. He felt a horrible pressure on his sides, and flexed his arms and chest against it, and the stone quarry shattered around him. He stepped out of it as the tanks continued their barrage, but they were so small now they looked like toys, and their metal slugs pinged harmlessly against his skin. More tanks hovered toward him over the horizon, and he stooped low to give them a good shot, desperate now to end his life before his unfathomable size destroyed the colony, but he was too big now, and growing so fast he couldn't even control where his limbs went; he tried to kneel before the tanks, but his legs grew so fast that by the time they hit the ground they were twice as long as before, the tanks were under him instead of in front of him. They crushed beneath him like thin metal foil. He staggered to his feet, stumbling backward in horror, only to smash into the massive solar collectors arrayed on the mountain behind him. Formerly massive, now tiny in comparison to his skyscraper body. They crumbled like dry leaves under his hands as he tried to stand up.

A helicopter came over what he'd used to think of as a ridge, rushing in from the settlement's airfield with guns blazing and missiles firing. He closed his eyes and spread his arms wide, welcoming destruction, but the ordnance popped against his head and chest like fireworks, painful but not remotely deadly. He brought his arms back in, clipping one of the helicopters as he did, his eyes wide in mounting horror. How big would he get? How far would this go? He turned back toward the mountain, heedless now of the destruction he might be causing below him, but saw that it was already small and flat from this vantage point. The far side of the settlement had bigger mountains—higher and rockier, like the craggy teeth of the Alps on Earth. He ran toward it now, desperate to end his life, barely even noticing the crunch of settlement buildings beneath his feet. Guns seemed to fire on him from every side, but they did nothing; he needed to do this himself. He gripped a mountaintop in both hands, braced himself, and slammed his head into the giant stone. The planet seemed to rumble in response. He smashed his head again and again, trying to crush his gargantuan skull, feeling the stone shatter and the mountain cascade in an avalanche, all the way down to the settlement below. He needed to die. He needed to die! He found the rocky peak of the mountain, now small and sharp as a dagger in his hand, and used the full force of his body to ram his face down onto the narrow tip.

**"CAPTAIN," SAID THE PILOT, "WE'RE** approaching the planet Elie."

"Roger that." Captain Yessica Bradley swiveled in her chair and thumbed the intercom button. "All hands, prepare for the drop to realspace." She gripped the arms of her flight chair, hoping they hadn't arrived too late to save the colony. Something had cut off their communications with the Elie Colony a few months ago, and she had been dispatched almost immediately on a rescue mission, but strange solar flares all through the system had made the journey far more difficult than usual, and the trip had taken almost twice as long as normal. Her ship was packed full of supplies, but if something had already happened....

The jump ended, and Captain Bradley felt the nauseating flop as they entered realspace. "I hate that part—" she started, but suddenly the ship was rocking wildly. "Status report!"

"We've jumped into a gravity well, sir—that's not supposed to happen."

"I know it's not supposed to happen," Bradley growled, "get us out of it. Navigation! What happened?"

"We used the exact jump coordinates the fleet gave us," said the navigator. "They were supposed to bring us in well outside the orbit of both Elie moons."

"Is that the problem?" asked Bradley. "Are we too close to a moon?" A rogue moon orbit wasn't impossible, but it certainly wasn't likely considering all the data they'd collected on this system. The ship was still shaking. "Damn it, Holst,

I said get us out of this pull!"

"I'm trying!" The pilot shouted, but the first officer cut her off.

"That's not one of the moons," he said, pointing to the window in front of them. "But it's not Elie, either."

Captain Bradley looked at the planet in front of them—far closer than she wanted it to be. The sphere looked... wrong. "Why isn't there an atmosphere?"

"Or moons?" asked the navigator.

"Sensor readings say we're not too close to it," said the first officer. "It's just... enormous." His voice was hushed, in a mix of awe and fear. "We're at the right coordinates, but Elie is approximately ten times larger than it's supposed to be."

"And the moons are gone," said the navigator. "It probably pulled them in to a collision--that's why it looks misshapen."

The ship shook wildly as the pilot fought the controls. "Full power to engines," said Bradley. "Whatever that thing is, let's give Holst everything she needs to get us away from it."

"It's got us in its orbit," said the first officer. "We're swinging around to the daylight side now; maybe we can see a little bet—"

He stopped, frozen in mid-word, staring at the thing in stunned silence. No one on the bridge could speak or even move; even Holst lost control of her steering, and the ship stopped shaking as it gave up resisting and settled into the pull of gravity. All four officers stared at the planet in horror. Because it wasn't a planet.

It was a man.

The arc of dawn moved across his body, pulled by his own mass into a fetal position that almost, but not quite, approximated a sphere. Sunlight revealed feet, legs, hands, arms, and finally a head, curled down into his knees.

"God in Heaven," whispered the navigator.

"He's bigger than Jupiter," said the Captain. "It's... it's impossible."

"What's going on?" asked the first officer.

The navigator shook his head. "I have no idea—holy crap it moved."

Captain Bradley stood up, taking a step toward the screen. The man's head moved, pulling up, fighting the pull of unimaginable gravity to raise his face toward them. He looked at them with tortured eyes, each the size of planet Earth, and opened his mouth in a silent scream.

"He's talking," said Bradley. "What's he saying?"

"How is he alive?" asked the pilot.

"I'm trying to read his lips," said the navigator. "It looks like...." He shivered. "It looks like 'Kill me.'"

"What is this?" asked Bradley. She looked at the size of him, growing larger in the window. "Why are we going toward it so fast?"

"We're moving toward it at standard speed," said the first officer. "But he's moving toward us even faster. He's—growing."

"Pull us up," said Bradley, sitting down. "Pull us up!" She jammed her finger on the intercom. "All hands, brace for impact!"

The ship impacted on the giant man, so tiny he didn't even feel it.

But he knew.

Soundless in space, Jim screamed and kept growing.

# TITANS AND HEROES

A TALE FROM THE WYRD

NICK COLE

**AT FIRST, WHEN THE WORLD** began to come apart, it was the zombies that were everywhere.

The world had ended, swallowed and drowned in a sea of rotting, dead, necrotic flesh. All that smothering oven of that final apocalyptic August, the world seemed to ignite all at once with wars and rumors of wars, seething with armed troops in the streets, when really all the reports had been about escalating tension between the nations. The signs were there. They'd been there all along, if you knew how to read them.

But it wasn't just the zombies who'd overrun everything like rats coming out of sewers *en masse*. It was all the other things that came out of the dark and extremely thin places in the universe.

There were all kinds of other names in use as the streets began to fill up with the Zekes, Zeroes, Dead Tangos, Walking Dead, and anything anyone else could think of to call them as

people ran, flew, drove, and did everything they could to get away from the rapidly spreading pandemic of supposed-to-be dead people, now tearing the barricaded living to shreds.

The governments sealed their gleaming bank-vault hatches on their bunkers and went dark, hunkering in brightly lit caverns beneath iron and rock. The news stations went offline, as did radio and the Internet. The world got all dark and quiet, if you didn't count the papery rasping moans and tormented cries of the dead, banging at the doors to your neighbor's house just down the way, as you prayed you wouldn't scream and draw them over to yours.

At first, when the world began to come apart... it was only the zombies that were everywhere. But the silence that filled the void of a dead civilization was like a yawning cavern, waiting to be filled by something massive. Something monstrous. Something coming this way across the nightmare landscape. And if you listened closely, you could just barely hear those first, distant artillery strikes of its steps as it made landfall down off the coast of San Onofre.

**FOR BILL PAPADOPOULOS, THE END** of civilization had been like a big game he'd been training for his whole life. Training for, though he'd never known it. No, Bill wasn't the typical prepper with a bug out bag loaded with everything from surgical scissors to chlorination tabs and six different kind of knives, each with a compass and a sewing kit secreted in the hilt and accessible through the pommel of the para-cord wrapped grip. Bill Papadopoulos hadn't been waiting desperately for the government to declare martial law, or the Chinese to invade, or for some sweet meteor of death to deal that final and oft-promised blow and do in everyone along the California coast with the big old Tsunami of Justice. He wasn't waiting to rebuild civilization in his image or become a barbarian warlord at the head of a savage biker gang, sweeping down out of the high desert wastes to wreak havoc while fighting over the last of the gasoline and the few remaining cans of dog food.

Bill Papadopoulos wasn't waiting for any of those things because he wasn't that kind of man. Truth be told, he was a kind man. A sensitive man. A dreamer really. He was not aggressive, or type A, but he was tough. He could deadlift four-fifty, and most of his friends were what society called gym rats. The women he began friendships with, and never quite managed to date, were gym bunnies, and corporate business women he spotted when they tried to lift improperly, or listened to when some guy dumped them or didn't call back after a big night.

Bill was that type of guy. He was the perpetual runner up. The bridesmaid, but never a bride. The kind of guy who'd sit in a coffee shop for hours with the girl of his dreams and listen to her talk about the jerk she was dating, never one being bold enough to say, "Maybe if you let that loser go... you might find someone who really loves you for who you are, instead of what you look like."

*Like me.*

He was that kind of guy.

And he was handy. Capable. A craftsman. His day job was installing and maintaining sprinkler systems for the uber wealthy at their coastal estates. Timers, pipes, and drip systems for newscasters, models, rock stars and pro athletes. In the circles of the elite, those ever in search of a front lawn status worthy of the successful Columbian drug lords of the 80s, his name was put forth as the go-to-guy for all your lawncare hydration needs.

This is very important in Southern California. Water is Power.

And so, since Bill was too nice to attract the right kind of women away from the wrong kind of dudes, and he was handy in that he could craft just about anything in his shop, he lived in a world of practical fantasy.

He was a re-enactor. That was his hobby.

Hobby, as you will see, is a poor descriptor for what he really was. The only word that comes close is that he was passionate in that way Stradivarius must have been to make violins that still went for a million dollars hundreds of years later.

In fact, he was a member of several re-enactor groups. A Civil War Regiment, which was okay—he didn't like sewing that much, and that was a large part of being an authentically accurate Confederate soldier. A medieval knight's combat league, in which they smithed their own armor, donned the armor, and then proceeded to beat the living hell out of each other with swords they'd also made. He liked that one a lot, mainly for the forging of the armor-aspects. He dealt out some pretty solid blows, but he wasn't a killer, even though he'd read every book, late into the evenings and in bed alone, on Medieval longsword technique.

Here's an inside bit. No one knows how to fight with a longsword like they used to. That's one of the things the historians and scholars don't like to tell people—that they don't know everything. That much of their job is just guessing at what once was. They can theorize. They can guess. But they have no idea how two guys actually did battle with swords. Here's a little more: no one knows how ancient armies fought when two lines of warriors, armed to the teeth with swords and spears, faced one another. Did they hack away at each other in unison? Was it man to man? Did the lines dissolve into a hundred smaller combats all at once? Was there any teamwork? No one really knows because no one wrote anything down about how it happened at the Battle of Thermopylae or Marathon, and no Herodotus doesn't count. That was big picture stuff, not Olaf and Pylus smashing away at each other with pointy spears and sharp swords. No one knew how to fight with bronze and iron age weapons.

But that didn't stop Bill and the other re-enactors from showing up on the weekends to "shoot" at one another with muzzleloaders in their hot wool uniforms and cook beans with a side of authentic recipe hardtack over an open fire in the park while someone worked their way through some melancholy "harmonica-I." Or spending Friday nights under the hot white light of an athletic field, sweating buckets inside forged steel as another guy whacked away at him with a sword while his girlfriend, purple haired, holding a leather flagon of mead, and wearing a Maid Marion cone hat cheered him on from the sidelines.

Those groups were nice, as was his war gaming miniatures group, and the *Dungeons and Dragons* meet-up he attended weekly, bringing coffee and baklava from his uncle's bakery. And of course, the gym before and after work every day.

All that was great.

Busy. Busy. Busy.

But the group that Bill loved the best was the one that called to him from his past. As you have no doubt discerned by his last name, Bill was a Greek American. His grandfather had immigrated here, worked his butt off, started a diner featuring the best char-grilled hamburgers in Anaheim, and subsequently established a massive Greek family proud of its heroic past. Grampa Andreas had raised young Billy on stories of daring-do as done by iron-faced Spartans and determined ancient Greek hoplites. And not just the battles of Marathon and Thermopylae, but the imagined contests and feats of Greek mythology. Theseus and Hercules. Warriors who fought multi-headed dragon dogs, and monsters that came up out of the sea to devour young maidens chained to rocks. These were the stories that never left him.

And so, late one night, when dithering over whether to join a new re-enactment group specializing in Roman Legions, he came upon a much smaller group that specialized in Greek Hoplite-ing, as it were. By the end of the first day he spent with them, he knew he was all in. For the next six weeks, every other activity in his life suffered in some way, though no outsider would have ever known because Bill Papadopoulos never let anyone down. He was a word-is-his-bond kind of guy, and it was a phrase he used often. It disconcerted most people when he did. Especially his customers when he promised to return with the perfect new part, or system, later in the week. When he looked them in the eye and said, "My word is my bond," regarding everything from which night they might meet for a movie to whether he would come and help them move that weekend into their new boyfriend's apartment, it felt, almost to everyone, like they'd just joined some suicide mission.

But once he'd joined "Thucydides Fist" he was all in. Before he began to craft his breastplate, helmet, greaves, kilt, sandals, spear, and short sword, he researched. He knew his way around the Internet, and, ignoring wild reports of some kind of mass plague raking inland China, he found his way into some university online archives regarding the subjects of Hoplites.

Four A.M. came when he finally tore his pinned open eyes away from the screen and went to stand out in his meticulous backyard. Dawn was in the east, and he stood there drinking a muscle protein enhancer drink packed with amino acids as he contemplated the life of a Spartan Hoplite.

Getting inside the mindset of the ancient warrior he was about to play was a big part of the re-enacting life for him. The Civil War soldier, 9th Alabama Irregulars, had been hard for him to nail down. His relatives hadn't even been inside the United States when the nation tried a very unamicable divorce. But, the detail, the buttons, the craftsman level of workmanship on a good canteen and musket had lured him in and kept him for a time. The Medieval Knights of St. George, Huntington Beach Chapter, had been more his speed. Putting together a set of armor took months and money—or just a whole bunch of money. But Bill was not the type to just throw money at his hobbies. Half the fun was in DIY.

He'd gotten that from Grandpa Andreas, who helped him build a soapbox derby the year before the old man's first heart attack. They painted it gold and called it the *Hermes*.

"Just like the messenger of the gods," Grandpa Andreas had proclaimed from around a cigarette. "As fast as the wind."

Bill always went all-in investing his time and energy. When his *Dungeons and Dragons* group wanted to move into hand-painted miniatures, a campaign Bill had carried out softly in his high pitched near whisper of a voice, they decided to set their homebrew campaign in the world of Middle Earth. Bill even volunteered to DM, which was not an excellent fit, in that he had a hard time killing characters. But the players had been flat out gobsmacked when they showed up at Bill's garage one early summer evening to see an entire diorama recreation of the Misty Mountains and the caves of the Goblin King spread out over several sheets of plywood. It was like looking at the glory of Middle Earth in absolutely realistic miniature. A pulley and chain system allowed Bill to bring in the sandbox maps full of monsters and dungeon denizens, each detailed down to the blood on the Goblin's blades and the half burnt torches along the cave walls. Even the lake where Gollum hides with his "Precious" was haunting in its simplistic and forlorn detail. It was like a window into a lonely wanderer's outcast soul. And Bill had painted over ten thousand miniatures just to finish the campaign.

All the players agreed there had never been any experience quite like that.

Especially when he brought out the Six-Headed Hydra he'd special ordered from an artisan miniature-maker in Ireland who charged an arm and a leg for his one-of-a-kind creations. That special fantastic beast had loomed over the player's tiny little figurines like Godzilla towering over Tokyo. Each golden green scale had been lovingly painted.

The irises of both sets of eyes in each head had been flecked with malevolent red bursts.

*Doing it yourself is half the fun,* Grandpa Andreas could be heard almost every day in Bill's mind. And, *We come from heroes, Billy. Heroes. We fought the Hydra and the Kraken.*

*They were called the Titans, Billy. Those monsters were Titans.*

Standing there at dawn, finishing the last of the protein shake and steeling himself for a body crushing day of benching at the gym before he had to see his clients, he vowed to go above and beyond anything he'd ever done in re-enacting, with respect to his Hoplite armor project.

Because he wouldn't just be a hoplite, or a Spartan... he would be a hero. A hero who fought the mythical beasts of an ancient golden age Greece. A hero who got the girl through bravery, and fortitude.

*We fought the Hydra and the Kraken.*

As you might guess, it got a little out of hand. Not that anyone could tell. That was the thing about Bill. He was background. Amiable. Can do. Always there to help. He'd long ago learned that he got to participate in the group activities by being the kind of guy that didn't make waves and was always willing to lend a hand.

This is what Bill thought being a hero was. Supporting everyone.

He missed all those parts in the Greek Mythology where the hero was anything but there for everybody. Hercules of all people didn't get along well with others. Maybe that's what it takes to be a hero of legendary make? Maybe those kinds of heroes do the things they do because, when everyone else is saying "run for your lives" from the fire, or the Kraken, they're the ones walking toward it with sword and spear. They're the ones bucking the trend. They're the ones looking Death in the eye to see if it'll blink.

Maybe.

It was a shame to Bill, as he stood in the wet grass listening to almost near perfect silence of another beautiful golden Southern California morning, that there were no monsters anymore. No quests. No mazes. No riddles. And no heroes.

What it must have been like to have been a Theseus, or a Hercules, or a Perseus, in that long lost golden age when deeds made mortal men into heroes.

But Bill was little more than a supporting character, at best, in people's lives. And so, most of his new friends in the Spartan re-enactment group didn't really notice the mania until later.

At the next meet-up, a weekend march through the woods around Lake Arrowhead and a one-night military camp, Bill showed up in pitch perfect period piece armor.

Say that three times fast.

The details on his kit were exquisite. The craftsmanship professional tier. So much so that several of the members suspected he'd bought it from the guy in Switzerland renowned for making the finest armor. A set from that cat cost an easy twenty large. But once Bill went into an almost withering account of his efforts, to his fellow jaw-dropped hoplites, they understood that Bill was that guy.

The guy who could make his own kit better than a pro.

Several of his new friends within the ranks of the Spartans asked for help crafting their next set of blazing glory Greek Armor.

Obviously Bill agreed.

A few even asked to buy a fitted set outright.

Obviously Bill would not charge them for anything more than the materials.

Which was so Bill. Get it?

And when he drove down the mountain that night, satisfied and yet somehow uneasy, casting loving glances at the clamshell case he'd designed for his armor as he stopped at stoplights, before making the freeway and the long trek along the coast toward Irvine, he decided he'd make another set of armor.

Except this time...

Now wait a minute, Bill, some sensible part of his mind spoke up. You've got the best set any of them have ever seen. And some of them have been to the European Hoplite conventions and seen the actual Swiss Artisan sets being worn by smiling German bankers.

Bill pulled into In-and-Out Burger and got two Double Doubles, protein style. Which means no bread. They're wrapped in lettuce leaves.

This was at the end of July.

The world was really starting to go nuts if you were paying attention. Bill wasn't paying attention because of his obsession with Greek armor and heroes and monsters. Politics made him angry.

*Titans. Those monsters were called Titans.*

Pakistan and India were on the verge of nuking each other into oblivion over a border closing incident. The "South East Asian Super Flu" was devastating China, and all air travel was suspended from that region.

Europe was on fire and rioting.

But as Bill sat there in the early blue twilight of summer, chomping on one burger after the other, he couldn't stop redesigning, improving the near perfect armor in the clam shell case out in his truck. Truth be told, the act of building that armor had been an almost religious experience to him. And he was not religious.

How could there be a Divine Being when there was so much pain and suffering in the world? That's how Bill would respond to people online whenever the subject of a Creator or the supernatural came up. That was what he would have said to anyone trying to shove religion down his throat. And then he was back to the armor in his mind. How could he improve on near perfection?

Except, he thought to himself, I don't just want to build a prop. And I don't just want to build something that would have stood up to Bronze Age weaponry.

No?

No, he thought to himself. Because he'd seen some of the images on TV of the riots in Europe and really, all around the world. Training with the Spartans, the question had been often asked: What was Spartan warfare really like?

Most thought it was as about as organized as it could be until it turned into the equivalent of a pell-mell mosh pit, as generals and commanders threw more and more men into the center of the line trying to break the enemy and roll up their flanks. Some thought there were real tactics in play that we never knew about. Shields phalanx-style protecting the front lines like an armored turtle. Spear men working over the top of the front rank. Commanders pulling the dead and wounded back and pushing the living forward to fill in the gaps.

But it was the riots that seemed to be on every TV channel now. Masses of almost insane poor people, starving like dying corpses, hurling themselves heedlessly into the lines of riot police protecting airports and government buildings. Someone at the campout even pulled some video, and for a long while they sat drinking the overly sweet wine someone else had made and watched the clash of riot police in full gear versus savage horde. Really, it was not that much different than a Spartan or Hoplite battle versus a mass human wave attack. Which really, when you thought of it, had to be the battle of Marathon all over.

Bill finished the last protein style Double Double and sat out front in the twilight as families in paper masks forced their children to eat quickly before they loaded them into luggage stuffed cars and joined the miles long traffic jams crawling away from the more populated areas of So Cal.

Belly full, Bill finally admitted something to himself.

He didn't want to just build another set of replica armor... he wanted to build the real thing. Armor for the modern age. Like something Boba Fett from *Star Wars* would wear.

But something that looked more like what an ancient Greek hero would wear, if such men still walked the earth and saved maidens from monsters the size of the tallest building in LA. If suddenly those Titans marched out of the sea, a prehistoric roar-screech echoing out like a trumpet issuing a challenge, rivers of sea water dripping off their scale-armored hides.

This new set, this armor for a modern hero, would consist of a bullet proof ceramic molded breastplate, arm guards, shin guards, and a helmet all styled like a hoplite, for good reasons. Ballistic cloth kilt and shirt. All of this protected the vitals, as the ancient Greeks well-knew. The hoplite design was a good design.

A cold-forged short sword honed keen and a graphite shaft ending in a cut-industrial diamond spear tip. The spear itself would be made of Teflon or graphite so that it was light and flexed when thrown.

He wouldn't bother with sandals, instead electing for steel-toed combat boots with some sort of spikes grafted onto the soles.

A shield like the riot police used. Something you could see through but big and round like a Greek shield. That was the biggest problem with period-correct reproduction Greek shields. You couldn't see through them. They obscured your opponent. A shield you could see through would be a big advantage.

Especially if he could get his hands on some of that new Transparent Steel everyone was talking about.

He drove home that night and threw himself into research immediately. Not bothering to shower off the camp grime and sweat until well after midnight. Not even returning the calls of Kimmy from the gym who really really needed to talk about Bryce, the scumbag she'd been seeing.

He cleared his garage workshop and began to get out his tools. He checked the forge he'd built and made sure he could get it up to temperature. He made a test fire and pronounced it ready for business. Then he hit the internet with an abandon he rarely exercised, ordering a lot of expensive materials. Some of which should have triggered an alarm or two at any of the government agencies constantly watching everything. Except... they were kind of busy with the world coming apart at the seams.

Over the next few days many of the materials had to be picked up in will-calls, as most direct home shipping was either too busy or cancelled.

The big box Home Improvement store he swung by after picking up the ballistic cloth looked like it was having some sort of incredible end of summer sale. People were buying plywood by the shipping flat. Cars and trucks loaded up and screeched off into the neighborhoods nearby.

Police cars formed up into long convoys and raced here and there as though they were some out of control wildfire up in the canyons.

Bill paid this no mind. Yes. He was not an idiot. Something, some new latest end of the world panic was going down. He was aware of that. But the news was always going on about that these days. Everything was "the end of the world" because the networks didn't particularly agree with the leaders currently in charge. Specifically the President. They really hated that guy. And it showed.

All of this... the spreading "Cannibal Riots" as they were being called, was just another Y2K to Bill Papadopoulos. Of course the President, according to CNN, was responsible for this one too. He was always responsible for every disaster, according to iron-haired serious-problem-glasses newscasters.

To Bill, just because the idiots in Pakistan and Thailand were burning their cities down, didn't mean Joe and Susie America were going to start torching the local KFC. "C'mon people!" Bill thought and slowly drove away from the near riot at the Big Box Home Improvement Complex. "We're trying to have a civilization. Just chill out."

Many of his customers cancelled appointments that week. And so, he dedicated the week to a full armor intensive construction project.

The re-enacting committee meetings, meet-ups, fund raisers, and charity events were all cancelled too.

Perfect, thought Bill. I'll get stuff done. Next week they'll find out it was all for nothing and my armor will be ready. Done.

When Bill finally pulled on the entire finished set late Friday night on the last night of August, he looked like...

Well...

He looked like a high-tech Alexander the Great.

Fitting everything to his tight, yet well-muscled frame had been the hardest part. And his eyes were bleary from the precision work. They'd been practically scorched by the mini-furnace he used to forge the weapons.

He'd wanted to put an industrial diamond edge on the tips of the spear and the short sword, but instead he'd taken the carbon fiber steel he used to craft them down to such an edge that the diamond, in his opinion, would have been redundant.

At ten P.M. he opened the garage door and turned off his favorite Moody Blues album as he stepped out onto the driveway in full high-tech armor.

He saw two things.

The sky was bright orange and filled with grey smoke off to the east. Probably over the City of Orange. Another massive firestorm rose up on the edges of Saddleback mountain off to the south east.

Together the fires were one of the two things he saw. Even though there were two and probably more in the distance. The fire, for purposes recounting what would happen next, counts as one thing.

The other thing was that a meth addict bent over Mr. Courso, Bill's neighbor, who was down in the middle of the small light post-illuminated quiet street.

"Hey!" shouted Bill and didn't think to draw the sword on his girdle as he immediately ran straight for the scumbag mugging his neighbor. He knew it was Mr. Courso because of Yorkshire Terrier barking ferociously a few feet away.

What Bill saw next, as he raced up to the scene of the crime, stopped him dead. His armored combat boots skidded, bringing him up short of a macabre scene unfolding before his eyes.

The meth addict, eyes wide and soulless, turned to hiss at him.

His mouth was full of blood and tendons.

Mr. Courso bled from a missing chunk of his throat.

Without thinking, Bill pulled the short, very sharp sword from his hip and thrust it into the body of the Meth Addict. He'd been reading about supposed attack styles of the ancient hoplites, and he'd been making practice cuts and thrusts, so the technique was in his muscle memory. Thrusting with a dagger was a standard attack.

The meth addict ignored the lethal wound and reached out with gore slicked hands to clutch at Bill. Bill pulled the dagger free of the addict's thin frame and back-pedaled, slashing at the emaciated kid flailing wildly with his blood covered claws. The meth kid all the while moaning through a mouthful of Bill's neighbor's throat.

Five quick slashes at the hands and shoulders did nothing to stop the mindless drug addict from almost getting a hold of Bill. In a last desperate slash, Bill took the top half of the druggy kid's skull clean off.

At that point the kid dropped. Just flopped over dead.

But other people along the street, other "meth" addicts came for him now. In seconds he was cut off from a path of retreat to his own garage. He attacked their heads as they came at him. When he managed to connect with the weaving targets that stumbled like drunken sailors, they went down. But his own strength quickly left him as his heart pounded blood in his ears like a jack hammer underwater. Even his armor felt incredibly heavy as the initial surge of adrenaline abandoned him.

One kid lunged viciously, a mouth full of dark broken teeth opened in a silent roar. The bite connected with Bill's ceramic molded arm guard; what remained of the kid's teeth shattered and popped off like a string of pearls suddenly undone. Still the kid tried to hang on to Bill's arm greaves with his bloody gums. Bill shook him off and stumbled back; he heard Chelsea Harrington, the cougar mom neighbor of his, beckoning him toward her open front door. In an instant Bill ran for the door she was barely holding open. Chelsea, her body covered in the latest high-end yoga wear, stepped back as Bill entered, and a moment later threw her curvy frame against the door to shut it.

It rattled and shook from a series of violent impacts that came all at once. The meth addicts silently beat on the other side of front door. Their silence despite their exertions disturbed Bill's fracturing mind most of all. There were no enraged, drug driven, psychotic promises of murder screamed from beyond the door. No breathy cursing or insane mumbling. If anything, there was little but the papery rasping moans of the drug addicts piling up at the other side of door.

A moment later one of them crashed through the front windows of the house. Her arms were now sliced open and bleeding, her fingers hanging by flaps of skin as she struggled to her bare feet amid the glass, like some drunk gone too far on that last binge of all binges. More were spilling in after her.

"Zombies!" screamed Chelsea Harrington.

At that moment, everything connected for Bill. The riots. The pandemic. Stuff he'd been hearing in news reports he hadn't been really listening too. It came together in a Matrix-like epiphany. The world hadn't been rioting from flu outbreaks and food shortages. Zombies. The living dead might have come back, or, it might just be fever-ravaged lunatics intent on murder and cannibalism. Either way... Zombies was what it was.

He nodded once to himself, as though accepting the state of the world for what it was now, and grabbed Chelsea.

"Kennedy!" screamed Chelsea as Bill dragged her through the perfectly appointed California hacienda decorated ranchero and away from the lunatics at the door. Kennedy was Chelsea's daughter from some long-term romance gone bad with an ex-basketball star who lived over in Newport Beach.

"Where is she?" asked Bill. Bill who was dressed like an ancient Greek Warrior meets Boba Fett. Chelsea gave him a quick look up and down, her green and azure eyes that had once made her one of the most alluring local swimsuit models taking it all in, and decided that a neighbor dressed like some mythic hero meets a *Star Wars* character was about par for the course considering the living dead overrunning every nation on Earth.

And besides that… there had been a lot of weird reports of other things happening out there.

"Back room," she said breathlessly. Her voice was soft and high.

"C'mon," shouted Bill and practically dragged Chelsea, and eventually Kennedy, out of there, through the backyard, around the side yard, through the wooden door alongside the house, and back across the shadowy street, avoiding the clustering mindless mass at Chelsea Harrington's smashed front door. They ducked from car to car to get into Bill's house. Bill lowered the garage, killed the lights, and the three of them stood there in the dark, not daring to breathe. Waiting for the not-drug-addicts, possibly the actually living dead, to surround the house and beat their way in.

Do they really eat brains? wondered Bill, shocked that he was having to ponder such a thing.

Later, after nothing happened, they moved into Bill's dark kitchen.

Bill turned on the radio and kept it low.

Emergency broadcast signal. A repeated message. Seek shelter. Stay inside. The government cannot help you at this time.

Bill went to the window.

It was three A.M.

The zombies were still out there. Milling in the front yard of Chelsea's single-story ranchero. He could see them moving through the house, crossing in front of lights that had been left on, like slow moving sharks through shallow waters. Languidly and haphazardly. Deadly of course.

He cast one last glance at the night sky. The fog had come in from the coast. The fires and sodium-lit street lights that crisscrossed Southern California turned the sky a hellish orange. The fog clustered and swirled about the house.

When he turned back from the window, the ex-swimsuit model and her daughter were curled up under the blanket he'd given them. Asleep on his couch. Safe from the monsters.

Bill watched the fog for a long time. Peeking out between the almost-closed venetian blinds. He swore things moved out there in the thick, swirling, fog. Big things. As large as dinosaurs or even bigger. But it could have just been the shifting fog. Or fatigue. The swirling mists. He heard no massive bombastic artillery strike footsteps of...

*We fought the Hydra and the Kraken. They were called the Titans, Billy.*

Just shapes moving out there in the fog at times. Ancient things. Lost from another age that never was.

Or another world that should not exist.

**WHAT HAPPENED NEXT WAS CLASSIC** Bill Papadopoulos.

Come dawn he had a plan. He'd been sitting at his kitchen table quietly thinking while making a list on a notepad and sketching out a few ideas that might be helpful if the government couldn't be relied upon.

*Seek shelter. Stay inside. The government cannot help you at this time.*

The Internet was missing.

But the power remained on. Which was strange...

The phones were dead. He stared at the landline phone, cradled on the wall. Hoping it wouldn't suddenly ring. Knowing that... that would somehow be weird. Too weird for reality.

It didn't.

But the power held steady.

After dawn he checked his supplies and made a quick inventory. He didn't have any guns. He supposed he could make one if need be. But using the tools in his shop would make an unnecessary racket.

First things first. I'll be brief here because what came next really isn't what this story is about. It's about who Bill was. Or rather what kind of man he was and why he ultimately ended up doing what he did.

That is what the story is about.

This weird little tale is not about zombies. Or survivors surviving. Because the world wasn't really about those things anymore. There was a group of survivors farther south, starting to come together. They'd make a good go of it. But most everyone was about to be wiped out by some little of bit weirdness leaking into the world at the seams. "Wyrd-ness" they would find out in time, and a bit too late. The zombies were just one of the symptoms of the fever racing across the known, allowing the unknown in through the back doors. The world, for want of a better word, had gone weird. Unexplainable phenomena began to happen over the next few weeks as Bill secured his house. Then the cul-de sac, and then most of the neighborhood.

The power stayed on. It never went out.

It remained hot. Like every day was that last day of August, even though the sun rose and fell and the moon came out. Sometimes in different phases. Sometimes in the same phase several nights in a row. Time progressed like it was moving on... but it didn't.

And the fog. The fog came in some nights like a living thing that could be felt, touched, and listened to as it breathed. It made all of them, all the survivors, uncomfortable. Little Kennedy was the first to voice this.

"Don't like dat fog, mama!" The girl had run in from the late afternoon, in from the secure area on the lawn where she could play, because by then Bill had secured the street. "They's monstahs all up innit!"

"I know baby girl," Chelsea had soothed the beautiful little girl with the blonde afro. Then held her close and stroked her.

"C'mon... let's go in for the night," Bill had said, casting a wary eye at the early fog seeping in, over, and around the houses along the street. Then they sealed up the fort, as Bill and all of them had taken to calling their safe cul-de-sac. It took hours for Bill to set the traps they'd made, the warning lines they'd strung, and lock each and every entrance into the fort, and finally the houses along the cul-de-sac.

A week later they rescued another family.

A week after that, one early morning, military transports flew overhead. All the neighbors had gone out to stand in the cul-de sac and stare up at the three massive, low-flying military aircraft.

"C-130s," someone said.

"We're saved," someone else had almost shouted in relief, or triumph.

"Finally," Chelsea had sighed softly.

Except a moment later, they watched a small battle take place in the sky over their heads. They watched one of the first planes get shot down by air-to-air missiles. A moment later a small fighter streaked past the other two lumbering planes and zoomed off over the city.

"That's a..." someone said, hands to shield their eyes from the low morning sun, "...a Warthog. A-10. Wonder why he's attackin' our own people!"

They heard the loud *burrrrrp* of the ominously humming cannon the smaller plane carried. A moment later another transport started to smoke and went down over Santa Ana. There was a loud but distant explosion as the big plane must've slammed into the city.

"No one survived that!" shouted the guy who seemed to know about military planes.

They only saw a little bit of the small fighter's next pass until Bill scrambled up onto a roof and watched the end of the battle. Bill saw the tiny fighter shooting straight into the last lumbering transport. A confirmed kill in the making, he thought.

Then he went blind.

In fact, they all went blind and remained that way for almost twenty-four hours. Unexplainable phenomena. By the next morning, they could see once again for no reason. That day, and then night, of unexplainable blindness had been a long night and some people had injured themselves trying to move around during the enigmatic sightlessness. Thankfully the most serious injury had been a twisted ankle.

A fracture of any sort and they were in serious trouble, thought Bill.

"World's gone weird," someone had said.

"End'a days," said another.

Bill merely tried to keep them all alive as best he could by throwing himself into a series of projects.

Over the next few weeks he set up more and more of the fort. For the first few days he cleared much of the surrounding streets of the zombies.

"They said it on the news... before it went ka-put," declared Chelsea, hands on her curvy hips. "That they were zombies. You have to destroy the brain to stop 'em."

So, spear in hand, kitted out in his high tech Spartan garb, Bill set to methodically clearing the nearby streets of zombie-meth-addict-plague victim-cannibals. He went out in his armor and only got into a few tight scrapes.

Though his first encounter went less than heroically, he refined his method by using the the spear and the long tongs he kept for smelting in combo attacks to deal with the zombie-junkies. He'd grab the zombie with the tongs, holding him at bay with his powerful right arm, while he stabbed straight into the skull in a jackhammer-like thrust with the spear he kept over and behind his left ear.

By the end of the first day he had the process down to a system and mental checklist he ran over and over inside his head.

Bill was all about systems.

Once the nearby streets were secure—that's when he'd found a few of the surviving neighbors—he began to secure the cul-de-sac with plywood walls and cars he hotwired off the street. Then he blocked off a few of the surrounding streets with more cars and other barriers. He'd learned that zombies, like children and water, sought the path of least resistance. Blocking off most of the entrances into their fort redirected strays away from their small community. Most of the zombies were out on the main broad streets and headed down toward the coast, following the natural fall of the land. One day there had been loud artillery fire down there that seemed to attract the wandering dead from the surrounding areas, drawing them off along the coast. In time, the survivors in the fort had the neighborhood relatively to themselves.

Bill worked day and night, even ignoring the bald offers of pleasure and comfort Chelsea put forth one night after Kennedy lay asleep on the couch.

Instead Bill had told her he didn't want to treat her like that. He told her she was more than that to him.

She liked that and lay in his arms, finally drifting off to sleep late in the night, both of them fully clothed. Bill stayed awake all night, going over and over in his mind exactly what needed to be done the next day to survive. To protect them all.

Three days later a soldier walked up to their ramshackle walls and pounded on their gate. He certainly looked beat to hell, but he wasn't a zombie. He carried a bloody entrenching tool. He'd run out of ammunition for his rifle days ago, and the shovel had been his only weapon. A good one at that. His name was Lt. Matt Stapelton, a military intelligence expert on China.

"How'd you end up lost out here?" asked Bill once they'd let him through the gates and given him a thorough going over to ensure he wasn't somehow infected.

"I can't talk about that," the young lieutenant told them. And then, "I probably could... I mean I'm not even sure if there's a government left to keep secrets for."

He paused. Then spoke again after taking a long look at the cornflower blue sky yawning above.

"I'm not even sure what's real anymore," he confessed emotionlessly. "But until I make contact with my commanders... I guess it's best if I don't say anything other than we got lost trying to find an objective. I was part of reconnaissance-in-force combat team. We were sent to gather intel on some terrorist organization we think might be behind all this... but we got cut off. And then we got ambushed. Except..." And then he stopped dead. Like he hadn't thought about the ambush since it happened. As though he were seeing it all over again once more, and not really believing he'd seen it. Or lived through it.

"Terrorists?" one of those gathered about prompted.

"Like they poisoned all the..." Bill didn't say zombies or dead people, "... all the sick with some kind... some toxin... a bio-weapon?" asked Bill.

"Maybe," continued Stapelton, as someone handed him a sandwich and a bottle of water. He took a bite and began to chew absently.

"Maybe," he said through a mouthful of food. Eyes far off. "But... what ambushed us... it doesn't technically exist. And whatever it was, it slaughtered half the convoy after we got ourselves boxed in down a street overrun by Zekes. Some of us managed to get away. I was with twelve marines. They're all dead now."

There was a long silence. No one said a word but each of them was thinking the same thought. If marines can't survive out there, what chance do a bunch of civilians have?

None, was the answer they all thought, except Bill.

And the answer wasn't one anyone much particularly liked.

"What attacked you?"

Bill asked the question. It wasn't like him. He'd always been the silent observer. The constant listener. But in the days since setting his mind to the fort, since he put together their little outpost... he'd become a driving force among the few, yet steadily growing number of survivors who found their way past the hordes of living dead, and into the walled off streets of safety.

Stapelton just shook his head. Like he didn't want to answer. But then he did.

"You know what a minotaur is?" he asked.

Bill did, though it didn't seem like any of the other survivors had a clue.

"Sure," said Bill softly. "It's a half man, half bull. In Greek mythology one..."

Stapelton cut him off after taking an angry chew of the sandwich.

"It wasn't just one at the center of a maze. It was a bunch of 'em. But it was a maze alright. Looking back now... they led us straight into a blind alley by blocking off streets and the freeway we were scouting along. Like they knew someone would come eventually and they could lead 'em into a trap and get us nice and lost. And like I said... it wasn't just the one. It was bunch of them. Big, strong, creatures that could pick up a small car. They drove the dead in at us and made us burn up our ammo trying to cut a path through. Then it was like they knew we ran out and they came at us with big axes like you'd see in some computer game. *World of Warcraft* or something like that. They were chopping guys in half. I barely got out of there."

He held up a hand like it was all suddenly too much to remember.

Then he said tiredly, "Just give me a few hours. I need some rest. I know it sounds crazy. It all sounds crazy, even to me. But it ain't even about them minotaurs. It ain't even about the dead. There's something going on out there. Something strange and weird that's tearing the whole world into a thousand little pieces. Like gateways from another world are just opening into this one. And stuff, nightmares and worse, it's just walking through those doors. And who knows... who really knows what's going to walk in next? My advice to you all... hunker down and wait this out. Don't leave these walls. Not if you want to go on living as long as you can. It's more dangerous out there than it ever was."

For the rest of that day the survivors let the soldier collect himself and even offered him a room in one of the houses along the cul-de-sac.

That night, after double-checking the perimeter, Bill decided he would begin to set up some kind of alternative power system they could tap into once the main grid went down. Chelsea, who was lying in his arms once more, spoke softly in the quiet.

"What do you think that was about today? Gateways to other worlds, Bill. Monsters coming in..."

But she didn't finish. And Bill said he didn't know. He had to force himself to focus on all the projects he needed to accomplish for the little community he dedicated himself to. Except his mind kept wandering back to thoughts of monsters and other worlds. Back to all the stories Grandpa Andreas had told him.

*They were called the Titans, Billy.*

Three nights later that fog came in. Thick and heavy. Tendrils crawled over the wall and across the still-well-kept lawns. The survivors bid farewell to each other for the night as the day surrendered the white embrace of something that claimed to be nothingness and wasn't. They locked their doors and windows as if committing acts of faith in the face of the terrible unknown. It had been mutually agreed upon that none of them liked the fog. It made them feel... uneasy.

Things were quiet for a couple of hours. Quiet until they heard what they all thought, at first, was a distant artillery strike. Then another. And another. The pause between them was slow and ponderous. As though whoever was firing was taking time to recalibrate their targeting between salvoes. A swift micro-adjustment to the calculations... then fire. But in the next few moments it was clear the impact strikes were coming nearer to the fort. Glass rattled in the frames of the windows. The houses trembled with each concussive *whump*.

Bill opened his front door, spilling light into the fog. Across the walled off cul-de-sac, he could see other survivors come to their doors. Standing in the open portals, not daring to walk just a few steps out into the mist.

"What is it?" someone shouted from across the cul-de-sac.

Bill shrugged and stared off into the swirling fog that clustered along their makeshift walls, covering the world in a downy white blanket. Even the orange glare thrown off by the street lights seemed to struggle in vain against the constantly curling shifting fog. As though the mist were a living thing trying to strangle the light.

The artillery strikes continued to "walk" forward, crossing the land, unseen in the fog. The frames of the doorways groaned ever so slightly with each powerful, yet distant explosion.

"Maybe the military is finally re-taking Orange County!" someone shouted out across the silence between strikes. Someone else whooped at this, and Bill winced. They'd all realized early that the noise attracted the zombies. In the days since forming their little band of survivors they'd practiced noise discipline like a religion. A faith based on not wanting to draw any more of the dead to their walls.

Because the dead didn't just go away. They waited. They had to be dealt with.

But it couldn't be that, Bill thought, unable to imagine the possibility of the military out there and on the move, wiping out whole sections of the city just to destroy the raving dead.

He thought about all things, everything really, returning to normal in the next few days as order was restored. And in that moment he could not name why he felt the way he did, but he suddenly felt extremely sad. Knowing that the last few weeks...

... would be over.

That what he was becoming... wouldn't be.

He was thinking about all those things when the monster in the darkness roared. It was a steely, hollow, titanic blast of an immense trumpet.

A noise like Godzilla would make, thought Bill as icy water and fear mixed in his blood.

*Gateways to other worlds.*

The survivors muttered among themselves in the silence that fell before the next footfall struck the earth, like shells fired from a comically large cannon. Yes, a massive foot falling from some great height... crushing the fragile landscape beneath it without remorse... because that's what it had to be. Because that's what it sounded like now. Not some artillery shell. But... a foot. Before the next footfall hit the ground, they began to mutter and yell. Pray. And there was, of course, cursing and disbelief. Noise discipline fled.

"What was that, Bill?" Chelsea asked, her voice edging into hysteria. He could feel her trying to hold him close and fight the compulsion to run at the same time. He could feel little Kennedy poking out between their legs.

The strikes grew closer moment by moment.

Whatever it was, it was headed their way. Definitely. The next few moments made that abundantly clear. Suddenly, some of the survivors ran for the gate. Within a minute they had it open, as Bill and other shouted at them from the doorways of the houses along the cul-de-sac. They were fear struck at the thought of whatever that giant thing out there in the fog was, the thought of it coming to crush them suddenly too much to bear. They pulled the gate open and ran off into the fog in ones and twos.

None of them were ever seen again.

*Gateways to other worlds.*

Five minutes later—when it felt like the entire world was coming down around them, the houses shaking, the children crying, more people bolting for the gate, or where the wall had fallen down—they saw it. They saw the monster. The thing that walked in the dark and the fog. It was... giant.

*They were called the Titans, Billy.*

They all saw it passing through the swirling fog down the street, beyond their flimsy little gate. It was enormous. It had to be—and this was incredible. People began to scream in horror... It had to be thirty stories tall.

Like some giant dinosaur walking upright.

But really, they saw only the shadowy outline of the thing, like some black mass, moving high above their smallness. It roared as though crying out a challenge to battle, seeking something to vanquish. Glass shattered. Pictures fell off the walls and smashed on the floor. The nearest footfall felt like a massive car bomb detonated down the street. Car alarms along the streets beyond the walls, unseen, triggered wildly. Their lights flashed on and off like neurotic ghosts signaling in the mist. They heard some structure suddenly explode outward. A moment after that, debris passed through the fog shrouded night, bouncing off the wall that protected the fort, knocking parts down.

And then, it—whatever it was—continued on along its course of destruction. The artillery strike footfalls rose to deafening in their destruction but faded ever so slightly a moment after that as the behemoth vanished into the fog and the night, passing beyond their safe place.

*Gateways to other worlds.*

The silence that remained in its wake was deafening.

**IN THE MORNING, ONCE THE** fog cleared, the survivors emerged from their houses to stare at the sobering damage. Most had not slept until sometime in the morning dark, if at all. All had lain there, listening to the unearthly and unreal quiet trailing in the thing's wake. All of them waiting for the artillery strike footfalls of the thing that walked in the fog... to return for them once more.

Even Bill eventually drifted and dreamed a little. Dreamed of other worlds, guarded by golden gates. And of maidens tied to rocks.

Yes, by morning's glare some of their flimsy ramshackle walls had collapsed inward. The gate still lay open, with no sign of those who fled into the nether. But beyond the gate they saw the giant footprint. A massive footprint embedded in the road and the nearby toothpick wreckage of a house.

A clawprint really.

Long and wide. Enough for a monster the size of a moderately tall building? It had landed on a house, crushing it underfoot. But the rest of the mega print crossed several lawns in width, then left an impression at least eight feet deep on the street that ran through the neighborhood. A car had been compressed into nothing but flattened metal at the dead center of the print.

The story of Bill's quiet madness began then.

In a way, all of them suffered a kind of madness. All of them, almost as one, returned to the walls, and, as silently as they could, worked together and got them back up with a kind of desperation. Everyone worked quickly, only using hushed whispers to accomplish what needed done. After all, the dead, though unseen, were still around. Somewhere out on those long wide manicured streets, they still wandered from house to house, looking for a way in. And if one of them got wind, or sound, of the prey behind the gates, there would be no stopping them.

One woman, a frightened, frazzled mother, lost it. She started to scream.

"What are we gonna do if that thing comes back?" she shrieked.

And she was right. What would these walls do?

Her husband clamped his hand over her mouth and took her inside one of the houses along the once perfectly manicured cul-de-sac.

*What were they going to do? If...*

They worked. Bill set to his projects, and the other's joined in.

It couldn't be killed, he told himself as he worked. But that was lie. A lie he'd told himself as he sweated and worked all that afternoon, laying wire and connecting house to house. Tomorrow he'd get some kind of solar, or even wind, power going.

Unless... he whispered in his mind. Unless you follow it. See where it's going? Kill it even?

*Gateways to other worlds.*

But that would be madness, he told himself. What could you possibly do against something like that? Except, at the end of the day, just before they locked up for the night, he went out beyond the gate and followed the debris and trail of ruin to the next foot print. No one had come with him, and even the soldier, Stapelton, waited at the gate with his shovel, watching Bill go out into the ruin and debris all alone.

Out there beyond the perimeter of the fort... it was a deep quiet. Bill stood amongst the destruction and wreckage left by the massive... what?

Monster?

Godzilla?

But none of those were right.

Thing from the outer dark?

At that a cold chill ran up his spine.

*They were called the Titans, Billy.*

He stood at the rim of the next footprint the thing had left in its wake. Now, with the afternoon turning to early twilight and the fading heat of the summer coming on, he could see the path—no, the *hall* of destruction carving its way into the hazy twilight of Northern Orange County.

It called to him.

This is how pyromaniacs must feel, he thought. Remembering some old movie in which a crazy old man had talked about fire being like a living thing that looked at you.

Which was exactly how he felt looking at all that wake destruction.

Grandpa Andreas had been right. As though the old man and all the talks of a lost heroic age of Greek Titans defeated...

Defeated by heroic warriors...

As if someday the world, even if it was coming apart at the seams, would need those warriors once again.

And then the Bill who'd always been the runner up, and the best friend, and the one who waits and is never called, that Bill reminded him that the monster, the mythic Titan of another world... was thirty stories tall. And Bill Papadopoulos was just Bill Papadopoulos.

He turned and looked back at the tiny little empire he'd made. The fort carved in the middle of a land overrun by the dead.

He had done that.

He had made a way where there seemed none. He had rescued them all from their barricaded last stands. First Chelsea and Kennedy. Then the rest, one by one. Finding them and getting them out of the tight spots they'd been in.

They were his responsibility too.

And... what if it comes back? he thought.

He began the long slow walk back to the gate in the twilight. The soldier, the bright good-looking kid with an Oklahoma accent who might have been a math major if the military hadn't needed him and he hadn't been so wiry and determined to stay alive, he looked at him with a look that read Bill's mind like it was written on a white board for all to see.

They closed the gate together.

Their chow hall, centered around one of the garages at the top of the cul-de-sac, was already serving the communal meal. Spaghetti. How much longer would the power stay on? How much longer would they have canned food? There were so many things to do. Farm. Water. Power. More houses to be cleared.

Bill stood there with Lieutenant Stapelton.

"Don't," whispered the soldier.

Bill turned to him, a look on his face that knew he was caught. And knew he didn't care in the same moment.

"It could come back," Bill replied softly.

Stapelton nodded.

Then, "What could you do about it?"

Bill thought for a long moment.

"I don't know. But I didn't think I'd ever have to do this. And I did." Bill finished chaining the gate shut.

"Don't be a hero, man," said Stapelton as they began to walk to the washing up station. Then he turned. "That thing's a monster. It's not from this world." He looked around. "I'm gonna tell you something I'm not supposed to. Shouldn't do it... but we need you. You're that kind of guy. You know how to fix stuff. Make things. That's the future. That thing... it came out of another world. A lot of stuff has been doing exactly that for a few years now. But the government managed to keep it quiet. Or at least they tried to."

"Like the gates? The one's you talked about?"

"Yeah. But not in the way you think. There are more thin spots in the space-time fabric. Places where other realties touch... and stuff walks through. Bad stuff. You can get lost in there. The fog. The fog is the gate. It's not like regular fog. You go in there... you might not ever return. I'm not kidding... there're things in there, man, that will mess you up without a second thought. So don't do it. We don't need any more heroes. We need to survive. Those things are actual monsters. And as far as the project I was part of was aware... there wasn't much we could do about it. We were looking for a way and not getting much of anywhere."

They ate dinner.

Chelsea and the rest tried to resume some sense of normalcy. All of them did. Bill watched them do their best to forget the night before... when the fog was thick... That thing might come back through, he thought and couldn't stop thinking about it.

He slept that night and dreamed of all the heroes Grandpa Andreas had ever told him stories of. At four A.M., when everyone was still sleeping, he went to garage and put on the armor. The high tech Spartan gear. It would be the best defense against zombies he reasoned. Whether he found what he was looking for or not... there would likely be zombies. He took the sword. And the spear. Some food and water in a pack.

And then, just before, dawn, he took a ladder and climbed over the wall.

And he too... was never seen again.

**HE FOLLOWED THE TRAIL OF** destruction through the silent golden morning. Followed the wake of debris all through Irvine, passing houses and even a shopping center that had been smashed into oblivion as the day rose in its heat. He followed the trail of debris into the big living goods store, marveling at how the thing's foot had collapsed a cinder block wall and exposed the store. The roof had caved in at the center of the massive building. There were zombies in there, milling about in the darkness. Trapped within the debris. He moved from car to car, avoiding those that lingered in the football field sized parking lot. He circled the building and picked up the path of destruction.

For the rest of that day he followed the thing's path through the ruins of suburban wasteland. At times he had to fight small groups of zombies who came stumbling out from buildings in ragged ones and twos. He cut, withdrew, and cut again, going straight for their skulls with each successive strike.

He carried the spear and used it to sneak up on lone zombies he could not get around. At the last second, he would jackhammer the haft once, fast and forward with as much power as his bulging bicep could deliver, driving the tip of the spear into the skull and through the brain. Then he shook off the corpse and moved on. There were other times when he simply had to run from swollen masses of them.

For three days he followed the broad trail of ruin through the heart of Northern Orange County and then into South Los Angeles. For three days, he kept telling himself "a little further and then I'll turn back."

But he never did.

Because that shape... that mass... that thing he saw moving through the swirling fog in the night consumed his mind.

*They were called the Titans, Billy.*

He passed downed jet liners that never made the approach to LA or Long Beach, coming up short on fuel, or lost in the fog. Zombies, people who'd been killed in the crash, waved their burnt and bloody limbs at him from inside the wreckage, and when he could, because he was kind, Bill dispatched them as best he could while still moving on quickly. Following the trail of the Titan.

In time he heard himself muttering the word over and over again, and he sweated and climbed, crawled and ran through the wide debris trail that led into West LA.

In the gloaming of the third night, somewhere near LAX, the fog rolled in off the coast. Its tendrils crossed the ground and air, suddenly becoming warmer, even filled with static electricity, instead of the cool mist it should've been.

Bill ducked inside a liquor store and barricaded the doors as best he could.

An elderly woman came out of the shadows like some hoary old witch just after he blocked the front door. He turned on her, short sharp sword pointing right at her gobbly old throat.

She was blind.

"Say I see..." she murmured in a ruined voice. "You smell of blood and steel, like all the lost heroes who died in the before."

She was dressed in rags. As though she were some actress from any of the dozens of Ren Faires he'd attended throughout the years. A special costume for each. An old woman who'd decided to play the part of the village crone. Or forsaken witch. Or crazy....

"I'm..." he stuttered once, unsure of his voice because he hadn't used it in days. "I'm Bill," he finished once he'd cleared his throat of the ash and dusty destruction he'd been trekking through.

"Where are we stranger?" she asked, hunching over as though doing some servile obeisance to him.

"LA. Near the airport. As best I can tell."

There had been no other survivors. Just zombies. No emergency personnel. No military. No state and local government coming out to pick things up and set things right. He had crossed it all by hacking and slashing his way through it, or running as fast as he could from it. For three days he'd been living off bottled water and power bars found in the various liquor stores he'd looted. Finding only occasional fruit, an orange off a tree that had somehow just barely escaped the passage of the monster.

"I have no ken of an 'L-Lay,'" she croaked uncertainly. "Be it a fey kingdom I've wandered into, sire?" she mewled. Though it was more like listening to a drowning frog try to imitate a cat than a kitten's purr.

Bill did not respond.

He sheathed his sword and began to devour the protein and power bars from a nearby rack. She asked more questions, all of it nonsense being spoken by a madwoman.

"Do you serve the Black Dragon?"

"What is the name of your Master?"

"Are you a demon from the dungeons of Umnoth for I known Xur'ilsyx, Master of Thousand Deaths?"

She's a vagrant, thought Bill, as the old woman sank down to the floor of the liquor store and began to root around in her rags in an almost obscene fashion.

He went to the windows.

The street beyond was lit up in the standard orange of Los Angeles night lighting. Strange that the power was still on.

The smothering white fog swirled in about the light posts, as though seeking to drown out the defiant dying light. How much longer can it last?

Down the street a dark figure wandered into an intersection where two cars had smashed into one another. Everything down there was just a dark silhouette, or a shadow. Bill looked away for a moment to unscrew a cold Gatorade he'd taken from the coolers, and when he looked up the dark figure down the street was gone.

"Musta been a zombie," he muttered. Thinking the thing had gone off, or was down in the wreck searching for some meal among the long dead victims.

"She brings the dead with her," muttered the old crone as she began to play with a doll made of straw on the floor. He turned and watched the old woman.

"Oh," she muttered. "I know you're still there... Bill." She gave a low and evil laugh as she continued to play with her clothes in the darkness between the pay counter and the coolers where she'd chosen to nest. Posters of bikini clad beach babes advertising the latest beer seemed a stark contrast to the withered old hag on the floor.

"Bill," she said again as though it were a joke. As though they knew each other and were sharing some joke known only to them. "I know what you seek, hero."

And the she laughed and brought the doll out into the light for a second. It was a doll with no eyes. A doll of a little girl that resembled the old woman.

"You're following the wrong Titan, Bill. She's afraid of him. Afraid of the Eye that Roams the Worlds. Even she, even the Black Dragon is afraid."

And then she began to laugh, telling him he would surely die. When he couldn't take it anymore, couldn't take her laughter, he was shocked at what he did next.

He didn't do anything.

But he did want to reach for his sword and thrust it through her gobbly throat shaking up and down in her hoary laughter as she repeated over and over that he was going to die.

He flung the racks aside that blocked the doors to the tiny liquor store and stumbled out into the fog and the night.

He wanted to get away from her, and before he realized it he was halfway out into the broad wide street that had once intersected LA east and west.

He turned back toward the liquor store. Its dark open doorway was like a blank space in the universe. He heard her still laughing, cackling at him, in there. And he turned and ran, following the trail of destruction into a fog that consumed him.

Later...

Later...

**THE POWER ON THE STREET** has been out for a long time, Bill thinks. He stops. He's been running. Running as fast as he could. For hours now. Maybe even days.

The damage here looks old. The streets covered in dust and debris. Ash everywhere. And when he turns to look up and around at all the tall buildings, he wonders if he hasn't ended up on Wilshire Boulevard. Where all the tall high rises of the rich once were.

Once?

They are still here.

Except these look old and gutted. As though they have been blown out by distant neutron bombs.

Neutron bombs?

Don't you mean nuclear weapons?

No, he thinks. They remind him of old comic book renditions of what nuclear warfare would have done to cities.

All that post-apocalyptic horror.

The destruction here in the night, is ancient. He sees the exposed girders, and eyeless sockets of the tall buildings, being consumed by the swirling fog above.

There is no one here, he thinks. And there hasn't been for a very long time.

A gate. I've gone through a gate, he thinks.

*Gateways to other worlds.*

And he wonders, not for the last time, if he is lost forever.

The roar comes. Loud and close. It is such thunder, such awesome power, that one of the skeletons of the ancient buildings farther down the street collapses in on itself in a sudden waterfall of rotting debris.

From off between the forest of buildings that now seem like skeletal trees in the fog, Bill Papadopoulos sees it. He sees the monster and there is no fog to obscure it this time. He sees it in all its terrible majesty.

What had the crone called it?

The Eye that Roams Between... Worlds.

That is what it is.

It's like a Godzilla. Claws, massive upright lizard body. Wide thick tail. Thirty stories tall at least. It howls, and Bill feels his legs wanting to turn to jelly.

He thinks of running. Just turning and running and trying to follow the path of destruction back to...

*Gateways to other worlds.*

And then he thinks of Chelsea. And Kennedy. Yes... in all that work, all those projects... he allowed himself the dream that they could be his. If he could earn their love by saving them.

And it didn't matter.

He loves them anyway. He would save them and never let that thing come back to terrorize them the way its passing presence had. He would end it here...

And then the beast turns its head and its terrible gaze falls on him.

It had one eye.

One massive eye filled the reptilian head.

An eye like a void in the world. A nether space in reality.

And the light that comes from it is a yellow glare that would destroy a sun.

Looking at it is like getting a million chest x-rays all at once. Bill feels paper thin and dehydrated. As though he's been photographed from the inside out.

A moment later the thing turns its head and continues up an intersecting street, seeking something Bill can't begin to guess at.

He runs.

I can kill it, Bill thinks. I can get close. From one of these roof tops. I can throw this spear into its one eye. For Chelsea. And Kennedy.

He runs toward the monster.

He runs through and around the buildings that line the street. His powerful legs churn ash and dust, crushing debris turned to bone shell fragments...

By the background radiation from the bombs, some distant part of his mind thinks.

He ignores this and runs, looking off to his right as he tracks the giant...

... Titan....

Yes... Titan, through the debris.

He manages to get ahead of it by running a diagonal course. It is coming his way, and ash is raining down from the sky all around him as loose debris comes away from the buildings above.

He finds the building he wants. A rotting skeleton that has been blasted to emptiness who knows how long ago. He dashes into its darkness recklessly and finds a stairwell leading up.

He takes the stairs two at a time, feeling them crumble and give way as he pushes his massive legs. Flinging himself from level to level.

The monster is close.

Its footfalls are not like artillery strikes, but like artillery barrages. At times the building feels like it is about to come down around him.

Bill makes the roof access door.

He smashes it open with a shoulder and heaves himself out onto the roof. In a moment he turns and sees the thing. It is coming abreast with the rotting building he has climbed onto.

The eye is still two stories above.

Bill runs, rearing back with the spear, and heaves it with all his might into the Eye of the Thing that Roams the Worlds.

*We fought the Hydra and the Kraken.*

The high tech spear he hand crafted arches out and lands in the monster's eye.

Dead center.

The howl that comes the next moment feels like it could separate his soul from his body. It is a depthless pain known by only those who have tasted eternity and found it a prison.

The light in the eye winks out as the monster cries at the nether fog and the apocalyptic wasteland. It writhes like lightning.

"We slew the Kraken, Grandpa!" Bill cries.

The building shakes as if hit by an asteroid. And a moment later the whole thing collapses.

In those last seconds, as the wasted world is suddenly obscured by the black ash and waterfall of debris surrounding

Bill, he remembers the great monster's massive tail. The wake he followed through all that debris.

It must have struck the building in its death throes, he thinks.

Horror washes over him as he realizes he is about to die. Crushed by hundred thousand pounds of debris.

But then he remembers the words he's just spoken. His mind falling on them like a soft and peaceful place to rest.

*Death throes.*

Which is how true heroes die.

The debris falls on Bill and the building collapses all the way down to its sub-basement, burying Bill Papadopoulos.

Burying a hero.

In that nightmare land that burnt itself up long ago, the dead Titan lies at the foot of a Hero's burial mound. Never to return to all the worlds it once roamed.

# THE HUNT, CONCLUDED

CULLEN BUNN

**YOU MIGHT THINK HUNTING SOMETHING** with a footprint the size of a tractor trailer would be easy.

You might think that, but you'd be wrong.

First of all, the world's a pretty damn big place. A monster might topple skyscrapers with a swipe of its spiny tail, rip bridges apart the way a baby tears through cake on its first birthday, and send concrete-cracking shockwaves through highways with a stomp of its foot. But there are still plenty of places for it to hide.

The depths of the sea.

The bowels of the earth.

Most of all—the Primeval.

"You will not see this again." Our guide, Aaron Connor said as he cautiously—reverently—slipped past a cluster of thorny, red-veined vegetation. His grey eyes swept across his

FBW
2018

surroundings. "These plants, they are not of this world, not of this time."

"Only—" I tapped at one of the leaves with the point of my knife. "—here they are."

Connor glowered. He didn't like me. That much was obvious. That was fine by me. The feeling was mutual. I found myself wondering if I could take him in a brawl. He was nearly as tall as me—just under six feet—and he looked fit if not ripped.

"Yes, Mr. Cole," he said. "Here they are. Don't fool yourself, though. So many people assume that because these plants—because creatures like the one you are hunting—exist in our world, that they belong here. They think because we breathe the same air as them, they are no better than us. They take them for granted the way they take everything else in the world for granted."

A woman's hand gently grabbed my wrist, guided my knife away from the plant.

"In his own way, Aaron is offering you a warning," Anaya, Connor's partner, said. "The oil from these leaves is lethal. If it touches your skin, you're done. It'll sink into your pores and go to work in seconds. Think of it as poison ivy... if poison ivy drove you mad and ate you alive from the inside out."

I looked from Anaya's deep brown eyes to the blade of my knife. The very tip of the blade glittered with a slimy wetness. I tossed the blade into the forest.

"Too bad," I said. "I liked that knife."

"Just try to show a little respect," Anaya said.

"You do know why we're here, right? I thought the assault rifles might have tipped you off. This isn't a sightseeing tour.

When we find our target, we're going to kill it."

"Once you see the beast, you might change your mind."

"It's not my mind that needs changing. It's his."

I nodded toward my employer. William Vanders was in his late sixties, but he was tough as nails and looked as though he could go toe-to-toe with any three men half his age. His watchful brown eyes were set deep in rugged, wind- and sun-calloused skin. His grey hair was cut short in an efficient, military-style haircut. He wore heavy trackers' boots, reinforced pants, a huntsman's jacket, and weathered safari hat. His shoulders were broad and strong; they had to be to support the weight of the modified, big-bore elephant gun slung across his back.

"When he sees this monster," I told Anaya, "it'll be his call. If he says, 'pull the trigger,' then that's exactly what I'm doing."

In the late afternoon sun filtering through the overhanging trees, Anaya's dark skin glistened with sweat. She was just a little younger than me, maybe in her late twenties, but when you looked into her dark eyes, you could tell that she had seen more in her life than most people ever imagined. She looked toward Vanders quietly, sizing him up, trying to decide if her first impressions of the boss still held true.

"He isn't the type to change his mind," she says. "Once he decides what he wants, nothing will stop him."

Vanders noticed Anaya's attention. He nodded at her, touching a couple of fingers to the brim of his hat.

At the end of the day, *finding* the monster isn't the problem. Hell—in my experience, if you wait long enough, the monster will almost always find you. The real trick, though, is not wetting your waterproof Taclites when you encounter one of the big-and-nasties. *Megalozoophobia*, a fear of massive wild animals. The term came into fashion only in the last twenty or so years, around the time the first giant monster rose up out of the Pacific and razed Sydney, Australia.

A death toll of over 200,000 tends to awaken primal fear in the remaining population.

Since that day—First Landfall, as it's known—twelve kaiju have gone on rampages in various places around the globe, surfacing from the depths of the ocean, burrowing up from under our streets, or—and this is the one that makes my bowels go watery—just flying down from God-knows-where above us. No two are alike in any way other than sheer enormity and potential for destruction.

There have been other giants, too, at least another dozen, that have made appearances around the world, but they've been less aggressive, peaceful even. It's not that they're inclined to "like" humanity or anything. We're just beneath their attention.

Destructive or "friendly," these creatures all inspire a deep-seated terror in humanity, a genetic survival mechanism that feeds one's senses to *run-run-run*. No one really knows where the monsters come from or why they've only started appearing in recent history. Speculation runs from nuclear testing to pollution in the air to climate change. But the fear is ingrained in our DNA, rooted in our very cells, which leads many, myself included, to believe the monsters have *always* been around us. Maybe they tormented our ancestors in prehistoric times. Maybe they've just been sleeping, and now the smog and the failing o-zone and the collective drone of our overpopulated cities is like an alarm clock that the creatures want to smash against the bedroom wall.

Up ahead, Connor stood still. He raised a hand, clenching his fingers into a fist, signaling for the rest of us to stop. Sweat soaked through his short, sandy blond hair.

Stepping lightly, I pushed my way past large, sagging leaves dripping condensation. Sweat trickled down the back of my shirt collar. I eased up next to Connor. He was looking across a great clearing in the jungle, a massive path of broken trees and crushed undergrowth. To me, having grown up in Oklahoma, it looked a bit like a tornado had cut a path across this section of the island.

"What is it?" I asked.

"Listen." His voice was barely a whisper.

I held my breath but heard nothing.

Not a damn thing.

Except—

Not hearing anything, that was the point.

"The insects," I said. "They've gone silent."

Seconds earlier, a cacophony of insects had been screeching from the thick undergrowth.

Now—nothing.

The bugs were still there, but a primordial instinct kept them from making a sound.

I stood frozen, poised to take another step, but not willing to commit to the action. The trees surrounding the clearing, too tall for their own good, creaked even though the air was hot and heavy and still. The sound, breaking the stillness, seemed thunderous to me. Carefully—quietly—I unslung the FN F2000 from my back. I clenched it tightly, trying to wring comfort from the weapon, even though I knew that it would do little to stop most things that might burst out of the jungle any moment.

"What is it?"

The voice—a hiss—came from behind me.

"Why are we stopping?" Anaya asked.

I glanced over my shoulder at her. She inched closer, scanning the foliage. Like our field guide, she carried no weapon.

Connor looked at her without speaking. A silent message, conveyed perhaps only by a narrowing of the eyes and flaring of the nostrils, passed between them.

"Oh," she said.

"Maybe we scared them." I glanced in the direction of the other men and women in our group. The others, unlike Anaya, had stayed still, waiting worriedly for me to give the go-ahead to continue.

"No." Connor shook his head curtly, turned and regarded the forest once more. "The wildlife in the Primeval operates on a different scale than their cousins in the rest of the world. To them, we're just other insects."

For a few seconds more, the jungle was silent. Then, the *chirring* of the insects resumed.

I shrugged.

I looked past Anaya, past the porters, the photographers, and the heavily-armed mercenaries, toward our employer. Vanders gazed back at me and nodded, urging us to forge ahead.

For hunters, finding prey is simply a matter of preparation, patience, and perseverance. Fright is the true roadblock when it comes to getting the kill. It takes a special kind of hard ass to fight through the quivering muscles, the racing heartbeat, the sweat running into your eyes. Your muscles betray you, either locking into a deathlike rictus or reflexively sending you screaming and scrambling to safety. Those who have never seen one of these creatures in the flesh can't possibly understand. I've seen many would-be "kaiju killers," hungry for the thrill or the glory, lay eyes on a giant for the first time, toss their weapons to the dirt, and start sobbing like children. One man, who claimed to have killed almost every kind of creature that ever walked the earth, fell dead from a coronary when he first encountered a true apex predator.

My boss, though, killed two kaiju in his time. He fought through the Megalozoophobia to claim his trophies. He was a proven "slayer of great beasts." Now, with me as his tracker, he planned to claim his third.

Vanders was a dying breed—

*You will not see this again.*

—and he had business of a personal nature with our prey.

We had abandoned the jeeps at the jungle's edge. For several hours, we'd traveled on foot, following the river. Connor and Anaya led the way as we trudged through the tangled vines and clouds of whistling mosquitos and thick, suckling mud. Vanders, myself, three photo-documentarians, three porters carrying thick plastic trunks of camping equipment and food, and a crew of hard-edged mercenaries. I knew some of these men and women—not well, but well enough to call some of them by name when issuing orders.

A couple of clicks in, we had stumbled across the carcass of a Gig-ant. The size of a bus, the massive aphid had crawled to the river's bank before dying; its armor-like carapace had been ripped open, three furrows through the shell made by three massive claws. The pulped meat within spilled out through the tears, swelling in the heat, attracting smaller, biting and stinging gnats. Three years ago, a horde of Gig-ants had crawled up from beneath the streets of New York and nearly destroyed a huge portion of the city. An F-16 squadron armed with poison-filled warheads drove the creatures back underground. They hadn't been seen since, and most everyone assumed they had all died.

So, of course, they would reappear in the Primeval.

The Primeval was a preserve of sorts, monitored by government agencies around the world but controlled by none. The island appeared—or should I say it erupted—in the middle of the Pacific Ocean three years ago. Miles of untamed jungles surrounding a mountainous active volcano, the Primeval was a mystery that the best geologists and zoologists in the world had yet to solve. For whatever reason, the island attracted giant monsters, lured them in droves. A reptilian vulture the size of a jumbo jet frequently circled the island. At least one megalodon haunted nearby depths. Enormous burrowing monstrosities lurked in subterranean tunnels. Three other kaiju were suspected to call the Primeval home.

And the Gargasaur was among the most fearsome.

"I didn't come all this way to see a dead monster," Vanders had muttered.

At the time, I noticed Anaya and Connor exchanging glances. It had been the first of the secret, silent language they shared, but I didn't give it much thought. They had worked together for years, just like Vanders and myself, and knew each other so well that they didn't always need to muddy the waters with words.

Vanders had stepped close to the Gig-ant, kicked its tank-thick shell a couple of times with no more consideration than if he was kicking the tires of a used car. He wrinkled his nose in disapproval. "I've invested a great deal of money in this expedition, and a great deal of money in you, Connor. I expect results."

"We're getting close." Connor's fingers moved along the tears in the Gig-ant's shell, tracing the path of the claw marks. "Those wounds were made by the Gargasaur, I'd stake my life on it."

A nervous murmur was passed back and forth among the porters and mercenaries. They could sense what I was going to say next.

"We're on the edge of a hunting grounds."

Vanders had stood tall, unslung his rifle from his shoulder, and sniffed the air.

"All right, then," he said. "Let's get on with it."

From there, we had moved away from the river (although the stench of the rotting Gig-ant seemed to coat the insides of my nostrils for hours) and moved through the rambling jungles, crawling down gullies and up steep inclines, ducking past low-hanging vines heavy with poisonous thorns, skirting lagoons and cascading waterfalls. We encountered no footpaths—at least, not those created by humans—and no man-made structures of any kind.

This place was pristine.

Pure.

From our caravan, I heard the crumpling of a plastic wrapper. One of the mercs—Reese, I think—was eating a power bar. When he was done, he brushed crumbs from his beard, then balled up the plastic wrapper and tossed it into the brush.

*You will not see this again.*

Early on, after the Primeval first showed up on satellite imagery, there had been debates among world leaders about destroying the island. Those ideas were squelched straight away by rational thinkers. After all, if the monsters were lured out to the middle of the Pacific, they were being drawn away from major population centers. Battleships patrolled the surrounding waters; drone aircraft cruised the skies. If the monsters tried to leave, someone would know, someone with a finger on the button to an extensive arsenal.

The Primeval was off-limits to civilians, of course, but that didn't stop the idle rich from sneaking into the region for a glimpse of one of the monsters. Illegal tour groups and safaris often ventured onto the island. Those who could fund such excursions could usually afford to bribe officials to look the other way. Some of those tour groups even made it back to tell the tale. Connor and Anaya had led six groups into the depths of the Primeval. They didn't have a TripAdvisor rating or anything, but word among the back-alley channels was they were good at their jobs.

But this was the first hunting expedition.

After all, who would be mad enough to try and hunt one of these beasts?

"I know what you're thinking." Vanders had caught up with me and walked by my side. He glanced at me out of the corner of his eye and smirked. "You think I'm insane for doing this."

I paused, weighed my response.

"I think you're the boss," I said at last.

"Don't," Vanders said. "Don't do that. We've known each other too long for you to try to appease me. Tell me what you think, Cole."

"All right, all right. I think… maybe… you've gone too far this time. Coming here, to a place like this, it's not the kind of thing a balanced person would do."

Vanders stared right down to my soul, waiting for me to continue.

"But," I said, "I know what this means to you. I understand why you had to do this. And if this is the way it's got to be, then I'm here 'til the end. Like I said, you're the boss."

Vanders was unflinching.

"And you're my friend," I said.

At last, his statue-like demeaner broke, even if it was for just a second, and he clasped my shoulder. "This has been a long time coming."

We followed the trail for a while longer. Every step seemed to be heavier than the last. I could feel it. I know for certain Vanders could feel it. And I imagined everyone in our group felt the same way.

Our guides were several meters ahead of us, but after a while I saw Anaya turn and walk back towards us. Connor, on the other hand, leaned his back against a prehistorically tall tree and slid to a sitting position.

"I think we've gone far enough for the day," Anaya said. "We should make camp."

Vanders looked to the sky. "There's at least another hour of daylight left."

"There's no point in continuing." Anaya motioned toward the trees that had been crushed flat, the wood that been pulped under tremendous pressure. "The Gargasaur follows this path to the river whenever it wants a drink. Back and forth, back and forth. It's a creature of habit, and those habits will bring it back this way soon enough."

"She might have a point, boss." I paced the clearing. "You want to set up a kill-zone, you could pick worse spots."

"All reports indicate that the Gargasaur is diurnal," Anaya said. "It sleeps at night, just like us. Locating its nesting place will be difficult as it is. In the dark, it will be almost impossible. And I doubt you're going to want to kill the beast while it's sleeping."

Anaya was playing Vanders, using his own pride against him.

Vanders watched her for a second, then spoke to me.

"Give the order, Cole. We set up camp here. Let's have it done quickly, yes? Twenty minutes."

It took closer to thirty minutes to raise camp. The mosquito netting, reinforced because the mosquitos in the Primeval could reach hummingbirds size, was more unwieldy than expected. Vanders wasn't really watching the clock, of course. Instead, he gazed into the jungle, almost as if willing his prey to present itself.

Camp was quiet as darkness fell. There were no bawdy jokes, no campfire songs. The team huddled together in little cliques, porters with porters, photographers with photographers, hired killers with hired killers. They spoke in whispers, not wanting to risk rousing whatever gigantic beast lurked in the shadows of the jungle.

Connor and Anaya kept to themselves, too, but they didn't appear to be talking.

I halfway considered striking up a conversation with Anaya. After this hunt, we'd have a few free days in Tokyo. I could think of less interesting people to spend the time with. But she was embedded deep with Connor, maybe having one of their silent conversations, and I didn't feel like suffering through the man's scowling glare.

Vanders sat outside his tent, his eyes fixed on the glow of the lantern. He absently cleaned his gun, but his mind cast back to another time. As still as he was, with the shadows gathering in the hollows of his sunken cheeks, with darkness pooling in his eyes, he looked like he was dead. Then, he stirred, a cough coming unbidden to his lips. He covered his mouth with his fist, tried to suppress the sound. The single cough broke into a dozen smaller expulsions, wracking his body again and again, despite his efforts to hide his sudden weakness. The movement did little to make him look any more alive.

I offered him my flask.

"Take a drink." I shook the flask, sloshing the contents around. "It'll help."

He looked up at me, and now there was a hint of life in his eyes, a glimmer of sadness I had rarely seen from the man in over fifteen years of working for him. His fingers trembled—just slightly—as he took the bottle.

"I haven't treated you fairly." His voice was a hoarse whisper.

"I have no complaints," I said.

"I've asked so much of you. Too much." He took a drink, closed his eyes and savored the smooth burn. "I've asked you to follow me into Hell itself."

"Not yet, you haven't." I took the flask from him, offered a quick salute, then took a drink. "My bet? Hell has less bourbon."

We passed the drink back and forth a few more times.

*This,* I thought, *is how we communicate.*

Vanders held his freshly cleaned elephant gun tightly. His head was down, as if in prayer.

"I don't blame the creature," he said at last. "Maybe you find that hard to believe, but I don't."

"You have every right," I said.

"At first, I did. Of course, I did. It killed my daughter. I was so angry. I wanted revenge, and so I started this hunt… this crusade of mine. I fed off that rage, maybe for too long. I let it—"

He coughed.

Once.

Dryly.

And I passed him the last swallow of bourbon.

"I let it make me sick," he said. "Now, though, I understand that the Gargasaur didn't target my daughter. It didn't know she would be in London on holiday. It's likely it didn't even know where it was. There was no malice in its actions, because it is just another stupid animal. Alice was… well… she was just there at the same time as the monster."

"If you no longer blame the monster," I asked, "why are you going to kill it?"

"We're both of us here, the monster and me, just like

Alice and the monster were in London at the same time."

Vander stood, taking his gun with him, and walked to his tent.

"One of us might as well die," he said.

For some time, I sat quietly outside Vanders' tent, like a watchdog guarding its master's lair. I watched as, one by one, the other members of our group called it a night. I should be bedding down myself, but I didn't feel all that tired. My mind raced. Tomorrow, I knew, we would likely find the Gargasaur.

And we would kill it.

No matter what my employer said, I knew he still hated the monster. It had taken his only child from him, and it deserved to die. He had been stalking the monster for nearly six years now, had killed two of its brethren in what some might consider practice runs. When he first took ill, he almost gave up the hunt. He was too tired, too weak. During a period of infirmity, maybe he convinced himself to "forgive" the Gargasaur to some degree. But when he found out he only had a limited amount of time remaining on this earth, he renewed his endeavors.

With the approach of death, he chose to live.

He was mad, yes, but maybe I was, too.

Because, God help me, I wanted him to see this through.

"You should be sleeping."

I looked over my shoulder. I hadn't seen Anaya creeping up behind me.

"What are you doing," I said, "avoiding the lantern light?"

She eased herself into a sitting position near me. "You were just too lost in thought to notice me."

"I wouldn't have thought that was possible," I said.

"Mr. Cole—" she smiled. "—are you flirting with me?"

"Maybe so, although this probably isn't the best place for it. Of course, if I die tomorrow, at least I took my shot."

"Is that what you think?" Anaya cocked her head slightly. "Do you believe you're going to die?"

"Somebody… something… is."

"Do you know that some people believe that's why the monsters come to this place?" She looked to the sky, her eyes dancing, as if she was counting stars that only she could see. "They say this is a kind of graveyard for monsters, that they come here to die."

"I'm not a monster," I said.

"Some might say it takes a monster to kill a monster."

I turned my attention to the camp once more.

"Where's your partner?" I asked.

"It's a big day tomorrow. He's sleeping." She looked at me, smiling again. "You should do the same."

She stood, dusting the seat of her pants with a couple of slaps, an act I thought she might have performed for my benefit.

"Hey," I asked. "I have a little shore leave after this mission. Maybe we could get together. We might even find something more interesting than monsters and graveyards to talk about."

"I think I'd like that." She smirked and winked. "Of course, if you're dead, I'll have to take a rain check."

I watched her slink off into the shadows again. I wished I had brought another flask of bourbon. I still wasn't feeling sleepy in the least, but after a while, I found my way to my tent, and, still in my clothes, crawled onto my folding cot and into my sleeping bag.

I was out like a light in less than a minute.

I awoke, only a couple of hours later, to screaming.

I tossed the sleeping bag aside. My gun was propped next to the tent flap, loaded and ready to go. Through the flap, I saw the bouncing glow of a flashlight, the shadows of running figures. I stepped off the cot—

And my booted feet sent a thunderous repercussion through the ground.

No—not my footsteps.

Something much, much larger.

I grabbed the rifle, threw aside the tent flap, and stepped outside.

One of the porters ran right into me, shoved past, screaming incoherently.

Another booming footstep.

Another.

I looked up and felt my heart leap into my throat.

The Gargasaur didn't sleep at night.

The creature stood nearly 200 feet tall, a cross between a crustacean, a land-bound stingray, and a chameleon. Colors danced across its rubbery hide, shifting, changing, adjusting to the surroundings. It crawled through the jungle on six segmented legs, each ending with massive, three-taloned claws. A long, serrated tail whipped around, tearing through trees, uprooting them, smashing them to splinters. The creature drew in three snorting breaths, then trumpeted deafeningly.

The sound sent a shockwave of fear rippling through the mercenaries and crew, eliciting gasps and screams. Guns and cameras and supplies were cast down.

To my right was the body of one of the porters, nothing more than a puddle of blood and mashed organs and fractured bones.

To my left, a photographer, had lost her mind. She mimed snapping photograph after photograph with an invisible camera. All the while, she sobbed uncontrollably. The real camera—the one she had dropped in fright—lay next to her foot.

I stood my ground. God help me, I didn't want to. I wanted to run screaming into the safety of the trees. A knot of icy fear palpitated in my belly. Sweat ran into my eyes. I took aim with the FN F2000, my finger grazing the trigger, but I held my fire. My gaze danced over the behemoth's form, from the armor-plated claws... to the curling, razor-sharp tail... to the clusters of bulbous, multifaceted eyes. I couldn't catch my breath as I drank in the sight of it.

*You will not see this again.*

A trio of mercs steeled their nerve, raised their guns, and took aim.

But the weapons didn't fire.

The mercs looked at their guns in horror. They tested the triggers, pulled the magazines to examine them in confusion. Then, they tossed the weapons down and started to scramble.

Too late.

The Gargasaur opened its cavernous maw, and three frog-like tongues shot out, grabbing the screaming mercenaries, snapping them back to be mulched by jagged fangs the size of church doors.

*The guns—why didn't they fire?*

The thought was fleeting, dancing through my head, lost

in the chaotic impulses to run-fight-run-fight-scream-run-fight.

"The ammunition! Cole! The ammunition's been tampered with!"

Vanders' voice snapped me out of my torpor.

Someone had sabotaged the hunt. Someone had brought our group here and laid us out like a breakfast buffet for the Gargasaur. Someone had compromised our weapons to make sure we couldn't fight back.

Not someone.

Connor and Anaya.

I scanned the surroundings, saw no sign of them among the tumbling trees, the cracking and churning earth.

They had lied to us.

They had brought us here—

—to the monster's feeding ground.

"Watch out!" Vanders shouted.

On instinct, I jumped, diving forward as one of the monster's striking tongues smashed into the ground where I had been standing. I rolled into a crouch, ejecting my gun's magazine without checking it. I knew it would be empty. I grabbed another magazine from the pouch on my belt, tested the weight, and snapped it into the tube.

Vanders stood nearby, taking aim with his rifle.

The cagey bastard slept with the gun, nuzzled it like a teddy bear. There was no way the traitors would have been able to monkey-wrench his kill. He fired, the rifle kicking in his arms with bone-numbing force.

A shuddering boom.

A wave of searing heat.

A fireball erupting along the creature's side.

Without hesitation, Vanders breeched his rifle, sending a smoldering shell casing the size of spray paint tumbling through the air. The acrid stink of propellant and sulfur wafted through the air. Vanders fingers danced over another diamond-tipped Inferno round, spinning it, sliding it into weapon.

"Cover me!" He moved past me with the sudden quickness of a man forty years younger. "I'm moving in closer!"

As my employer bolted past, I raised my gun and opened fire. The F2000 was loaded with armor-piercing incendiary rounds. Not as effective as Vanders' ammunition, but far less expensive. It would get the monster's attention, but it wouldn't kill it.

Which is how Vanders wanted it.

It probably didn't bother him that the weapons the rest of his team carried had been sabotaged.

The kill shot was for him alone.

As my bullets tore across its side, blossoming into fireballs, the Gargasaur turned away, moving in what seemed like slow motion. Its claw rose—deceptive in its speed—and whipped earthward.

Toward Vanders.

I dove again, this time throwing myself at my employer, tackling him, knocking him to the ground just as the monster's immense claw crashed behind us, sending a ground-splitting shockwave through the earth. Dust and debris pelted us as we slammed to the jungle floor, our bones jarred.

Vanders scrambled to his feet. He kept hold of his precious gun—his god-killer—as we fell. He snapped it to his shoulder and fired once more.

The Gargasaur reared back, screeching, as a cloud of flame erupted alongside its head.

The ground heaved. Great, jagged cracks zigzagged beneath us, chunks of rocky plates rising, venting steam in hot gouts. I had only just gotten to my feet from the fall, and the quake almost sent me sprawling once more. I grabbed Vanders arm for support, but he was "in the zone." He pulled away from me as if barely noticing my presence. Marching forward, he breeched his rifle, a mechanical motion, and loaded it once more.

He never saw the beast's tail coming for him.

The Gargasaur spun around, and its spiny tail cracked the sound barrier just before it struck Vanders, like a tree slamming into him with the force of a runaway semi. Vanders didn't make a sound as he flew, tumbling like a rag doll, through the air, smashing through tree branches before vanishing into darkness.

The monster roared in triumph.

I cried out, too, and the sound that escaped my mouth must have been inhuman.

I charged after my employer—my friend—stumbling through the darkness as the ground bucked and quaked beneath me.

The leaves of trees and creeping vines slapped me in the face as I bounded through the jungle, leaping over fallen trees, slipping in mud slicks. The Gargasaur had thrown Vanders away from the cleared path, deep into the bush. I didn't know where I'd find him. I didn't know *if* I'd find him.

The towering trees shivered as the ground quaked, the roots of some of the sentinels erupting from the wet earth as the trees came free of their anchors and crashed to their sides nearby.

Behind me, I heard the Gargasaur's cry.

And somehow, the island answered.

I burst out of the brush and into another clearing. A tangle of weeds snagged my foot and I sprawled forward, landing hard, tasting blood as I bit my tongue.

Looking up, I peered into the empty eyes of a massive skull.

I clambered to my feet. Before me, I saw before me a vast field of gargantuan bones. The remains of dozens of giant monsters littered the area, sprawled where the great beasts had fallen. Almost all the bones had rotting, stinking flesh upon them, and massive parasitic centipedes and leeches crawled over them, feasting. The moon—bone white itself—shone down upon the skeletons.

It was like an elephant graveyard—only for monsters—the place where great beasts come to die in peace.

And suddenly I realized that the flattened trail we'd been traveling wasn't the path the Gargasaur walked to and from the river. No, it was where it paced, impatiently awaiting its own demise.

There, among the bones, lay Vanders' broken, twisted body.

I flew to his side, dropped to my knees. He was still alive—just barely—his breath coming in ragged gasps, bloody bubbles popping on his trembling lips. His eyes had already glazed over, but he saw me just the same.

"C-Cole," he wheezed. "It… it killed me, didn't it?"

"Be still," I said desperately, lying to myself that there might be some way to save him if he just didn't move. "Don't try to move. I… we're going to get help."

"N-No. No, we're not. They led us here to die."

The earth trembled beneath us, as if something was crawling up from Hell itself to invite us down into the depths.

Then, the tumult eased, fading into an uneasy peace I knew wouldn't last for long.

"Sacrifices," Vanders said. "We were offered up as an offering… an offering of blood and bone and meat."

"A… a sacrifice?" I asked. "To… to who? To what?"

A woman's voice answered me.

"To Echidna," Anaya said as she walked, accompanied by Connor, across the boneyard. "You were meant to appease Echidna."

"The mother of monsters," Connor intoned. "She waits here, waits for her children, who are as mayflies before her own endlessness, to come home to die."

Vanders' arm was outstretched, and he clawed feebly at the dirt.

"You honor her," Anaya said. "You honor her with your death."

I didn't bother giving them a warning. I jumped to my feet, took aim with my F2000, and fired.

*Click!*

I had emptied the magazine firing at the Gargasaur.

The ground shook again, and this time I recognized it as the approach of the monster. It was following me, hunting me the way we had hunted it.

I ejected the magazine, fumbled for another.

"Don't fight it," Connor said. "You weapon is useless against the children of Echidna."

"I'm not going to shoot the monster," I said. "I'm gonna make sure you die before—"

The Gargasaur burst through the trees behind Anaya and Connor. Chunks of wooden shrapnel flew. The monster stomped forward, kicking at the bones of the creatures that had come to this place of death before it. It kicked at a great, ape-like skull and sent it flying.

Connor screamed as a shadow fell over him. He raised his arms futilely. The skull smashed down on top of him, ending his horrible cry.

The Gargasaur shrieked, and the island trembled in response.

Whether or not the gun would harm the creature, whether or not I had intended to kill Anaya with my final act, I opened fire at the Gargasaur, the bullets impacting ineffectually on its impenetrable skin.

Anaya, scrambling across the unsteady ground, ran for her life.

The Gargasaur's tongue was faster. Her eyes snapped wide open as the sticky appendage struck her back. She was yanked the through air, hard enough to shatter her spine. She vanished into the yawning maw.

Vanders gasped. He clawed at the ground.

The Gargasaur turned—slowly—toward me and took a step. Air and bone dust blasted out from beneath its colossal feet.

"Cole—"

Vanders coughed once more, then breathed his last breath.

The monster thundered forward. Its mouth opened, viscous saliva dripping between its teeth.

I took a step back and tripped over Vanders outstretched arm. I landed on my ass, hard enough to make me think I'd broken my tailbone. I looked at Vander's fingers frozen now where they had been digging furrows in the ground.

Nearby, concealed under a shell of cracked bone, was Vanders' elephant gun.

The Gargasaur's mouth opened wide, and the three tongues coiled around one another, soon to strike.

I scrambled for the gun.

The beast's tongues exploded from its mouth.

One of the tongues struck the bones of a long-dead creature. Another strafed across the dirt. The third smashed into my foot with enough force to pulverize every bone.

I cried out.

My fingers latched onto the rifle.

Just as the Gargasaur started to drag me towards its mouth, I pulled the gun up, took aim, and fired.

The shot hit the monster in the roof of its open mouth, punching right into the soft tissue. The explosion that followed ripped the Gargasaur's head in half. The monster took an unsteady step backwards, then toppled, smashing down onto the bones of those who had died here before.

The island screamed.

A shifting of tectonic plates, the screech of steam from newly-formed fissures, the bones of the earth scraping against one another.

Great spikes of jagged stone erupted from the ground.

Geysers of sulfuric gas sprayed from cracks in the earth.

I could barely stand. My ruined foot would support no weight. But I pulled myself to a standing position, using the bones of a fallen monster for support.

I chanced one last look at my fallen employer, and I saw his body slipping into a developing crevice beneath him. His corpse plummeted into nothingness.

Every movement brought a wave of agony, but I hopped on one leg, fleeing through the jungle as the island came apart around me. When I could no longer hop, I fell to the ground.

Above me, I saw smoldering debris flying, trailing black smoke.

Ash fell from the sky.

My fingers were raw when I finally pulled myself to the edge of a great cliff overlooking the ocean. The drop might have been 50 feet—it might have been 200. My mind spun. Pain numbed my senses. I knew only that I would die on the island if I remained, and so with the last of my strength, I hauled myself over the edge.

Head over heels, I plunged to the churning waters beneath. I thought I saw boats in the distance. I thought I glimpsed a horribly large shape gliding beneath the surface. I thought I heard the Gargasaur… or maybe my terrified colleagues… screaming. I smashed into the water with shocking force.

And all went black.

**WHEN I CAME TO, I** was being pulled across the slippery deck of one of the sightseeing vessels. A half-dozen tourists in rain slicks looked down at me, all asking frantic questions. Some spoke in languages I did not understand, but others spoke English.

"Where'd you come from?"

"What's happening to the island?"

"The Primeval—did you come from the Primeval?"

I muttered unintelligible responses, and someone helped me sit up.

A cataclysmic *boom* rippled through the air. The tourists gasped, turning from me, running to the deck railing so they could get a better look at the Primeval.

From the deck, I watched the truth of the Primeval laid bare.

The volcano at the island's heart spat out columns of blood-red lava. A pyroclastic cloud surged into the air, then receded, then billowed once more, giving the impression of gasping breaths. The trees trembled and shook and fell in waves. The entire island shuddered and bucked, and frothy waves rippled away from the coastline.

"Dear God," I heard someone say, "the island—it's rising!"

"It's not an island," I muttered.

Thundering white waterfalls of seawater fell from the sides of the Primeval as it rose. Beneath the rocky surface—beneath the facade of an island—something fleshy and grey and horrible squirmed.

I turned away.

Instead of looking upon the true face of the Primeval—the true face of the thing we *should* have been calling Echidna all this time—I looked across the deck, looked at the terrified crew as they scrambled to and fro, the tourists as they screamed senselessly. Tears ran down my face as I felt the ship buck beneath my feet, first as the waves crashed against the hull, then as the engines roared, churning water in full reverse. The boat turned, and I heard someone else—there was no point in learning their names—cry out "Full throttle!" Another shift beneath me, and we were heading at full speed back to civilization.

Still, I didn't look back at the creature—the Mother of Monsters—rising behind us.

I studied the faces of the people around me. Many of them were gazing past me, watching in horror as the most terrible monster of all, roused by a sacrifice gone wrong, rose from its slumber. Even held in the grasp of Megalozoophobia, I could still see a hint of the people they were on their frightened faces. These were people who had homes, loved ones, lives back in the "real" world—lives they had, until seconds earlier—thought they might return to.

I sobbed and laughed at the same time.

*I will not see this again.*

# THE DEVIL IN THE DETAILS

SABRINA VOURVOULIAS

*:: 1735*

**DEBORAH WAS A WELL-FORMED WOMAN** of twenty-six. Tall, long of leg, and wide of hip. Under the white muslin cap and black bonnet, her hair was arranged in thick, springy coils. Her dark eyes were kind but canny.

Like many of the women of the Pinelands, she had some wortcunning that she plied in an attempt to keep each of her twelve children alive through gripe and fever, abscessed tooth and bloody flux. That Deborah was more successful at this than most made her neighbors believe the family was especially blessed.

Her husband, some thirty years older than Deborah and bemused by the attention, was fairly certain they were cursed, instead.

The first time he had seen his wife wild-crafting herbs by the light of the moon, she was in the company of ghosts—a

coven of spectral elderly women, as tall and unbowed as Deborah herself. He had barreled into the silver dappled glade as she was harvesting honey mushrooms, and struck her full in the face.

When he tried to hit her a second time, she caught his fist in her hand. For a few seconds, the shock of it paralyzed him. Then, he threw his full physical weight and the weight of his burgeoning ire behind it. Deborah's grip didn't falter. In fact, it grew surer as the ghosts moved closer to her.

"Respect, Japhet. Do you not see that my mother and foremothers stand beside me? Our fortunes rest in their hands. You do not want them for enemies." She released him after a moment, and went back to cutting the fungi.

In the days that followed, Japhet was tentative around her, even though Deborah was as stalwart, industrious, and placid as she had been before the encounter. But, she became more forthright with him about the nature of her craft.

"What is that tea you are drinking?" he ventured to ask one night as they readied for bed.

"It allows me to enjoy our coupling without fear of bearing another child," she said. Her eyes danced as she shed her green homespun dress and undid her stays. "You have your eleven boys, and I have a dear little daughter with whom to share my foremothers' wisdom. With twelve good and healthy children, what business have we to seek another? Surely that would display inordinate desire and mark us with the sin of greed."

After taking their pleasure, Japhet stayed awake and hatched his plan in the dark.

He journeyed outside the Pinelands, as he always had, to

examine lands to purchase. Before returning home, he sought out those members of his father's family whose love of arcane and esoteric knowledge had led proper Quakers to ostracize them. Through their broadsides, almanacks, and pamphlets, Japhet became a student of astrology and natural magic; of Christian occultism with its parallel strands of demonology and angelology.

Several months into his plan, he brought home a handsome rendering of his family crest: a white shield bisected by a red band, with two creatures of claw and wing above, and one below. "They are wyverns," he told his sons as they pored over the drawing with him. "Creatures of magic very much like dragons. They represent valor and protection."

He noticed Deborah raise an eyebrow as he told his tale, but she did not stop him or interfere until their daughter toddled over to him, climbed on his lap, and reached for the parchment unfurled on the table.

"Not her," Deborah said swooping down to pluck the girl away before she touched the crest. "She is a child of my world, not yours."

Japhet would forever swear that it wasn't until that moment that he realized their youngest shared her mother's swarthy skin and dark hair, while their sons favored his own fair coloring and light eyes. The realization sealed his resolve. Less than a week later, while Deborah served as midwife to a thirteen-year-old Piney giving birth to her first child, he left his children at home and found his way to a spot in the Pines where the decaying honey mushrooms formed a circle of foxfire, Folklore had it that an otherworldly black dog sometimes let himself be seen there.

There is no record of what rite he performed on the spot, and Japhet's recollection of it fled with each step homeward. By the time he opened the door to his warm and cozy home, he would have vowed that his foray had been to gather wood to dispel the uncharacteristic chill of the night.

Deborah tried by root, bark, and leaf to prompt a miscarriage, but nothing worked. Every night, after Japhet had retired to bed, he could hear her speaking to her ghosts in some language he did not understand. Come morning, he'd clear away the detritus of her ever more desperate magic—bits of feather, red threads, and seed pods punctured clear through by a hot metal awl.

But as Deborah's stomach grew larger, she grew haggard and ashen-faced. By the last month she seemed, Japhet thought, like a skeleton weighed down by a fifty-pound sack of grain. He was solicitous, and thought to secure the services of one of the best midwives in the Pinelands, but Deborah stopped him.

"My foremothers will attend to me," she said, "and to this birth you have forced on me."

He protested his innocence, but she just studied him with those canny eyes, stripped now of all their kindness. When her time came, Deborah bade him to take their sons to a neighbor's home and bide there with them until the next day.

"This is women's work," she said calmly. "Only our daughter should witness it." He corralled the boys, and as they were leaving, Japhet saw every corner of the house come alive with the shades of women summoned by the first pangs of birth.

He returned, as instructed, a day later, alone. Their

daughter slept in a nest of quilts on the floor in front of the woodstove where the cheerfully leaping flames best threw out their warmth. His wife sat in the rocking chair a few feet away from her. The ghosts were all gone, and he saw no movement in the house at all, except for the slow motion of the chair.

As Deborah heard his footfall, she turned to him. "Come meet your new daughter," she said, patting the shawl covered bundle at her breast. "This one takes after your side of the family."

As he drew close, she pulled the shawl away. He caught a glimpse of a dark little body covered in mousy fur, with delicate, translucent wings tucked close to the body. Small claws at the joint of the wings moved in the aimless way of all infants. The preternaturally elongated head was shaped something like a horse's skull, with four prominent teeth fully formed. The creature made suckling sounds as Deborah pulled the swaddling cloth from around its tail and legs. "Look," she said. "Have you ever seen such perfect little hooves?"

As if it knew Japhet was there, the thing in his wife's arms opened its eyes. They were red, and glowing, and almost before Japhet could register the fact, the creature's mouth opened and a piercing scream rent the air.

Japhet took a couple of stumbling steps away as Deborah made soothing noises and stroked the creature's long nose until it stopped wailing. Japhet took another step back, and heard a yelp emerge from under the quilts that covered his daughter. "Get away from here, as fast as you can," he hissed at her. "I'll come find you when I'm done."

He felt rather than saw the child get up. Deborah watched him silently as he opened the door of the woodstove. "Give that devil to me," he said, arms outstretched. "We'll burn it and let its evil taint be dispelled with the smoke in the chimney."

His wife looked down at the creature's upturned face. The red glow of its eyes played over the planes of Deborah's face, making her cheeks rosy, and for the first time in nine months, his wife looked healthy.

"How strange," she said, raising her eyes to Japhet again, "you are."

At her words, their daughter went to stand by her mother's side; Deborah acknowledged her with a quick one-armed hug.

"You want what you want so relentlessly, so righteously, that you think nothing of forcing it on another," she said as she held Japhet's gaze. "And yet when the result of your actions is clear in front of you, you will not admit responsibility. You would rather deny it, you would rather have proof perish and the truth go up in flames than to have to examine the impact of what you provoked."

Japhet saw the shadows behind the rocking chair coalesce into figures. He didn't count them, but he guessed there might be ten women. Many of them were elders (with just a few who had died young among them) and had countenances made formidable by hard experience. Some were clothed simply and modestly, but others wore flamboyant ornament and flashy garb. All of them looked at him with contempt.

"My foremothers ever adopted those cast aside as irredeemable, and those left alone in the world by others' doing," Deborah said. "I will raise this daughter wrought of your English witchery and hubris, and love her as if I had chosen willingly to bear her. She, in return, will love me and mine. Thus, we will be safe from whatever she becomes.

"But you and yours will be cursed, Japhet," she said. "For as long as she lives."

His hands shook so badly he had to clutch at the hem of his waistcoat to steady them. The brush of his fingertips against the sensible, plain fabric restored his sense of moral certitude. "For the love of God, Deborah, you are clinging to a devil."

She turned her face to the thing in her arms. "Who's the devil?" she cooed at it. "Who's the devil in this house?"

Japhet shook his head, extended his hand to his daughter still standing quietly by the rocker. During the course of the exchange, she had stuck her thumb in her mouth and was sucking furiously on it—something she hadn't done in months.

"Let's go," he told her. "Your brothers are waiting."

The child's eyes got big, but she shook her head, and as he stepped forward she shrank back. When he grew exasperated with her timidity and roughly grabbed her arm, the devil let out an ungodly shriek.

It launched itself out of Deborah's arms. Japhet had enough time to note that the translucent wings unfurled into a wingspan roughly equal to that of an eagle. Then the devil's teeth were at his throat.

*:: 1909*

**BEE HATED HER NAME. NOT** "Bee," which was the nickname she earned by her golden skin, but Deborah—a name one woman in each generation of her family was fated to bear. Fated, mind you, not forced, because there was little a Smith woman hated more than to be forced into something she didn't want to do.

But there was always someone in the family who was all too happy to raise a Débora, Dvorah, Deb, or Debbie.

Bee sighed as she pinned up her thick coil of hair. Her family had some odd customs, no question. A foremother from time immemorial had decided to forsake both husband's and father's surnames and picked Smith out of a hat. Literally. And every daughter thereafter kept it, married or not.

That was another thing: the marriages. They never lasted. Just long enough to produce a healthy number of children. Then, after the separation the father took custody of the boys and the mother retained custody of the girls. Sometimes, after some years had passed, a child protested this and, mostly, was accommodated.

Bee intended to be the first to break some of those customs. She had no desire to marry, finding men's conversation mostly tiresome and far inferior to that of her girlfriends. She felt no need to bear children, though she didn't discount fostering one or two—another Smith tradition. But she was invested in her job as a nurse and loved her life in Camden, so she didn't foresee that as a possibility for a long time yet.

She finished her ablutions and headed downstairs. Mrs. Sorbinski, the rooming house owner, wasn't much of a cook, but her breakfasts always included the one dish she made to perfection: potato pancakes. Bee could easily eat four of them in one sitting.

But the only living being she found in the dining room was Pepper, Mrs. Sorbinski's elderly collie, looking forlornly at the empty table from which, usually, a few scraps of food were forthcoming at this time of day.

Bee found Mrs. Sorbinski in the sitting room with one of the boarders, Mr. Kremezi, poring over the latest edition of the *Camden Daily Courier*.

"The devil's on the loose," Mrs. Sorbinski said to Bee, her voice midway between alarmed and gleeful. "One of the councilmen in Trenton heard the monster flapping outside his window in the middle of the night. He says it was enormous, much larger than its legend would have you believe. He took a shot at it, but he must have missed because the police could find no blood trail."

"Probably an owl and an overactive imagination," Mr. Kremezi scoffed as he continued to read over Mrs. Sorbinski's shoulder.

"I can't speak to the imagination, but if he heard it flying it was no owl. They are absolutely silent in flight," Bee said.

When Mr. Kremezi turned his bespectacled eyes on her, she added. "I grew up in the Pinelands, and my family's all from there. We know the ways of wildlife."

"They're saying the monster attacked the trolleys in Trenton," Mrs. Sorbinski read on. "And in New Brunswick too. Then it flew to West Collingswood, where the firemen at the station turned their hoses on it."

"Did it kill anyone anywhere?" Bee asked.

Both Mrs. Sorbinski and Mr. Kremezi shook their heads.

"Some farmer's chickens," the old woman added after a moment. "The farmer went at it with a shotgun but said it was impervious to the shells."

Bee frowned. "Poor creature. Like us, it has to eat. Who is it really hurting that it should constantly be harried with bullets and water?"

Mrs. Sorbinski looked so scandalized at her sympathy that Bee quickly said goodbye and went to work early. And hungry.

Despite the bitter cold, Bee chose to walk home to the boarding house after work rather than take the trolley. A servant from one of the wealthy residences in town had turned up at Cooper Hospital with blue-red papules on her arm, and Dr. Cooper feared it might be leprosy.

The servant girl understood immediately what that diagnosis would mean: she would lose her job, no one in town would rent a room to her or allow her to enter the stores where food stuffs were for sale. An immigrant living alone in Camden, she would surely die—of poverty if not of the shame heaped on her.

Despite her dire circumstance, the girl had been lively and witty. Her words sang and her eyes danced. Perhaps one of the kindly Smith aunts could be persuaded to foster her...

Bee was so lost in her thoughts that she didn't see the crowd gathered in front of Mrs. Sorbinski's rooming house until she was right on top of them. "What's going on?" she asked a policeman, newly arrived and parting the crowd to get inside the house.

"The Jersey Devil!" someone from the crowd answered with a shout, and as soon as he did, other voices followed.

Bee grabbed the back of the policeman's jacket so she wouldn't lose him in the crowd as he plowed through. "I live in that house," she yelled when he turned at the tug. He thought for a second, gave her a nod and started throwing elbows again. Once inside he made a beeline for the kitchen door and out into the backyard.

There, in the center of the yard, with a circle of silently

stunned police and spectators all keeping their distance, stood the Jersey Devil—with the inert body of Pepper, the collie, in its mouth.

The creature was some ten or twelve feet tall, a muddy dark shape in the dusk's gloaming. It shifted from leg to leg, hoof to hoof, keeping balance with the weight of its thick, scaly tail. The red eyes darted from person to person in front of it, as if it was waiting for them to give it a cue about what it needed to do next.

Bee didn't consciously make the decision to push through the gathered people, or to traverse the empty buffer space between them and the devil, but she soon found herself face-to-face with it. She was close enough to see the shreds of wood caught in the fearsome claws on its folded wings, close enough to notice the pink nub of teats poking out of the mouse-brown fur on its chest and underbelly.

Close enough to see that Pepper, while undeniably dead, wasn't bleeding and the devil's massive, prominent teeth were merely holding a dog it had found already dead.

The monster put her head down to look at Bee, first out of one big red eye, then the other—like a horse. The long nose was less than a foot away from Bee when she reached a hand out to touch it. The creature softly bumped her hand in return.

Without thinking, Bee started stroking the length of the creature's nose. "Sweet girl, put the dog down," she said. "It is well beloved by the lady of this house, and she will want to properly mourn it."

The devil looked long at her, then did as she had asked.

"Thank you," Bee said. "Go back to the pines that shield you, the river that soothes you, the wilderness that loves you.

These people can't do any of those for you, what's more, they don't want to."

The devil made a strange noise, something like a baritone chirp, and ducked her head so it almost touched the ground—but not before Bee saw the gulf of loneliness in the creature's eyes.

The monster moved to spread her wings, but Bee caught a glimpse of something barreling toward the creature.

Mrs. Sorbinski skidded to a stop beside Bee and swatted the devil—full in the face and a hard as she was able—with her best broom. And then she did it again. And again. She screamed Pepper's name with each strike.

As if the old woman's attack had been a prompt to action, the spectators started shouting and the policemen started shooting. Bee was close enough to see that those bullets that hit their mark were absorbed by the creature's body without inflicting harm.

Which is more than could said for the stray bullets that hit the surging bystanders.

Some twenty people of assorted ages went down before the policemen stopped to reload. In those few seconds, the devil stepped delicately over the prostrate bodies, spread her wings and flew away, screeching and raging.

In the weeks that followed, Bee heard that someone had built a cage large enough to house the devil and was offering $10,000 for its capture. The newspapers were filled with stories of people too scared to send their children to school or to go back to work themselves. Mrs. Sorbinski, neither frightened nor forgiving, formed the First Camden Civil Anti-Devil Brigade. She also asked Bee to vacate her room within the month.

Dibella, the servant girl, was found not to have leprosy but a skin condition called Erythema multiforme, so Bee packed a supply of carbolic acid, zinc wash, and boracic acid ointment in their leather satchels, and they boarded the Camden and Atlantic Railroad.

Bee fed Dibella milk, and sweets as pillowy and soft as their kisses, all the way to the Pine Barrens, and when they disembarked, the house that passed from one generation of Smith women to another, was waiting for them.

*:: 1937*

**GERALDENE WAS A SMITH TWICE** over.

That is, she was born to one of that long line of Smith women, and as chance would have it, she ended up marrying a man whose surname was also Smith.

In all other ways, she had broken with the custom of her foremothers.

She had been happily married for nineteen years with no intention of leaving her husband. She neither gave birth to, nor fostered, children; in fact, she wasn't overfond of sharing space with them in public or in private. She had kept away from the house in the Pine Barrens as soon as she was emancipated from her mother's care, and then she fled the state of New Jersey altogether. She lived in Pennsylvania, in a small paper mill town some forty miles west of Philadelphia—near her father, with whom she was determined to establish a relationship after the years of estrangement.

She wasn't a Smith fosterling, but she looked nothing like her mother, aunts, and cousins. She was short of leg and round of shoulder. Her hair was the color and texture of fresh corn silk. While the Smith skin tones ranged from deep brown to light with an olive cast, Geraldene's was uniquely pearl white.

Still, there were some things no Smith could escape.

She had recently attended a memorial service for one of her Smith aunts—the Deborah of her mother's generation—at tiny Jenkins Chapel, deep in the Barrens, which the living aunts and cousins had rented for the occasion. The shadowy Smith ghosts, not used to her presence at family gatherings, all swarmed around her.

Geraldene ignored them. She pretended not to see them. Pretended not to hear the words in Portuguese, Tupinambá, Yoruba, and Ladino that the ghosts whispered to each other about this most strange child of their strange line. She was tempted—just once during the hours-long service—to stand up and proclaim it loud and clear so both the living and the dead could understand it: the past simply did not interest her.

Her passion was the future, and at night—after her wifely duties were done—she wrote pulpy science fiction at her kitchen table in Downingtown. She'd even had a few stories published, under the masculine pen name Debron Smith, at the *Thrilling Wonder Stories* and *Amazing Stories* magazines. Alien planets, swashbuckling rocketeers, and heroic scientists left no space for ghosts—ancestral or otherwise.

As the years passed she almost convinced herself she had beaten the curse that no Smith woman would admit was a curse. Then, one night while sharing coffee cake and gossip with her neighbors after dinner, the happy construct of her life tumbled down around her ears.

It started with blood-curdling shrieking.

Then all the dogs in the town started baying at once.

She and her guests ran out of the house and followed the sound. In the sky above them an enormous winged creature slowly beat its wings as it circled the town.

Geraldene had a writer's attention to detail. She noted the silvery moonlight glancing off the leathery wings and bony head as the creature flew. She marked how it avoided the columns of grey smoke as the paper mill's stacks spewed particulates and stench into the hot and humid night. She saw, even from afar, the moment the devil's glowing red eyes lit on her.

It landed a short distance from them, its massive hooves crushing two of the cars parked across the street from their homes. The dogs that had come out to howl at the creature scattered. So did Geraldene's neighbors—she heard their heavy oak door slam loudly.

Geraldene's eyes slid up the length of the Jersey Devil's body—all twenty feet of it—until she met its eyes. When she was young and attending all the Smith gatherings that her mother forced on her, she had heard the cousins' whispers and conjectures. That the creature was their relative. That it was daughter to the first Deborah, and sister to the second. No aunt had ever confirmed or denied the possibility, but perhaps they simply didn't know.

The creature lifted a hoof as if to take a step. The flesh around the hoof was thick with scars, as if it had healed from a terrible burn.

"No! Stop!" Geraldene yelled, flinging her hand up in a warding gesture. "Stay right there."

The devil shifted restively but didn't take a step.

Unbidden, a scene she had written just last night surfaced in her thoughts. In it, the strapping, blond rocketeer was trying to communicate with a huge, crab-like creature on the alien planet where he had just landed. Some of the rocketeer's lines seemed suited to this night.

"I can see you understand when I speak," she said to the devil. "But can you talk?"

The creature gave a strange sort of chirp.

"Who are you?" Geraldene asked. "What do you want?"

Words started tumbling out of the creature's mouth, but she didn't understand any of them. When it stopped, Geraldene shook her head, and the creature echoed her motion.

"You should go," Geraldene said. "Before they come after you. Because they always come after you, don't they?"

It cocked its head at her, then unfurled its wings and took flight. She watched it fly eastward until it was no more than a speck in the sky. The dogs started baying again, and as she stood there twenty or so men with leashed hounds in one hand and shotguns in the other came running pell-mell to where she stood.

"Where'd it go?" one of the men asked. She recognized him as the deacon in the church her husband attended.

"Away."

"It didn't hurt you?"

"No. But it killed my car..."

"This is no joking matter, Mrs. Smith," he snapped at her.

"No, I guess not," she said. She turned around and went back inside her house, and wrote down phonetically the few words she could remember from the devil's speech:

*Kuento. Danyo. Ermana.*

She looked at them for a long time, then stuck them in her wallet and resolved to look for them in every one of the town library's foreign language dictionary.

Three hours later she finished the story she had been working on. The rocketeer decided not to zap the crab-monster with his ray-gun and tried to speak to him instead. Despite his efforts, and the crab's, they came to the conclusion they were never going to understand each other. The crab monster chirped sadly when the rocketeer walked back to his ship. The rocketeer shed a tear for what might have been. The end.

*:: 2018*

**THREE-THOUSAND ACRES OF THE PINE** Barrens were on fire.

Not near the Smith homestead yet, but DB was keeping watch via remote. Not even two years before, another 1,000 acre-stretch had burned when some dipshit improperly disposed of the charcoal briquettes from his grill. Those were nothing compared to the fire of 1936 (which had burned 20,000 acres) or the one in 1963 (which had burned 183,000 acres) of course...but every bit of lost habitat had a real impact.

She punched a new set of coordinates in the mapping console, and watched another remote sensing satellite camera come online to stream in real time.

The stretch of deep forest where her sister was living these days was intact. DB felt her shoulders unclench, and she stretched to work any remaining tension out of them. She wasn't the first trans Smith woman, but she was the first one named as the Deborah for her generation, and all of the title's expectations weighed heavy on her. She had started noticing some gray strands as she did her twists, and she was still a few months from turning thirty.

The thought drove her to punch in an appointment request at her favorite beauty shop. The other Smiths teased her about being vain, but the media really liked to run photos of celebs looking awful, and that just wasn't how DB rolled. *It's okay if I look old and haggard* said no woman ever.

She found herself humming a couple bars of music that would make a great opening for a new composition, then moved to another section of the mothership. In addition to all the monitoring and communication consoles, the mothership had a keyboard, sound mixer, and state of the art recording equipment tucked into it for just these moments. You never knew when (or where) your next million-dollar song was going to worm its way into your consciousness.

A resonant chirp drew her to the balcony.

The forty-foot Jersey Devil had picked its way—very carefully on the harmless track DB had meticulously plotted for her—to the huge Navy Yard building in Philadelphia where DB was the only tenant. The behemoth could have flown, but the tremendous wings, unfurled, would have been visible from the more developed and congested parts of the city.

"Ermana," DB said. Sister.

DB had long ago decided, regardless of any other Smith woman's ambivalence, that the Jersey Devil was indeed kin.

DB couldn't remember which Smith woman had figured out that the words spoken by the Jersey Devil in the early 20th century were in Ladino (the language that the earliest of Deborah's antecedents, Sephardic Jews, brought with them from Brazil when they settled in the U.S. in the 1600s), but one of the first things she did when she assumed the role of Deborah was learn it.

Then, when the devil initially showed herself to DB—as she customarily did once per generation with every Deborah, whether written record of the sighting existed or not—DB made sure to speak to her in Ladino.

The devil went stock-still and practically prostrated herself trying to get eye-to-eye with DB. Finally, DB climbed up a fire-escape so there wouldn't be some calamitous, forty-foot belly flop. That first conversation had lasted an hour. It was when DB learned that the Jersey Devil's name was Reina. Queen. Appropriate.

"What do you need, my queen?" DB asked in Ladino.

"Lonely," Reina said.

DB leaned over the balcony and Reina ducked her head for her nose to be stroked.

"I can't hang with you tonight, sister. I've got a date and celebrities get lonely too."

Reina made a sound that DB had come to understand was akin to laughter.

"But I've got a present for you," DB said, stepping back inside her apartment. "Wait there."

She came back with an odd-looking gold ring about the diameter of a PVC toilet drainpipe. It was hinged, had a locking clasp and big pendant with a round, red push plate on it. Despite the gold, it really wasn't much to look at, and nobody would have guessed it cost her about a half-million to have it custom-made. The most expensive part was the guarantee that it would last for at least 75 years.

"I thought I saw a healing tear in one of your wings," DB said. "Let me see it."

Reina very cautiously unfurled the tip of her left wing, where a hole gaped in the membrane between the second and third finger.

"Can you touch your nose to it?" DB asked. When Reina showed her she could, DB motioned for her to bring her wing closer to the balcony edge. With a lot of finagling from both of them, DB finally clicked the huge earring in place so that the push plate was permanently affixed to the inside of the wing where Reina could reach it.

"Is it uncomfortable?" she asked.

"Yes," Reina said, "but it doesn't hurt. It's just...strange."

"Nudge the red push plate with your nose."

When Reina did, DB's voice, singing a lullaby in Ladino, rang out from the earring.

"Nudge it again to turn it off," DB said. "I recorded two lullabies for it, plus a song I wrote for you, 'Queenie,' which is in Ladino, Portuguese, and English all sort of mixed together, that I think might go on my next album. When you get bored with those, I can record other ones and just swap out the chips. I thought it might be good for when you get lonely out there in the Pinelands, in between our visits."

Reina was so quiet, DB got worried. "If you don't like it, just tell me. I won't be mad."

"It makes me happy," Reina said. "Thank you, DB."

"Okay, then," DB said. "Now, shoo. I've got to get beautiful for tonight."

Reina chirped once, and started the slow process of trying

to get out of the industrial complex without unintentionally destroying the city.

*:: 2018*

**PHILADELPHIA—DB SMITH, A TRANSGENDER WOMAN** and platinum selling artist, was killed in Philadelphia Saturday night according to family members and transgender advocates.

Smith was stabbed and left for dead in a hotel parking lot on the 1800 block of Market Street just before midnight. Police say she was stabbed multiple times in the face and her throat was slashed.

Smith earned Grammy nominations for her songs "30 to 50" and "City of Women" from her breakout album, *Identidade.* She had recently started recording tracks for her third album.

Latinx and Black Trans Women, an advocacy group with which Smith was associated as an advisory board member, released a statement after her death, decrying the brutal murder as a hate crime. "2018 is on track to be the most violent year on record for transgender people," the statement said. "In the first 60 days of the year there have already been seven killings of trans women of color—a rate that DB was committed to bring to light through her songs and her activism. It is to be noted that not even celebrity trans women are safe from the escalation in violence we are experiencing."

Police have not commented on whether the murder will be investigated as a hate crime, and no suspects or motive have been named.

*:: 2018*

**NATIONAL DESK—AT LEAST 1,000** people, mainly workers and residents in its downtown, have died in a bizarre attack in the city of Philadelphia attributed to the legendary Jersey Devil.

Local media has reported the death toll is expected to rise as first responders begin to excavate bodies believed to have been crushed as the creature demolished City Hall and toppled the historic Billy Penn statue that crowned the edifice.

Dilworth Park, on the apron of City Hall, has been cordoned off to remove bodies and to clean out the fountain, which is reportedly covered with a scrim of blood instead of the usual water.

Hundreds of people are believed to have been injured, some critically, as the monster rampaged through other areas in the Center City district. Multiple injuries were sustained by people stampeding to take cover in the underground trolley, subway, and train stations along Market Street.

The district's hotels appear to have been especially hard hit by the flying creature. Few have any remaining glass, and images on social media showed people laying on the ground, impaled by pieces that fell as windows shattered.

Eyewitnesses say that when the Jersey Devil landed between aerial attacks, it caved in cars and SEPTA buses. Many of the disabled vehicles still line the streets of downtown Philadelphia. The eyewitnesses also describe the creature singing songs at different moments during the attack. Its voice was allegedly reminiscent of that of electro-samba artist DB Smith who, in an eerie coincidence, was found murdered in the city yesterday.

The city government has declared martial law and set an 8 p.m. curfew until order can be restored to the district. National Guard and Reserves from New Jersey and Pennsylvania have been deployed. In a statement, the mayor's spokesperson said that "measures will be taken to help the victims and their families."

For its part, the Philadelphia Zoo has offered a $10,000 reward for the live capture of the Jersey Devil and is said to be consulting with architects and a planner for a potential safe enclosure that would enable the creature to be on display should it be trapped.

The Jersey Devil was last sighted flying in the general direction of the Pine Barrens, the million-acre preserve that includes first- and second-growth forests from which its legend emerged nearly two centuries ago.

*.: 2018*

**REINA ALWAYS KNEW IN HER** bones when a new Smith had been named as the generational Deborah. She usually waited until the young one had settled into her duties before showing herself. She knew she was monstrous to them and that even those who were kind to her when they were alive did not consider her kin—else their ghosts would have shown themselves to her. In the nearly 250 years she had been alive, she had never seen one.

The earring hung slack from her wing, but the bullets that could not harm her had hit it multiple times, and DB's voice was silenced. Reina would never hear it again. She wished DB had never spoken to her in the secret language of the first

Deborah. You can bear to lose language once, but not twice.

She approached the Smith homestead as carefully and stealthily as she could hope to—flying from her deep, old forest to the younger one, and then allowing the river to carry her within a few miles of the house. She became like a shadowed statue amid the hundred-foot trees that opened into a clearing in front of the house. It was dusk, and through the windows of the house, the lights winked on and off following the living cousins and aunts in and out of the rooms they transited, readying for the memorial.

She had a vivid imagination—all creatures that live alone successfully do—so she got caught up in envisioning what might be happening inside, and missed what was happening in front of her, down near the ground.

A child—skinny, light brown skin, long black hair midway down the back—was standing about ten feet away from her, head tipped all the way back to encompass the magnitude of the devil standing in the trees.

"Hello, Reina," the child said in halting Ladino. "I am Dev, the Deborah of my generation."

"The only living Deborah." It hurt Reina to say it.

"Yes." Dev cocked their head. "Don't you want to know how I know your name?"

The dusk had turned misty, so Reina ducked her head as close to ground as she was able. Her flashing, fearsome red eyes were only a few feet from the child. "Your family ghosts told you."

"Your family ghosts too," the child said.

Or maybe it was the flickery, shadowy semblance of DB who said it. Or any of the other ghosts stretching all the way back to the first Deborah who stood tall, now, in the mists around Reina.

She couldn't feel the ghostly hands that reached up to stroke her nose, but they were there. And that, as ever, was enough.

# MORITURI

MELANIE R. MEADORS

**THE MUSCLES IN MY ARMS** burned from the morning's grueling routine of jabs and parries, rivaled only by the scorch of the sun on my dark shoulders. I sparred with Pugnax, a giant oaf of a Gaul, who looked more like a beast one would find in my mother's world than in Rome. Bent, monstrous, and deadly.

Every time someone in the practice yard of the *ludus* slid across the sand to avoid a thrust or take an opportunity for a low strike, a plume of dust rose from the parched ground, drying our throats and eyes even more. The sweat dripping from our bodies gave the ground more water than it had seen in weeks from rain. Yet still we fought, still we toiled, because we had to.

The weight of several gazes hung upon me from the balcony above, but I paid no heed. A Discordian fed on the attention of an audience, the roar of a crowd. Instead of pressuring me, the scrutiny gave me strength. It gave me focus.

Swing, stab, block, feint, thrust. We moved in a dance I knew well. The fight seemed endless, and hunger gnawed at my innards, weariness at my limbs. Yet if this mock fight ended, another would only begin. Why bother?

*Glory*, said a voice within my mind. *End this fight and gain honor for your kind.*

The voice of my uncle. He made himself known now and again.

*Glory for a slave*, I returned. *That would be a novelty indeed.* I dodged a thrust from Pugnax. The giant's movements became slower, heavier.

*Do not question our motives, girl. You are Discordian, not some mere slave. Your entire existence is a paradox. Use your trident, vault, and end this now.*

I met Pugnax's gaze and did not look away. *Yes, Uncle.*

While he was caught by my amber gaze, I planted the base of my trident into the sand and pushed off, swinging my feet in front of me to hit Pugnax square in the face. He, his blood, and a few of his teeth flew backward. The other gladiators fighting around us leaped out of the way, and he landed with a thud on the ground, skidding before his body came to a halt. He did not rise.

After a shocked silence, the training yard filled with laughter and cheers. I took a moment to touch my hand to my forehead, thanking my uncle Mars for reminding me of my purpose.

"Canna! Step forward!"

I stood at attention before the words had even registered in my mind. Then I turned and made my way across the yard to stand before the balcony where my master and his guests stood.

"Undefeated," Gaius Venario said, his chest puffing out with pride. "And no indication of forfeiting that distinction any time soon."

One of his guests, a fit man of obvious noble stature, laughed. "There's always a first time, Venario. Always. Everyone loses at some point."

"You see how she fights," Venario said. "She was *bored* out there. She's a prodigy even among Discordians."

"A true child of the goddess Discordia," said the other guest, a tall, slender man younger than the other two. His voice was tinged with wonder. He turned his attention to the other man. "And worthy to fight on behalf of the best ruler known to Rome, *ne*?"

The other still looked down at me. "Don't you worry about having such a deadly person in your house? I'm reminded of some parables of old."

It was my master's turn to laugh. "Will she be the death of me? Perhaps. But what a death it will be. It certainly beats choking on a fig or dying peacefully in my sleep. Where is the notoriety in that?"

"You'll pardon me, dear Venario, for preferring to be remembered for my life rather than my death. I wonder if I might have a closer look at her."

My master looked surprised at this request, and I was likewise surprised when he gave a smile that didn't quite reach his blue eyes and replied, "Certainly. Who am I to refuse?"

He looked down at me and nodded sharply. I'd seen that look in my master's eyes before. No toying with this one. His guest was someone of great importance.

---

**MINUTES LATER, I STOOD AT** the barred door which separated the *ludus* from the rest of the house. My master and his noble guest faced me, the latter giving me an appraising look.

"You allow her to stay with the men?" the stranger said. "Aren't you concerned for her safety?"

A laugh exploded from my master. "Concerned? *Her* safety? I pity the man who approaches her without permission. One man made that attempt, Caesar. He attempts nothing more in this life."

Caesar? I'd heard my master discuss Rome's dictator, but had no idea he was on such friendly terms with the man.

"I've never seen a Discordian up close before," he said. His tone was casual, yet somehow managed to hold the power of a command, something my master did not miss.

"Say the word, and I'll have her cleaned and brought up for your closer inspection. It's hard to get a proper view of her here in this dim light. Though where she truly shines is in the arena."

Caesar looked down his nose at me. "I would not have myself end up like that fool she sent to Hades. Tell me, girl, do you know who I am?"

My master had a glimmer of worry in his eye. He often underestimated me. I stood tall and gave salute.

"You are Gaius Julius Caesar, Father of Rome."

My words had the desired effect. The slightest twitch in his eyebrow betrayed a pleased surprise at the title. I silently thanked my goddess mother's inspiration. While the role this man would play in my life remained obscure, Discordia made clear my own purpose. The purpose of all Discordians.

To watch.

To listen.

To wield men like weapons, one against the other.

Caesar nodded. "I am that, indeed." He turned his attention back to my master. "Yes, I think she will make fine company. I'm pleased you understand I'm not just looking for physical might, Venario. Your *ludus* is among the finest I've visited, truly worthy of its reputation."

"Thank you, Caesar. You honor me by saying so." They walked off down the hall that would lead them to the *domus*, where more civilized discourse would take place, but not before Venario jerked his head at one of the other slaves. I'd be bathed and oiled and perfumed.

*Mother Discordia, Uncle Mars, I know not what lies before me, but I shall prove my worth. I shall make you proud.*

**THE MEN RECLINED WHILE I** stood before them, my hands behind my back. I kept my gaze neutral while they chatted and ate their figs and olives and drank their wine. I was accustomed to such meals. Being a champion meant extra time on display at the whims of rich men. Unlike many gladiators, I didn't begrudge gawkers. While others might feel objectified—and indeed, they were, as was I—I drew a certain power from these men's underestimation of me. I was a mere animal in their eyes; a curiosity. And while they stuffed their faces and never so much as offered me a cup, I knew in the end they would grow fat and lazy, and I would be hardened and ruthless.

Incense hung thickly in the air of the *triclinium*, and the fans the slaves waved did little to alleviate the hot, stifling air. An orange curtain separated the room from the rest of the house for privacy. The men discussed games and strategy, Caesar being the owner of several gladiators himself. My senses told me there was another conversation happening in the room as well, one without words, but with intention. Every move Caesar made, every word he spoke, was done with careful consideration, like a cat stalking its prey. My master's gaze shifted, and he fidgeted. As light and casual as their conversation seemed, the room lacked any comfort. Then the dictator surprised me from my musings with a question.

"Discordian, do you know why I am here?"

I chose my words with great care. "Because you're interested in the inner workings of the finest *ludus* in the Republic."

He'd taken an unfortunate sip of wine at the time of my answering and choked on it. I stood patiently while he recovered. My master sat frozen, his eyes narrowed the slightest bit. I knew my game well, however, both in and out of the arena.

"This is the fourth gladiatorial college I've visited this week, all of which were labeled the best by someone. Seldom, however, did they label *themselves* as such. I'd be tempted to accuse one that did so of hubris."

"It's not hubris if it's true. If my word is faulty, let the gods judge me in the arena."

I caught my master's eye, and he attempted a glare, yet his anger could not match the hope in his eyes. I was his *gladiatrix*, after all. Was it not my duty to fight for him? The rules of society may have prevented him from directly pursuing his goal, but as an animal of the arena, I was not bound by such pettiness. Sometimes, being considered less than human gave one an advantage.

"Let the gods judge you, indeed," Caesar said thoughtfully. "I've seen your record. And I've witnessed you fight. You're the first Discordian I've sat across from, and certainly the first I've exchanged words with. You are indeed everything they speak of. I'm planning a spectacle of a sort. A celebration of the glories of Rome—and of her strengths. Your name, Canna, has come up repeatedly around the Republic as one of the best fighters in Rome. Indeed, of the known world. Is this warranted?"

Again, I remained stoic as I answered, "I'm undefeated. I will let that record speak for itself."

Caesar tapped his fingers together, his dark eyes calculating. "Indeed. How would you like to take part in my spectacle? How would you like to be a part of something that will make your name legendary?"

"What I want is irrelevant. I don't have the freedom to make that choice for myself."

At this, Caesar shifted his weight and sat up.

"Tell me," he said, leaning forward with his elbows resting on his knees. "Were you born a slave?"

"No, *Domine*. My village was taken by Rome when I was about seventeen summers. I became a slave after that."

"I see. And did you have family?"

My heart gave a flutter as memories I'd struggled to block for long years came trickling forth. "I was found by villagers at the edge of a forest. A family was kind enough to take me in and call me their child. They didn't know until later what I was. And… there was a child. Of my own blood. She was taken by the same men who captured me when Rome came to my village. She couldn't be sold as a gladiator, so they sent her elsewhere."

"And the father?"

I thought of the father. I couldn't conjure his face. Only blood. Every memory I had of him, every sight, sound, taste, smell. All tinged with blood.

"Dead," I replied.

"Very well," said Caesar. I glanced at him, daring to meet his gaze. He met mine squarely, not looking away from my odd amber eyes. He understood. "I'm going to have some words with your master. I thank you for your displays today. May the gods continue to grant you favor."

"And you, *Domine*," I said.

Before I left, I looked to my master to gauge his reaction to the encounter. There was a crease between his eyes which betrayed his pleasant outward countenance. I could see he wondered the same thing I did.

What sort of "spectacle" did Caesar have in mind?

**"HE WANTS YOU," ONE OF** the house slaves called through the bars of the *ludus* door. It was the closest they usually came, and the most they usually spoke.

It hadn't even been an hour since I had come down to have my dinner of bread and porridge. Caesar had seemed sufficiently impressed with my skill in the arena and with my answers to his questions. I hadn't any doubt I'd be selected for his game, whatever it was. My master's summons surprised me.

I followed the slave up the stone steps. I hadn't even reached the top when I heard my master's voice bellowing. The closer we came to my master's *tablinum*, the more the slave hesitated. Once I saw the flow of slaves coming and going from the office, I didn't blame him.

I dismissed my escort with a wave as I entered and stood against the wall, assessing the situation. Slaves milled around the desk, offering our master food, drink, medicine. Venario sat with his face buried in his hands, fingers woven through his short brown curls. His chest rose and fell with each breath, his tension emanating throughout the room. With each offering, his reactions escalated, first with a "No," then, "*No*," until, finally, he swore and swung at the next person within reach. I stood and nodded at the remaining slaves in the room. They took my meaning and fled, drawing the curtain closed behind them.

I glanced around the room. I'd only been invited there on a few occasions. Shelves of scrolls I couldn't read lined the walls, and the desk was piled with wax tablets and bits of parchment. Everything had a purple cast from the sunlight of the atrium coming in through the curtain.

I might have been his champion, but I was still a slave, and so had to wait until Venario spoke first. After several minutes, however, I grew restless.

"*Domine*?" I prompted.

The word triggered him. He stood from his desk, the chair scraping loudly on the floor. He flung his hands downward, like a child taking a tantrum. "*Futue*!"

I couldn't resist a smirk. He'd cleaned up his language so well for his guests. "If you don't tell me what's wrong, I can't help you."

"How can you help me? You're a *damnatoria* slave," he spat, glaring at me.

"That doesn't stop you from telling me every other cursed thing that happens to you."

He flopped back down into his chair and ran his hands through his hair. "Best *damnatoria lanista*, he says. The glory of *Romae defututae*. So why not *pedicare me*?"

"Who?" I asked, ignoring his curses that rivaled even the worst plebeian street talk.

Venario smacked his hands down onto his desk and looked at me as if I should have known. "Our glorious *Imperator*, Julius Caesar. What reward do I get for having the finest gladiatorial college in Rome?"

I raised an eyebrow but didn't move otherwise. "Honor and glory."

Venario snorted. "You didn't see this… this… *thing* he has, this horror. He wants me and every other notable *lanista* in Rome to throw away our best gladiators to fight this monster he claims to have dragged from the depths of Tartarus itself. A show of might for his enemies, to show them the monsters he commands. Something to impress his friends, make friends of the people. It will be a show like none has seen before, he claims, and all who take part will be honored with notoriety, whether they live to tell the tale or not. He'll pay handsomely in case of death, but it's not enough to pay for your lifetime of appearances in the arena. It's not enough to offset the loss of reputation and ability this school will suffer with your loss."

"My loss?" I said. I stepped forward and leaned on the front of the desk with my hands. "Then he's chosen me. And you've already assumed I'll lose."

Venario rolled his eyes. "Of course it's to be you. Was

there any question? You're my champion. The entire Republic cries your name. You were Caesar's first choice."

*Remember who you are*, Mars said. I had a duty, no matter how terrifying my opponent was.

"You've not actually seen this creature, correct?"

"I've seen a drawing of it. I've heard it described, as well as the carnage it causes." He scrubbed at his forehead. "There will be no escaping it."

I crossed my arms in front of my chest. "It had to be captured in the first place. Therefore, it's not invincible."

"The thing supposedly killed half a cohort during its capture, and drove many of the rest mad."

"These soldiers were not Discordians."

My master shrugged. "Hearing this thing described… I can't even imagine it truly exists."

"Perhaps Caesar is having a bit of fun at your expense."

He laughed weakly. "Does he look like the type to have fun?"

I remembered what I saw in the man's gaze. "No, he does not."

Something wasn't right. I looked at my master, who buried his face in his hands once more. He didn't involve me in his politics, never spoke to me about his loyalties. And why should he?

I stepped over to the wall of scrolls and ran my fingers over them. "If the best gladiators of the best *ludi* are killed, those *lanistae* will lose money. Reputations. Power."

My master looked up at me and gestured impatiently with his hands. "Yes, that's what I've already said."

I narrowed my eyes and looked at him in a new way. Not

my master, not as Gaius Venario the *lanista.* But as Gaius Venrario, the threat to Caesar.

*Remember who you are.*

I was Discordian.

"Caesar wants to ruin you," I said. "And he wants to ruin others like you. Publicly."

With those words, all outward anger and annoyance fled my master's eyes. It was replaced by a shrewd focus, something I'd only ever seen when he spoke to his peers. I took heart from this and continued.

"The shows, the arena, these things have power over the people. If Caesar shows he has power over them, he gains respect. But that's just the surface. I think Caesar believes you're a threat."

Venario tented his fingers and leaned his chin on them. He didn't seem surprised by my words, nor did he deny their truth.

"Go on," he said. "Cautiously."

"You have power over the people as long as you have gladiators who will put on a good show," I said. "But with those gladiators you also have an army of men at your command. Powerful fighting men. If you were to combine forces with other *lanistae*, as well as the rest of Caesar's enemies, whatever leader commanded your loyalty could be unstoppable. Caesar would be a blind fool if he didn't see this."

"And Caesar didn't get to where he is today by being a blind fool. The fact that he wants to wipe out our most popular gladiators with this new monster..."

"It would even things out a bit for him."

Venario rubbed his temples. "Are you making me paranoid, Discordian? What you say makes sense. Yet, why couldn't they just be games? He's had them before."

“Look at who else he invites to the spectacle. Look where their allegiances lie. If you see someone who is a strong Caesarian, then you may doubt me. If all you see are people who oppose him, perhaps question his motives. When going into an arena, it is always best to know exactly who and what you are fighting, *ne*?”

“That bastard. I can’t afford to lose you, and he knows it. He must be hearing rumors.” He visibly thought for a moment, his expression becoming even more serious than before. “*Mehercules*, I think you’re right.”

My cheeks burned with a heat unrelated to the temperature of the room. “You speak as if I’ve already lost. I’ve beaten impossible odds before. That’s how I came to be your champion. You can’t tell me there’s no hope.” I pounded on the desk with my fist. “I won’t accept that.”

Venerio leapt from his seat. A loud crack sounded off the plaster walls of the *tablinum*. It took me a moment to realize he’d slapped me. Again, he struck, and again, with what must have been all his might. I made a show of stretching my jaw and blinking. It would take more than the palm of a pudgy, pink Roman to do me harm, but I let him get his frustration out.

He panted as much as I might have after a harsh training session. His eyes held a challenge, though he knew I wouldn’t retaliate. I allowed him his triumph, hollow as it was. He was the only one in the world allowed to strike me without fear for his life. He was also my weakest opponent. I could kill him in a heartbeat. But why hand Caesar his prize so easily?

**JUST AFTER THE CALENDS OF** the month, I stood upon the sand behind the gate of the Circus Maximus. I’d been there before, peering out at races and giant spectacles involving rare animals from around the world, usually fighting gladiators. I'd always been an alternate, however. I should have felt proud to finally be featured in such a place, in front of the eyes of the best men of Rome. Instead, trepidation wormed its way through my entire body.

The crowd chanted and cheered, excited for what was to come. Caesar kept the thing we were fighting a great secret, only calling it a monster of legend. Romans loved a good show and clamored for any chance to see bloody sports in their arenas. This would be an audience to rival all others.

"There are only six of us," one of the gladiators beside me said. "How bad could this beast be?"

"Pompey had a bunch of fighters face twenty elephants in here," one of the others said.

"Silence," the gladiator closest to the gate snapped. "Stay focused."

The stench of unwashed bodies and anxious sweat made my stomach cramp. I forced myself to be calm. Sweaty palms would only make my trident slip.

I'd met three of the five others in the arena before, and had bested them all. The other two didn't seem remarkable, but I knew there was no room for complacency in the arena. That would only get a person killed.

When the ground shook, when the walls of the building shuddered, we had our first indication of what we might be facing. Then the thing unleashed a roar.

It wasn't the sound so much as the feeling, a vibration in my chest that shook me to my core. A couple of the men cried out. Were these the champions of their *ludi*?

*Mars, hear me*, I said. *I henceforth dedicate my life to your purpose, to do with as you may. Let me beat this creature. Let me stand in glory, and let your enemy, darling of Venus, suffer the pains of defeat by my actions in your name.*

As soon as I finished, the doors opened, and all Hades broke loose.

Instead of using caution, the men ran out as if they were going to face other gladiators. Idiots. Then one man turned.

"There's to be only one winner, and it shall be me. I'll give whoever wants it a quick death before we even face that creature. Who shall be the first to feel my blade?"

Before conscious thought could even take root in my brain, I thrust my trident out with lightning speed. He looked down at the weapon in his gut with surprise, his open mouth letting his last breath escape.

The others turned on me instantly, as if I were the one threatening their lives.

"We can't fight against each other now," I said. "That can come later, if any of us are left. We need to face the creature first, together. Then the winner shall be decided."

The men all stared at me warily, but slowly each of them nodded. I pulled my trident from the gladiator's guts, spat on him, and proceeded forward to pay my respects to Caesar, as should have been done in the first place. This was no way to win favor with the gods.

The dictator yelled some words for the crowd, which we, of course, could not hear. Suddenly, an unearthly sound came from beyond a huge gate in the side of the arena, next to the one from which we had emerged. All of us turned to face it. Caesar couldn't blame us for being disrespectful to him. It was his beast, after all.

I breathed slowly. My net was hooked in my belt, where I could pull it free in an instant. My trident was sharp and had already tasted blood. I lived in that moment. I didn't know if I'd live for another.

The gate shook as the thing on the other side rammed into it. Then it exploded, splinters of wood flying all the way across the arena from the force of the impact. That thing, that… horror, sprang forward, its clawed feet buried in the sand when it landed. For a moment, my entire world was teeth as it opened its mouth and roared.

It was indeed a thing from legend. From a nightmare, yet not one of my own. My mind wasn't capable of imagining such a shimmering, writhing monstrosity. It was a perfect combination of things known, yet impossible. It loomed before us, eclipsing all else.

"*Dei immortales*," one of the gladiators said with a gasp. "What is that?"

I realized I'd stopped breathing. "Chimera," I said, my voice croaking. "Of some sort."

Perhaps my eyes deceived me. Maybe the heat from the sun played tricks on my mind. I'd seen lions before in the arena, fought them, and won. I bore scars from the experience. This was no ordinary lion.

Instead of fur, its body was plated in white scales, which glistened iridescently in the sunlight. It did have a mane, of sorts: a fringe of purple tentacles writhed around its feline head. Its tail curved upward and over its back, almost like a scorpion's. It took me a moment to realize it was no ordinary tail.

A snake peered back at me from its tip, its eyes holding an intelligence to rival most humans'.

"Don't look at the snake," I said, feeling myself swaying the longer I was trapped by its gaze. I jabbed my sandaled foot with the end of my trident, the dull pain breaking the beast's spell. "It will hypnotize you."

One of the gladiators vomited on the sand beside me. The action attracted the monster, and it charged, a white flash against the golden sand. I leapt to the side, not backward, colliding with one of the men, and we landed in a heap. But I knew the monster would be going for the other man and wanted to be as far from its path as possible.

The man in its path disappeared into the maw of the beast. He didn't have time enough to scream. The monster shook its prey and sprayed us with his blood before gulping it down, all the while watching us.

Four of us remained.

"We have to split up," the fair-haired man under me said. I could barely hear him over the roar of the crowd. "Run in all directions, surround it. Confuse it so it doesn't know where to strike next."

He was right. I rolled off him, never looking away from the creature. The thing stood twice the height of a man at its shoulders. Pompey's elephants were one thing. They weren't starved carnivores. They were large and angry, violent, tusked, but this… this was another matter entirely.

"I agree," I said. "I'll go to the back, distract it while you three get into position. I'm the fastest," I added, when the fair gladiator looked at me quizzically. "You'd all just die."

With that, I gripped my trident and ran, trusting, perhaps

foolishly, that the others would do the same. I gave the thing as wide of berth as I could, always keeping it in sight. I'd wait until it had someone in its sight, wait until it charged them and was fully engaged, and then I'd strike. And I'd strike true. For I could not lose to this thing. I would not allow Caesar that glory.

Besides, no one expected us to leave this arena alive. What sort of Discordian was ever content to let things go as people planned?

As the other three gladiators took position around the beast, it looked from one to the other. Myself and the fair gladiator closed in a bit from behind, not too close, but close enough to attack when the beast struck.

And strike it did.

This animal might have had the appearance of a lion, but it didn't behave like one. It attacked with fearless, reckless abandon, like a creature who knew it had no match. It thought nothing of a counter attack. When it lunged forward, so did I, slashing at its hindquarters with my trident, hoping to hamstring it, or at least slow it down. I was thankful my partner on the other side had a similar idea, and the skill and experience to see it through.

My first slash made contact, but the blades of my trident merely slid across the surface of those cursed white scales. I immediately retreated before the creature could react to what must have equated to a gentle caress.

"Pierce it!" I screamed, hoping I would be heard over the roaring of the beast and the screaming of the crowd. "Slashing is useless, you must pierce it under its scales!"

The monster faced me, as I knew it would. Its jaw dripped

with blood from its second victim. It was making quick work of us. I ran before it could lunge—toward the beast, yet across its path. Using every instinct, I leaped just before it struck and twirled my trident as I flew past it. I felt my weapon impact, felt the spatter of blood, and heard the sickening wet flop of several tentacles onto the ground. I landed on the sand and rolled so I stood once more. The beast gave a shriek I expected the gods to have heard on Olympus.

Then another shriek sounded, and I realized it came from me.

Where the blood had hit my leg, the skin bubbled and blistered in burns such as I had never felt before. Without even knowing where the idea came from, I grabbed a handful of sand and clapped it to my leg. I rubbed it until my leg was dry, the acid-blood coming off with the sand. The pain distracted me, however, and I could not afford that.

When I looked up, my fair-haired partner was caught in the monster's tentacles. He twitched and squirmed as much as they writhed and squeezed. He provided the distraction I needed. I ignored the pain in my leg and charged at the beast from behind once more, this time with the points of my trident. I stabbed upward to get under the scales and found my mark. Then with all my strength, I pulled the weapon from the beast and avoided the blue blood that spurted from the wound.

The Furies themselves inhabited the creature's roar. I barely saw a flash before moving, and realized I'd just missed being struck by the thing's vicious tail. I slashed at it, but it moved too fast. My breath burned in my chest as I ran away from it with everything I had before it could claim me as its next victim.

With only two of us left in the arena, our previous plan

wouldn't work. I ignored the voice in my head that told me survival was impossible. I'd given the creature a limp, after all. A couple more strikes like that would surely slow it down and provide an opening for the kill. But first there had to be an opportunity for those strikes.

After running and dodging strikes from the creature, I finally came across the other remaining gladiator, who was nursing a severe slash to his arm.

"Come on, we have to—"

Before I could finish speaking, horns sounded. I didn't dare look to see what was happening, knowing as soon as I looked away, I'd be dead. The beast, however, did not have such concerns about us. We were as insects to it. It turned to face the balcony seats where Caesar sat, where the horns were sounding. As it turned, I made a move to strike, but then was grabbed by the arm by someone behind me. I spun with my teeth bared, ready to kill whoever it was.

I came face to face with a terrified slave who had all but wet his tunic. My blood-lust raged, and I almost cast him aside before he quickly said, "A reprieve, to regroup and tend to your wounds. Swiftly!"

He didn't have to tell me twice. I grabbed his arm, bolted, and saw the other gladiator bolt as well. He wasn't so considerate of his slave, however. The poor man fell behind. I didn't think of what that meant for him. For us, it meant a diversion standing between us and that beast. When I came to the gate, I dove into the space beyond, and lay where I landed on the cool hard ground. My breath came in ragged gasps.

Barely a second later, the other gladiator tumbled in, followed by the clawed forepaw of the beast, swiping and reaching for its prey like a cat with a mouse.

"What game is this?" I asked hoarsely. "Since when do we get a break from fighting?"

"Perhaps Caesar wants to prolong the inevitable," the other gladiator said, wincing as he flexed his arm. It was his right arm, his sword arm. He was all but useless now, and he knew it.

The *medicus* came and looked to our wounds. Slaves brought us cups of water. I drank, but my stomach immediately seized.

Something was happening out in the arena. The creature seemed to be occupied with some new toy or other, at any rate. Neither of us peeked out, knowing we'd see soon enough.

"When we go out..." the other gladiator said, "I'll go straight for it. You follow me. I'll leap into the thing's mouth and as soon as its head is up, stab it in the throat."

"What?" I said.

"I'm done. You know it. I know it. I can't fight like this. I'm worthless, except as bait." He snorted. "My master said this was all a ploy for Caesar to kill his political opponents without actually killing them. Killing their reputations, their careers, by taking away what makes them great. Looks like he was right."

"My master agrees," I replied.

His plan was decent, if we were fighting lions or other animals we were accustomed to. It wouldn't work with this beast. I didn't tell him, however. I'd let him believe he would die a noble death of sacrifice.

My breath slowed, but as the rush of battle faded, my limbs felt heavy and tired. Was this Caesar's plan?

"Bubo..."

A woman's voice called out as if in a dream, echoing unnaturally through the arena and into our hiding space beyond. What further madness was this? My fellow gladiator bolted to his feet.

"Bubo, I've missed you. I've wanted to visit you so many times..."

"Don't," I said, rising myself. "Don't go through that gate."

"My wife," he said, wide eyes staring at the leather flap that separated us from the arena. "That's my wife."

"The only things beyond that door are the monster and those it's killed. If your wife is indeed out there, do you think she'd last long even if you went to rescue her? Four other highly trained fighters met their deaths out there."

"One by human hands, not the beast's," he said, as if it made a big difference. "We have children."

His voice cracked. I didn't mean to be heartless. He was just a man. I knew men had their weaknesses, men loved. I wished at times I were capable of such things. But Bubo was all there was left. I had no idea how I would defeat the beast on my own.

"I got a letter last week saying she disappeared. Just vanished off the street. How could she have ended up here?"

I'd heard the voice, too, so he wasn't hearing things. Yet it was too loud, too... *invasive* to be a normal human voice. Venario had mentioned people driven to madness because of the beast. I'd assumed it was from fear, but now, I wasn't so certain.

Bubo reached for the gate. I grabbed at his arm, but he snatched it from my grasp.

"Only one of us can win, right?" he said. "I have to see what's over there. If she dies by that beast, then I will welcome the afterlife by her side."

"How can only one of us beat that thing? It's impossible!" My voice had a frantic note to it, but I couldn't bring myself to be ashamed. I couldn't imagine feeling any differently, facing that thing.

"I have to help my wife. I have to save her."

With that, he jerked away and swept the leather flap aside, disappearing behind it.

There was no question. I had to use his action to my advantage. The gods remained silent. I had to keep my wits and use every possible chance that came my way.

"Bubo," the voice said again, at the same time there was a sound like Bubo crying out. Perhaps it was my imagination, because a moment later, he spoke.

"Stella, what are you doing here? How did you get here?" There was a pause, and then he said, "Why is it so dark?"

She answered him, but I couldn't make out the words. They must have been close together.

Bubo said it was dark. How? The mid-day sun streamed in around the leather flap. Part of me wanted to peek out, but I didn't want to attract the beast's attention. If somehow the presence of Bubo and his wife escaped its notice, I didn't want to be responsible for calling it. Yet, how could Bubo not see it? Why didn't he just grab his wife and return to safety?

Before I could even begin to consider answers, Bubo let out a scream, a blood-curdling, inhuman sound that didn't just echo of pain or fear, but heartbreak as well. The soul-rending noise shook me more than the roar of the beast. But something else shook me more.

I was alone, now. And time was running out. I couldn't

hide behind a leather flap forever.

I took a deep breath and put my hand to the flap. I clutched my trident, and a strange calm washed over me. I would not escape this time. My blood would water the sand of the arena, added to that of hundreds of gladiators who died before me. But I would die a warrior's death, a death to make Mars and Discordia proud.

I pushed the flap aside, and the bright sun dazzled my eyes. Then a sharp pain bit into my shoulder. I gave a weak cry and clutched the wound, but the pain disappeared. I opened my eyes, though I didn't remember closing them.

"Mama," a voice said. A familiar voice. A voice I had never even dared hope to hear again.

Out of the darkness stepped a girl. My girl. My dark skinned, ebony haired child, who'd been ripped from my arms those years before.

"Mama, you came. You came for me."

"Of course I did," I said, if for no other reason than to buy time.

She walked closer, still wearing the same tunica she'd worn when last I saw her. The sight of her was a blow to the heart. A heart I'd all but forgotten I had.

"Dear child," I said. "I'm sorry. I'm so sorry. I should have protected you. I should have killed them all."

She shook her head. "You did protect me. You could have gotten away. You stayed for me."

*Stayed for her.*

The child stepped closer still. Something tickled my ankle, but it barely registered. Only my daughter walking toward me mattered.

*Walking.*

I fought a battle in my mind. A far away part of me raged and fought, but I *wanted* this.

*Walking.*

*Caesar.* The single word was hissed not in the voice of my thoughts, but in that which I heard only in my darkest moments. The voice of my mother.

I looked at my beautiful daughter, my impossible daughter.

"I'm here, my daughter," I said, gripping my trident. "Come to Mama."

I help my arms out, and the child ran—*ran* toward them. At the very moment my arms, my whole body and soul screamed to embrace her, I brought the trident up and thrust it with all my might.

A mighty roar split the heavens, and pain followed, flowing over me, through me. A heavy weight slumped upon me and I couldn't move, couldn't think.

Death. Where was my death?

*Drink,* a voice commanded, a voice I dared not defy. *Drink.*

I drank the pain that threatened to drown me. The sun returned to the sky, the sand of the arena turned to blue mud under me. I could not discern the rushing of blood in my ears from the screaming of the crowd. Perhaps they were one in the same. Still, I knew my duty as a gladiator.

I raised my arm to the crowd even as I lay there. My trident gleamed blue with blood where it emerged through the top of the beast's skull.

I was victorious.

**A WEEK PASSED IN A** burning haze of pain. Venario ordered me to rest, to recover as quickly as I could.

I didn't see the *ludus* around me. I didn't see the other gladiators' concerned faces or hear their congratulations. I saw only one thing.

My daughter's face when I stabbed her through the heart.

I healed faster than anyone expected. While others attributed this to the gods, I knew it was my raw hatred that made me stronger. Strong enough to make Caesar pay.

During my few hours of consciousness, Venario explained what had happened in the arena. The pain I felt after stepping from behind the leather curtain was the bite from the beast's snake-tail. Caesar had told him the snake spoke with the voices of its last victims, which the crowd had watched the beast devour in the moments before Bubo and I had come out.

"Disgusting," Venario said. "Monstrous. And he had the gall to tell the crowd they were prisoners. No one cared who they were, of course. Blood thirsty animals."

The poison from the snake's bite made us hallucinate. Hearing the voices of our loved ones, our poisoned minds made us see them, too. Or see what the beast wanted us to see.

That was its fatal mistake.

"My girl ran to me in the arena," I told Venario when he asked. "She couldn't run. She was born with a twisted foot. That's how I was caught by the Romans. I stayed with her because she couldn't run. Somehow it was all warped in my vision. Perhaps the gods intervened, as they did when they made me drink the blood as the antidote to the venom."

There was a party. Of course there was a party, and Caesar demanded I come, to parade me around like a trophy. It was easy for him to pretend his spectacle was to show off Rome's wonderful gladiators, that he was proud the beast could be bested by another of Rome's curiosities, a real Discordian.

I didn't greet him as one would a gracious host. I didn't even greet him as I would the dictator of Rome. I looked him in the eye, and asked,

"Was my daughter well when you found her?"

He didn't seem surprised by my question. His expression didn't shift in the slightest. "She was in a brothel. I saw it as a kindness, really. I believe if you could have seen her, you would understand."

There were knives everywhere. Fine glass cups; I'd only need a shard. I was the best gladiator in Rome. I didn't need much to end the life of this man, this monster, who thought so little of the lives of innocents. Bubo's wife, my daughter. With rage as my fuel, my bare hands would be sufficient to snuff out the life of this tyrant.

I inhaled, gathered my focus, and stepped forward.

*Stay your hand, Discordian.* Mars suddenly made himself known. After all of this, he spoke to save the life of a monster?

*It is not your place to decide this. Serve your purpose.*

The battled that waged within me seemed endless, yet it was over in a breath. Quelling my fury took as great an effort as besting that creature in the arena, but I prevailed.

I looked at Caesar, and simply nodded. "I only hope someday, someone can be equally kind to you."

The room fell silent at this. Someone gave a nervous laugh. But Caesar... Caesar didn't laugh.

His dark calculating eyes did not betray his thoughts, but he must have felt no small amount of bitterness toward Venario. His bid to render my master powerless had failed.

Yet I knew we hadn't seen the last attempt to seize power from his opponents. Power was far too important to him.

"I would keep an eye on that one, Venario. Perhaps I should make an offer to buy her from you."

"I'm sorry, Caesar, but no *lanista* in his right mind would part with such a gladiator. Every day she proves her worth more. I must thank you, truly, for giving her a chance to show off her skill in such a way. I see golden days ahead for my *ludus*. Golden days, indeed."

"Well deserved, to be sure," Caesar said. "Though I admit, I feel the loss of such a great creature. Finding another will indeed be a challenge. Now, if you'll excuse me, I must make the rounds and give my regards to my other guests. But I'll be watching your career in the arena with great interest, Canna. And yours, Venario. Perhaps someday, my soldiers will capture another beast for you to fight. One that will prove a more formidable opponent."

"We look forward to that day, of course," my master said in a strained voice. "I hope we shall continue to please you, Caesar."

As Caesar walked away, he whispered something hastily to his secretary slave, who followed him like a dog. His expression was sharp, but as soon as he came across someone else, he was all smiles once more. I watched him make his way around the room, aware of a presence at my side. I turned to see the thin man who had watched me from the balcony alongside Caesar and my master, that day a lifetime ago. I'd heard Caesar refer to him as Brutus, his dear friend.

"We don't often see gladiators at our parties," he said. "Your wounds are not too grievous, I hope?"

"Nothing I won't recover from, *Domine*," I said. I glanced over at Caesar, who now laughed with some other men. I felt a familiar tingle along my spine, a warmth in my cheeks. *Inspiration*. "Caesar makes a fine king, does he not?"

At this, Brutus let out a chortle. "Oh, no. No, he's not king. Rome is a republic. We have no kings."

Brutus's eyes were on Caesar, however, and therefore he didn't miss the way people bowed to him, the way people deferred to him as he went around the room.

"Caesar has taken up the mantle of dictator—*legal* dictator—just while Rome needs him," he continued. "He'll relinquish power when his term is done, when we've recovered from the civil war. He's promised."

*Watch.*

*Listen.*

*Wield men like weapons, to carry out our will.*

"Caesar has always proven he can be relied upon to relinquish power, has he?" I asked. "A rare man indeed. But then, why was there a war in the first place?"

"Caesar overstepped..." A crease formed between Brutus's eyes as he considered my words.

"That's the good thing about a republic, though, isn't it?" I said in a softer voice. "So many people care about the city's wellbeing. So many noble people defend it."

He turned to look at me, but I'd already started across the room to join my master. My seeds of discord had been planted.

Let them be watered with blood.

# MAUI'S HOOK

LEE MURRAY

**THE BOAT SKIMMED ACROSS LAKE** Taupō. Marie gripped the fibreglass side, her heart pounding in time with the thumping hull. It was exhilarating. Glorious!

And at 6 a.m., they had the entire lake to themselves, her husband having insised on picking up the keys from the boat hire people the night before.

"Lived half my life in and around boats," Matthew had told the girl on the desk. Technically, it was true. They could *see* boats moored in the marina from their Florida apartment.

"How hard can it be?" he'd told Marie. "You gonna tell me these Kiwis drive their boats on the left, too?"

As it turned out, he wasn't too bad a skipper, manoeuvring them out of the marina and across the lake to Mine Bay without any trouble.

"So where is this place?" Matthew called from the driver's seat.

FBW2018

Marie checked the guidebook for the location of the rock carvings, which were only visible from the water. "I think they're over there, to the right."

Matthew brought the boat around, the wash sending spray across the lake's mirrored surface. The vessel rocked a moment, riding the swell of its own making before coming to rest in the little bay.

"Matthew Barbeler," Marie scolded, but she stopped when she saw the carvings. She sucked in her breath. Rising from the lake and etched into the grey volcanic rock, they were as high as a second-floor balcony.

"I'll bet these carvings have been here for centuries," Matthew said. Bracing himself against the rocking boat, he lined up his smartphone for a photo.

"Hmm. Those centuries only go back as far as 1976," Marie replied. "The sculptors were led by a local man called Matahi Whakataka-Brightwell. The face carved into the rock is his ancestor. Guy called Ngātoroirangi." She stumbled over the Māori pronunciation.

"Hey, Marie. Get over there on that little outcrop, and I'll take a picture."

Marie hesitated. In the muted dawn light, the raw beauty of the primitive design made her uneasy.

What the heck! They were here for an adventure. "Can you get a bit closer?"

Matthew manoeuvred the boat closer to the ledge and Marie dropped one leg over the side. "Hold it steady." She giggled. It took a couple of goes to clamber out, but eventually she was teetering on the outcrop.

Matthew puttered away. "I want to get the whole carving

in," he called. He held up his phone and snapped off a few pics. "Smile!"

All at once the water foamed white, the surface roiling.

"Matthew!" Marie called. "What's happening?"

Matthew grabbed the steering wheel. "It'll be an underwater geyser. This whole place is a geothermal hotspot."

"Well, come and get me."

"Can't. If we overturn the boat, we'll be stuck with the excess on the insurance. We'll let it grumble a bit and I'll come back when it's died down."

"What if it hits me?"

He wasn't listening, already moving away from the simmering water. Marie hugged the steep rock face while the lake boiled and spat. There was nowhere to go. "Matthew, I don't like this."

"It'll be fine—" Matthew broke off, his face contorted as a creature, a monster, emerged from the water, lake-weed sluicing from shoulders as wide as a truck.

Marie blinked in disbelief. Her heart skipped a beat.

*Omigod! What the hell is that?*

As high as the rock face, its form was vaguely human, only it was fleshless, with cruel shark-like jaws. The limbs and torso of solid bone were smeared with blood. Narrow white eyes scanned the water.

Her knees sagging, Marie shrunk against the rock.

Matthew's face was a rictus of fear. He revved the outboard.

What was he doing? Abandoning her to the monster? But the noise alerted the creature and, oozing blood, it surged forward. The boat rocked violently. In just two steps, the creature blocked the little craft.

Frantic, Matthew backed up, the motor screaming.

Reverse. Forward. Throttle.

Marie had to admit he was an incredible skipper, turning the boat on a dime and scooting away.

*Don't you leave me here, you bastard!*

The monster slammed a bony limb down on the boat, breaking the vessel in two as if it were nothing more than a toothpick. The crack of the hull echoed off the rocks and Matthew plunged into the water. He swam for his life, arms and legs churning. Almost nonchalant, the monster picked him out of the lake, its bony, bloodied claws flinging him wide.

*Ohmigod!*

Marie didn't dare scream.

Surfacing, Matthew swam again. Marie held her breath. Within seconds, the monster was looming over him, grabbing him up and slapping him bodily on the surface of the water. The sound was chilling, like a walnut hitting concrete. It was playing with him, flaying him, the way a seal flays a penguin. Marie marvelled Matthew could still scream, so little flesh remained.

When the monster crammed the ragged remains of her husband into its toothy maw, Marie could only whimper.

It turned.

She scrambled, hot urine running down her legs, fingernails tearing and knees scraping as she tried to climb up, get a foothold, get away!

*Help!*

She clutched at the slippery rock, slipped, and climbed again, desperate to evade those grasping claws. Hurry! She glanced back. Her stomach dropped.

The swell gathering around it, the creature surged towards her. Mercifully, the wave hit her first, blood and water blurring her view as the monster's teeth punctured her back. If only it could have spared her the sound of her spine cracking…

**BEFORE LOCKING THE BOATSHED, AWHINA** glanced across Lake Taupō. Cradled in its caldera of grey-green mountains, the lake was calm. There was no sign of those tourists who'd insisted on an early start. She'd expected them to return the boat hours ago. Probably stayed over in one of the bays. Awhina imagined they'd ditch the boat tomorrow to avoid paying the late return penalties. She sighed. People never would have dared to do that when her dad and Granddad Koro were running the boat hire.

Well, she didn't have time to wait for tardy tourists. Setting the alarm code, she clicked the screen door padlock and gave it a tug to check it was closed. There'd been a spate of vandalism recently—someone smashing up boat houses on the lake's edge and getting into the boats—and Awhina didn't need the disruption.

She pressed the door opener of her car key as she crossed the carpark, the car lights flashing in recognition.

"Awhina!" Andrew Thurston was making his way to his car. He was new to town this summer, working as a pilot for the heli-adventure tour company. "You're here late."

"Waiting on a return that didn't eventuate."

"Welcome to the hospitality business, eh?"

"Tell me about it."

"Stolen?"

Awhina didn't think so. In the first instance, the

Americans didn't have a trailer to pull it, and even if they were able to get one, what were they going to do with the boat? Take it back on the plane to Florida? "No," she said, shaking her head. "Probably just dumped it somewhere."

"Well, there were only so many places they could leave it. If you like, I could keep my eye out for it when I take the bird up tomorrow."

"That'd be cool, thanks."

Andrew scuffed his foot on the curb, kicking up gravel. "You have time to head across the road for a drink?"

Awhina hesitated. He was nice. She liked him. And unlike most of the blokes around here, she hadn't done her primary school swimming lessons with him or played netball with his sister. But she'd promised she'd pop to out to Rainbow Point tonight. "I really should go to the rest home to visit my granddad."

Andrew nodded. "Sure. No worries. Some other time." He turned to go, his shoulders slumped.

"Maybe I could meet you afterwards?"

His brown eyes lit up. "Yeah? That'd be great. If you text me, I'll let you know where I am." They exchanged phone numbers, and Awhina pulled out of the park, but not before taking a last look down the mouth of the Waikato River to the lake.

**JUDE FREER TURNED OFF STATE** Highway One into Hatepe and slowed for the speed bump meant to deter the hordes of sightseers from entering the village. Hordes? Chance would be a fine thing. The perfect spot for quiet holidays, the agent had said all those years ago, and she was right. Even now, there wasn't a single shop in the village, just a hundred holiday homes sited for the sun and views of the lake. Which meant taking trips into Taupō any time you ran out of milk. Jude didn't mind too much; if she was honest there was only so much reading a person could stand, but, despite the lack of excitement, Phil and the kids loved it here. This was their eleventh summer holidaying on the lake.

She pulled into the rear of the lakeside cottage as a shadow passed over the house. Rain maybe? Looked like she was in for some more reading. She was getting the groceries out of the back seat when Phil came careering out the back door, the toddler in his arms, Bella and Jordan running after him.

"Get back in the car!"

"But I only just—"

"Get in the fucking car, Jude. Jesus!"

Dropping the groceries, she got in the back seat. Phil thrust Robbie at her, leaving Jude to fasten him into his car seat.

"Jordan, get in the front."

*Does he have to snap at the boy?*

Jude fumbled with baby's seat belt. "Phil, what's going on?"

A long sharp creak put Jude's teeth on edge. She craned her neck. A falling tree? Which direction was it coming from?

"Fuck!" Phil reversed, then zoomed forward, just as the back wall of the neighbours' bach collapsed outwards, the corrugated iron roof skewing sideways and off.

It was going to slice the top off the car!

Phil braked, throwing them forward. Jude hadn't had time to get her own seatbelt on. Her face struck the front seat and she came up, her eyes watering and her nose pumping blood.

Shit, that was a close call. Another metre and the roof might have decapitated them all.

Bella screamed as a shadow came into view.

Every hair on Jude's body stood on end. What the fuck was that? It looked like something out of a Halloween Amusement Park. Spliced from gristle and bone, the creature towered above the pile of timber, glass and iron. It was dripping blood. So much blood. *Who's blood?* The slanted white eyes turned their way, and Jude didn't care so long as it wasn't theirs. "Phil, go!"

Spinning the steering wheel, he gunned the engine, cutting across the empty corner section and onto the road.

Jude scrambled for her seatbelt.

The thing was on the move. It clambered over the collapsed bach, long clawed limbs extended. *Reaching for them!* It grabbed the back bumper, tearing it half off the car, then thrust a bloodied limb through the back window grasping at the head rests. Glass sprayed across the seats. Bella shrieked. Jude threw her body over Robbie, but she could do nothing for her daughter.

A bony, fleshless, limb patted the back of the seat. Jude shuddered. It was looking for her baby girl. And it was going to find her. "Phil!"

He put his foot to the floor. The wheels spun and the car lurched forward.

*The speed bump!*

It was too late to slow. The car flew forward, up on two wheels, and flipped sideways heading for a ditch. Everyone screamed. Jude waited to die. But sliding along the length of the sandy ditch, the car slowed and righted itself. Phil didn't waste any time, engaging his inner boy-racer to get them the hell out of there, as if he'd planned for it all along.

Jude glanced back at Hatepe. People were running out of their houses, looking for the source of the commotion.

*No, no, no. Go back inside!*

The people veered the minute they saw it, but it was like a monkey searching for fleas. Scooping up three people in its skeletal claws, it separated a figure out, and stuffed it in its mouth. Blood trickled from its jaws and mingled with its own bloody slick.

*Omigod, it ate someone!*

Horrified, Jude couldn't look away. The creature flung the other two people away. One, a woman, landed in a tree, her sun-browned bare limbs contorted grotesquely. The second thudded on the hood of their car, the windscreen shattering in place, broken pixels obscuring the road.

Jude screamed.

Phil slowed but didn't stop. Jude felt rather than saw the broken body slide away. One hand on the wheel, her husband used his metal coffee cup to smash out the shattered glass. "Cover your face, Jordan," he yelled.

For once, Jordan didn't argue. The way was clear. Phil put his foot on the gas. Through the broken windscreen, the wind hit them full in the face. No one complained.

Fifteen minutes later, Jude's heart was still on overdrive when Phil pulled in to a rest area just before Taupō at Four Mile Bay. He checked the rear vision mirror.

"I can't see anything," Jude reassured him. Phil got out of the car and removed the dragging torn-off bumper, while Jude picked pieces of glass out of the baby's car seat. She used the corner of his blanket to stem her nosebleed. Bella and Jordan were quiet.

When Phil was back in the driver's seat, she said, "We've got to call the authorities and tell them what's happening."

Phil shook his head. "What the hell *is* happening, Jude? What was that thing?"

His face like cement, Jordan twisted in his seat, "It came out of the lake, Mum. I saw it. There were men fishing in the water. They were wearing waders…" His voice trailed off.

"When I saw…" Phil's voice cracked. "I just got the kids and ran."

Leaning forward as far as her seatbelt would allow, Jude squeezed her husband's shoulder. "You did the right thing. Who knows what might have happened?"

She wondered what had happened to their neighbours. The Mackies had been packing up to leave today because Lila was due back to work tomorrow. Had Jude seen their Hyundai when she'd pulled in? Were they still at the bach when the creature attacked? She recalled the shadow, the creaking of the building as it fell, and, through the windscreen, blood streaming down bone.

Phil could probably tell her, but Jude couldn't bring herself to ask.

**AT RAINBOW RESTCARE, AWHINA SIGNED** herself in, then shot some antibacterial gel into her palm from the container on the desk, rubbing it in on the way to Koro's room. He'd been here almost a year, a necessity really. Dementia. Not Alzheimer's—there weren't any plaques on his brain, but the end result was the same. Thirteen years from start to finish, they said, depending on how aggressive the disease was. It hadn't been so bad when he was just forgetting the bathwater and flooding the house, but the stove was another matter. When the fire service had been called out twice, it'd been time to pack up the house and call it a day. At least he had a lovely room here overlooking the lake.

"Hey Koro."

Her grandfather stood at the window, his forehead pressed against the glass. He looked up, his expression strangely lucid. "Hello, Awhina." He remembered her name! But almost immediately, he turned back to the window, his eyes fixed on the lake. "Have you come to get me out of here? I need to get out," he whispered, his breath fogging the glass. Not so lucid, then. He still believed he was in prison. Some days Awhina felt like his jailor, keeping him here when all he wanted was to be back in a boat, back on the lake. Before his diagnosis, when he was still working at the hire shop, he used to take a boat out every day.

"He's been at that window since this morning, pacing back and forth," said a voice from behind her. Awhina turned. Katrina Varisi, the health care assistant, was leaning in the doorway. Awhina knew Katrina well; a lifetime ago they'd had shared a desk at Taupō-nui-a-Tia College. It'd been a relief to find a familiar face working here.

Because putting Koro in care had been just as hard for Awhina as it was for him.

Entering the room, Katrina faffed about, tidying the bed. "Something's been bothering you today, hasn't it, Mr Te Heu Heu?" she said. Koro continued to stare out the window. "You wouldn't eat your lunch. Been doing a lot of mumbling about tipua."

"Demons?"

Katrina smoothed the bedclothes, leaning closer to Awhina so Koro couldn't hear. "It might be nothing. Most likely it'll be all over tomorrow and he'll be back to his old self. It's the progression of the disease: these ups and downs."

Awhina frowned. "But demons? You don't think someone's mistreated him, do you?"

"Here? Of course not! Everyone loves your granddad here—the staff and the residents. It's not the first time he's mentioned tipua since he joined us. I wonder if it's his way of interpreting his confusion."

Awhina nodded. "Maybe." Stepping away from the bed, she tucked her arm under her grandfather's. He was mumbling again. Chanting in Māori. He'd been doing that more and more lately, reverting to the old tales and language of his youth—apparently this sort of thing was normal in dementia sufferers. "What's that, Koro?"

He murmured something. Awhina's Māori was pretty sad, but she recognised a few words: lake, demon, sacred, and a name, Māui… That last one wasn't so surprising. The crater lake was said to have been created by Māui's fishhook, which the demi-god had fashioned from his grandmother's jawbone and baited with his own blood. The lake bed was the place where that mighty hook had snagged its greatest catch ever: New Zealand's North Island. Naturally, the legend was epic in these parts, retold every day in schools, cafés, and on holiday tours. It was as common as the pumice stone locals collected from the lakeshore.

Katrina sucked in a breath.

Awhina looked up. "Is something wrong?"

Her school friend's eyes were wide. Shoulders trembling, Katrina pointed across the lake. Awhina followed her finger, squinting against the sun on the glass. A swell was rising in the lake. A tsunami. But this wasn't the ocean. How was that even possible? Had there been an earthquake?

Then, from the mountain of water, a monster rose. Awhina felt her jaw drop. Still yards off shore, the massive creature, grotesque and vaguely human, surged north towards the township, water sluicing off bone.

Katrina staggered backwards, sitting heavily on the bed.

"Tipua," Koro said, patting Awhina's hand. "I told you, you needed to let me out."

**"DAD..." JORDAN'S VOICE SHOOK. BELLA** moaned softly.

Jude looked across her daughter towards the lake. Its torso emerging from the water, that fucking monster was striding towards Taupō, pushing a small tidal wave before it.

*Coming this way.*

Jude wanted to scream. It wasn't fair. They'd escaped death once already today. Phil jabbed the ignition and the car roared to life. "Take the northern bypass," Jude shouted. "It's staying near the lake, so maybe if we get away from the water..."

"On it." Phil swerved right heading towards Mount Tauhara and the bypass.

In the back seat, Bella rocked back and forth. Helpless, Jude stroked Robbie's hair.

**"KATRINA, THE RESIDENTS! WE NEED** to get them out of here," Awhina shrieked.

"Omigod." Katrina bit her lip. "I don't know what to do. It's too... I can't..."

Awhina grabbed her by her shoulders. "Katrina, go to the office and get the keys to the minibus. Bring the vehicle out front. Koro and I will round up the residents and meet you there. Can you do that?"

Katrina nodded. "Get the minibus. Yes." A plan in place, she darted away.

Awhina didn't watch her go. Instead, she picked up Koro's alarm clock and used it to smash the glass of the fire alarm. She flicked the switch. Alarms blared.

"Fire drill," Koro shouted. "We better get out, love." He patted her on the shoulder. Awhina almost cried. She glanced out the window. Already the creature had hauled itself onto the shore, tossing aside a catamaran and bowling a hire cabana. At full height, it had to be four storeys tall, maybe more. Suddenly, the air changed, the windows vibrating. Awhina's hair stood on end.

*What the hell?*

Grabbing Koro by the arm, she thought she heard him say, "It's angry," but with all the noise, she couldn't be sure. "Come on," she urged.

The residents were already streaming into the corridor, staff ushering them to the assembly area at the front of the building. Thankfully, only eighteen people lived at the rest home, its intimacy one of the reasons Awhina had chosen it for her grandfather.

"Must be a big fire," Koro said, already forgetting about the monster. Her pulse racing, Awhina wished she could be so lucky.

At the front of the building, residents swirled around the minibus like kids at a tuck shop.

"How many can it take?" Awhina shouted to Katrina over the wail of the fire alarm.

"Sixteen. Including me." It'd be tight.

"I'll take Koro," Awhina said.

Katrina didn't argue.

Awhina was getting Koro's safety belt on, when her phone buzzed. "Awhina, it's Andrew. Are you still at Rainbow Point? You need to get out of there. There's reports… You're not going to believe this, but the reports—"

"They're true," Awhina interrupted. "We saw it on the shore at Wharewaka Point, heading this way. We're leaving just as soon as everyone is loaded up. Can you get to your chopper? A bird's-eye view would help."

"I'm half way there now. Call you back when I'm in the air."

No time for niceties, Awhina cut the call, stuck the phone on the dash, and ran back to the minibus. It was taking an age to load everyone. None of them were disabled, but none of them were young either, and the fire alarm, while effective, had them rattled. It didn't help that some of the staff were fleeing.

"For crying out loud," Awhina said.

"Let them go," Katrina said from inside the van where she was buckling in one of the older residents. "They have families to see to."

"My photos are still in my room," wailed a woman near the front of the bus. "Can someone get my photos?"

"We'll come back for them, Margaret," Katrina said, closing the sliding door. She turned to Awhina, her face pale.

"Where do I take them?"

"I don't know. Inland?"

"There's a sister facility in Rotorua—"

The ground shook. The demon was on the move.

"Go, go go!" Awhina screamed as she ran for her own car. Katrina was already on the move, pulling out of the carpark and onto the road. Awhina dived into her car, the door of her old Hyundai rattling as she slammed it.

Koro turned to her. "I was going to tell you something," he said. "Something important."

"Not right now, Koro," Awhina said. She didn't bother to reverse, just drove over the grass verge. At the highway, she looked left.

*Shit.*

The minibus was already 500 metres away. At the bottom of the hill, it was scooting along the waterfront. Katrina was heading for Control Gate Bridge and the old highway to Rotorua. Going inland, taking the route closest to the lake.

Awhina's chest tightened.

The monster was on the shore. Blood streamed off bone-white flanks as it strode across the sand, making a beeline for the minibus, the largest vehicle on the road. Cars veered for side streets. A man flung himself beneath a park bench.

A bony claw reached for the bus…

Awhina held her breath. The minibus shot forward. At the wheel, Katrina was trying to outrun the monster. How fast could a loaded minibus go? Awhina willed her to make it. *Go!*

Beside Awhina, Koro mumbled an incantation in Māori. If it was meant to soothe her, it wasn't helping! Awhina should really go: turn right onto the highway, take the bypass and get the hell out of here. Only she couldn't bring herself to leave. Her friend was down there.

The monster stamped a gristly foot in front of the vehicle. The minibus skidded, the rear fishtailing.

*Oh God, no.*

Before the bus came to a stop, the monster lunged and picked it up. Just like that. As if the bus didn't weigh a couple of tonnes. It shook the minibus, like a child testing the contents of a gift, and looked inside. What must that bony eye look like, pressed up against the window? Just thinking about it made Awhina tremble.

The bloody creature hiffed the vehicle aside like a petulant toddler with an unwanted toy. The bus sailed through the air and crashed into the water. There was a belly-flop of a splash and then it bobbed on the lake a moment, before it slipped silently under, the surface of the water rolling inwards on itself.

"Katrina! No, no, no…"

The monster charged towards the township.

Awhina watched the lake. *Come on, come on.*

She wanted to race down to the water, dive in and haul them out, but she'd never get there in time. And even if she did, how deep were they? She stared at the surface, her heart in her throat.

*Katrina please. Come on…*

The lake was smooth. There wasn't even the slightest ripple.

Awhina waited, praying for an air pocket that would give Katrina time to smash the back window. There was that movie, the one about people escaping a submerged van and breathing air from the tyres…

The emergency sirens screamed; the town's civil defence operation finally getting wind of the threat. Whatever they did, it'd be too late for the holidaymakers in the third-floor balcony room of a lakeside hotel. The tipua punched its bony claw through sliding doors and hauled them out. Too distant to hear their screams, Awhina couldn't bear to watch it stuff them into its razored jaws.

She took a last look at the lake.

Still nothing.

Eighteen people, entombed beneath the water.

No air pocket, then.

Awhina turned right and headed for the bypass, her hands shaking on the wheel.

"He's too angry," Koro said. "Nothing's going to appease him now."

**IN THE BACKSEAT, JUDE STROKED** Robbie's downy hair. This bypass road was swift. Everyone agreed. Cutting out the dog-leg through Taupō's CBD could save you twenty minutes travel time, depending on the traffic and the time of year. Still, Jude couldn't relax. Maybe it was because the road here was walled on either side by steep cuttings, funnelling cars like cans in a vending machine. There was no escape. It might be fast, but it made her uneasy.

Phil must have felt the same, because he stomped on the accelerator. Only it was high summer and Taupō was crawling with tourists; he was forced to slow for a caravan, lumbering down the road.

"Come on!" Phil moaned.

"Just drive, Phil," Jude shouted over the wind. "Go!"

Phil zoomed around the caravan, only just missing an oncoming SUV which came within a hair's breadth.

Jude looked in the windows where two children were strapped in the back seat. The family were heading towards the lake. Jude should warn them, but it would mean going after them, going back, so she said nothing.

Minutes later, they emerged onto the flanks of Mount Tauhara, the township nestled in a crook to their left. Wairakei geothermal plant was just ahead. Get past that, through the round-about and it was a straight run north to Hamilton. They'd be home and hosed.

They passed over the bridge, light steam and sulphurous odour drifting across their path. They'd nearly reached the round-about when a shadow fell across the road.

**AWHINA ZOOMED DOWN THE HIGHWAY.** "Koro, what do you know about this? What is that thing?"

"What thing?"

"The thing in the lake."

He gave a lazy wave. "You'll have to ask your dad."

"Dad's not here, Koro. He died. Heart attack, remember?" His face crumpled. It wasn't new news. The heart attack had been two years ago, but every time Awhina reminded him, it was if he was hearing it for the first time. It had to be the cruellest thing, experiencing that loss over and over again. Like poor old Prometheus having his liver pecked out. These days, Awhina avoided mentioning it, but today she needed answers. "You were waiting at the window. You knew it was coming: the lake monster."

"It's a sacred tipua."

"You're kidding me? That thing is sacred?" Awhina didn't question how he knew. Koro was a seer.

"I should think so. It's Māui's hook, isn't it? Made from Māui's own blood and his ancestor's jawbone," Koro replied.

*Made from blood and bone.*

Is that why Koro had insisted on going out on the water every day? He'd never missed a chance that she could remember. Once, when he was still working at the boat hire, when he still had all his marbles, she'd asked him why he did it.

"To placate the demon," he'd said. She'd thought it was a metaphor, thought he found peace and solitude there. But just maybe the truth was something else. Maybe he went out there to placate this creature cobbled together from blood and bone. Maybe he'd spent a lifetime whispering sweet nothings to it, crooning softly so it would stay quiet at the bottom of the lake.

"Why is it here?" Awhina asks, checking the sky for any sign of it.

"Why is what here?"

"The tipua."

"That's bad. That lake demon doesn't belong here. It's supposed to stay in the water."

"No kidding."

"None of your cheek, young lady, or I'll be telling your father."

This time Awhina let it go. "How do we get rid of it, Koro? Is there a way to kill it?"

"Kill it?" He shook his head. "It's not alive."

"Oh, it seems pretty alive," muttered Awhina, slowing

for the bridge near Wairakei, where drifts of steam ghosted across the road.

On the dash, her phone buzzed. She checked the screen. Andrew.

All at once, the demon appeared out of the wafting steam.

**JUDE WAS DRAGGED FROM HER** stupor by the sound of helicopter rotors. The baby was crying. Phil and Jordan were gone, the front of the car obliterated. One minute, they were there, and the next, the bloody creature had stamped them out. Jude had seen Phil's arms go up to cover his face, and then nothing. Flattened like a Coke can.

On the other side of the car, Bella moaned. Her daughter was stuck in the footwell, squashed in tight by the caved-in roof.

A thin shadow loomed over them. For the moment, it wasn't interested in them, occupied with the helicopter overhead.

Suddenly, Jude was overwhelmed with anger. Fuck that monster. Fuck it to hell. It had taken Phil and Jordan. Well, she was damned if it was getting any more of her family. Unclicking her belt, Jude kicked open the door and crawled out of the car. She lifted out the baby.

Bella panicked. "Mummy!"

"I'm coming." Jude circled the car. She didn't know how much time she had. Not much. She had to get Bella out now. Sending up a prayer to the chopper pilot, she put Robbie on the ground. "Don't move," she said. The car was a mess, the rear door warped and twisted. Would it open?

*I'll have to make it open.*

Jude grasped the mangled doorframe. Bracing one foot on the side of the vehicle, she held her breath and pulled, every muscle fibre shrieking. She pulled and pulled. The gap opened. A bit further. Jude strained harder. Gave it everything.

"Come on, you bitch of a door!"

Finally, it was wide enough for the seven-year-old to squeeze through. "Hurry!" Jude shook with effort as Bella wriggled through the gap. Jude's hands slipped, Bella just getting clear, the metal relaxing with a tinny sigh. There was no time to hug the children. If she wanted to keep them, she had to get them off the road, somewhere safe.

But where?

**"LOOK OUT!" KORO YELLED.**

Straddling the lane, was a crushed car, pancaked under the monster's mass, the front of it flatter than a credit card. The driver had to have been reduced to mush.

Awhina hit the brakes, her heart cartwheeling. She'd have to reverse. Go back. But that would mean driving back through the bypass. If the demon followed them, there'd be nowhere to escape to.

A chopper whumped overhead. Andrew! Thank goodness. He hovered and swooped, teasing the monster, dragging its attention away from the road.

He was giving her a chance to get past! Far be it for her to look a gift chopper in the mouth. Awhina gunned the accelerator, changing lanes to zip past the crushed car.

"Awhina," Koro said. "Stop!"

"Can't, Koro."

A woman and her kids were standing on the side of

the road. She hadn't been able to do anything for Katrina... Adrenaline pumping, she slammed on the brakes, thumbing the button for the passenger window.

"Get in!" she screamed before the glass pane was fully lowered. The woman was already pushing the kids into the back seat. The instant the door closed, Awhina put her foot down.

"Thank you," the woman breathed. Seatbelts clicked.

Awhina put the window up. "We're not out of the woods yet. That thing is right behind us. My friend is doing what he can to distract it."

"The guy in the chopper?" More clicks.

"Yeah. Trouble is, I don't know how long its attention span is."

"Where are the police, anyway? The army? Why isn't anyone doing anything?"

"Caught flatfooted is my guess. Water demons aren't exactly in the manual."

Koro chuckled. "In the manual. That's a good one."

"Mummy," the girl said. "The monster's coming."

Awhina checked the rear-view mirror.

*Shit.*

**THE CAR ROLLED. FOR LONG** moments, Jude didn't know which way was up, or even how many times they'd rolled. Too terrified to scream, she hung on and prayed for it to stop.

Finally, in a shriek of metal and gravel, they slid off the road and smacked against an old pine, jolting hard, forward and back. The car was lying on one side, Bella and the old man closest to the ground. At least, the children were fine. White as sheets, and likely bruised to all hell, but they were both crying, which meant they were still breathing.

"Everyone okay?" the driver asked, unclipping her phone from the dash.

That's when Jude got a whiff petrol. *Shit.* Her heart raced. She fumbled with her seatbelt "Petrol. We've gotta get out!"

"Oh fuck," the driver said. "Koro, come on, we have to move!"

Sitting on the side of the car with her legs in the window, Jude hauled the kids out, lifting them bodily, while the driver did the same for the old man. But now they were out, petrol wasn't the only thing they could smell. Striding towards them on weighty limbs of bone, the monster was as ripe as a day-old tampon.

"Look out," the driver screamed.

There was no time to run. Not if Jude wanted to get out of there with Bella and Robbie. Slow it down! Casting around, Jude spied a hubcap on the ground. It'd have to do. Scooping it up, she held it like a Frisbee and hiffed it as hard as she could, striking the monster on its knee.

Caught by surprise, the demon gave a strangled squawk and stumbled backwards as the helicopter came at it again.

Equally surprised, Jude snatched up Robbie. Her pulse thundering, she grabbed Bella's hand. The driver pulled on the old man's wrist and together they raced through the trees, more of a hobble than a run, their rag-tag group heading away from the road. Going over the hill, Jude glanced back to see the helicopter bank away just as the fireball went up.

"Nice throw," the driver said, when they stopped. Spent, the old man leaned against a tree. No spring chicken, the run had to have taken it out of him. They'd covered nearly a kilometre over rough ground through the pines.

*Away from the demon and the wrecked, burned-out car.*

"I didn't expect to hit it," Jude said, though ragged breaths. "Although, you've got to admit, it's a pretty big target."

The driver grinned. She put out her hand. "Name's Awhina, and this is my grandfather, David Te Heu Heu."

Jude used the mother-with-her-hands-full manoeuvre and showed her an elbow. "Jude."

The woman took it. "Pleasure. You must be shattered. I can look after your little girl if you like."

Jude gave Awhina Bella's hand. "This is Bella."

"You've been so brave, Bella," Awhina said. Bella smiled, and Jude was grateful for Awhina's kindness.

Suddenly, Jude's heart vibrated, the pain deep and intense. Bella squealed. Awhina's face paled. "It's not dead," Jude said.

"They don't die," David said.

Jude's head snapped around. "You know something about this thing?"

"I know enough," the old man replied. "My family are the guardians of the lake."

Awhina frowned. "I'm your family. How come I don't know about this?"

The ground rumbled, halting their conversation.

"We need to find some cover, at least until it's left the area," Awhina said.

"Craters of the Moon geothermal boardwalk is just over that hill," said Jude. "Otherwise, it's a five kilometre sprint back to town." They exchanged a glance.

"Craters of the Moon it is," Awhina replied.

**THEY'D REACHED THE BROW OF** the hill, when the ground shook and the sky darkened. The monster loomed into view. Awhina couldn't believe it. Why them? Why couldn't it just leave them alone?

"What do we do?" she said, tilting her head in Bella's direction. "We'll never make it to the cabin."

"Hide in the steam?" said Jude.

It was better than nothing. They ran down the slope and onto the winding boardwalk where they were enveloped by the steam. In this thermal hot spot, steam just didn't come in drifts; in places it came in boiled clouds, the boardwalk weaving its way through craggy rocks pitted with treacherous vents and sulphurous sinkholes. They were safe enough on the wooden boards. Safe from the boiling mud and scalding water. Although, supernatural demons were another matter.

Through the moving wisps, Awhina caught sight of the monster stepping on the boardwalk. The boards groaned, splintering and cracking under its colossal weight. Its bony grizzled limb plunged into a boiling geyser. The demon screamed, and Awhina's ears rang. She held tight to Koro and Bella, keeping them steady while the damaged boardwalk shook.

Maybe the scald would send it running? Her hope died as the monster hauled itself out of the crater to straddle the remains of the boardwalk. It peered down into the cloud, huge white eyes fixed on Awhina. Her heart plummeted. It could see her, but why was it hesitating right at the edge of the billowing steam? "Don't move," she whispered.

The demon gave a long silent screech, jangling her nerves.

In Jude's arms, the baby whimpered.

The boardwalk trembled as the creature picked its way through the rocks, circling the spot where they were standing. An elongated claw penetrated the steam.

Awhina tucked the girl behind her. She held her breath.

In the distance, the chopper whumped.

Andrew, no! If the chopper got too close, its downdraft would blow away the steam. But the demon was losing its fear anyway, coming closer and closer. It was only a matter of time before it reached in and grabbed someone.

Jude was coming to the same conclusion. "It's going to find us. We have to go," she said.

"The children won't make it."

"We have to try."

"I'll go," said Awhina. "I'll lure it away."

Jude stared at her. "It'll kill you."

"Someone needs to do something, or it'll kill all of us."

Jude nodded, and Awhina remembered the car the woman and her children had crawled out of an hour ago. Who had Jude already lost? "Can you look after my grandfather? His memory's a bit rusty."

"Of course, I'll look after him. You take good care of yourself." Awhina wished they'd met in different circumstances. They might have been friends.

Firing off a text to Andrew, she squeezed her grandfather's hand. "Back soon, Koro," She sprinted out of the steam and onto the intact end of the boardwalk, doubling back to take another path out of the park. She ran as hard as she could, not looking over her shoulder. She didn't need to; it was coming. She had to stay head of it long enough to lure it away from the others. And if it got too close, she hoped Andrew would swoop in and distract it.

Awhina darted left, right, from tree trunk to tree trunk, following the general direction of road, from time to time letting the monster get a glimpse of her. The craziness of her plan hit her. She was offering herself up as bait!

*Good one, Awhina.*

Well, sounds like she was born to be a guardian. Was Koro really able to keep the monster at bay? If so, then this was all on her for putting him in the rest home.

So many deaths. So much damage.

Maybe she was being too hard on herself. Maybe the problem wasn't the rest home, so much as Koro's encroaching dementia. Why on earth hadn't he told her about the demon when he started losing his memory? She could've taken him out on the lake. Or taken over his responsibilities. Suddenly, it dawned on her. The guardianship should have gone to her father.

But Dad had died.

Koro was old school; he never would have given her the responsibility because she was a woman and the demon was tapu. As a woman, her presence would have drained away the power of Māui's sacred fishhook.

*Like that demon needed more power!*

Well, it certainly didn't have any trouble killing women. It'd killed Katrina and all those poor old ladies from the rest home.

Behind her, the demon was getting frustrated. Angry. It yanked out a small pine, throwing it like a cable toss. The tree thundered overhead and smashed just metres to her left.

Awhina's spine tingled. That was close! She darted across the motorway and plunged into the bush on the other side. Andrew circled, like a pesky fly at a BBQ. Through the fern fronds, she saw the demon thrash at the chopper, trying to swat away the nuisance. How much longer could he distract it? He was forced to be more and more daring, coming closer to the demon at every pass. They weren't going to be able to keep this up for much longer. She had to think of something.

Nothing came to her, so she kept running, lungs heaving, another half mile to the Wairakei geothermal plant. Hopefully, the army or the police would get their act together soon, or she'd find somewhere to hide.

The compound was a labyrinth of pipes and funnels carrying steam from the site's underground geothermal source. Awhina sprinted for the main office building on burning legs. She could hide in there. But how long would it protect her? She might be spared the shark tooth jaws, only to be buried under a pile of rubble.

Steam! The monster hadn't liked the fuming vents at Craters of the Moon. What if she rammed the pipes? Sprayed the creature with a bigger dose of steam? It was made of bone. Maybe a good steaming would turn it into soup… She gave a hollow laugh.

Quickly, she glanced about. She'd need a vehicle. A big one. A few Contact Energy service vehicles were parked haphazardly near the facility entrance. She ran from one to the next, peering in the windows. Yes! Someone had left the keys in the centre console. Awhina didn't question her luck; she jumped in the driver's seat and hit the ignition. The truck purred. She checked out the pipeline, selecting a spot close enough the demon to reduce it to broth, and stepped on the gas.

Would a direct hit be enough to crack the pipe? No idea, but she had to do something. Even if it meant she sacrificed her own life. Unless it was stopped, more lives would be lost…

The truck sped on, towards the pipeline that stretched across the horizon. Awhina almost laughed. Even she couldn't miss that.

She felt a twinge of sadness. She probably wouldn't survive the collision. She'd be another dead relative Koro would have to hear about again and again.

On the other hand, at thirty-one years old, living was a nice option.

Wait! What if she jimmied the accelerator! Surely, that only worked in the movies?

There was nothing in the front. She glanced into the back seat. A faded umbrella lay in the footwell. It was destiny, as if the universe had given her a sign. The truck swerved wildly as she leaned back to grab it.

Her foot still on the accelerator, she jammed the umbrella spike down on the pedal and pulled the hook over the steering wheel. Slowly, she let her hands go. The truck kept a steady pace.

Thirty metres! She opened the door. The gravel road skimmed by in a flash of colour. *Fuck!* Time to go. Awhina jumped.

She tumbled on the road, the world a blur. She didn't see the truck hurtle into the pipes, only heard the squeal of metal on metal and the groan as the pipe burst. It wasn't until she stopped rolling that she felt any pain. It was enough to make her see stars. She could barely breathe. Quick assessment. No broken bones, but there were grazes on her hips and shoulder. It hurt like hell. If she survived, she was going to have some wicked bruises.

If she survived.

The monster bellowed.

*Fuck.* She looked up to see the pipes whipping through the air, spewing steam in a ghostly spiral. It was like someone had let go of the garden hose, the pipes circling in a crumpled mash of metal. How did metal even do that?

Trying to avoid the scalding stream, the demon struck the chopper's landing skids.

*Oh God, no.*

Damaged, it spiralled out of sight. Awhina held her breath waiting for the crash. But there was nothing. No fireball on the horizon. Relief was short-lived. The monster gave a silent bellow and stomped out of the steam, grey gristle hanging from its limbs. The smell was vile. It was cooked, but not dead. Well, it was supernatural, wasn't it? A tipua.

She, on the other hand, could die at any moment.

*Damn.*

Awhina scrambled to her feet, taking a few tentative steps as her knee burned with pain. She ran through it. She had no other choice. The demon gave a noiseless bone-shattering bellow. It was on her heels. Now there was no helicopter to slow it down. She was on her own.

**SHE HALF-SPRINTED, HALF-HOBBLED THROUGH** the maze of little jetties that made up the shrimp farm alongside the geothermal plant. Why was she running? She was only delaying the inevitable. One way or another, it was going to kill her. She knew that now. Because tipua don't die. She should have listened to Koro. Although he had dementia, he still knew this lake demon better than anyone. "It's supposed to stay in the water," he'd said.

Only it hadn't. And now it was free, could it be put back?

The Huka Falls jet boat company did tours to the bottom of the falls. It had its set-up beside the shrimp farm. Awhina limped down the slope to the river. She sprinted along the pier. Leaping into a boat, she fired it up and spun into the river, trailing foaming white water.

The lake demon waded in after her.

*Another crazy plan, girl. This lake demon comes from the water. You want to fight it on its own home turf? Pandora couldn't put all the evil back in the jar, what makes you think you can?*

But Awhina had lived in and around boats all her life. She might be woman, but she was also a Te Heu Heu. If she was going to die today, she may as well go out doing what she loved.

Gunning the throttle, she headed upriver for the falls. Minutes later, they appeared before her. They were spectacular: fifteen metres wide and eleven metres tall, pumping 220,000 litres per second of thrashing, frothing, thundering white water through the gorge.

But the giant falls meant a dead end because even a Te Heu Heu can't drive a boat up a cliff. This would be where it ended. She turned to face the demon and imagined she saw it smile.

She revved the motor, and headed right for it, zipping between its legs. Skimming over the water she wove in and out. She confused it, at least a little, because it turned and turned, like a cat trying to catch its own tail. The water foamed and bubbled, the jet boat bobbing on the swell. The air stunk of fuel. The tipua swatted at her again and again, trying to push the boat under. Several times the rear submerged, only to bounce back again. While she was swinging wide to come back inside its legs again, the monster caught her off guard, lunging and swatting the boat sideways. It smashed against the rocky cliff. Awhina's teeth rattled in her jaw. The boat crumpled, the fibreglass cracking. She slammed the throttle, pulling the boat away from the crags. The lake demon slapped the boat again. This time, the vessel plunged beneath the water, taking Awhina with it.

Grey water churned about her. The boat would be sucked below the waterfall. She was going to drown. Something bumped her elbow. Dizzy, she clung on. At last, little craft bobbed to the surface. She was still in the boat. Still alive. But the outboard had died. Too much water.

The lake monster turned. Bony, narrow eyes stared at her.

Well, there were still the safety flares, tucked beneath the console at the front of the boat. She almost laughed. David fighting down Goliath. With safety flares.

There were six smoke sticks and a flare gun. Overkill really. Health and Safety gone mad; the base of the whitewater basin was only 100 metres across. Most people could swim that.

Providing there were no demons in the way.

Each smoke flare would last a minute. What the hell. She pulled the caps off all of them. Orange smoke choked the canyon.

The monster smacked the water, barely missing the boat.

The craft shunted sideways. It was taking on water. Jeepers.

But the jet boat wasn't just carrying flares; it had a life raft, too. Awhina hauled it from its cradle, and, ensuring it was still attached to the painter line, she heaved it overboard. Pressurised gas exploded the boat open alongside. Not fast enough, though.

Hurry up!

When it was only half way open, she dived into it, away from the flares. Cutting the painter, she leaned over the side and used her hands to paddle away. Not out of the smoke, but out of reach of the enraged demon swatting blindly in the fumes.

She stood up and the life raft swayed wildly. It didn't help that her legs were shaking, from fatigue and injury as much as from fear. This was her last chance. She squinted into the haze, and raised the flare gun, aiming for its eye. Not for the bony plate of its forehead, but right into its narrow white orbit. One chance. She braced herself. Pulled the trigger.

And fell back into the raft.

The lake demon staggered, its soundless roar setting her teeth on edge. It collapsed, its hulk of bone and blood sinking beneath the giant falls.

Swamped, the life raft was sent surging across the basin. She did nothing. She had nothing left. When she looked up upstream through the orange haze, Maui's bone demon was slipping beneath the churning water. Awhina thought she heard the sound of bones cracking and for a moment, the water ran red. She sat up, bobbing in the inflatable, her chest heaving, and waited.

Water roared over the falls.

The tipua didn't come back up, pinned beneath the deadening force of 220,000 litres-per-second of water which tumbled over the giant falls and carried on its way as if nothing had happened.

Inside the life raft, Awhina floated gently downstream.

**AWHINA WAS ON THE JETTY,** about to cast off, when she saw Andrew leave the heli-pad and stroll across the car park towards her.

"What's up? Stopping work already?"

Awhina jerked her head to Koro, who was sitting at the back of the boat. "Thought I'd take Koro for a ride down river."

"You're checking on it," Andrew said, and Awhina smiled. Half the people who'd seen the monster hadn't survived, and the other half couldn't believe the truth of their own eyes. The story circulating on the national news was that a freak tornado had run amok in the township, upturning vehicles and trees and flattening structures. Several people had been killed by the freak twister, including the residents of a local rest home, drowned in a submerged minibus. Scientists were baffled about how a cold water lake, with cool air on top of it, could create a tornado.

Nobody mentioned seeing a monster.

"Koro says tipua don't die."

Gazing back towards the heli-pad, Andrew nodded.

"Hey, you want to join us?"

Turning towards her, he grinned. "Sure." Slipping the stern line from its mooring, he climbed in.

Awhina fired up the outboard.

# SOLEDAD

STEVE DIAMOND

**"WHY DO THEY KEEP SENDING** us down here?" Donovan asked. Pale green light from holographic navigation displays illuminated his face. "Doesn't the UN have anything better for us to do?"

"Maybe we'll find something new this time," Villanueva replied. He lounged in his captain's chair, waiting for the next part of the ritual from Edgar Donovan. Donovan—pilot of the UN submersible *Soledad*—was the most superstitious person Villanueva had ever met. Every dive had to start the same way. He was also the best pilot Villanueva had ever dived with.

Donovan spun around in his chair and cocked an eyebrow. It was all part of process.

*Here it comes*, Villanueva thought.

"Fifteenth time's the charm?"

"Fifteenth time's the charm," Villanueva said. His part of the ritual. "Let's get going."

FBW 2018

"Sure thing, Captain," Donovan said. "Beginning descent."

*Soledad* was a nice ship. The nicest, in Cisco Villanueva's slightly biased opinion. She had been built specifically to handle the pressures of the deep. Earth and Mars had their little alliance going on in space, trying to figure out FTL drives for ships, and doing a decent job of avoiding going to war over trivial matters.

In their grand wisdom, the UN decided to completely explore the seafloor on Earth. "Understand Earth, Understand the Universe." It was a horrible motto. But no one had ever accused the UN of being marketing geniuses.

Cisco pulled the New Orleans Saints hat down low over his eyes and let the hum of the ship's nuclear-powered engine speak to him. There was something beautiful in that constant hum. The music of it was the most comforting sound in the world to him. It carried notes of power. Promises of reliability. More than a hint of mischief.

When he was home, he barely slept. A baby without the white-noise machine.

It was good to dive again.

*Fifteen dives*, he thought. *Fifteen dives into the Mariana Trench, and not a thing to show for it.*

Back in the old days, the pressure of the trench made fully-manned explorations impossible. Then came the single-manned dives in submersibles that had more in common with coffins than subs. But that was before *Soledad* had sailed out of the UN shipyards in Norway. No one had ever explained to Villanueva why the submersible had been given the name *Soledad*. But he liked it. It was a peaceful name that encapsulated how he felt when he was on a dive. Just him, his crew, and the *Soledad.*

Villanueva pushed a button on his chair, opening a comm channel to the crew quarters. "Anderson, we are on the edge of the trench. I need you and Makoto up here at your stations."

"Sure thing, Captain," came Anderson's voice. "Be there in five."

Villanueva closed the channel and said, "Donovan, take us down lazy. Our orders have us exploring right down the middle this time. Let's give *Soledad* time to adjust."

"How far are we traveling along the bottom?"

Villanueva smiled. "I'm of a mind to take it slow. We can easily spend a few days skimming the bottom of the trench."

"Deep-sea poker game?"

"You know me too well, Donovan."

The clanking of shoes on steel rungs announced the arrival of Anderson and Makoto, the ship's scientists. Dmitri Anderson was a mountain of a man, almost to the point of being precluded from serving on *Soledad.* He was six-seven, three-hundred pounds. All of it muscle. Chie Makoto, on the other hand, was barely five-five. She claimed she was descended from some Japanese warlord. Of all the people on the ship, she was probably the most dangerous.

"Cap says we're having our poker game at the bottom," Donovan said without turning.

"Awesome," Anderson said.

"I look forward to taking all your money," Makoto said. "Then your booze. Then your firstborn."

The green holographics at Donovan's display flickered.

"The hell was that?" the pilot said.

"You said all electronics were green before the dive,"

Villanueva said. "What's up?"

"No idea, Cap… uh… Cap?"

"What?"

"I'm… I'm picking up something at the bottom of the trench."

The room went completely still, then Anderson and Makoto burst into a flurry of action, cycling on their own systems.

"Cap," Donovan said, "it's massive."

"Where?"

Donovan's fingers flew over his controls, then he flicked one of the displays over to the scientists. Anderson stared at it for few moments, his normally jovial face now ridged in concentration.

"That can't be right," Makoto said.

"It is," Anderson said, though he didn't sound like he believed it himself.

"There's a whole lot of talking going on, and not a lot of updating the damn Captain," Villanueva growled. He got up from his chair and stood behind his scientists, looking at their data. He wasn't an expert at all the scientific mumbo-jumbo—which was why he had scientists on board to begin with—but any captain worth their salt knew how to read 3D maps.

There, at the bottom of the trench, and a few hundred miles north of their position. A giant, pulsing anomaly, vaguely egg-shaped. Debating its existence was futile.

Except it—whatever *it* was—hadn't been there on *Soledad's* last dive two months prior.

Villanueva was opening his mouth to voice his thoughts,

but Makoto was already pulling up survey records from that dive. She compared the archival record to the current readouts. Overlaid them.

"Do I keep diving?" Donovan asked. "Cap, I need to know—"

Villanueva held up a hand, cutting of the pilot.

Makoto shook her head and looked at Anderson. The other scientist shrugged, then sighed.

"It's the damndest thing, Captain," Anderson said. "I can't explain it by looking at these maps. That thing wasn't there before."

"Then how did it get there?"

"Impossible to know," Makoto said. "Either our records—and memories—are wrong, or it just showed up."

"Or there is a third option."

"Which is… what exactly?" Anderson asked.

Villanueva shook his head, then stepped back to his chair and sat down. "I don't know. And I won't know until we are down there looking at it. Donovan?"

"Captain?"

"Keep diving."

**DONOVAN TOOK THE DIVE SLOW** and lazy, just as Villanueva initially ordered, and they reached the bottom of the trench in two hours. The depths of the ocean in a submersible—even one as advanced as *Soledad*—were just as perilous as the depths of space. One mistake could mean their deaths, and he wanted to give himself time to order the ship to surface if something started feeling off. And now the Soledad moved along the bottom of the fifteen-hundred-mile trench.

By all rights, he could have scrapped the dive. Maybe he should have.

But that brand of cowardice wasn't in his nature.

Villanueva wanted to know. *Had* to know. Why did mankind go to the moon? Because it was there. Why did mankind colonize Mars? Because it was there. He could read his own emotions reflected in the body-language of the crew. Were they uneasy? Of course. Definitely concerned, as well. But they needed to know, too. That desire to continually quest for knowledge was why he'd picked them to crew *Soledad* in the first place.

Some were motivated by greed. Promises. Sex. Power.

Villanueva was motivated by *discovery*.

As *Soledad* creaked and groaned under the intense sea-pressure, he stopped by his cabin to pick up two glasses and a bottle of Blanton's. He had one last crew member to bring up to speed.

Chela Aldego sat on the floor of the engine room, legs stretched out, reading a magazine. She wore a lazy expression. Perhaps too lazy. Calculated lazy.

This meant Villanueva was in trouble.

"Nice of you to come down," she said. "Finally."

"It's been two hours."

"Which is one-hundred and eight minutes later than it should have been."

Villanueva took another look at the magazine Aldego read. Luxury timepieces in the old, twentieth-century way of construction. It was her thing.

"We found something at the bottom of the trench."

"I gathered."

“It’s in the exact same location as some of our previous dives,” Villanueva said. “Neither Anderson or Makoto can explain it. Something this big should have showed up before.”

Aldego set the magazine aside and gave Villanueva a considering look. “Maybe it has.”

“What do you mean?”

“You don’t feel it? In the engine?”

“No…”

“You need to spend more time in with the heart of *Soledad.* Come over here and put you hand against the engine wall.”

Villanueva crossed the room and placed his hand against the steel wall separating them from the actual engine. The humming of the ship reverberated through his arm and into his body. It was completely normal. “I don’t—”

“Wait.”

He kept his hand pressed there. He was about to comment again when he felt it. The thrumming pulsed heavier for just a moment. A double *whump.*

“What was that?”

“I’m not sure,” Aldego said. “And it isn’t the first time I’ve felt it.”

“Why haven’t you reported it?”

“Because the trench is a weird place filled with strange sounds. But now I wonder.”

“About what? A random sound?”

“It isn’t random. It’s regular.” Aldego pulled out an old-fashioned pocket-watch and held it up. “I’ve been timing them. Every fifteen minutes, to the second. I only noticed it the last few descents. It’s stronger now than it was before. It could have been there on every dive, but only recently has it been strong enough to feel."

Villanueva had the feeling his engineer was ramping up to a theory. "Spit it out. What do you think it is?"

"If I didn't know any better," Aldego said, "I'd say it's a heartbeat."

**IT WASN'T LONG BEFORE THE** thrumming became noticeable to the crew.

Villanueva instructed Donovan to slow the descent, and now at twenty hours in, the pulsing could be felt through the floor of *Soledad*. He set a timer on one of the displays to track the time between sets of pulses. Just as Aldego reported, they came every fifteen minutes.

Donovan didn't tell his normal jokes. Makoto and Anderson didn't engage in their usual banter. Aldego didn't join the rest of the crew for meals.

A simple *whump-whump*. It shouldn't have been anything but a curiosity.

And yet, Villanueva couldn't shake the feeling that something was waiting for them.

That unknown filled him with dread.

**AT THE TWENTY-SIX HOUR MARK,** Villanueva decided to try and get some sleep. A look in the mirror showed red eyes with dark circles under them. Sleep wasn't normally an issue aboard the *Soledad*. In fact, he usually slept better here than ashore.

But the heartbeat—if that's what it actually was—left him unsettled.

His personal cabin was small, but comfortable. As

advanced as *Soledad* was, it still kept room for personnel to a minimum. A small bed, and a smaller vanity. A cabinet for his clothes held a trunk at the bottom for his personal items; Blanton's, glasses, a few books—actual paper editions that were worth a fortune—and a few other odds-and-ends.

He took out the Blanton's and poured himself another drink. He tried to keep himself limited to three glasses per dive, and here he was with a second glass before reaching the bottom of the trench.

But maybe it would help him sleep.

Villanueva downed the liquid, savoring the hints of vanilla and caramel. He took a deep breath, dimmed the lights and laid down. When he closed his eyes, he could still see the display counting up to fifteen minutes. Then he felt the *whump-whump*.

He let his mind wander, thinking of prior dives. Wondering—imagining, perhaps—if he had felt the pulsing before.

How had they not spotted the anomaly before? It didn't make any sense.

He gave himself over to the thrumming of the engine, and eventually drifted off.

Villanueva dreamt of swimming.

He kicked his way along the bottom of the trench, which pulsed with green, oily light. He looked back over his shoulder and saw the *Soledad* behind him. None of the running lights were on, and the submersible looked to be completely powered down. Thick, almost tangible shadows enveloped his ship.

He turned back and continued swimming. Dreams being dreams, he wasn't worried at all about being out in the pressures of the ocean outside his ship. All he wanted was to see the anomaly with his own eyes.

The green light began pulsing faster as he neared its source, and his heartbeat pounded in time with it.

The water grew thicker, and he struggled to swim through it. The anomaly was just ahead, a dark mass in the center of the putrid light. It looked like… an egg. In the green, flickering lights, Villanueva could see shadows writhing around it; some appeared to be emanating from inside the oblong shape. One of the shadows reached out from the depths, passed him by, and wrapped around the *Soledad.* It pulled the ship toward itself, and Villanueva tried to swim faster to follow his ship as it moved past him.

Another shadow detached from the green and black murk and writhed its way toward him. For the first time, Villanueva felt fear. Not unease. Heart-freezing fear and terror.

It reached out, and moved to wrap around him…

…and he woke up.

He didn't move for several moments. Just stared at the bulkhead above him. His heart pounded, and he was almost surprised he couldn't see it jumping out of his chest.

Then he realized he could feel the *whumping*, and it was coming faster than every fifteen minutes.

**"DONOVAN, I NEED YOU TO** get us the hell back to the surface."

Donovan was staring at the controls in front of him, head cocked to the side. The green glow from the holographics reminded Villanueva of his dream.

"Donovan?"

The man didn't answer, just stared down into the green.

Villanueva walked up on the man from behind, a chill creeping upon him. When he was just a few feet away, he noticed a dark trail snaking down from Donovan's ear. It ambled down his neck into a stain on his collar. Blood.

"Donovan? Buddy? You OK?"

Villanueva reached out, hesitated for a moment just an inch from the pilot's shoulder, then spun the man around.

Blood hadn't just leaked from the man's ear, but from every orifice on Donovan's face. Twin lines spilled from his nostrils, and his chin was red from a sheet of blood. His eyes wept russet tears, and the whites of those eyes had been painted crimson. In the pilot's lap was a red, bloody lump. Villanueva leaned in. It was a tongue.

Villanueva gasped in shock. He backed up until his legs met the edge of his captain's chair, and he fell into the seat. He keyed the intercom.

"I need everyone up here. Now"

Aldego was the first to arrive. She was usually the last to arrive when he issued these sorts of commands, but she practically threw herself up the ladder leading to the bridge, her face a mask of concern.

"What's wrong, Cisco? You sounded like you saw a gh—oh…" Her face went pale when she saw Donovan.

Makoto and Anderson came up a moment later. They stood silently, staring at the scene.

"Dammit… what… what…" Anderson couldn't even finish his thoughts.

"How?" Makoto asked.

Villanueva shook his head. "I just found him."

"We need to surface," Aldego said.

Villanueva found he was nodding in agreement, his head bobbing up and down like a demented child's toy. "Do it," he finally managed to say. "Get us out of here."

Aldego pushed by him and only hesitated for a moment at Donovan's side. Her gaze took in the blood, and the severed tongue. She shuddered, then began keying commands into *Soledad's* navigation systems. She wasn't as good a pilot as Donovan, but she could hold her own. Villanueva let out a breath. This was bad, but at least he'd found the... issue... in time to get them back to the surface.

Then he noticed the expression on Aldego's face, and that her hands were moving over the controls in the exact same pattern as before. She paused, then did it all over again for a third time.

"What is it?" Villanueva asked. His heart felt like it was being squeezed in a fist. Somehow, he knew what she was going to say.

"We can't. Navigation is locked."

Villanueva pushed aside the horror and the blood, his mind focusing. He brought up is own controls, and keyed in his override.

=ERROR=

He blinked at the message, then executed the command for a second time.

=ERROR=

He opened the communications network, intending to have someone on the surface access the navigation remotely and adjust *Soledad's* course.

=UNAUTHORIZED=

"What the hell..."

"Captain?" Anderson asked.

Villanueva cycled through all his systems. Anything having to do with navigation or external comms returned the same error messages.

"I'm locked out," he said in disbelief.

"You're the captain," Makoto said, confused. "You have access to everything."

"Not anymore," Villanueva said. "We can't turn back, and we can't call for help."

**THEY WRAPPED DONOVAN IN A** pressurized body-bag and stored him in the ship's freezer. Just like the ships navigating the stars, those exploring the depths of Earth's oceans all carried the specialized body-bags. Accidents happened.

Though it was difficult for Villanueva to consider Donovan's death an accident.

Aldego plugged directly into the ship's root systems and still couldn't get in. She was able to see the last few commands Donovan entered, but none of them made much sense. He'd queried an unknown sound picked up on his sensors, then he'd locked the ship into its current depth and heading. None of which explained why Villanueva couldn't override navigation or comms. Aldego couldn't do anything to fix the issue on her end either.

"We could reboot the entire system," Makoto suggested.

"Do it," Villanueva said.

Aldego pushed herself under the main control bank on the bridge, removed several panels, then said, "Here we go."

The power flickered briefly, all the holographic displays momentarily when blank, then came back on. Thousands of lines of computer coding Villanueva didn't understand scrolled down all the screens until the systems were fully back online.

He keyed in all the same commands as before and received the same errors. A status check confirmed the *Soledad* was still moving along at the same depth and speed as before.

Somehow, nothing had changed.

"Now what do we do?" Anderson asked.

**WITH THE SHIP ON AN** autopilot of sorts and external comms down, Villanueva had little to do but sit in his chair and worry.

Aldego had locked herself away in the guts of the ship, looking for some way to restore control to the needed ship systems. Anderson and Makoto were lost in analysis of the anomaly.

Villanueva felt about as useful as Donovan's corpse.

The images from his dream ate at him. Those shadows from the depths wrapping around *Soledad* and pulling her toward the anomaly. A few days ago, even the thought of it all would have seemed absurd. But now? Against his better logic, Villanueva knew the dream, Donovan's death, and the dive were all related.

The worst part of all of this—besides Donovan's death—was the helplessness. Aldego, Anderson, and Makoto each had tasks to keep themselves occupied. Villanueva felt, for lack of a better term, adrift.

"Captain?"

Villanueva blinked, noticed both Anderson and Makoto staring at him. Had they been saying his name?

"Yeah?"

The two scientists glanced at each other, and something

silent passed between them. Anderson cleared his throat, then said, "Got a sec?"

"Of course," Villanueva answered. Not that he was busy, but even now—especially now—they adhered to custom and protocol.

"The anomaly has grown."

Villanueva stared at the other man, not quite sure of he'd heard right. "I'm sorry?"

"It's grown," Anderson said again. He ran his hands over his head, then pointed at the screen in frustration. "I don't know how, but it's true. Makoto didn't believe me either, so she checked my work."

Villanueva looked to the other scientist. "And?"

"He's right."

"OK... how much bigger are we talking? A few inches? Could our sensors have been affected by distance distortion through the water?"

"Doubtful," Makoto said. "A few inches wouldn't have merited attention. That's not statistically significant, in my opinion."

"So...?"

"It's doubled in size," Anderson said. "It used to be about twice the size of *Soledad.* Now it's four-times our size."

"No way our sensors are off by that much," Villanueva said.

"Exactly," Makoto said."

"Cap," Anderson said. "I have a really bad idea."

"OK..."

Makoto didn't look happy about this apparent bad idea, but neither was she stopping her partner. Anderson said,

"What if… what if our sensors have been wrong for the all our prior dives, and are now getting more accurate?"

"I'm not sure I follow."

"Something Aldego said got me thinking," Anderson said. "I was down by the engine room, trying to clear my head."

"Drinking," Makoto said.

"Drinking," Anderson confirmed. "I took a pill to neutralize my BAC, don't worry. Anyway, I heard Aldego swearing up a storm, and she said, 'I swear this thing doesn't *want* us to surface.'"

He stopped talking and looked at Villanueva expectantly.

Villanueva waited for a few moments, then said, "And this means…?"

"What if she was right?"

"You're gonna need to explain that to the non-scientist in the room." When Anderson looked momentarily confused, Villanueva sighed and clarified, "Me."

"Oh. Right. Well, what if Aldego is right, and whatever this anomaly is had some sort of camouflage that kept it hidden from our sensors all this time?"

"Is that even possible?"

"It's as possible as it magically appearing, and suddenly doubling in size, all in thirty-five hours."

"Point. Animals use camouflage to keep themselves safe from predators."

"Or to keep the hunter hidden from its prey," Makoto said.

**VILLANUEVA LEANED HIS HEAD AGAINST** the cool door to the freezer. The chill felt wonderful against his skin. The last hour had greeted him with a growing headache. His paranoia screamed at him that this was due to the anomaly. The rational part of his mind reminded him he hadn't slept since the nightmare.

The *whumping* was almost audible now. Sure enough, it reminded him of a baby's heartbeat on an ultrasound.

They had mere hours before they reached the anomaly. He feared for his ship. For his crew. He should have surfaced the ship at the first sign of the anomaly. But then what? The UN would have sent him back down immediately to check it out, and they'd be in the exact same situation.

He lifted his head and thumped it into the door with a *thump*.

A *thump* answered back.

Villanueva shoved himself away from the door, a hoarse scream choked off in his throat.

In the small circular window of the freezer door, a hand flattened itself against it from the inside, wiping away the small layer of frost. The hand was pale. Bloodless.

Donovan.

The hand slid away.

Villanueva stared at the window for a few moments, heart pounding. He slowly edged toward the door, then peered through the window. In the middle of the freezer floor, where they'd left it, was the body-bag. It was ripped open from the inside.

Donovan's bloodstained face suddenly slammed into the small window. The force of it smashed Donovan's nose to the side, hideously broken. Villanueva flinched back. Donovan's mouth opened, moved. One of his front teeth hung loose, dangling by the thread of its root. More damage from the impact. In that mouth, Villanueva could see the bloodless wreckage of where the man's tongue had been.

Villanueva wanted to run screaming, but he was transfixed.

Donovan's mouth moved in the same way again and again. Words. He was trying to say something.

Taking small, cautious steps, Villanueva approached the window to get a better view. He felt tears stinging at the corners of his eyes. Donovan mouthed the words over and over until Villanueva grasped their meaning.

*It's killing them. Run.*

*It's killing them. Run.*

Donovan's corpse backed away from the door. Lifted a hand. Pointed.

Villanueva felt a presence behind him. He looked down at his feet, saw the shadows from his prior nightmare slide around his feet. Dark, writhing tentacles whose ends opened into mouths with bristling teeth.

He opened his mouth to scream...

The cool door of the of the freezer had numbed the skin of his forehead. Villanueva jerked away from it. The corner of his mouth was wet from a small line of drool. He reached out and yanked the door to the freezer open.

There, in the middle of the floor right where they'd left it, was the body-bag containing Donovan's corpse. The body-bag remained closed. Unmoving.

Another dream.

He could still see Donovan's ravaged face mouthing the words, *It's killing them. Run.*

The last time he had a nightmare like this, Donovan had turned up dead.

In the distance, he heard shouting.

Villanueva sprinted from the kitchen, down the short hall passing the crew rooms, and up the ladder onto the bridge.

The scene that greeted him was pandemonium. Makoto had a long-bladed knife—Villanueva had no idea where the hell she'd produced it from—and was slashing the air in front of Anderson. Anderson's face was beet-red, twisted in anger. Makoto's visage was dead-calm. Flat. Completely emotionless. Hers was easily the more terrifying of the two.

Before Villanueva could do anything, Makoto darted in and buried the blade into Anderson's stomach. She slashed it to the side, ripping a jagged, horizontal gash in him. Anderson's eyes bulged, and he gasped in pain as she pulled the blade free and stabbed him quickly once, twice, three times.

Anderson's knees buckled. As he fell, one massive arm wrapped around Makoto's neck. He dragged her down to the deck of the bridge. She stabbed him over and over as he tightened his grip around her neck. Anderson roared, blood spraying from his mouth, and jerked.

The sound of Makoto's neck snapping was louder than Villanueva expected.

Anderson collapsed to the deck, sobbing.

Villanueva pulled himself the rest of the way onto the bridge. The whole scene had played out in seconds. Blood was sprayed and splashed everywhere. His stomach roiled, but he kept himself from vomiting. He crossed the room to Anderson's side and cradled the dying man's head in his lap.

"Cap," Anderson gasped. Blood streamed from the sides of his mouth. "It's killing us. We… we gotta… we gotta… we… run…"

Tears poured from Villanueva's eyes. "What happened? Dammit, Anderson… what happened?"

The other man coughed, spraying more blood. "A sound… on sensors. Got in our head… Makoto went crazy… anomaly… kill us all… sorry… so sorry…"

Anderson's head lolled to the side, and all life left him.

**TWO MORE BODIES IN TWO** more body-bags. The freezer was fuller than ever intended, and with the wrong things.

Aldego sat on the floor, knees pulled to her chest. She stared off into space, shaking her head occasionally in what Villanueva imagined was mute defiance.

He looked down at his hands, still covered in Anderson's blood. How had this happened? Why was is happening? He replayed scene of Makoto and Anderson killing each other in his mind. Over and over. He was going to die down here. If events continued as they had, chances were he'd watch Aldego die somehow, leaving him all alone. On *Soledad*. He almost laughed at the irony there… and then he almost wept.

He was dimly aware of a distant chiming. Villanueva shook his head, clearing—albeit, temporarily—the cloudy misery.

Proximity alarm.

"Well," he said aloud. "I guess we should go see what has been killing us."

Aldego nodded and pushed herself up. She walked out of the kitchen quickly, and Villanueva followed behind. The bridge was still a disaster. They hadn't bothered to clean it up. *What's the point?* Villanueva asked himself.

He tapped a quick series of commands into the controls

on his chair, half expecting another error. Instead, the Soledad's scanning software built a holographic representation of the view outside and projected it on the front-inner bulkhead—like a viewscreen.

Both he and Aldego gasped at the sight.

The anomaly was a massive oblong shape ahead of them. Using the earlier scans, they'd described it as egg-shaped. Now, he couldn't see it as anything else.

"It's a damn egg," Aldego said, echoing his thoughts. "A massive one."

"Anderson was right. It's got to be four-times our size. Maybe bigger."

As they watched, shadowy tendrils reached out from it, grasping denizens of the deep. Some of these creatures had no business being in the depths, but here they were, likely lured just as the *Soledad* had been. One-by-one, the sea-creatures were pulled inside the egg.

Fissures appeared in the surface of the egg, and the anomaly stretched out, expanding. In the spaces between, Villanueva caught a glimpse of a creature so massive, so alien, that his mind shrunk in on itself, gibbering in terror. The spaces filled in, and the egg was now larger than before.

A small light blinked on his chair. It was an alert indicating a new, unidentified sound. He didn't want to push the button. Nevertheless, his hand reached out. From the corner of his eye, he saw Aldego push something into her ears. *Huh*, he thought. *Why would she do that?*

He pushed the button.

Sound flooded the room. It clawed into his mind, screeching and screaming. Images filled his mind and vision.

He couldn't tell what was real, or his imagination. Visions of him pulling out Donovan's tongue, hacking it out. Stabbing Anderson over and over. Breaking Makoto's neck. Gutting Aldego. Their corpses pointed in accusation, then begged and pleaded for him to kill them again. And again.

For eternity.

*Set me free*, they all said with one voice.

He turned and saw Aldego studying him. He had to kill her. Set her free. Just like the others.

He took one step, then another.

Aldego raised her hand, and in it was a small gun. He knew it. Even as we went mad, he knew its type. Strong enough to kill, too weak to pierce the bulkhead.

Villanueva wanted her to die with every fiber of his being...

...and the tiny sliver of this brain that retained his shrinking sanity hoped she would kill him.

He saw the muzzle-flash.

**ALDEGO STEPPED OVER VILLANUEVA'S BODY,** and keyed in the overrides into the ship's system. Immediately, the ship began to rise. She opened the comms.

"Aldego to top-side."

"Top-side, here."

"It's as you said. The 'thing' is growing. It's sentient enough to make itself known, just like the others."

"Casualties?"

"The whole crew," she said. She was almost sad about it this time. Villanueva had been a good man.

"Recommendation?"

"Same as the rest," she replied. "Send the egg to space. Hide it in an asteroid belt. Feed it. I still think we can weaponize these 'things'."

"Understood. Return to the surface. We'll send a retrieval team. Top-side, out."

Aldego looked down at the corpse of Villanueva. He'd been a good man and a better captain. She glanced around the bridge, and found she was smiling.

A job well done.

She wondered if she would be allowed to keep the ship…

# WHEN A KAIJU FALLS IN LOVE

ZIN E. ROCKLYN

**"BLACK LIVES MATTER!"**

*"Say her name!"*

*"Black Lives Matter!"*

*"Say their name!"*

Gertie snorted and shifted her weight from one swollen foot to other while arching her back to pop that sweet spot just above her dimples. The position was getting harder to keep the older she got, but this window was her newscast night after night, the program running for the last sixty-three years. She'd watched this neighbourhood be built up by Black and Brown hands only for it to be systemically dismantled by invisible pale ones. Still, they tried, including her parents and, later on, her, but nothing changed. Nothing—until more than a few bad loans gutted out the souls of some pre-war brownstones, leaving them vulnerable to the claws

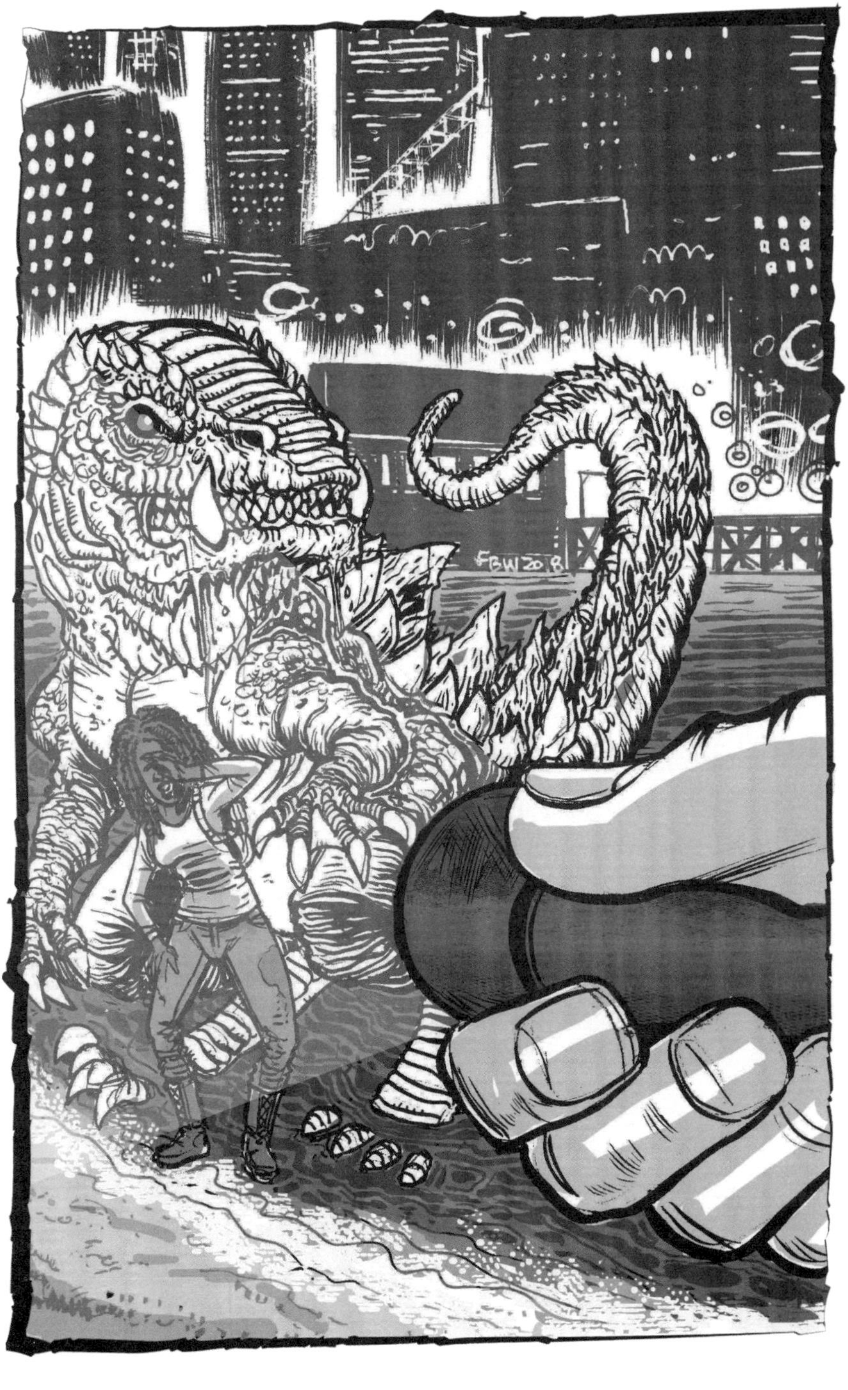
FBW 2018

of predatory real estate and new money. A few people held on tight, those lucky enough to breed generations of money knowledge, of legacy wealth, no matter how little it may have been. But the neighborhood was changing yet again, turning over a whiter shade of pale and victimhood.

More of that pale in the form of soft-handed fists stabbed the air.

*"Black Lives Matter!"*

*"Say his name!"*

"What's the matter, Grammie? Mad you can't be down there?" Nettie asked from her perch the next window over. She'd been a little smarter, having dragged a chair to the spot. Her view was slightly obstructed by the lip of the windowsill, but at least her back didn't ache.

Gertie rolled her eyes at her granddaughter's familiar tone, though the corner of her mouth upticked a bit. "You should be marching for all of us," she shot back, just as sarcastic.

"Please. Our lives don't matter enough for them to stop taking over the goddamn place," Gertie's daughter interjected as she shuffled into the living room. Angela plopped onto the couch and groaned as she pulled off her heels.

"What I tell you about that mouth of yours, Angie?" Gertie grumbled.

"And I told *you*, I get it from my mama, Mama, so how about that?"

All three women chuckled and sighed, shifting in mirroring ways. Silence briefly chilled the room as Angela let her head fall back against the couch cushions.

"What's for dinner?" Nettie asked as her eyes trailed the last of the pathetically drawn crowd. All fifteen white people rounded the corner half a block down, police escorts lazily flowing behind.

"Whatever your Grandmother made," Angela mumbled sleepily.

"Leftovers," Gertie said. She'd have to stand in a moment, and the prospect made her tired.

"Aw, Grammie!" Nettie whined playfully. She stood up in the chair and twisted her back this way and that, mimicking her grandmother like she had since she was a child, while also releasing the anger that clenched her belly.

"Shut'cho ass up, lil' girl, and eat what's heated up for you," Gertie groaned as she straightened up. "Oh, good Lord, heal this fuckin' back!"

Immediately, Nettie launched into a censored version of the rap ballad, twerking her waist and popping her chest. "*She get it from her Mama!*"

Being the only one to get the reference, Angela busted out laughing, now wide awake with hunger and love.

Gertie shook her head, shuffling from the room with a grin she hid from her daughter and granddaughter as the nerves of the night ahead tickled her chest.

**HOWARD WALKED IN JUST IN** time for the table to be set while Nettie's twin brother Hannibal miraculously managed to avoid contributing anything but his after-practice body odour, sending Angela into a frenzy.

"Go wash up! Ruining my damn appetite!"

In retaliation, Hannibal swept his mother up into a bear hug, briefly lifting her from the ground to set her right back down when her scream hit fever pitch. "Damn, Ma! The neighbours gon' call the cops!"

Angela sucked on her teeth and fidgeted with the oven. "Please. This building ain't that white yet."

They waited until Hannibal exited the shower before dishing the food, and by the time they sat down to eat, Hannibal was joining them along with his cell phone.

"Uh-uh, put that damn thing away," Angela muttered in between bites of baked chicken.

"I was just checking for funeral arrangements," Hannibal explained, though he did darken the screen and plant the device face-down towards the middle of the table.

Nettie shifted, her eyes on her plate as the middle prongs of her fork toyed with her food.

"You okay, Netilda?" Howard asked, his deep voice softened by genuine concern.

Nettie winced at her full name being spoken. Her nickname eased the sting a bit, but she still hated the old sound of either of the monikers she was given. "Yes, Daddy," she said, her eyes not meeting his. She knew the moment she did look at her father, her resolve would crumble.

"Did y'all know her well?" Gertie asked. Nettie automatically sighed, her fears being realized, although she was sure both of her responses hadn't helped the possibility of avoiding the subject.

"Nah," Hannibal answered for her. "She dropped out, like, a year ago when she got pregnant."

Nettie lifted a shoulder. "I had a class with her in sixth grade." She paused, pushing her green beans to one side of the plate. "She was a bitch."

"Nettie!"

"Netilda Denise Anderson."

"Oop!"

"Netilda, you don't speak ill of the dead, baby," Gertie said with a sigh.

"And you damn sure don't talk like that at the dinner table!" Angela added.

"I'm sorry, but she was!" Nettie whined. "I'm not saying she deserved to die or anything."

"*Especially* like that," Hannibal said, shaking his head.

"Hmph. Thirty-two bullets—"

"Three alone to the dome—"

"Like she was some kind of... *beast*."

Stillness rushed the room as everyone nervously scraped at their plates, eyes glued to food that now tasted like cardboard. The butterflies Nettie had been fostering were now taking full flight, obliterating the appetite for the courtesy bites she'd been taking.

"They're going to find him, Daddy," she said, her voice smaller than her sixteen years. "It's only a matter of time."

Forks clattered against Corningware, and several sighs went off as Nettie kept her gaze down. Another regret of the night. She should've waited until she and Howard were alone. But she'd been worried about this for some months now, ever since that white couple bought the old trap house three blocks over on Harrison, right in the middle of a territory battle. Everyone and everything paused then, the gravity of gentrification weaving its way into the bloody fabric of the city's most notorious neighborhood. It was like watching a white dude jog his baby through the center of a gunfight, not one bullet touching him or his towhead progeny, AirPods blocking out the screams and shots.

"Finish your plate," Howard said, his tone not much changed from the last time he spoke. "I have something for you to deliver."

**NETTIE WASN'T ALLOWED TO GO** anywhere near her father's study until the kitchen and dining room were spotless, so she and her brother decided on a Best of Aretha Franklin and set to work. It was easy enough, nothing like a Sunday dinner clean-up, but Angela had let them slip the last couple nights by allowing them to do the minimum. Now sweeping, scrubbing countertops, the table, and the stove, and a wipe-out of the oven were required.

It hadn't been lost on either of them that Angela was also delaying the inevitable.

Everyone was on edge, and it had begun long before the murder of seventeen-year-old Estelle Dubois at the hands of their city's finest. Trayvon Martin, Michael Brown, Sandra Bland, Kalief Browder, Akai Gurley; the hashtags and the bodies attached to them were no strangers to their city. They held their own protests, ran their own programs, built their own safehouses against gun-violence, gang initiations, and drug addiction. All funded from their own pockets. But none of it mattered to outside optics. The housing collapse meant most programs collapsed, too. Employment was on the rise, but it was too late for their homes. The entire city was ready to explode.

And explode it could, had they just given the word.

But that would've been selfish. Would've called for wielding an indiscriminate power none of them could handle nor recover from.

It was best to hold on as best they could without losing their minds.

And so, deliveries like the one Howard was about to give his daughter were necessary. She'd been doing runs like this ever since she was a child, usually at Howard's side, and then since last year, alone. The family hadn't been too happy about it, but Nettie insisted she was protected, and not just by the neighbourhood itself.

"He knows when I'm coming," Nettie'd said dreamily after one of Angela's tsk-filled scoldings. "And everyone else knows where I'm going, so nobody messes with me." She'd tried to hide it, that wistfulness, but it'd been hard, especially after spending hours at the rocky shore with him.

Howard blinked at his daughter, not quite grasping the situation. He'd discussed it later that morning with Angela and she popped a laugh in response. "At least she won't walk up in this house pregnant."

They both stopped and looked at one another, faces contorting as they tried to imagine the impossible.

"Never say some shit like that again," Howard said, shaking his head.

"Yeah, I'm kinda mad at myself for that one," Angela agreed.

"Daddy? You got a package?" Nettie said from the door, snapping Howard from the reverie.

"Yes, babygirl, come in," he said, straightening his posture as the study door slid open. Nettie slipped inside as if sneaking in, her curvy body slithering through an opening wide enough for her alone. She slid the door shut behind her, careful of the squealing wheels and loud catch awaiting connection. She'd been doing this since she was a little girl, when she couldn't sleep and wanted to "assist" her father's projects. He worked as a data processing manager of the telecommunications giant that, at one point, had over half the neighbourhood employed. By the grace of his ever-adaptability, Howard survived six major layoff seasons over the last ten years, but even he knew he was running on borrowed time.

"Isn't it too early?" Nettie asked excitedly. It seemed she hardly cared for the answer, but was trying not to be so eager to get out and be on her way to visit her... paramour? It was such a strange thought, but it was clear his daughter was in puppy love. Obviously, she'd grow out of it as soon as she realized the extent of their relationship could only go so far. She was still young. The practicality of a partnership had yet to befall her as a challenge. Until then, until college and a career, he'd allow this... whatever it was. He'd keep Angela at bay and allow his babygirl some happiness, wherever she could find it. Especially on a night like tonight.

"Nah, it's not," he finally said as she sat down in her favourite seat: the rocking chair where her mother had nursed both she and Hannibal until they all fell asleep. Nettie never wanted to be too far from her father from the time she was born. Angela swore it was even before that. She blamed him for having to be put on bedrest; Nettie wouldn't stand for Angela going to work and being away from her father's scent. Howard thought the both of them ridiculous, but secretly adored the idea of both his girls being close always. "With the neighbourhood upset, Sister Ulen thought we should head off any issues by being proactive."

"Keep him distracted," Nettie said.

Howard smirked. "Yeah."

Nettie shrugged. "What am I bringing?"

"More parts. Our boy likes puzzles."

Nettie grinned. "Yeah, he does."

Howard tilted his head as his daughter gazed at nothing, her eyes glossy and her smile serene. "What do y'all do when you're there, Nettie?"

Nettie's head snapped up then, her body going rigid as she stared wide-eyed at her father. "Uhm—"

"I mean, do y'all *talk*, do y'all—wait, *how* can y'all talk?"

Her smile was small, accidental, but warm. "Well, remember how obsessed I was with radio waves, sonar responses, shit like that?"

Howard narrowed his eyes and Nettie shrugged. "Sorry. But, yeah, I mean, we started out with Morse code—"

"Gramps would be proud."

Another shy smile, the stained mahogany of her skin flushing red. "I hope so. Well, yeah, so one night I was tinkering around and came up with a device that combines—"

And this is where Howard lost his daughter. Antiquated communications had been the foundation to his career, but with quickly advancing technology, he was bound to forget the details and nuances of the old. Zoning out unnecessary information had become his specialty since becoming a father.

"And that's that!" Nettie announced proudly. A twinge of guilt made Howard wince; she was obviously sure her efforts would make him proud, and proud he was, but heaven forbid she ask him for advice.

"Well, damn, Nettie," he said, hoping he sounded as honored as he actually was. "Then y'all will have a field day with this old junk. They're cleaning out Gibson's place."

Nettie shifted, and Howard struggled to move on for a moment. Jedidiah Gibson had been a relic on their block, the example of refusing to be strong-armed out of his brownstone. But they'd all known one day he'd be gone, and, having no living relatives, the house would be sold out of their hands. Howard cleared his throat.

"You know he was in the Korean War?"

Nettie smiled softly. "Yeah, Dad. We talked about it sometimes."

Howard nodded. Of course, they did. Nettie had a knack for getting along with even the most cantankerous of elders. They adored her or, at the very least, grunted a little softer at her when she passed by with her friends.

"Well, did he show you this?"

**NETTIE TRIED NOT TO RUN,** she really did, but two factors kept her pace just above cool-calm-collected: the equipment she carried and her destination. She waved off a few friends, dodged more hugs, and cut off several starts to long conversations she couldn't pretend to be interested in.

That was, until Snow spotted her.

"Ay, girl, where you rushin' to?" he called from his perch against the six-month old BMW. He was due for an upgrade in about another two. The nickname wasn't from his alleged occupation, but a joke at birth about his partial albinism which turned into affection as he grew older.

Nettie rolled her eyes and kept her pace, but turned and said, "You know where I'm going. Don't play dumb." Several of his boys, their friends, cracked up laughing, exaggerating the impact of her comeback. Nettie snorted and shook her head, her mission renewed as she side-stepped a small group of Snow's employees. They all nodded her way, and she nodded back with a small smile, throwing the youngest of the set a wink.

"Damn, Tilly, you in a rush?!" Snow said, suddenly appearing at her side. Snow was one of the few people to call her "Tilly," a slight upgrade from the "Tilda" he used to throw her way back in seventh grade. When he realized just why she was ignoring him, Tilly was born.

"You and your light-skinned tendencies," Nettie snapped back. "Always gotta know where I'm goin'. All up in my face!" She palmed her own face, twisting her neck. "Chill out, Drake, and let me live."

"Aight, you got jokes tonight," Snow said, keeping pace. It was easy, being 6'4" against her 5'9" stride. "Where your twin at?"

"In his skin," Nettie said with a snort. "What do you want, Snow?" She stopped walking so suddenly, Snow progressed another six feet before realizing. When he turned to her, her pointer finger was an inch from his eye. "You better not be talking to him about pushing shit, you hear me?"

Snow put up his hands in mock surrender. "Nah, nah, nothing like that, Ma, just wanted to confirm if y'all gon' go to the protest, that's it."

She narrowed her gaze at him, deciding whether she should scold him again for calling her 'Ma.' She hated that term, and Tilly had been their compromise for it, but it was clear she was making him nervous, so she backed off. "Yeah, we'll be there," she said softly, turning on her heel and resuming her walk towards the bay. Snow fell in step beside her. He liked to think he was keeping her safe this way. Even sometimes had her call him if she felt nervous walking back. She rarely did. "You see that wack-ass Chad-and-Becky march earlier?"

Snow busted out laughing. "Yeah, we all did. Wack as fuck, man. They always gotta take over, don't never think about talkin' to us first."

"Cuz they don't actually think about us," Nettie mumbled back.

"True."

They walked another three blocks in comfortable silence, each of them briefly greeting associates along the way. Half a block from the abandoned lot that would take Nettie to her meeting place, Snow slowed down, nervously eyeing the shoreline. Nettie smirked as she turned to him. "You scared?"

"Shut up, Tilly," Snow grumbled, still not looking at her. "That muhfuckah eyed me kinda hard last time."

"You were kinda rowdy last time," Nettie said, fidgeting as they stood. "His hearing is sensitive." She really wanted to sprint the last thousand feet to the rocky shoreline, though it wouldn't be necessary.

He wasn't there yet.

"Look, I know you can't stand it when I get all up in your face, but call me when y'all are done, no matter what time," Snow said quickly, his eyes darting everywhere around them. "These white people are making me nervous."

Nettie nodded, not having the heart to even joke about his justified paranoia. They were going to have to discuss this wave of change, all of them. Including him. Relocation was going to be nearly impossible, but something was going to have to be figured out.

Before he was by the wrong people.

"Aight, I will," she said.

Snow smirked at her. "Do you even *have* your phone?"

Nettie patted her pockets, then the small tote bag at her side. A faint glow lit up one corner of the canvas and Snow chortled. "Yeah, I got it."

"Surprised, wit'cho old ass. That shit a flip?"

"Fuck you, Snow," Nettie said through a chuckle of her own.

"Aight, stay up, Tilly," he said, sobering again and beginning his walk backwards. "I'mma watch you 'til he gets here."

Behind them, the rustle of a wave larger than most disturbed the darkness. Nettie smirked.

"I'll see you later, Snow."

Snow nodded his acknowledgement, his pale cheeks rosying before he turned away, practically jogging back towards home.

**THEY WERE CALLED COMMUNICATORS.**

Each family had one, and the responsibility skipped from block to block within the three-mile radius with each new generation. No one really knew how far back it had gone, but it was a duty most willingly accepted. Hannibal was supposed to be the next, but while introductions had been tossed around at a safe distance from the shore, little Netilda had waddled her way towards the funny looking mound making all those bubbles in the water.

"And look at this!" Nettie exclaimed excitedly as she pulled out another long male-to-male cord, thickly braided with bungee line. "I haven't seen this in *years*!"

The night sky was crystal clear. City lights polluted the darkness, but the gutted factories surrounding them provided enough privacy and enough cover to dim the amber radiance of his gaze. Most of his body stayed below water line; only the rough surface of his elongated head, the serpentine eyes, and the gaping abyss of his nostrils graced the air. Nettie guessed him to be lying on his belly at that point, not unlike his evolutionary cousins with short arms, keeping him in place. The freighter-truck sized talons on his toes would be dug deep into the bedrock under the city, his tail stretching like an incomplete bridge to the mainland they were just outside of, about six miles away. He was small for his kind and still young. The elders predicted he'd hit puberty in another ten years and a growth spurt with it. The bay wouldn't be able to hold him then.

The hope was he'd transform then, lay eggs and leave, like his kind do. They'd take care of feeding and caring for the next hatchling, more than likely just the one of three eggs to survive, much like he himself. It wasn't known what happened to them when they left, whether they met up or if they just swam out into the vast ocean until the darkest trench claimed them. It was fun, to a point, to speculate, but no one ever investigated. They just did what they had to and moved on.

Nothing like *this* had ever happened before. The threat of occupiers who didn't know, who didn't *care* to know. The new world that held no beliefs in anything but themselves and their moment.

A human falling in love with one them. And most certainly, not the sentiments being returned.

"I've got some good parts for the thing I built. We should come up with a name for it," Nettie mumbled as she picked through. She avoided looking at him. Had been since sitting down after her initial greeting of a small headbutt to his massive philtrum.

A burst of thick, wet air hit her like a foghorn and she fell back, her crossed legs flailing as she clawed at rocks for purchase. "The fuck, Wani?! I *just* washed my hair three days ago! You know how hard it is to get Grammie to braid my shit and here you go, fuckin' it up wit'cho hot-ass breath!" She continued mumbling as she wrung out the frizzing strands of natural hair. Ignoring the scraping of her voice against his sensitive ears, he snorted again, this time completely soaking her from head to foot in viscous fluids.

Her Kaiju had snot-rocketed on her.

Nettie squealed, stomping her frustration and disgust from foot to foot in a jittery dance. "Fucking gross, Wani!" He raised up, threatening to do it again until she glared at him, pointing a finger. "Don't you fuckin' dare!" His second lid blinked wetly at her as he settled back into the water. He eased backwards, giving her room as she continued to eye him. He then nodded, sending harder waves to the shore, lapping them at her sneakered feet. She softened. "I can't swim with you tonight. It's too cold." He snorted within the water, creating bubbles, before lifting and spraying enough to rinse her jeans. She squealed again, shivers settling in next. "Keep it up and I'll have to head home early!"

He stopped then, pulling back further and settling deeper

in the water until only the very tops of this eyes could be seen.

"Oh, god, Grammie's gon' kill me," she groaned, swiping at her box braids. It wasn't as bad as she thought, but bad enough that she'd have to rinse her hair, more than likely drying it out. "Fuck it, I'll say I needed a trim. Take it all down and have Katura do it for me." She knew he wasn't really listening at this point, but she needed to keep talking about idle things, tiny things that hardly mattered. Not when it felt like her entire city was threatening to explode.

He neared her again, soft and silent, until his short snout was brushing rocks aside to nudge her. The nudge was just short of a punch to her middle and she collapsed onto him, arms spread for an awkward hug. The roughness of his skin never bothered her. She often found it fascinating, the scales that sometimes harboured barnacles and plankton and, even rarer, whole fish.

"The neighbourhood's changing, Wani," she mumbled against him. She was getting colder the longer she embraced his snout. "All these white people are moving in. Not the kind that help. The kind that yell that they do, but still colonize. The kind who are scared." She sighed and shivered. "When does the self-fulfilling prophecy stop and inevitability begin?"

"Ma'am! Ma'am! Are you okay?! Are you hurt?!"

The flash of an LED light startled the both of them, and Nettie drew away, her next instinct to fan herself out in front of him hardly effectual, but she did it anyway. His massive head still flanked her and the low growl emanating around her body solidified the spotlight.

"Oh, my God, what is that?! Oh, my God!"

The scream that followed came from neither of them,

but sent both of them scattering for their respective habitats.

**"HMPH. WHITE PEOPLE DON'T KNOW** how to blend in nowhere. They always gotta take over, then got the nerve to get mad when shit gets as bland as they are."

Nettie and Gertie were standing in front of the new chic restaurant, the one that boasted fake bullet holes and a 40oz bottle of cheap champagne served in a paper bag for an exorbitant amount of money. The soft opening resulted in terrible reviews of the food and overall atmosphere. Still, people flocked. At least the newer residents did. Those of the old neighbourhood curled their lips in disgust and enacted weekly protests.

"Girl, where is yo' head at?!"

Nettie started, her whole body jolting as she turned around, frantically looking for her grandmother who had been at her side seconds ago. She spotted her a good fifty feet away, already at the corner. "Sorry, Grammie!" She hurried towards her, the light changing in their favor.

"What's wrong with you?" Gertie asked softly. "Been actin' real strange all mornin'. And I saw that Blizzard boy in front the house late last night. He better not have been dropping you off."

Nettie smirked. "His name is Snow, Grammie, and he was just making sure I was safe."

"Why? Something happen?"

Nettie's face fell as they walked into the dollar store. She could feel new eyes on her, questioning eyes. Or it may have been her fresh paranoia.

"Did it? I noticed your hair is a damn mess. I ain't tugging at them naps for you, girl," Gertie warned.

"Nah, Katura said I needed a trim anyway, so I'mma go over by her later."

Gertie stopped short, narrowing her gaze at Nettie. "Netilda Denise, you better tell me what happened last night, and you better not lie to me again, acting like I ain't comb through not even a week ago to feel them ends smoother than warm butter."

Nettie immediately began to fidget, her eyes stinging and throat tightening. "I-I think I fucked up, Grammie," she said through a strained breath.

Gertie suppressed the urge to cup her granddaughter's chubby cheek, her stance hardening. "Tell me."

"They saw us," she sputtered. "Last night. He was out the water, head kinda high and they *saw*."

"'They,' who?"

Nettie's shoulders fell, but she held back the smart-ass response. "*Them*, Grammie."

"Ayo, Tilly, Tilly!"

Both women turned to see Katura rushing towards them, her nephew on her wide hip, dark skin flushed. "Mad cops is down by the bay. Somebody said they lookin' for your boy. Some white lady lost her fuckin' mind, talmbout some big-ass alligator or some shit. Y'all might need to step back for a while." Katura took a breath, then said, "Hey, Ms. Gertrude, how you doin'?"

"Hmph, now I ain't so damn sure how I'm doin'," Gertie said. "They say anything else? They lookin' for anybody?"

Katura shook her head. "Not that I heard. Just an alligator."

"Okay, thank you, young lady. Y'all okay? How your sister doin'?"

Katura shook her head, her chin dimpling for a moment. She shook it off and straightened her back. "She aight. They treatin' her okay."

"Good, good, you writin' her? It gets lonely in there, don't forget to write her."

"I am, Ms. Gertrude, promise."

"Okay, good. Be on now and tell your mother to stop by some damn time. She owes me her Auntie's pound cake recipe!"

Katura giggled. "Yes, ma'am."

It wasn't until after Katura left that Nettie took a shaky breath. "Oh, shit, Grammie—"

"Calm down, girl, you ain't do a damn thing wrong," Gertie said. "It was bound to happen. Now, c'mon. We need to talk to your father, see what we gotta do."

**LAY LOW.**

That was it. It was all they could do.

They couldn't draw attention to themselves or to the bay. The bay that was dragged for twelve hours the first day, and patrolled since then.

No communication, so Howard had Nettie strategically disassemble the communication device, ensuring no transmission could occur, but allowing her fast reassembly when the coast was clear.

So, stay low.

Nettie visited once, maybe twice a week normally. But something about being forbidden from him, especially at such a crucial time...

It was excruciating.

On the third day, they were to attend the funeral of Estelle Dubois, the procession of which would double as an official Black Lives Matter march. Permits were approved with hours left, but the neighhourhood was ready.

While Nettie's assessment at the dinner table had been uncouth, it wasn't entirely inaccurate. Estelle had a fresh mouth with a sharp tongue and loose eyeballs to top it off. She rubbed plenty the wrong way, but none of that truly mattered. The neighbourhood let her be, and she kept mostly to herself and her core family, which had expanded to her baby girl in recent months. She was mostly quiet when she wasn't bothered. Some speculated more was going on with her, maybe depression or some other mental illness.

But, in the end, none of it mattered.

It started with an accusation and ended with an immediate execution. She wore the cloak of societal guilt before even opening her smart-ass mouth that day in Manny's bodega on the corner of Cambridge and Vine: her skin. And now her daughter would be raised without her mother in a fog of grief she herself would never quite understand.

"Ayo, you sure you aight?" Hannibal asked as he stepped into his sister's room.

Nettie jumped within her skin, but nodded immediately.

"Nervous?" Hannibal poked.

Again, Nettie nodded, her top teeth worrying her bottom lip. She, Gertie, and Howard kept the situation amongst themselves. Though neither were as close as Nettie, Gertie and Howard knew Angela and Hannibal would never quite understand the bond between a Communicator and their Kaiju.

"Go ahead," she whispered. She cleared her throat, smoothed her hands over her black skinny jeans. Before running out of the door, she would slip on a black hoodie with the Black Lives Matter logo on the front, Estelle's hashtagged name on the back. Her brother would mirror her in dress as well, just like the projected hundreds of protestors who were to join them. "I'll be right down." Her voice was a bit stronger, although it still shook.

Hannibal stared at her a moment longer, expression open and searching. They had the bond most twins did, but lately they'd been growing apart. Neither questioned it when they undoubtedly had each other's backs. Still, Hannibal worried for his little-sister-by-four-minutes.

"Aight," he said. "Don't take too long. Ma's already being extra."

Nettie rolled her eyes and Hannibal snorted a laugh. "I'm sure. Just tell her I have my period or some shit."

Hannibal scrunched up his face. "Way too much info."

"Goodbye, Hannibal," Nettie insisted. Hannibal waved her off and skipped down the hallway, the front door to the apartment slamming closed behind him.

Nettie wanted to go after him, but she stood in front of her window, an arm wrapped around her middle as she tried to will her dread away. But it had taken root in the center of her chest, constricting her breathing, setting her face ablaze.

She sat down on her bed and tucked her legs up, hugging her knees to her chin. "It's okay. It'll blow over in a few days. People will move on, if they haven't already," she chanted to herself, much like she had for the last three days. The dread only grew. "Fuck it." She stood up in one swift movement, her toe knocking into something as she rummaged through her closet for her black leather Timberlands. Frowning, she knelt down and pulled out the hunk of metal.

Her radio.

The very first one she'd created to talk to him, her Wani, before she understood that he heard her. Always. He'd indulged her, though. Allowed her to communicate this way so he could respond in kind. They barely needed devices now, since she saw him so often—

Used to see him so often.

The once or twice a week were the official times. There had been others. Like after school in winter, since the sun set so early. Or during the summer when curfews were lax and her friends knew she was safe. She saw her Wani as often as she could.

So, this was torture.

Relief and panic flooded her at once as she scrambled to her desk. The muscle memory fell into place as she reconnected the wiring and adjusted the headset.

One message. That's all. Just to let him know she was okay, that this would be over soon, and she'd be back.

She turned the dial and was immediately assaulted by what most would mistake as whale songs. He'd been crying for her this whole time, waiting, not understanding what had happened. Her eyes stung as she listened. She couldn't decipher most of it, but the lilt of those notes tore at her.

"Okay, okay, real quick, let me just—"

But her bravado failed her for a moment and she popped a sob.

He'd missed her. Much like she'd missed him.

And, so, placing her fingers on the straight key, she began tapping out her message.

**"WHAT TOOK YOU SO LONG?"** Angela snapped as she watched her daughter skip down the stoop.

"I thought I got my period," Nettie said, smiling hard.

Angela eyed her daughter suspiciously. While the condition would explain her mood shift for the last few days, it sure as hell wouldn't explain that moony expression on her face now. If she was late, that was a problem. If she wasn't, Nettie was prone to whining, baby-like behaviour, usually up under everyone and seeking pity. While the pity was well-deserved, Nettie tended to push the boundary of decency when explaining her plight.

And she *loved* explaining her plight.

"Stop it, Ma, I'm fine," Nettie said with a giggle. She even planted a kiss on Angela's cheek, setting off more alarms. "Promise."

Angela decided to let it go, considering what the day itself would entail. She was going to allow her daughter whatever bit of happiness she could find.

And keep an eye on her while she was at it.

**"YOU OKAY, GRAMMIE?"**

"Hell no, girl, this back is *killin'* me!" Gertie said, placing a hand on her lower back to emphasize. The cane wasn't doing shit to relieve the pressure, but her granddaughter slipping an arm around hers helped a little more than a little bit. "I'm gon' head back, start on dinner."

"You sure? You want me to walk with you?"

But Gertie was already shaking her head. "It was a beautiful service, but I can't do no protest. Shout loud and proud for me, girl."

Nettie beamed down at her grandmother. "Will do."

Gertie hugged her granddaughter a little tighter and longer than usual. Nettie tensed at first, but then allowed it, planting a large smack of a kiss to her smooth cheek. They let go and Gertie started off without another word. When she was almost out of range, Nettie shouted, "Make something good, old lady!"

By the time Gertie turned around to cuss her little insolent ass out, Nettie had been swallowed up by the crowd of black on black.

**THAT DREAD HAD RETURNED. THIS** time a bit different, but it was just as heavy, just as breathtaking.

Nettie had fucked up.

She wasn't sure how yet, but she felt in her chest that last transmission was pushing what little luck she had left.

But still she marched. She hollered for Estelle, for those she didn't know. For herself. For her future. She raised her fist in the darkening sky and she yelled along with her neighbours who were desperate for change, desperate for the chance to be human, to be seen as such, to be treated as such within their lifetime.

She cried for the present.

At the end of the route, the crowds dispersed into huddles of planning. Sign-up sheets were going around for volunteering and for the next round of protests. The vibe was electrified, emotional, yet filled with hope. Nettie smiled.

Until she saw Snow running straight for her, his pale face flush with exertion. And stained. The closer he got, the more she recognized the dark smears as soot. They'd heard sirens nearly an hour ago, but they kept going, pushing forward.

Nettie wished she'd gone back. She wished she'd walked with Gertie, had insisted to stay with her, maybe make her lie down and make her a snack. Start on dinner. Watch television. Anything.

She should've been there.

"Ayo, Tilly, they raided y'all's building," Snow said breathlessly. His eyes flicked about him as he watched his crew inform others of the news. Murmurs came alive as the crowd started to close in.

"Wait, what?" she screeched, calling attention to a few others surrounding them. In the next moment, Hannibal was at her side with Angela and Howard hustling towards them.

"The cops. They had some bogus warrant, wanted to search the place for a radio or some shit," he said sounding much more collected. "Said there was some kind of suspicious transmission—"

"Grammie," Nettie rushed. "What about Grammie?"

"They burned the building, Tilly," Snow explained, hoping he didn't have to say the words. "They fucked up. Tear-gassed the fuck out of the spot and one of 'em hit Prissy's heater."

Priscilla. Their downstairs neighbour who was always cold.

"The whole shit is gone, Tilly. The whole block burnin'."

"Young man, explain this to me," Howard said, stepping forward and grabbing the front of Snow's hoodie in a clenched fist. "Where is Gertrude?"

Snow grit his jaw, letting himself be humiliated as he said,

"She's gone, Mr. Anderson. She ain't make it out. Nobody did."

Howard's fist loosened in time for him to catch his wife as she fell, unconscious. Next to Nettie, Hannibal clenched his fists.

"You sayin' everything is gone?" Hannibal pressed, shifting from one foot to the other.

Snow nodded, his body language mirroring Hannibal's.

"I don't know about y'all, but I'm about tired of this shit." The crowd quieted as they turned to see Elder Ulen hobble towards them, adorned in all white. The only two who didn't were Nettie and Howard, the latter of whom was still clinging to Angela. "We can't even go to the corner store without bein' accused, tried, and executed for some shit. Now Gertie's paying the same price?" Ulen snorted and shook her thin head. "A seventy-eight-year-old woman they probably ain't even see. Fuck 'em." Her blue-ringed eyes flickered over to Nettie. "Call 'im."

Nettie's jaw loosened, her tongue lolling for a protestation that wouldn't come.

"We'll be aight. We know these parts. They don't. We been rebuildin' since Tulsa and Rosewood. We can do it again. *Call him*. It's time we used our own executioner."

Without another word, Nettie stepped off, breaking into a full-on run towards the bay.

**THEY WERE MORE THAN COMMUNICATORS;** they were Caretakers, they were Creators. Lovers, families, friends. They were a People unto their own, a People forced to make do with what could be taken. They were Protectors, they were Keepers.

And tonight, they would be Destroyers.

Netilda ran as fast as her legs could carry her, her lungs on fire as the cool air snatched at reserves, hardly having time to replenish her. She felt the neighbourhood at her back, heard Snow calling for folks, smelled the smoke, the char of burnt flesh, of lost hope, of dead Generations.

Or it may have just been her imagination. Her guilt threatened to singe the back of her throat as tears blurred her vision. Yet still, she pushed. She ran until her Timbs crunched glass, kicked rocks, slapped at the awaiting shore.

Only then did she stop. Hands on knees, mouth gaping, sucking at the air for a steady breath that her sobs wouldn't let her claim. In all her years, never once had she cried like this. Never had she *lost* like this.

But as the waters ran towards her, engulfing her boots, climbing up the darkness of her jeans until she was waist deep in the adjusting shoreline, she realized just how much she was set to gain.

The low growl hit deep within her belly and she held a hand there, the smile slow and sad.

"They killed Grammie," she whispered.

The water shifted again, a soft whine piercing the air loud enough to make Nettie's neck twitch as she winced. The whine eased into an open-throat groan, oddly melodic, filled with pain. Nettie felt her knees give way and she collapsed into the shallow pool, head submerged, body colliding into a rough patch of scales, barnacles, shells, and the ever-so-rare whole fish.

A catfish this time. As Nettie felt the chill of the night air against her skin once more, she rescued it, pulling it from the clutches of Wani's skin and tossing it below. Below became farther and farther away as Nettie belly-crawled to the edge of Wani's snout.

Four stories. Seven. Ten.

She held onto the curve of his nostril, her nails digging deep, her grip secure. Her Wani had grown since the summer, since they'd last gone night-swimming together. Even then he hadn't stood tall like now.

Fifteen. Twenty-two. Twenty-seven.

Still they climbed, as if in slow-motion, the air singing around her as wind hit his scales and other detritus. She was reminded of her father's job, the one before last, the one with the view of the world from its windows. She'd felt on top of it all then, had gaped at how tiny the people and all their problems had become. She thought of her Wani. Is this what he thought of them? Insignificant in their fickle struggles? Inconsequential to anything outside of their moments?

Thirty-three. Thirty-four.

Their ascent slowed. A moment later, Nettie could hear the distant rhythmic thud of a helicopter—no, *several* helicopters coming their way. The music of her lullabies as a child. The big bad monsters coming to tear apart another home.

Except this time, Nettie was the monster. Wani was the monster. And they were ready to tear it all down.

Wani stiffened and popped one short squawk. Immediately, Nettie scrambled backwards, carefully gripping his skin before scraping forward until she was set against the top of his skull. Her hands were cut up and bleeding, making her hold slippery, but she tried her damnedest to hold on as Wani stepped forward, one arm swiping at the clouds above them and colliding with two of the three helicopters. There were no explosions like the movies, just the ear-scraping sound of crunched metal, the stink of exhaust and gasoline, the faint cries of four men falling to the dark waters below. Wani swung around, his other arm smacking the last of the first fleet into the watery oblivion.

Wani stepped forward for the first time since he'd hatched and swam to shore. Since the first time he'd met Nettie. Nettie liked to think he'd fallen for the city much like he'd fallen for her, but she knew that couldn't be true. Their tradition revolved around his secrecy. What kind of life was one lived in the shadows, alone and without the warmth of family? Of your own kind?

Nothing could have prepared her for the movement. Nettie crouched as Wani stepped again, his left foot grinding the empty buildings that had shielded him into dust. Sure, she had ridden on his head during those forbidden swims deep under the night sky, but they'd just crest the surface as she held on, cackling with glee as he glided along. This was unsteady and unpredictable as his weight shifted, compensated for the deliberate destruction of a neighbourhood that had held her people captive for generations, a neighbourhood they'd turned into a home, a neighbourhood being stolen from them, brownstone by brownstone, block by block.

And now they were taking it back. If only by leaving rubble in their wake.

Wani was careful, concentrating on makeshift blockades, kicking objects with lights flashing so bright the slit of his pupils tightened into a blade of black. He let out another squawk and Nettie lay flat, facedown into the sea-smell of his flesh as he swooped down, laying waste to Manny's bodega, Estelle's apartment building, and three of Snow's cars.

Everyone who mattered were well on their by then, carrying only what they had in their hands, much like their pilgrimage generations before them. They would settle, they would be fine, just as Elder Ulen said.

Wani just made sure they were never truly forgotten.

**THE CITY'S ARTILLERY WAS NO** match for Wani's evolution. His hide ate the impact of AR-15s, brushed off canon-projected tear gas and flash bangs. He ignored it all, did what he was taught with care, with consideration.

Though they deserved none.

By the time emergency state marshals moved in, Wani was heading back to shore, his back to the destruction. It was then they struck, hitting him square between the shoulders with a missile meant for buildings. It hit him like a punch, and he dove forward, shocking both himself and Nettie. Nettie felt his surface give way, her arms and legs flailing for purchase, her breath stolen.

Wani wailed after her, his eyes widened in panic as his maw opened wide. Nettie wanted to protest, wanted to give him a sharp "No!" but choice was stolen from her as she headed straight for the abyss of Wani's throat. The thick blackness closed around her and still she fell, the stench of rotted fish and aged salt making her gag. She landed with a thud against the spiked roughness of his tongue. The sea of buds grasped at her, bulbs the size of the lamp posts in her neighbourhood swaying and splitting as she slid further and further into darkness.

Finally, she grabbed at a fatter bud, her body swinging round it as her momentum continued. She was lathered in spit, but she had no time to be disgusted: the sounds of the sea crashed around her, small buckets of it splashing towards her, washing over her. Pressure began to build in her head, her ears muffling too fast for any bit of swallowing to make a difference. A sharp pain jabbed both of them and she could hear again, the agony nearly unbearable. She screamed and the world halted, if only for a second, the pressure in her head easing. A mournful whimper vibrated around her and she nestled deeper into the buds, taking hold of the root of the one she clutched. There she felt warm, comforted. Held.

Nettie passed out.

**WHEN SHE AWOKE, THERE WERE** people standing above her, smiles on their painted faces and long spears in their fists. One extended a hand, the other a bowl of water.

Nettie took both, and then promptly passed out again.

**THE NEXT TIME SHE OPENED** her eyes, she was lying in a hammock, swaying gently with the evening breeze. It was warm wherever she was, tropical, if she dared assume.

By the look of the bay, she was not wrong.

Blue-green waters, slate grey plateaus overgrown with moss-like forests, and massive, raptor-like birds cawing as they flew overhead.

And one massive ape sitting patiently amongst it all. Watching her. Waiting.

Next to it, her Wani. And behind him, his kind. Two

of them, smaller, but still his. They all watched her. They all waited.

**IN THE COMING DAYS, NETTIE** would find her strength through the meals provided first by the tribe, then hunted by her. They communicated in rudimentary ways, all giving way to her leadership, her Wani.

She came to know the names of the others. Gojira. Minilla. Kong. They would come to know her, respect her. Listen to her.

Because a war was set to come. And this time, they were staying.

# ROGUE 57: HOME SWEET HOME

JEREMY ROBINSON

**INTERSTELLAR TRANSMISSION: CAPTAIN MARSHAL GUNN,** you are in violation of Interstellar Resource Division terms of service, section 236-S: dereliction of duty. If you do not respond within 72 hours of this message's confirmation receipt, your contract will be considered forfeit, and your survey mech, serial number HMJ 091795, will be collected for reimbursement of any outstanding debts.—IRD Command

Message sending...

Message Sent...

Awaiting confirmation...

Awaiting confirmation...

Awaiting confirmation...

Awaiting confirmation...

Awaiting confirmation...

FBW2018

Awaiting confirmation...

Awaiting confirmation...

Awaiting confirmation...

Awaiting confirmation...

Awaiting confirmation...

*:: 1*

**THE LYRICS AND TUNE OF** Die Antwoord's old-Earth classic song, "Scopie," repeat over and over in my head. Most people don't consider songs like this to even be music now, but tunes like this keep me awake, and amused. It takes all my concentration not to lapse into humming, whistling, or singing the song aloud. The last time I made that mistake it nearly cost me my life.

Rogue 57 isn't just alive, it's deadly. An untamed wilderness tumbling through space. There might have been a time when the planet circled a sun, during its formative years, but it's been alone long enough to develop a complex web of self-sustaining life that's not dependent on the light of any star.

I stop at the clearing's edge in a crouch and glance up at the luminous sky, alive with billowing clouds of tiny bioluminescent microbes. When it rains, and holy hell does it rain here, the drops glow as they fall. And they explode with light on impact. It's beautiful to witness, and it results in a rebirth of life as the planet's smallest creatures—fast moving worm-things—emerge from the soil to feed on their glowing prey. The worms attract leather-winged bat-things, hairless rat-things, and predatory, featherless bird-things, which I took for prey animals at first, but have since learned are savage pack hunters.

While some Rogue 57 species actually do eat plants, nearly all of them are omnivores, which means no matter what I encounter, I'm potentially on the menu. Especially during a rainstorm. When the first drop hits, I make my way to the top of the nearest, tallest, thickest tree to wait out the bloodbath that follows.

As dangerous as most of the lifeforms on Rogue 57 are, none compare to the planet's monarchs. I call them "assholes" mostly, but on Earth, the term for them is kaiju, first used to describe a fictional genre of movies, comic books, and novels, and later a harsh reality of the twenty-first century. What I wouldn't give to see Nemesis dropped down on Rogue 57…

It's been hundreds of years since kaiju were spotted on Earth or on any other inhabited planet, but here I am, marooned on a rogue planet where the apex species are kaiju, ranging from 75 to 150 feet in length. I've never seen the big ones on land—they tend to stay in deep waters—but the smaller ones hunt the shorelines, and deeper into the forest during rainfall. They're also extremely territorial, so any venture to the coast must be done with the utmost care.

A breeze carries the smell of my prey's dung—something like a cow patty doused in vinegar. It's odd, but the scent makes my mouth water—not because I like to eat shit, but because the smell's strength means it's fresh.

A mewl confirms it.

I call the rabbit-sized creature a "yummy-thing." Of all the animals I've managed to kill and eat, it is the tastiest. Its meat is tender and sweet, which is important, because I'm forced to eat my meals raw. The smell of fire would attract unwanted attention, though I've never been able to confirm that theory. The rubbery trees and squishy moss-coated ground don't burn.

I slip into the beige grass, which provides prefect camouflage for my naked body. After the defeat of *Daikoku*, my survey mech, it took a week of uncomfortable, sweaty living before I realized my clothing was more burden than help. It took another two months for me to shed my underwear. Now, I live like a primitive, with the exception of my Model K, sound-suppressed assault rifle.

I recovered the weapon from one of six survival pods, which sustained me as I acclimated to life on Rogue 57. They contained water, food, medical supplies, and weapons. I ran out of the first two within months, but I still have a cache of first aid gear and a small armory, which I depend on for self-defense and in case of injury. I hunt Rogue 57's smaller animals for food, and use a portable water filter for drinking. While I've managed to ration my rounds, I have just two months' worth of ammunition left—if nothing goes wrong—after which I'll have to find a way to hunt without modern tech assisting me.

A second mewl stops me in my tracks. The pitch is higher. Agitated.

*Hungry.*

To the yummy-thing, like to all living things on Rogue 57, I am a meal waiting to happen. Now that it's detected me, we're hunting each other, which is the very best way to hunt a yummy-thing. "I got what you want," I sing aloud, then mutter, hopefully, "Come and get it."

My voice triggers the expected reaction.

A snort. And then the stomping of broad feet.

I aim through the reeds, tracking the sound. The creature's hard and narrow snout allows it to slice through the grass unhindered. If it strikes me, the bony blade will cut through me just as easily.

I twitch to the left as the creature breaks out of its charge. The weapon coughs a single round, but the lack of a squeal means I've missed. The stomping feet fade into the distance.

I've never known a yummy-thing to run away from a fight… unless there's something nearby it can't eat.

*Shit.*

I lift my head above the four-foot grass blades. Standing fifty feet away is a bird-thing. The twelve-foot-tall, long-necked creature lacks the wings of a traditional bird, but its long legs are built for speed, and its long talons for gripping prey, which it consumes in chunks, cleaved by its foot-long, razor-sharp, hooked beak.

Its head is raised, four yellow eyes focused on the fleeing yummy-thing. But it doesn't pursue. Instead, it raises its beak and sniffs through what I think are a dozen nostrils lining the sides of its neck. The black beak claps together, beating out a rhythm that rolls across the field.

It's been six months since I first heard that sound, and it still gives me chills. The familiar beat has a very specific meaning, which I translate, roughly, to, "Food here's, let's eat!" It's a dinner bell, and as usual, the bird-thing's flock emerges from the forest of broccoli-like trees, anxious and squawking.

Lying low, I sniff-check my armpits. I reek. Too long without the potential for a woman—not to mention the kaiju lurking near the shore—have made me lazy about hygiene. Then I check my ammo, the number of rounds displayed on the side of the weapon. Twenty rounds and eleven bird-things.

My aim will have to be exceptional. Body shots won't do. The creatures have thick hides and round bodies. Killing them requires a headshot, and, like the birds on Earth, these things bob their heads with each step.

In short, I'm screwed.

The lead bird-thing agrees with a squawk and starts thumping its wide-splayed, three-toed foot on the ground. The tactic is meant to flush out prey, and it nearly works. Every fiber of my being says to run. But I remain rooted, hoping death will pass me by—but knowing Rogue 57's death bringers have a keen sense of smell.

*.: 2*

**CONCEALED BY THE TALL GRASS,** I have a few minutes, at most, before the first part of my body slides down a bird-thing's throat. I place the assault rifle down and carefully open the satchel bag hanging around my naked body. Inside are my first aid supplies, a water pouch, and my flightsuit's left-hand glove.

I remove the glove, slip it over my forearm and hand, and then flex the fingers twice to power it on. After a two second boot time, and a ten second connection time, I'm logged into *Daikoku's* system.

The giant survey mech took a beating, and many of its systems were disabled, but it was designed to take a beating, and it's capable of self-repair. While I've been fighting for survival, *Daikoku* has been lying motionless, not far from the shoreline, fixing itself. Taken for dead, its motionless, now moss-covered, body is disregarded by the kaiju. I've even spotted them lounging on the mech's broad chest.

I check in with *Daikoku* on occasion, monitoring repairs, checking for incoming messages from Nina, or from anyone else who might have received my two reports. But I kept my distance, allowing the mech to complete its repairs, at which time, we would have retreated from the fresh water ocean containing an untold number of kaiju, and moved inland. With *Daikoku* as a safe haven, I would have been able to survive on Rogue 57 indefinitely.

But that's no longer the plan, because without *Daikoku*, I'm not going to survive the next five minutes.

I scroll through the machine's menus, bringing up diagnostics. Repairs are at 90% out of 95%. A perfect report is impossible, as some of the mech's interstellar capabilities are beyond restoration, which means I'm stranded on this paradise/hellhole.

But the mech is fully mobile, and right now, that's what's important. I tap in a command, hit the Engage key, and flinch when I receive an error message.

[[[ PROXIMITY ALERT ]]]

One of the first things I did after realizing *Daikoku* had been knocked down, but not out, was instigate a proximity protocol. The mech won't move, or self-repair, if any lifeforms are detected nearby. And if something is nearby, it's almost always a kaiju.

Dead if I do. Dead if I don't.

But I'd rather go down fighting.

I start to override the protocol when something in the atmosphere changes. It starts as a subtle shift in pressure. Then a temperature drop. I glance up. The sky is thick with shimmering clouds, bright enough to make me squint.

*You've got to be kidding…*

To prove it's not a joke, the cloud unleashes its first drop. I track its luminous passage through the sky, descending toward me. It splashes against my naked leg, traces a blue-green path down my limb and to the ground—which instantly roils with hungry worms.

It takes all my self-control to not lunge away from the squirming tendrils as they twist and coil around my feet, eager for the incoming feast. It will result in a feeding frenzy the likes of which only one human being has witnessed since the beginning of time. And, judging by the cloud's positioning, I'm going to be at the center of it all.

Adrenaline pumps.

A lopsided smile slips onto my face.

*God, I'm messed up.*

Death's imminence is making me feel alive for the first time in a long time. Eking out a living, alone on a planet of predators, is a slow, tedious, and quiet life. Every day, I do my best to avoid fights I can't win, and now that I'm finally the star of my very own shit-show, I feel a lot less depressed about my situation.

Sure, I'm probably going to die, but at least it will be with a smile on my face.

*If* I die, I tell myself. There's still some fight left in me, and in *Daikoku.*

I return to the mech's interface, undoing the proximity alert. I tap out a series of commands that will bring *Daikoku* running—and fighting, if need be. I'm about to hit the Engage key when I'm interrupted by another message.

[[[ TRANSMISSION RECEIVED ]]]

"Holy..." The whispered word is barely audible, but enough to get an excited squawk from the nearest bird-thing, which starts running in place, building up to a frantic crescendo. The rest of the flock joins in. As soon as they have a direction, they'll spring forward at full speed, like windup toys released by a child.

The transmission displays onscreen.

[[[ TRASMISSION ]]]
Captain Marshal Gunn, you are in violation of Interstellar Resource Division terms of service, section 236-S: dereliction of duty. If you do not respond within 72 hours of this message's confirmation receipt, your contract will be considered forfeit, and your survey mech, serial number HMJ 091795, will be collected for reimbursement of any outstanding debts.—IRD Command

My first thought is, *Dick move, Nina.* But I quickly realize that nothing about the message sounds like my IRD contact. It's a form message, likely sent from the legal department. But that it happened at all means Nina is no longer at her position. She's either moved up, or out.

My second thought is more pressing. I've long since determined Rogue 57's atmosphere reflects transmissions, which means that this message came from something…

The sky above glows brighter.

Clouds billow downward as something big shoves a pressure wave toward the planet's surface. The clouds shimmer and spill their insides like a wrung-out sponge. My eyes widen as a wave of glowing water falls from the sky.

Even the bird-things seem taken aback by it. Their stomping stops, but it's replaced by a series of clapping beaks from various locations. They're confused. Talking it over. And when I hear their thumping feet again, fading in the distance, I know they've decided what's happening above us is a very bad thing.

While I have yet to come to a verdict, I don't really want to be in the open when the glowing torrent slaps into the ground. I rise from the field, my gloved hand gripping the assault rifle, and sprint toward the tree line. A quick glance over my shoulder confirms the bird-things' retreat, and then the first cool drops strike my skin.

I don't bother looking up. I just run into the shade of the nearest broccoli-like tree and dive toward its light green trunk. The tree shakes as it's struck from above. The ground thumps with the weight of thousands of gallons of water all landing at once, flattening the field's grass and covering it with a layer of glowing liquid.

As the ground comes to life with furiously feeding worms, the rain falls normally, cascading to the ground in sheets. I step toward the canopy's fringe. I would normally try to avoid the rain, but there's still the lingering question of what they hell is up in the clouds.

I peek out from beneath the tree and gaze up in time

to see the storm open and disgorge a massive structure held aloft by hundreds of booster rockets.

*Oh no...*

The IRD sent an entire colony, and it's setting down a short distance from the coast.

*:: 3*

***WHY IS THAT HERE?*** **I** wonder. The IRD never received my transmissions about Rogue 57. So why send a colony?

The obvious answer makes me angry—they assigned someone else to the rogue planet. Someone who didn't nearly pancake into the planet's surface. Someone who wasn't assaulted by kaiju. Someone who brought a habitable planet to the IRD and is getting *my* two percent.

"Like hell they are," I grumble, striking out through the broccoli forest, heading toward the still descending colony. I didn't spend the past six months fighting for my life for someone else to claim what's mine. At the same time, I recognize the colony as my ticket off planet.

If the facility isn't destroyed by kaiju.

Colonies arrive months in advance of colonists, so there are no people to worry about. They set down in optimal territory, close to water sources, and go through the automated process of self-deployment, spreading out over a landscape, expanding its interior, putting down roots, and prepping for the five hundred people who will eventually call it home. They also come with everything I need to fully repair *Daikoku*.

"*Daikoku*," I say, activating my glove's verbal interface. "Proximity status."

With the bird-things in my rearview, I don't want to risk a fight with the kaiju.

"Proximity status red," *Daikoku's* feminine electronic voice says. I'm not a fan of the voice. I'd prefer a text interface. But running and typing aren't good bedfellows. The red status means there is still an alien lifeform in direct contact with the mech's body.

As waterfalls of glowing rain water pour through the gaps in the lush canopy, I break into a run. The white noise of falling water hides the sound of my bare feet striking the ground. A side benefit of living in this harsh land is that I'm now in excellent shape. I kept myself in decent physical condition before, but *Daikoku* did all the heavy lifting, and I spent a lot of time confined to a chair. Now, I can run miles at near full speed without stopping for a breather.

Within minutes, water permeates the moss-like forest floor. Each step brings a glowing soup of water up between my toes, sometimes with worms.

I round a stand of trees and come face-to-face with a veritable horde of rat-things. On their own, or in a small group, they'd be on the dinner menu. But there are hundreds of the creatures, bounding, writhing, and gnashing their teeth. If they decided to have a Marshal Gunn snack, there'd be nothing I could do to stop them.

Water sprays around my feet as I slide to a stop, bumping my way past a few of the small creatures. There's a horrible pause as the creatures look up at me, but they don't attack. They go back to their worm feast, unconcerned with my presence. Knowing it won't be long until the vast number of rat-things attracts larger predators, I continue my sprint straight through the pack, slowing only to avoid stepping on them.

The forest ends atop the crest of a hill, providing me with a view of the fresh water ocean, *Daikoku's* prone body, the kaiju laying over his legs, and the descending colony still several thousand feet up, but performing a controlled descent that will deposit it just a few miles from the water.

Too close.

The kaiju lounging atop *Daikoku* watches the colony's progress through the sky, intrigued by the massive, fiery circle, but not yet aggressively so.

Because the sky isn't its territory.

I'm at a crossroads. I could head for the colony and attempt to activate its automated defense systems after it sets down. But that will take time, and if I'm honest, the defense system wasn't designed with kaiju in mind.

I scan the creature on top of *Daikoku*. It's at least eighty feet long—big, but not the biggest. Its beaver-like tail, the sides lined with spikes, pats the ground behind it—the only clear sign that the kaiju isn't pleased with the colony's appearance. Its wide, black head is craned skyward, the four small black eyes on either side watching. The armored plates rising from the back of its skull and tracing a path down its salamander body flex and retract. It reaches out a long arm, slips the talons at the ends of its two fingers into the soil and drags two troughs into it.

The kaiju's agitation is building.

Ignoring the lessons learned over the past six months, I head for *Daikoku* and the kaiju perched atop it. With the colony still descending, and the rain still pouring down, I doubt the beast would even react to my presence if it spotted me… which I'm not going to let happen anyway.

Moving through trees and tall brush, I run toward my fallen, moss-encrusted mech. The closer I get, the deader *Daikoku* looks. The survey mech is technically a tool, but for me, it was a home. At times, my only friend in the universe. I imagine the kaiju's surprise as *Daikoku* springs to life beneath it and puts a drill through the side of its head.

Adrenaline pumping, my smile returns.

And then, the kaiju roars. The massive beast leaps to its feet.

But the colony hasn't set down yet. Something else has agitated the beast, and it isn't me. I follow the monster's beady, black-eyed gaze up above the colony and spot a familiar, humanoid shape, far too big to be human.

A survey mech.

One of the new models.

The robot stands seventy feet tall. Its blue hull shimmers with color as it reflects the clouds, and the rain douses it with glowing microbes. Whoever claimed my planet is on board that mech. As much as I'd like to backhand-slap the pilot, I also need to warn them.

I tap a message into my glove's interface.

[[[ DANGER CLOSE. DO NOT LAND. RETURN TO ORBIT. ]]]

When I receive no reply, I resume my sprint for *Daikoku*.

The kaiju is on its feet now, held aloft by its powerful hind legs and wide-splayed, three-toed, webbed feet. I could probably fire my assault rifle at the thing and it wouldn't notice. The beast is locked on target. But so far, it's alone.

Luckily for me, when *Daikoku* fell and powered down, it did so with its head turned to the side, allowing me to reach the hatch at the back of its head without having to climb. After punching in a quick numerical code, the locks *thunk* open. I freeze for a moment, listening for any signs of movement, but the hissing rain, and now the roar of rocket boosters, drowns out all other sounds.

Inside the airlock, I pull the door closed and flinch again when the locks reengage, the sound much louder within *Daikoku*. But the mech's thick hull muffles the white noise from outside. After climbing up through the sideways second airlock door and closing it behind me, the sounds outside fade to nothing. For a moment, it's peaceful, then I look up to where my command chair once sat before it, and I, were launched through the ceiling, escaping what seemed like certain death at the time.

"Ahh, crap."

*:: 4*

**PROBLEM NUMBER ONE: *DAIKOKU'S* CONTROLS** are 20 feet above me. Reaching them without first having the mech right itself will mean somehow scaling the floor.

Problem number two: no command chair. I'll have to control Daikoku from a vertical position, something I've never done. It's common enough in newer mechs but unheard of with the old analog controls that I prefer.

A blaring roar sifts its way through the mech's hull. Then the quake rolls through the oversized head, knocking me to my knees.

*It's the kaiju,* I think. *It's moving.*

*How long until more of the monsters heed the roar's call?*

*How long until they overwhelm and destroy my ticket off this world?*

I run to the rear of the command room, climb up the angled wall of the octagonal space, and then lunge upward, gripping hold of a hatch handle. I hoist myself up, using the hatch's frame as a handhold and getting my foot up onto the handle.

"That wasn't too bad," I whisper, and then I turn around to look at the control console. The outer most edge is just ten feet away. A good leap might get me there, but it could also damage the hardware. I need to reach the secondary support system—basically a series of straps dangling from the ceiling designed to keep a standing operator from flying all over the control cabin. And that jump… is too far.

I scan the front of the control room and look for handholds. If I can climb to the top, I might be able to drop down to the straps… which will either work, or kill me.

"*Daikoku,*" I say. "Power on visual array." A circle of viewscreens extend from the ceiling. Nearly all the screens show views obscured by moss. Damn.

"Open window shields." The protective flaps over the windshield visor snap open. Brilliant splashes of blue and green explode across the glass, sliding to the left in long rivulets. Beyond the rain is empty sky. No kaiju. No survey mech. No colony. We're facing the wrong direction.

I'm about to order *Daikoku* to turn its head to the right when the rain stops hitting the window.

*The rain didn't stop,* I realize. *It's being blocked.*

A broad black face slides into view above me. The kaiju turns its head to the side and leans in close, getting a better look with its four small eyes. I remain perfectly still until the thing snarls.

*It sees me…*

*It's going to attack!*

"*Daikoku*, sit up!" The big mech obeys without hesitation, sitting up hard and fast, catapulting the surprised kaiju off, and me into the front of the command center. My naked body tumbles and then squeaks to a stop against the smooth floor. I right myself and then leap for the secondary support system, wrapping the straps around me and cinching them tight.

Hands on the familiar controls, I take command of *Daikoku* for the first time in half an Earth year. And it's just in time. The kaiju righted itself just about as fast as I did. Its arms stretch out as it charges, reaching for *Daikoku's* head.

The past year has taught me a lot, but the most useful skill I've picked up is how to fight things that aren't human. Step one is to not let their ferocity frighten you. Step two is to frighten them with your own.

I grasp the kaiju's outstretched wrist, squeezing down with enough force to compress titanium. It makes short work of the monster's wrist bones. Then I fling *Daikoku* back, plant the mech's feet against the kaiju's core, kick hard, and fire the boosters at full.

The kaiju launches.

I twist my head to track its spiraling course up into the atmosphere, and *Daikoku* mimics the movement. The kaiju's rigid form twists through the air, a scorched hole in its chest.

I smile. Round two is going to be different.

It takes just seconds to get the mech on its feet and ready to brawl. I scan the area, expecting to see an army of kaiju rushing me. Instead, I see rain, a still sea, and the colony, hovering a thousand feet up.

*Did the mech pilot receive my warning?*

I scan the sky for the survey mech and find nothing.

*Where did it go?*

A rumble shakes *Daikoku.* I assume it's the kaiju crashing back to the ground, but then a proximity alert sounds. Without looking, I dive low and forward, performing a roll it wouldn't have occurred to me to attempt six months previous. Back to the ocean, I get my feet under me and stand, extending two drill bits above *Daikoku's* fists.

But I don't strike. Confusion assaults me, locking me in place.

My attacker isn't a kaiju, it's the mech, and now that I can see it up close, I realize the horrible truth: it's not a survey mech.

It's battle mech.

My comms ping. The pilot is calling me.

"Accept," I say, and I look upon the face of a man I hoped I'd never see again—Rich Taylor. His name might not sound like that of an animated villain, but he's an asshat in the extreme. He's been flagged multiple times for questionable activities that were never enough to get him booted from the IRD, probably because they generally worked out to be profitable.

And there is no more profitable prize than Rogue 57.

"Wish I could say it was nice to see you alive," Taylor says, "But I was hoping to find your corpse."

I say nothing. Offering any kind of retort is going to play into his game and distract me. Instead, I scan his mech and find myself woefully outclassed. It's got rocket bays, chain guns, and bladed weapons, and it's built for power and speed. *Daikoku* is tough, and powerful, but it's not built for a fight, let alone against a battle mech.

Of course, that doesn't mean it *can't* fight. And my theory on ferocity applies to humans as much as to kaiju.

Speaking of which…

I disengage the lasers tracking my head's movements and adjust my viewscreens to display the view behind Daikoku without turning the big head. As far as Zorn is concerned, I'm still looking at him.

"What was that thing?" Taylor asks. "Big sonuvabitch, yeah? How many of them live on my planet?"

I'm not sure about that. Rogue 57 is a big planet. The kaiju could be a local species, but given their ocean-going ways, I suspect they populate most of the waters and coastal regions. There's probably millions of them. Instead of relaying the facts, I can't stop myself from saying, "*My* planet."

When I see waves rising in the distance, I return my view to Taylor.

His high-pitched laugh tests my patience. "There's the Captain Gunn everyone loves so much. You know, Nina actually cried when you were finally declared MOD last month."

That's why he's here. When they didn't hear from me, and I didn't respond to their TOC transmission, which was broadcast by the colony's repeater as it descended past the atmosphere, I was declared "Missing or Dead," meaning any available mech pilot could claim my job.

"As much as I don't like you," Taylor says, "I know you're a good pilot. For you to be MOD meant you'd encountered something you couldn't handle, and since you can handle damn near anything in space, I figured…" His mech opens its arms at the surrounding lush planet. "Life."

His smile becomes a scowl. "And death."

When his mech's shoulders snap open, I drop to a knee, form a shield out of *Daikoku's* tough forearms and retract the window shields.

Rockets twist toward me, striking the ground all around, and *Daikoku's* arms. Damage reports flash to life. The left arm's drill is ruined, but I managed to survive the attack with mostly superficial damage.

Without standing, I extend my right forearm and eject the drill. The twelve-foot diamond tipped drill launches out. Had Taylor's mech been a survey model, it would have taken the bit in the chest, but the battle mech has no trouble dodging the projectile. While Taylor moves left, I lunge forward, forcing him to keep moving. If I were able to get ahold of him, this fight might go a different way.

Taylor circles as his shoulder rockets reload. It won't be long before he's able to launch another barrage. When I stop moving, Taylor does the same, squaring off with me once more.

"This hardly seems fair," Taylor says as chain guns snap out of his forearms and his rocket bays open again. "But fair never got me anywhere."

As tough as *Daikoku* is, Taylor is going to tear me apart.

"Any last words?" Taylor asks, smiling like a dick.

When I smile, it unnerves Taylor. He knows what it

means. Knows there's something he's missed. "Just two," I tell him, and then I say, "Proximity alert."

*:: 5*

**THE KAIJU RISES FROM THE** ocean behind Taylor, shifting from a rapid swim to a thunderous run when it reaches the shallows, which for it are several hundred feet out.

Taylor spins around to face the incoming monster, and I'm given the pleasure of hearing him squeal in fright before he remembers he's in a battle mech. But there isn't a mech in the universe designed to handle the two-hundred-foot-long behemoth rising from the sea. It's by far the largest kaiju I've ever seen, and it shows no fear as it lunges, opening its broad, toothy jaws and two-fingered claws.

Taylor unleashes with the rockets and chain guns, all of the ordinance finding its mark on the creature's softer underside. None of it is enough to kill or even slow the thing. If anything, the assault fuels the kaiju's territorial rage.

The battle mech's shoulder's compress under the kaiju's powerful grasp, its strength more than a match for even *Daikoku.*

Twin blades extend from Zorn's arms. If he can strike the monster's core, he might actually deliver a killing blow. As he thrusts the blades forward, the kaiju pulls outward, wrenching both of the mech's arms at the shoulder joints, thwarting Taylor's attack.

Still connected via comms, I hear the man's scream and can't help but feel a smattering of mercy for him. His neurologic connection to the mech lets him feel the arms' removal as if they were his own. The feeling would have been momentary as the emotional compensators shut down the link to the missing limbs, but Zorn's scream isn't just from the faux pain of amputation—it's also from the realization that he's now defenseless and about to die.

The kaiju roars with enough force to send a wave of distortion through the glowing rain water. Then it lunges down, clamping its massive jaws over Taylor's mech. The robot is lifted off the ground and shaken back and forth. Sheets of metal tear away. Insides fall out. And then, the mech's lower half breaks away and falls to the ground. The monster crushes the mech's torso and head between its teeth, again and again. The kaiju then determines the mech can't be consumed and spits the mashed hunk of mangled metal to the ground.

"Taylor?" I say, but I already know he's gone. The silent comms confirm it.

The kaiju lowers to all fours, standing over the ruined mech. It's impossible to tell exactly where its solid black eyes are looking, but I have a strong sense they're staring straight at *Daikoku.*

At me.

I take a slow step back, lowering myself down, hoping that a submissive posture will help.

It doesn't.

The kaiju matches my pace, stepping over the remains of Taylor's mech.

I continue back, wondering how far I'll have to go before I'm outside the kaiju's territory, or it decides I'm not worth the effort. The kaiju are giants, monsters in every sense, but they're not stupid. It knows *Daikoku* isn't food. Probably knows *Daikoku* has been lying beside the ocean for the past six months, which might be the only reason the behemoth hasn't torn me asunder already.

I consider lying back down, but putting myself fully at the mercy of the kaiju doesn't sit well with my "go down fighting" personality.

When it takes another step closer, lowering itself into a pouncing stance, adrenaline flows anew. But this time, there's no smile. As good as I might be at surviving, and fighting, I can't stop this kaiju any more than I can calm the storm overhead.

And I can't eject this time, either.

*Fight or die,* I think, and some annoying part of my mind reworks the statement to something more accurate: *Fight and die.*

My eyes turn up to the sky. At least the last thing I see will be beautiful... if you don't count the inside of the kaiju's mouth.

Then I see it—the colony.

It hovers a thousand feet above the ground, its booster rockets shimmering heat, turning the falling rain into steam. It's a giant circle, a quarter mile across and densely packed with compressed walls, floors, and heavy machinery.

With Taylor's destruction, the colony is obeying his last command, and will, until it runs out of fuel and crashes.

Unless someone with an active comm and an IRD clearance takes over.

I begin working my customized keyboards while continuing to back off.

A roar announces the kaiju's assault. It leaps forward,

halving the distance between us with a single lunge. Its thick hind legs bunch for a second bound. Knowing escape is impossible, and fighting is hopeless, I do the only thing I can. "*Daikoku*, brace for impact!"

The big mech folds in on itself, ducking its head down and folding its arms and legs into a protective barrier. Everything cinches up tight, as the strongest armor plates shift to the outside. The result is a crude square of armor designed to punch through an errant comet or asteroid encountered in deep space.

I'm thrashed about during the transformation, but I keep on typing, overriding protocols and sending a series of commands.

I can no longer see the kaiju, but I don't need to see it to know it's picked up *Daikoku* in its massive maw. Alarms sound. Warning lights flash. How long until the command center is crushed, and me along with it? I hit a final key on the keyboard and I'm thrashed about even more. Restraints dig against my naked flesh, rubbing it raw. My head feels like it's going to snap as I'm whipped back and forth.

And then… weightlessness.

*What the hell?*

I glance at my altimeter and find myself several hundred feet above the ground. The damn thing catapulted me!

*Daikoku* unfurls, grinding a bit as its body returns to its humanoid form. The kaiju is below, watching my course through the air, completely oblivious to what's behind it. I fire the mech's undamaged boosters as I descend. It's not enough to fly, but it slows my fall.

The kaiju flexes, ready to charge as I land with a ground-shaking thud.

*Too soon,* I think, triggering *Daikoku's* external speakers, cranking them to max, and unleashing the most ferocious scream I can manage. The aggressive stance catches the kaiju off guard. Its head retracts in an almost comical "what the fuck?" kind of way, like when a mouse stands its ground against a cat.

And it's enough.

The kaiju senses the colony coming, the roar and heat of its boosters giving it away, but there's no time to move. The outer edge of the plummeting structure slams into the kaiju's head, cratering it inward. The stunned monster falls, allowing the colony to pass over it, but a roaring booster spews white hot fire over the creature's body, which bursts into flame.

Then the colony's entire weight comes down, smearing the kaiju into oblivion and forcing me to run. *Daikoku* isn't built for speed, but I manage to give each step a little rocket boost, keeping myself ahead of the crashing colony and the wave of soil rising ahead of it.

When my proximity alert flashes, I leap into the air, ignite all functioning boosters, and surge ahead. My landing is far less graceful. *Daikoku's* foot snags on a broccoli tree and I'm sent sprawling forward. I roll to a stop, facing the colony. A wave of forest crashes over me, before I'm struck by the colony's outer edge and launched out. I roll to a stop again, but this time when I look back, the mound of ground between me and the crashed colony lies still.

*Daikoku,* on hands and knees, climbs to the top of the mound. A trough of ground has been scoured clean by the colony, which lays still. I'm not sure if the massive structure is functional or not, and I'm not going to get the chance to find out. Beyond the fallen city, the smeared remains of the kaiju, and Taylor's mech, the ocean roils with massive waves.

More kaiju are incoming, and if I stay, my odds of surviving are as slim as they were when I faced the flock of bird-things. Using the mound of soil as cover, I slide down and do the only thing I can—I run.

Still stranded.

Still without help.

Still alive and now with my home returned to me.

"Okay, big guy," I say to *Daikoku*, giving one of the keyboards a pat. "Let's have a look around."

Within ten minutes, I'm beyond the range I previously explored on foot. Thirty minutes later, we're atop a mountain, sitting on a ledge overlooking the ocean, which is shimmering in the rain storm that doesn't reach this far. The view is stunning, if you ignore the kaiju stomping around through the colony as it attempts to expand and deploy.

I stand atop *Daikoku's* head, clothed in only a glove, breathing the freshest air in the known universe, free of humanity's ambition-fueled drama. Life is simple on Rogue 57. I smile. Life is good.

For the first time since setting down on this rogue planet, I think I'd prefer it if no one ever found out about it. Rogue 57 isn't mine to profit from… it's just mine.

# THE GENIUS PRIZE

MARIE BRENNAN

**THERE ARE ABUNDANT RECORDS OF** the Twentieth Annual Metzger-Patel Genius Prize championship in 2131. Everything from the entry forms for each Contestant Team, to the judges' notes on each creation, to the home videos filmed by proud parents, to the helicopter footage of the aftermath.

Finding out what happened isn't the hard part.

Believing it is.

**AFTER THE CONCLUSION OF THE** nineteenth championship, Immis Chae interviewed Anjale Metzger for *Globeline*. Metzger and Tahira Patel usually retired out of the public eye after the competition was over, but Patel had given a similar interview after the ninth year, and this time it was Metzger's turn.

"It's become a cliche," the interviewer says in the recording, smiling under the broadcast lights, "but the

FBW 2018

entries this year really were bigger and better than ever—with an emphasis on bigger. What are you going to do for the twentieth anniversary of the Genius Prize? How are you going to make it stand out, when escalation has become the expected norm for your competition?"

Metzger is less fond of the camera than her wife, but she looks crisp and collected in her tailored silk suit, the grey threading through the black of her mathematically precise cornrows almost more decorative than a sign of age. She does not smile. "Well, Immis, in part that is up to our contestants. It's their creations that the world tunes in to see, and so if those are more impressive every year, that's because these young people keep on coming up with new and more astonishing innovations. But yes, Tahira and I have plans for the twentieth anniversary, just like we did for the tenth. This time we'd like to look back at the history of the prize and honor those who have come before—and that's all I can say for now."

Chae faces the nearest floating camera, and their smile grows wider. "You heard it here, folks: next year you won't just see *one* Genius Prize, but twenty years' worth. I'm sure it will be spectacular."

**THE CAMERA IMAGE FROM THE** warehouse in Bamako rocks unsteadily as a parran-alloy arm slams into the wall. "Careful!" Akua Fonghoro shouts, as if her teammate Kisi Abouta is deliberately being careless.

Their mecha staggers drunkenly. "I'm trying!" Kisi shouts back, even though the microphone inside the suit picks up every whisper with perfect clarity. "It's just—this thing—won't—"

The days of simple humanoid shapes are long gone. Everyone knows that Dr. Metzger and her judges score the entries on more than just size, power, agility. Anybody can slap together a mechanical suit, piston-driven arms and legs and a thundering engine to make it go; without style, you're no better than the average middle-class tinkerer in their garage.

The device lurching with a stiff-legged gait toward the cinderblock wall has the head and beak of a skeletal pterosaur, and wings that are extending and retracting in a stuttering rhythm. They aren't used to fly like a bird; no amount of flapping up and down could lift the mass of machinery beneath them, even with modern lightweight alloys. That's what the spinjets are for.

"Breathe," Ye Tangara says from a prudent distance, as one of the spinjets fires briefly, incinerating a stack of fiber rods. "Like you practiced."

Panting comes over the loudspeakers. Kisi manages to turn aside before she runs headfirst into the wall. "Okay. I think I'm getting the hang—"

The left wing shoots out full-force and slams against the cinderblocks. Kisi's curse is lost within the grinding screech of the collision.

Almost out of frame, she stops the mecha and levers back the top of the pterosaur's skull, exposing her face, which leaks sweat like a crushed sponge. "I swear, I'm going to just rip that thing out of here. We did fine without it before. Why do we need it now?"

"Because," Akua says, as Ye brings Kisi water and mops off her face. "What we've got was good enough to win the Songhali Nationals, but not the Genius Prize. *Everybody* there is going to have a Truong sympathy net. Without one, you won't be able to keep up."

"And with one, I'll fall on my face and be the laughingstock of the world." But Kisi nods away the last of the water and claps her mecha shut again. The machine hums as the sympathy net activates, and the wings rattle shut, unevenly. The loudspeakers pick up her voice again, restored to its usual focus and cool. Nobody lacking in those qualities makes it to the three rounds of the Genius Prize, much less through them.

"I have two months," Kisi says as she stumbles out of the camera's view. "I'll get this."

**"GOD, THAT STUFF STINKS."**

For all that the robotics teams mock the bioengineers as being "squishy" and not knowing which end of a computer is up, the truth is that the bios know their way around a program or two. They couldn't possibly design their handcrafted genomes, much less produce them, if they didn't.

But it is true that they're more prone to being careless. Chango Benitez used his laptop to call his parents back in Guatemala, and while the camera is off now, he forgot to disable the audio pickup afterward. With enhancement, it's possible to make out his team's entire conversation, right up until the point where Miguel Cobar asks if he remembered to kill the mic and Chango swears, running for his computer.

Before that happens, their team leader and kaiju handler speaks. "I don't care what it smells like, as long as it works." Rico Sarabia's bitter words are undercut by a gagging noise. "Okay, maybe I care a little."

Faint noises register on the mic as he fills the cartridge,

loads it into the hypospray, and hooks up the pressure hose. Their organism, a creature best described as an armor-plated, six-armed gorilla with the many-rowed teeth of a shark, is only vulnerable to such a device in one location, but the boys have it well-trained; there is no sound of shuffling, and only a small grunt of complaint, as Rico crawls between its legs, levers up one of the armor plates, and shoots a dose of cutting-edge chemistry into the creature's bloodstream.

"We should have done this months ago," Miguel says as Rico crawls back out. "I can't believe we lost, man. This is our only chance to redeem ourselves."

The Tlachi Institute is the most respected secondary school for biological sciences in the world. They've won fourteen of the last thirty Patel Bioengineering Tournaments, dating back to before the foundation of the Genius Prize. For Rico and his friends to lose the Central American Regional Championships to the Nicaraguan national team was humiliating. Had the Nicaraguans not been disqualified after the fact for outside assistance—a consultation with the leader's aunt at the Shinrasen Center, not covered up quite well enough—Rico, Miguel, and Chango would be staying home this year.

The Tlachi team's chat logs, subpoenaed during the later investigation, reveal that Rico was the one who successfully argued against using obsequium on their kaiju before regionals. Although ruled legal by Dr. Patel and the advisory board of her tournament, he felt the agent was not "in the spirit of things," and preferred to direct his kaiju the old-fashioned way, with shouted commands and hand signals.

He changed his tune after the Nicaraguans' obsequium-dosed three-headed serpent dodged every one of their gorilla's six arms, got it in a pin, and nearly put one head's fangs through its skull. There's another hypospray hiss on the audio from Chango's laptop as Rico doses himself with dominatio, the companion drug to obsequium.

Scruples don't last long in the face of defeat.

**EVERY YEAR, THERE ARE NEW** developments. More efficient engines. A carbon nanotube splice that makes the bones lighter and more resilient. Stabilizer systems that mean the mecha spend less time knocking each other over. Fast-coagulating blood. What starts out as secret tech becomes standard military issue, then the plaything of the rich, then fodder for teenagers working in their garages and backyards and high school bio labs.

Many of those things are invented by past winners of the Genius Prize. Some of the new techniques make their debut in the competition. After all, that's why Metzger and Patel founded their respective championships: to encourage innovation, to find and nurture the brightest young minds in their respective fields.

As for why they joined those championships together, pitting the top wonders of each side against one another in a no-holds-barred fighting extravaganza?

They've answered that question a thousand times in a thousand interviews. A polished answer, focus-tested and vetted by lawyers as being non-prosecutable. But Tahira Patel gave the real answer once, when she'd had a bit too much sake at a reception in Tokyo.

"Because it's *fun*."

---

**WHAT ANJALE MEZTGER MEANT ABOUT** history becomes clear during the inaugural parade of the Twentieth Annual Metzger-Patel Genius Prize.

Although not quite as extravagant as the opening ceremonies of the Olympics, the Genius Prize parade is still quite astonishing. For the billions of people worldwide who only tune in to the realms of high school competitive robotics and bioengineering during the third week of June, it's their first chance to see the competitors: massive robots and equally massive kaiju, shaped to look like creations out of science fiction or national folklore or someone's worst nightmare, all stomping or rolling or slithering or flying around the arena where they will soon be demonstrating what they're capable of.

When the masking field drops, revealing the stage at the center of the arena, Metzger and Patel are not alone. Together with the usual array of judges, officials, and security forces, they have the winning entries from the previous nineteen years of both their respective competitions.

The effect is initially comical. In the early days, the standards for what teenagers might be expected to create were a good deal lower than they are today. It is a tradition almost as old as the Genius Prize itself to bemoan the loss of those simpler, more innocent days, before the attention of recruiters and the sizable cash award drove the teams to ever-more ambitious heights. The top mecha from the first year of the competition is little more than human-sized—essentially just a souped-up exoskeleton. The top kaiju from that year isn't even present in person, having died of lung failure six months after the competition. It is represented instead by one of its ninth-generation offspring, having displayed a capacity for budding that surprised its designers as much as anyone else.

But with each subsequent year, the creations get more impressive. Simple human-shaped mecha give way to things with more arms, more legs, more spikes. The kaiju leave nature behind and take hybrid forms even the ancient Greeks never conceived of.

And they get bigger.

A *lot* bigger.

The winners from the previous year—a scythe-armed Cuisinart with no discernible head and a creature that resembles the love child of a squid and a rhinoceros—dwarf Metzger and Patel, towering nearly forty feet tall. The technology for creating such things may fit into a suburban basement, but the creations themselves do not.

So in the end, the effect is exactly as the two women intended. As laughably simple as the early entries may seem, they're the foundation for a progression that has escalated through the years. They make clear the sheer magnitude of what Metzger and Patel have wrought.

In the footage of that evening, there are close-up shots of all the individuals who would become so important a few days later: the Songhali team of Akua, Ye, and Kisi; the Tlachi team of Chango, Miguel, and Rico; the Canadian hacker Tiennot Ahenakew, nearly the only member of his team to survive; Nevali Jones, the head of security for the event; and, in a panning shot across the stands, the Canthorpe twins.

**IN THE FOCUS PIECE THAT** ran prior to the nineteenth championship, ambition burns within Arthur and Arnold

Canthorpe like a flame. You can see it blazing in their eyes, feel the heat of it in every gesture.

"We've been planning this since we were six," Arthur says, slinging one arm around his twin brother. "Eleven years of work. This is the year it's gonna pay off."

From outside the frame, the interviewer asks, "Why did you decide to split up? Why not join forces, work together on the same team? Then you could both win the Genius Prize."

Arnold laughs. "Because we want *all* the prizes. The way we've got it set up, Arthur will win the Metzger Robotics Championship, and I'll win the Patel Bioengineering Tournament. Then we'll face off in the final round, and whoever walks away with the Genius Prize, it'll still be a Canthorpe."

Their confidence is infectious. You can see it in your mind's eye: Arthur Canthorpe holding the robotics trophy, Arnold Canthorpe the one for bioengineering, and between them, the enormous twined helix and gearing of the Genius Prize. The interviewer says, "It's quite a plan. Aren't you competitive with each other at all?"

Arthur laughs. It's indistinguishable from his brother's laugh; their hairstyles are identical, save for the direction of the part. They worked hard to create their public image, the cooperative opposition of the Canthorpe twins. "Oh, sure," he says, and lets go of his brother to punch him gently in the shoulder. "I'm going to kick his—"

Although the courtesy filter transforms his final word to "butt," anyone who reads lips can tell what he really said.

There are no interviews with the twins after their defeat. Although most leaders of losing teams are gracious enough to speak at least briefly with reporters, the Canthorpes left in a fury before the dust had even settled.

**INVESTIGATORS SCOURED ALL THE RECORDS** of the first few days of the twentieth competition, not because they were unclear on what happened, but because they wanted to answer the question: could it have been prevented?

The answer, of course, is *yes*. There were countless opportunities for someone to notice what was going on and put a stop to it before the chaos began. But those opportunities all came in the months between the nineteenth and the twentieth competitions—not at the event itself. The government of the Rocky Mountains Federated States, exceedingly eager to pin responsibility for the disaster on as many people as possible, did its very best to flay Nevali Jones alive for being negligent, but the truth is that she wasn't. By the time the various competitors arrived at the stadium outside Aspen that had been chosen to host that year's Genius Prize, there was nothing she could be expected to see, no action she ought to have known to take. Not until the trouble began.

The documents from the investigation describe the first few days as utterly routine, the recordings showing nothing suspicious. Demonstration trials for each of the kaiju, each of the mecha, in alternating turns. The panels of judges inspect them up close, questioning the teams who built or bred them, conducting various tests. Then they back off to a safe distance while the team leaders put their creations through their paces. The robotics pilots climb into their mecha; the bioengineering handlers shepherd their beasts along like proud owners at a dog show.

But the differences are visible. With the aid of a Truong sympathy net, the linkage between the mecha pilots and their suits is far more fluid than before, the mechanisms responding to thought instead of controls. With a fresh injection of obsequium rendering them docile, the kaiju almost seem to have a telepathic link with their dominatio-dosed handlers, never hesitating, never balking.

Even knowing what will happen, it's mesmerizing to see. More people tuned in to watch the first round than ever before, just to enjoy the balletic dance of these creations across the arena.

As usual, the judges choose eight in each category to progress to the second round. This is the point at which the whole world starts watching, because who can resist the appeal of watching giant robots slam each other with titanic force, giant beasts tear each other apart? It's better than a movie, because it isn't scripted; it's better than the Olympics, because it's mecha vs. monsters. Metzger and Patel judge this round themselves, basing their choices not simply on the brute question of which entry can beat up the other entries, but on subtleties of movement, speed, elegant engineering.

If there's one downside to the creation of the Genius Prize, it's that it has taken a little of the shine from the awards—the lesser awards, the preliminary awards. People these days use a whole host of deprecatory words to refer to the Metzger Robotics Championship and the Patel Bioengineering Tournament, so thoroughly have they been subsumed into the spectacle of the final round. You can even see it in the faces of the winners, Kisi and her Songhali teammates, Rico and his Tlachi friends: they're happy, of course they're happy, but they're also thinking ahead to the next day. And so are all of the losers, because it's happened before that an entry has lost the individual competition, but won the final prize.

This is where the real fun usually begins, the temptation that led Metzger and Patel to combine their two events into one. The top eight finalists from each category—those still in good enough shape to move, after a night of frantic surgery and repair—march into the arena, for a grand melee of metal against flesh.

In the year 2131, this is when the chaos starts.

**THERE IS NO FOOTAGE OF** how it happened, of course. The Canthorpe twins were far too clever for that. They both placed a close second in their respective competitions, and came near to winning the Genius Prize itself; no one ever accused them of being stupid. They made sure the cameras and microphones where they settled in to work transmitted only what the twins wanted them to.

But it's possible to re-create it from the evidence. Arthur found a security vulnerability in the Truong sympathy net about one month after Truong Industries hired him, and chose not to report this to his employers. Arnold had the more difficult challenge, contaminating an entire production batch of obsequium with a custom-designed virus—and in fact, one of the kaiju entries was dosed from an earlier batch, and failed to be suborned as expected.

Every single recording of the main event agrees: precisely thirty seconds into the melee, the twins take over.

Fifteen of the titanic figures thudding and whirring and

flying toward one another across the huge arena stagger to a halt. The sixteenth, the French scorpion that has escaped the trap, pulls up short a moment later; its handler has noticed the sudden stillness, and thinks someone has given a signal to abort the competition.

In unison, the fifteen under Canthorpe control wheel to face the box from which Metzger and Patel are watching. Every loudspeaker in the arena, every mecha's external output, and quite a few personal devices that have been insufficiently shielded, suddenly boom out the identical voices of Arthur and Arnold Canthorpe, speaking in eerie (and pre-recorded) unison.

"Peoples of the world," the twins declare into the growing silence. "Last year, Anjale Metzger and Tahira Patel judged our creations inferior. Insufficient. Unworthy of their respective awards, and of the Genius Prize itself. They judged *us* unworthy. We have come here today to show them—to show all of you—how wrong they were."

The French handler, Amina Beausoleil, breaks the stillness. Her scorpion wheels and charges the nearest kaiju.

Some people later claim that Amina thought she could win the Genius Prize while everyone else's backs were quite literally turned. But with eight mecha and seven kaiju under Canthorpe control, she had to know her creature didn't stand a chance. Footage from a thousand angles shows the scorpion spitting a tangling web at the legs at the Greater Irish kaiju that sends it crashing to the ground, but Japan's teddy-bear-shaped mecha breathes fire that crisps the web into ash—fire-breathing still being popular for its visual effect, even though it's easy to engineer and useless against any competitive creation. The whip arm of the Brazilian mecha duels briefly with the scorpion's extendable tail, but three seconds later it's over. A camera in one of the exit tunnels from the field shows that Amina abandoned her charge the instant the rest of the entries turned on her beast, running for cover—an action that certainly saved her life.

During this brief fight, one of the mecha begins to spasm. Then another, then another, until all of them have twitched and then fallen still.

Only when that is done do they turn against their surroundings, unleashing their firepower on the shielded stands that surround them.

**CREDIT GOES TO THE SONGHALI** team for observing appropriate safety standards, and installing a purely mechanical hatch release in their pterosaur. Thanks to this, Kisi is able to pop open her construct and dive free after Arthur takes it over. Not all of the other pilots were as diligent, and so they remain trapped, helpless passengers in their own creations, as the Canthorpe twins begin to wreak vengeance for what they saw as their unfair defeat the previous year.

The teammates of the pilots, and all of the kaiju engineers, are on the field. They know first-hand exactly how destructive their creations can be. A few of them waste precious seconds trying to regain control; others realize the futility, and begin fleeing immediately.

Nevali Jones is in the judges' box with Metzger and Patel at the start of the attack. Her body cam shows the first rocket exploding against the front window, and (contrary to those who would like to accuse her of negligence or incompetence) less than two seconds go by before she takes action. The judges' box is defended, of course, because accidents have happened before. But anything that offers visibility to the outside world has certain innate vulnerabilities against focused attack, and so you can hear Jones shouting for Metzger, Patel, and their various guests to retreat to the much more heavily fortified chamber behind. She covers their retreat herself, even though frail flesh isn't much of a shield against a kaiju or a mecha; her own body armor is only rated to resist threats up to Hellstop rockets, Class B plasma drills, and fluoroantimonic acid.

Once the dignitaries are secured, she descends to the arena below, shouting orders to her subordinates as she goes.

**CHANGO, AS THE TLACHI TEAM'S** tactical coordinator, had a drone circling the field so he could advise Rico in handling their kaiju. Its auto-tether drags it after him when he and a dozen others retreat into one of the tunnels, and so unlike most of the drones in the air when the Canthorpes took over, it escapes the destruction outside long enough to memorialize what comes next.

The shot is from above, but the figures are recognizable. From the Tlachi team, Chango and Rico; Miguel has escaped, but via a different tunnel. From the Songhali team, Kisi, Akua, and Ye. From the Canadian team, Tiennot; all three members of the Brazilian team; two from the Pakistani team; from the Sinai team, Muhammed Najjar, badly injured by shrapnel; and Yankton Robins, an arena employee responsible for supplying food to the kaiju.

Akua immediately begins applying first aid to Muhammed. Most of the others are shouting in a medley of languages; isolation analysis later teases out their words, the majority of which are profanities supposedly unsuitable to their tender years. Then Kisi's voice rises above them all. (Her words, and most of the subsequent conversations, are in Kotava.) "What the hell is going on out there?"

The Canthorpes' message is still broadcasting. Despite the noise from outside, it echoes through the tunnel in which the group shelters.

"Who else has the capacity to hijack the sympathy nets in all the mecha built by the newest crop of supposed geniuses?" the twins boast. "Who else can brainwash kaiju that supposedly answer to no one but their handlers? The display of coordination and skill you see before you now—"

"What fucking coordination?" Kisi yells toward the mouth of the tunnel. The flames consuming that end of the field are not visible in the drone's view, but their light dances across the huddled figures. "You're destroying everything!"

Tiennot stands up from his crouch against the wall. "Listen to the message! The ambient sound—it's pre-recorded, not live. I don't think this was supposed to happen."

Rico answers him with a well-chosen vulgarity in Spanish, then says, "Who cares what was supposed to happen? There are people dead out there!"

(At the moment he says it, the death toll stands at thirty-four, all individuals who were on the field when this began. It will climb fast as the stadium's shielding begins to fail.)

Tiennot's hands flap in the air, beating out a swift rhythm as his mind focuses on the problem. "The sympathy nets. He hijacked them—must have been Arthur. But one mind can't control eight at once. He must have daisy-chained them together, so that he's controlling one and that controls the next and so on—but that only works if he can maintain the focus necessary to stop sensory input from washing back through the chain. Did you see them spasm? He must have let that slip on the first link. Then he'd be hit by the second, and his odds of resisting that are lower, so—"

He doesn't finish the sentence, but he doesn't have to. The image of dominoes falling is so clear, it might as well be on the video feed.

Chango and Rico are kaiju crafters. They've never worked with sympathy nets. "What does that *mean*?" Rico demands.

Kisi slams her hand against the wall. "It means Arthur Canthorpe has gone insane. Taking all the mecha with him."

"What about that *comemierdas* Arnold?" Chango says, gesticulating wildly toward the tunnel entrance. "What's his excuse?"

An explosion cuts short any answer the others might have given. The shock wave knocks Chango's drone into a wall, destroying it. The next record of this group comes from inside the west loading dock, whose security barriers Tiennot has hacked. By this point Akua has taken Muhammed toward Infirmary Station D, and two of the Brazilians, along with Yankton Robins, have chosen to flee into the surrounding mountains, hoping to find safety there. Thanks to Robins, all three will make it to Aspen, the nearest town. Others who try the same escape do not fare so well.

"We've got to do something," Rico says. "We can't just let a pair of insane losers rampage around with kaiju and mecha—*our* kaiju and mecha." He says that last part with venomous fury.

"What do you think we can do?" Ye asks wildly. "Throw wrenches at them? Carve them apart with welding torches? We built ours to be indestructible!"

One of the Pakistanis says, "The contest authorities have their own kaiju and mecha—"

"Which also use sympathy nets," Tiennot says, with bitter amusement.

Chango nods. "And obsequium, I'm sure. They have all the best tech before we do, unless we invent it ourselves."

Ye snorts. "Right. So all we have to do is invent some brand new bit of tech out of whatever we've got in our pockets."

While all of this is going on, Kisi drifts a few steps away from the group. At first her posture is limp and hopeless, her movements dazed. But as Ye speaks, she straightens, her gaze going into the distance.

"No," Kisi says, not looking at any of them. "Not something new."

**IN THE TUNNELS UNDER THE** arena stands, Nevali Jones is hunting Canthorpes.

They have prepared for this, of course. She's already walked into several booby traps, not because she failed to see them before they triggered, but because she cannot afford to take the time to disarm them. Instead she trusts in her armor. It is now blackened and smoldering, the silencers destroyed, such that each step she takes clangs against the concrete floor.

The final defense is a good deal subtler. It has been growing for weeks, seeded by Arnold Canthorpe via an "accidental" spill the janitor did not realize should have been cleaned with hydrochloric acid.

By the time Nevali Jones walks into it, the creature has grown to coat the hallway in something that will pass for concrete, if you don't stab it to see if it will bleed.

It's smart, too. It lets her get halfway down the hall, halfway to the door of the generator room where the Canthorpes are holed up, before it moves.

Then the entire corridor comes to life and closes in on her like a fist.

**TIENNOT THROWS THE SWITCH IN** the west loading dock. The lights come on in rows, a gunfire volley of illumination rattling from the near end to the far, revealing in true color what, until that point, had been recorded only in infrared.

The mecha stand silent along one wall. The cages facing them from the other wall are quiet only because there are sound dampeners on each one; Metzger and Patel wanted all attention on the new entries for the Genius Prize, not the old ones. But they're there: kaiju and the descendants of kaiju, and the mecha they once battled.

"You've got to be kidding me," Chango says in Spanish, before collecting his wits and switching back to Kotava. "None of those things can stand up to what's out there!"

"They're all we've got," Kisi says. "And they don't have sympathy nets or obsequium."

Ye utters an oath in Igbo and runs down the line to the robotic winner from six years before. "He's here! Anansi is here!"

The construct in front of her can only be called a spider

as a courtesy toward its eight legs; unlike the French scorpion that died on the field a little while ago, it does not spin webs. But its Nigerian creators named it for the famous West African spider god, and so that is the name by which the world knows it. Although the two countries have been longtime rivals, Songhali robotics students have a great deal of respect for Anansi, whose sheer agility and ability to climb larger mecha to find a better angle of attack made for a thrilling display in 2125.

"Do you even know how to pilot that thing?" Chango demands.

Kisi doesn't look at him. All her attention is on Anansi. "I've watched the recordings of the Nigerians. We tried building our own six-legged mecha a few years ago—couldn't resolve some center of gravity issues with the weaponry. But that won't be a problem here."

Meanwhile, Rico is studying the various kaiju. Nine of them are Tlachi creations, the legacy of a long tradition of victorious teams. His gaze lights on the 2128 winner: La Diestra, who resembles nothing so much as a deinonychus the size of a tyrannosaurus rex. She, too, is memorable—albeit for a different reason.

Tiennot makes a sound like he choked on his tongue. "You can't be serious."

"What choice do we have?" Rico asks.

The ensuing silence breaks Kisi's attention away from Anansi. Her gaze meets Rico's. Then she says, "Oh."

Finally Rico says, "We need more than just us."

Kisi nods and faces the Pakistanis. "You in?" She doesn't even wait for their answer before she adds, "Ye, round up anybody you can find. Pilots, handlers—anybody brave enough to try. But hurry."

Outside, the destruction is mounting.

**THE RECRUITER FOR THE SHINRASEN** Center left his standing camera rig in his private box. The various explosions have shaken it out of its original alignment, leaving it pointed at the mouth of one of the tunnels—the one nearest to the west loading dock.

It records, with astonishing clarity, the moment when the tide turns.

Rico charges out first, mounted bareback atop La Diestra. The huge, dinosaurian kaiju—the only one ever to win while carrying her handler—provides cover for fast-moving Anansi, whose faceted pilot bubble refracts the face of Kisi, bellowing a war cry. Behind them comes a herd of other mecha and kaiju, winners of the previous competitions, piloted and directed by more than a dozen brave contestants.

It is the grandest grand melee the Genius Prize has ever seen. Anansi swarms up the back of the Canadian grizzly-shark and blows open the hatch; two legs reach in, snag Tiennot's compatriot Miigwan, and drop her to the waiting arms of a small naga kaiju below. Rico on La Diestra kites several of the Canthorpes' enslaved mecha around the field, and one of them falls into a pit dug by the infamous Tlachi-crafted Mole Man from the 2117 competition. (He is not under anyone's control; he is simply burrowing for the sheer joy of it, as he does whenever given access to dirt.) Anansi leaps from the grizzly-shark across to the Lovecraftian monstrosity the Norwegians brought, then leaps again just as the Japanese teddy bear breathes fire across its supposed ally. The Holy Angel of 2120 defends a large portion of the stands, where the collapsing structure has trapped several thousand spectators.

Chango was right. Very few of the previous winners can hope to stand up against the most recent entries; even Anansi and La Diestra are outmatched. But the young people who have taken the field can and do save lives, covering the evacuation of the stadium, and giving the crazed Canthorpes something to focus on other than mass slaughter.

And Kisi manages more. When three of Anansi's legs are crushed by her own pterodactyl, leaving that construct helpless on the field, she doesn't hesitate. She leaves the pilot's compartment and climbs the pterodactyl's leg while it finishes smashing the Nigerian spider. Like most mecha, it's built to tackle things its own size; it can't grab Kisi, and has no weaponry it can point so close to its own body. When she arrives under its jaw, Arthur Canthorpe can't even see her on the mecha's external sensors.

The Songhali team installed the sympathy net only after their national championships. It's an add-on, not integrated into the frame the way it would have been had they built it in from the start.

Ye's toolbelt is around Kisi's waist. Clinging to the outside of the pterodactyl even as it turns its attention to the rest of the field, she removes the panel on the underside of its jaw and shorts out the sympathy net. The pterodactyl stops dead.

The hatch is still open, left that way during Kisi's earlier escape. She climbs back inside, and as the spinjets fire and the pterodactyl takes flight, the interior mic picks up her next words.

"I'll show you who's a genius."

**THE LENS OF NEVALI JONES'** body cam is smeared with blood and ectoplasm, but it still shows the furious, horrified, defiant face of Arnold Canthorpe when she blows the door off its hinges, and the twitching body of Arthur Canthorpe on the floor, overwhelmed by the sensory input of too many sympathy nets at once.

She doesn't bother with speech. She just stuns Arnold, then Arthur, and then shoots them both again for good measure.

On the field above, the remaining enemy mecha stop. The remaining enemy kaiju stagger and fall.

The arena is silent, except for the crackle of fire, and then the agonizing, metallic screech of La Diestra finishing what she started: tearing the arm off the Japanese teddy bear.

Wheeling overhead, the Songhali pterodactyl lets out a victorious cry.

**OUT OF RESPECT FOR THE** dead, there was no competition in 2132.

Metzger and Patel gave no personal interviews during that time. They testified before judges and committees, gave public statements, and spoke privately with the families of those who had lost loved ones. They donated enormous sums to charity. And they made sure the heroes of the day were honored as they deserved, from Nevali Jones down to Yankton Robins and an arena janitor who led fleeing spectators to the shelter of a supply closet—anyone who helped save lives. Kisi Abouta and Rico Sarabia were named the joint winners of the Genius Prize: the first time the award was given to two individuals from separate teams.

They shared the cash with everyone who had helped them that day.

A little over one year after the disaster, Metzger and Patel appeared together on Immis Chae's show. After a brief review of the previous year's tragedy, Chae cuts straight to the question on everyone's mind.

"Will the Genius Prize continue?"

Patel glances at Metzger and says, "My wife and I still believe in the principles that led us to create our respective competitions, and the Genius Prize itself. But it's undeniable that the entries have grown far beyond anything we envisioned when we started out."

"And with that," Metzger says, "the danger has grown as well."

Chae says, "So you plan to end it?"

It's a sensible idea, but you can hear the disappointment in their voice. Metzger smiles. "Not exactly. We'll be back in 2133 . . ."

". . . but we'll be taking it in a different direction," Patel finishes.

In unison, they reach into their pockets and set two objects on the table before them, neither more than three inches tall.

"Miniaturization."

# END CREDITS

**EVEN BEFORE MARVEL STARTED PUTTING** two stingers at the end of its movies, I was one of those people who stayed until the very end credits rolled. Without the names of those people, films like *Pacific Rim: Uprising* and *Rampage* and *Kong: Skull Island* would never be made. You Kickstarter backers? You're our end credits. We could not have done this without you, and we are so grateful that you believed in us enough to make this stompy dream of ours a print reality. Thank you. Stay safe out there where monsters roam—you never know where their feet are going to fall.

Alana Abbott, March 18, 2018

..........................

@JamesFerguson • Aaron "Foxx" Garcia • Aaron Boss
Aaron Hanoff • Aaron Zsoldos & Emely Pul
Adam McLain • Aimee Morgan • Alfred Haus
Anders M. Ytterdahl • Andrew Alvis
Andrew Carrick • Andrew Hatchell

Anthony "HachiSnax" Giordano • Anthony R. Cardno
Arthur Dixon • Ashli Tingle • Atalay
Bill and Laura Pearson • Bill Mills • Brandon Wolff
Brian Griffin • Brooks Moses • Bryan Geddes
C. L. Werner • Cassie Barden • Chad Bowden
Chandra Reyer • Chris Callicoat • Chris Matosky
Chris Roby • Christian Juventino Martin
Christian Wiessner • Cliff Winnig
Clyde Lee Graham • Cullen 'Towelman' Gilchrist
D-Rock • D. Mancini • Dakkaramazariah
Dan Delgado • Dan Paddock • Dan Rabarts
Daniel Southwick • Danny Keith • Danny Lore
Darren Forbes • Dave Cox • Dave Hermann
Dave Versace • David Banes • David Doucey
David Rains • Debbie Cowens • Dee Haddrill
Dennis Davison Jr • Derek "Ray Gun" Boudreaux
derek elder • Donald Cullen Brawley
Dren Productions • DrLight
Dustin Michael Dreyling • Dylan Murphy
Emily Williams • Eric Brooks • Eric Wei
Erin G. • Evan Berkow • Ezzy G. Languzzi
Flo Beys • Floyd Brigdon • Frank Gawryla
G-Man Josh • Garrick Dietze • Gary Phillips
Gavran • Geoff Englebach • Geoff Strayer
Geoffrey Kidd • Gerd Van Buggenhout
GMarkC • Grace Bridges • Greg Brunell
Greg Noneman • Guy McLimore
H. Lee Mathes • Happy Apple • Hattie Quinn
Heather Eberhardt • Heather Parra
Heide Goody • Hollow Harbor • Hoss Keen

Ian Alexander Casey • Ian Chung
Indigo R. Pohlman • Jacob Rubin
Jake M. Spencr • James F Tillman • James McKelvey
Jamie Sands • Janice Giles • Jason Breining
Jay Barnson • JayC • Jeff Lewis
Jeff Richards • Jess Turner • Jessica Enfante
Jim Dowell • Jimmy Chang • Joanne Burrows
Joaquin Blount • Jobeda Ali • Joe Kontor
Joe Monson • John Heine • John Lambert
John MacLeod • Jon Morin
Jonathan Edward Smith • Jonathan Vallier
Joseph S. Fleischman • Justin Bell • Kalu Ekeh
Karl Markovich • Katherine Shan
Ken "Merlyn" Mencher • Kévin Fuster
Kevin Henderson • Kevin Schroeder • Kilbaro
Kory & Braedyn Keller • Kyle Spencer
L. Ratliff • Lark Cunningham • Lasse R. Olsen
Lawrence vs gamera • Lee Turner • Leowyn
Lilly Ibelo • Liz • Luke Morton
Mac McClintock of Titanic Creations
Madison Keller • Marcus Polk • Marcus Tsong
Mark Roman • Martin Gallo • Martin Greening
Matt Hufstetler • Matt Leitzen
Matt Zitron • Matthew Burgess
Matthew David Goodwin • Matthew J. Barbeler
Matthew Mastrogiovanni H.P. • Matthew R. Gaglio
Max Kaehn • Mechatarrasque • Melanie R. Meadors
Meredith Jeanne Gillies • Michael Farrah/Kaiju Battle
Michael Feir • Michael Feldhusen • Michael Leaich
Michael Shoemaker • Mika Koykka • Mike and Axisor

Mike Pastore • Mountain Barber • Nathan McCullough
Neil "Thunrashi" Gorman • Neil J Murphy
Nicholas Frame • Nicholas Johnson • Noah Bast
NXPS's mama • Osye E. Pritchett III
Panos A P • Patti Short • Paul Cooper
paul dever • Paul Hawke • Paul McMullen
Paul Osentowski • Peter T • PrairieZombie
R.J. Lewis • Rachel Sasseen • Randi Rainbow
Raymond Pegoraro • Rebecca Scott
Rhiannon Raphael • Richard BrimstonePrime Taylor
Rms • Rob Mattison • Rob Robinson • Rob Voss
Robert B. Battle • Robert Connick • Robert Hood
Rodney Rodgers • Role Playing Public Radio
Rolf Laun • Ron Searcy • Ross Hathaway
Sabrina Vourvoulias • Sachin Suchak
Sally Novak Janin • Salvador Bernado Sala
Sam & Ben Sharps • Saz Wells • Scenarex
Scott "Smiticles" Smith • Scott Macauley
Scott MAynard • Seamus Quigley
SeanMike Whipkey • Sebastian H.
Seth Lee Straughan aka TrashMan
Shawn Carman • Shawn Hanna • Sheldon Hicks
Sheryl R. Hayes • Shiro • Simon Davidson
Stan Bundy • Stanley Chau
Stephen "Quinn" Thomas Bayley • Stephen Redmond
Steven "Sammo" Simmons • Steven Mentzel
Susanne Schörner • The Great and Mighty Poo
Thomas E. • Thomas Hunter Broussard • Tim Elkins
Tim Rodriguez • Tim Rosolino
Tomas Burgos-Caez • Tommy Acuff • Tony Heugh

TraciandBrian Belanger • Tracy "Phoenix Djinn" Benton
Trevor A. Ramirez • Tyrone 'tiggertq' Queensborough
Umar Abbasi • Ven & Nikki Sio • Vincent E. Hoffman
Wayne L. Budgen • Wendy Shaffer
Willhameena Power • William C. Tracy
William Caudill the villainess mr. C • William Katt
WolfDawg • Yankton Robins • Your Mom

OUTLAND
ENTERTAINMENT
BLOG
FICTION
COMICS
GAMES
CREATIVE SERVICES
STORE
KAIJU
RISING II